Rune Romance

Amelia Wilson / J.A. Cummings

Rune Sword
Rune Series Book 1

Amelia Wilson / J.A. Cummings

Contents

Prologue
   Chapter One – Exhibit
   Chapter Two - Hunters
   Chapter Three - Revelations
   Chapter Four – The Draugr
   Chapter Five – Interlude (Erik)
   Chapter Six – Interlude (Nika)
   Chapter Seven – Soul to Soul
   Chapter Eight – The Calm Before the Storm
   Chapter Nine – Enemies
   Chapter Ten - Flux
   Chapter Eleven - Casualties
   Chapter Twelve – Blood Eagle
   Chapter Thirteen - Choosing
   Chapter Fourteen - Transformation
   Chapter Fifteen - Destruction
   Chapter Sixteen – The Chosen
Epilogue

Copyright © 2018 by Amelia Wilson
All rights reserved.

In no way is it legal to reproduce, duplicate, or transmit any part of this document in either electronic means or in printed format. Recording of this publication is strictly prohibited, and any storage of this document is not allowed unless with written permission from the publisher. All rights reserved.

Prologue

An icy wind whipped across the field where the people stood, flickering torches in their hands. The laborers had finished digging a pit, and longboat had been lowered down into the hole. A sheet of silver was laid on the floor of the boat, with silver shackles attached to its four corners.

From the village behind them, a solemn procession approached. The warriors and the vala – the wise woman and shaman – walked at the forefront. More warriors, heavily armed with double-headed axes, brought up the rear. In the middle, bound with silver chains, the Draugr chieftain rocked and screamed his fury and his fear.

The warriors took the Draugr and wrestled him to the pit. He was shaped like a man, but his vampire nature was clearly revealed by the long black fangs he gnashed as he struggled. His bloodshot eyes were wide with fear and rage.

He fought like a wild beast, but the silver around his body weakened him, and they were able to overcome his resistance. They flung him onto the silver plate, still bound by his chains, and shackled him at the wrists and ankles. He screamed in agony as the silver burned into his flesh.

The vala intoned the words of a binding spell as she held a mighty sword in her hands. The runes inscribed into the blade glowed brightly. The power was alive.

They placed the sword on top of the Draugr, sealing him into his grave. They could still hear him screaming after the last heap of earth was added to the barrow. The screaming would last for weeks.

Chapter One – Exhibit

Nika Graves hurried through the museum, headed for the special gallery. The last guided tour of the day for the traveling exhibit was scheduled to start in just a few minutes, and she had promised Tamara that she would be there. A long meeting with the museum docents had made her late... again.

She reached the velvet rope just before the guard snapped it shut, closing off the exhibit for the day. She saw Tamara waiting by the massive wooden gate that marked the entrance to the display, and her friend smiled when she approached.

"About time you got here! I thought you were going to leave me all alone with these Vikings."

They were as different as two women could be. Tamara was blonde and blue-eyed, but with an edgy style that hinted at her job as a bartender on the rough side of town. Nika was lithe and elegant, with long, flame-red hair and bright green eyes. Her style was more conservative. Despite their differences, they had been friends for years.

The exhibit was on loan from the Royal Museum of Stockholm, and it featured priceless artifacts recently discovered in the remains of a Viking ship burial. The wooden gate that Tamara was standing beneath was a replica of two dragon boat figureheads. The dragons roared silently above them as they entered the gallery.

Nika had always been fascinated by the Vikings, and having this exhibit in her museum was a personal thrill. As the assistant curator, she was delighted to have the opportunity to present her passion, Nordic history and mythology, to the general public. She hoped that people enjoyed the exhibit as much as she did.

Tamara's reactions would be her guidepost. Her friend was not a stupid woman, but she had a tendency toward flightiness that verged on the annoying. She had virtually no sense of history and certainly would never have studied it on her own. If the exhibit could grab and keep her attention, then Nika could rest assured that the general public would enjoy it, too.

They strolled through the temperature-controlled boxes in which the artifacts were displayed. The glass was specially treated to block UV rays, protecting the fragile treasures within. They were also bullet proof and airtight, which would prevent accidental damage or excessive moisture from causing the objects to decay.

"This is weird," Tamara said.

"What is?"

"I can't believe that they buried a whole boat."

"It was common for a Viking chieftain or person of note to be buried in his or her boat. It was a mark of status and a great honor."

She looked at the label on the case before them. Inside, the Swedes had created a perfect scale miniature replica of the burial as it was first laid in the ground. She pointed.

"See, the man they buried holding the sword - he was a very important person in his day. It's just a shame that they haven't been able to figure out his name."

"But why the boat?"

"He'd need it in the afterlife."

"But he's dead."

"He would live again."

Tamara shook her head. "It still seems like a waste of a perfectly good boat."

She laughed. "To each their own."

They continued through the rooms of the gallery, following a path that roughly matched the outline of the longboat that had been the unnamed chieftain's coffin. In the very center of the exhibit, in a darkened area illuminated only by carefully-aimed spotlights, was the central artifact.

It was a Viking sword, the one that had been buried in the cold hands of its master all those centuries before. The lighting was arranged so that the runes etched into the blade could be seen, the play of shadow making the symbols appear more clearly. Nika was well versed in Futhark, both

Elder and Younger, but she could not make out the words that the runes were spelling.

"That," Tamara said, "is one hell of a pig-sticker. That bad boy would leave a mark."

Nika smiled but did not reply. Instead, she leaned closer to the glass, peering at the runes.

A deep, resonant voice spoke behind her. "I don't think you'll be able to read it."

She turned, surprised, to see a tall man in a black suit, his blond hair perfectly coifed. He had an earpiece in one ear with a curling wire leading down into his suit coat, and he looked for all the world like a member of the Secret Service. He smiled.

"I'm sorry to startle you, Miss Graves."

Tamara drifted to stand behind the man, but where Nika could see her face. She mouthed 'wow,' to the embarrassed curator, who quickly turned her attention back to the stranger.

"I'm afraid you have me at a disadvantage, Mr. ..."

"Thorvald," he said, offering a handshake. She accepted, and her hand vanished into his huge grip. "Erik Thorvald."

"A pleasure to meet you."

"Likewise." He smiled. "I'm an attaché from Stockholm."

"Oh! Then this is your baby," she said, gesturing to the sword.

He looked at the ancient weapon with a jaundiced eye. "Not mine, I assure you."

"Has anyone been able to determine what those runes say?"

Thorvald looked back to her with a smile. "No. Not yet. Some scholars in Sweden believe that it might be encoded, which of course makes no sense at all."

She laughed. Behind Erik's back, Tamara was waving good bye, winking at her friend as she backed away. She put her hand to her face, mimicking a phone in the universal sign for 'call me,' and then vanished into the crowd.

Her companion looked over his shoulder. "It seems your friend has abandoned you."

"Well, history isn't really her thing."

"Too bad." He looked around the room, a flash of sudden anxiety in his clear blue eyes. His tone abruptly changed from warm and friendly to all business. "Please enjoy the exhibit. I have to -"

A black blur erupted through the floor, shattering marble tiles and scattering hapless bystanders like autumn leaves. Erik flung Nika behind him, dropping into a fighter's crouch.

The black blur coalesced into a tall woman, her white-blond hair pulled back into a wild tangle of braids and beads. She was clad in a black cat suit, and when she saw Nika's protector, she laughed.

Alarms blared. People screamed and ran from the gallery. The woman looked at Nika, then back at Erik.

"Which one are you protecting?" the newcomer asked him. "The sword or the girl?"

"Both."

The woman laughed, revealing long, feral teeth that should never have been in a human face. Nika shrank back, retreating toward the fire extinguisher.

"You can't do both. I would have thought you'd have learned that by now."

The woman in black lunged at Erik, and they tumbled together across the broken gallery floor. Nika ran to the extinguisher and pulled the pin. When she turned around, the Swedish man and the fanged intruder were facing off, trading punches and kicks. The strange woman landed a roundhouse kick to Erik's head, and when the man reeled, Nika blasted his opponent.

The intruder pulled away, hissing, and Erik scrambled to get out of the jet of chemicals. Security guards raced into the gallery from the main body of the museum, and the woman in black leaped onto the display case holding the sword. Erik produced a knife from under his suit coat and threw it at her, and the blade struck her in the shoulder.

The woman shouted in rage and pain, then punched her good hand through the reinforced glass of the display case. She wrenched the sword free of its setting as Erik flung himself onto the case, as well, trying to grapple her. The sword came up, and the runes on its blade began to glow an eerie green. Erik grabbed the blade and screamed. The sound of sizzling and the smell of burned flesh filled the air.

One of the guards pulled his pistol and started firing. The bullets bounced off of the thief, but one hit Erik in the thigh, a grazing wound. The woman saw his injury and laughed.

She pushed Erik off of the case and spat at him, "Osterkligr veithimathr!"

The guard fired again, and the woman shot up through the air, passing through the roof of the museum like a missile. Nika dropped the extinguisher and ran to Erik's side.

"Oh my God," she said, her head whirling. "You're hurt."

He turned his face away from her and pulled himself to his feet. Blood stained the leg of his trousers, and he was cradling his left hand. The palm was blackened and cracked. "It's nothing."

"You're bleeding," she protested.

"What the hell was that?" one of the guards demanded.

Erik took a deep breath and turned at last to face them. "Just a thief."

"Just a thief? I just saw her fly!"

The Swedish man brushed past the guard and hurried out of the gallery. "I don't have time for this."

Nika raced after him. "Mr. Thorvald! Erik!"

He did not wait for her, and she had to run to catch up with him. He was slowed by the injury to his leg, which was in her favor, but she still had to kick off her heels to run faster.

"Mr. Thorvald, wait."

He turned on her. "I do not have time to wait! Go away, Miss Graves!"

"Where are you going? You need a doctor."

Erik growled in his throat. "I need to get that sword."

"I can help you."

He shook his head and started walking again. "No, you can't."

"I saw her fangs!" He stopped short, and she caught his arm. "I am responsible for that sword, too. You can't just leave me out of this!"

"The Rune Sword is my responsibility!" He pulled his arm free. "I am telling you for the last time, Miss Graves. Stay out of this. You will get hurt if you persist."

"If I don't, I lose my job and the museum loses millions of dollars."

The Swede snorted. "Money and jobs are nothing if I don't get that sword back."

A woman in a smart gray business suit emerged from a side gallery, and Erik stopped when he saw her. She spoke to him rapidly in something like Swedish, but different. Erik responded, clearly ashamed. The new woman snapped at him, then seemed to notice Nika for the first time.

"I apologize, Miss Graves," she said. "I am Astrid Sigurdsdottir. We spoke on the telephone."

Nika remembered. Sigurdsdottir was the curator from Stockholm, the one who had negotiated the terms that had brought the Viking display to Central City in the first place. "Yes, I recall. I'm so sorry about the sword. We will get it back, I promise you."

Astrid fixed Erik with a harsh look. "We had better."

"We have to get Mr. Thorvald to a doctor," Nika told Astrid. "He's hurt."

She Swedish woman looked at Erik and smiled strangely. "Hurt? No. He's not hurt. Are you hurt, Mr. Thorvald?"

He pulled himself up straighter, almost like a soldier coming to attention. "No. I'm not hurt."

"But your hand -" Nika grabbed his left wrist and pulled his hand away from his side.

The burn was gone.

Erik pulled free of her grip without rancor. "As I said, I am unhurt."

Astrid interposed herself between them, slipping an arm around Nika's elbow. "Come, we must see to the rest of the exhibit. I hope there is no damage to the other artifacts..."

As Astrid pulled her away, Nika looked over her shoulder. Erik was already sprinting for the front door.

Chapter Two – Hunters

Erik raced out of the museum, holding his earpiece with one hand. He could hear his partner, Gunnar, speaking rapidly.

"I've got a visual. She's heading across the rooftops toward the east."

"Copy that," he replied. He shook his left hand, which still stung from the unexpected blast of burning magic it had received. "Is she alone?"

"Negative."

Shit. "How many?"

"I count three."

He made it to his rental car and threw it into reverse, barely looking to make certain that there was nobody in the way. He rubbed his hand over the wet blood on his slacks and scowled at the stain.

"Known quantities?" he asked.

"Yes," Gunnar answered, sounding regretful. "They're the brothers."

Erik cursed in every language he could muster, spewing foul invectives to vent his anger. This was not supposed to happen, not now. The barrow had been plundered, and Hakon's body was lying in that museum, just waiting. Now the brothers were in town.

His team had crossed paths with the brothers before. Ivar, Knut, Arne and Bjorn were formidable fighters and hired killers. They had been Erik's particular enemies for years.

"I see you," Gunnar coached from his over watch position. "Keep heading east three blocks. They've gone into the fourth building on the left."

"Residential or business?"

"Residential."

"Get Rolf and Magnus to guard the museum vault and meet me at the building."

"They're already on the way."

He drove as quickly as he could in city traffic. The urgency of his need to intercept that sword made his heart race, and he gripped the steering wheel to calm himself.

Don't panic, he thought. That won't help.

He managed to make it to the building without killing himself or anyone else, which he counted as a victory. There were no parking places on the street, so he simply parked the car and turned on the hazard lights. Over the honking objections of the people behind him, he sprinted into the apartment building.

It was a surprisingly rundown place, with the smell of rats and urine in the entryway. He found the stairwell and took the steps two at a time, charging up toward the roof, hoping that he would meet the thief and her accomplices on the way down.

"I'm in," Gunnar said in his ear. "Taking position to watch the exit."

"There had better be only one way out."

"I've got Hrothgar coming to mind the back."

He heard rapid footsteps approaching, racing down the stairs toward him. He pulled his sidearm and pointed it up the steps, waiting.

Bjorn was the first one to appear. His name meant 'bear,' and it suited him perfectly. His eyes widened, and then he grinned, flashing long black fangs. Their tips were a stunning red.

"Huntsman!" he called to his fellows.

Erik shot him in the face.

The man's big body tumbled down the stairs, and Erik stepped around it, heading up. He could hear one of the brothers shouting.

"Sigrunn! Give me the Sword!"

He proceeded cautiously, with his gun still aimed upward. Above him, the largest of the brothers, Ivar, leaned over the railing then ducked back, avoiding the silver bullet that Erik shot in his direction. The projectile clanged off of the metal beams supporting the stairs and ricocheted twice before it buried itself into the wall.

Another of the brothers, the youngest, Arne, leaped over the rails and landed in front of Erik. He slashed at him with his left hand, his fingers hooked into claws. Erik ducked, and the vampire caught a fistful of plaster from the wall behind him. He growled and tried again with the other hand.

This time when Erik shot, he didn't miss. Arne's body rolled down the stairs to join Bjorn's on the landing below.

"Arne!" Sigrunn, the woman who had stolen the sword from the museum, screamed.

Erik charged up the stairs just in time to see the middle brother, Knut, dragging Sigrunn through a doorway and into one of the interior corridors. Ivar, the last brother on the stairs, whispered words of power and threw a handful of dust at him. In mid-air, the dust became an impassable wall of tangled branches, studded with long, glistening thorns.

He knew from past experience not to touch that wall. Cursing again, he raced back down the stairs to doorway on that level, heading into the interior of the building, as well.

He reached the corridor just as the elevator dinged to mark its passing. He activated his earpiece and spoke.

"Coming down."

"I've got them."

Gunnar sounded confident, but Erik was less sure. He went back into the stairwell.

He should have known that a single bullet, even a silver one, would not keep the Draugr down. Both Arne and Bjorn were struggling to sit up, recovering and healing as he emerged from the corridor. He didn't have time to properly decapitate them, so he shot them each in the head once more. At least it would keep them quiet for a few minutes longer.

He ran down the stairs, hearing the sound of battle in the foyer as he approached. Shouts and the clang of metal led him like a beacon. He reached the bottom floor just as a brilliant flash of green light erupted, searing his eyes and making his ears ring with the hum of magic. Sigrunn was using the Rune Sword.

Ivar saw him coming and flung a hand axe at him. Erik dropped to one knee and fired, hitting Sigrunn between the shoulder blades. She screamed and turned away from Gunnar, who was lying on the ground, bleeding heavily.

Knut, the last brother, grabbed her. "Let's go!" he shouted to her in their native tongue, Old Norse. He caught his brother by the arm, as well. "Go!"

Erik pursued them out onto the street, where the three Draugr took flight. He emptied his clip, trying and failing to bring them down.

"Damn," he spat. Astrid would have his head for this.

He went back into the building and found Gunnar cradling his arm, which had been deeply wounded by Ivar's axe. Erik knelt beside him.

"You're lucky to still have that hand."

"I know. Hopefully I'll have it a while longer." He glanced at the stairs. "Where are the other brothers?"

Erik grimaced. "Down, but not out. I'll be back."

He picked up the axe and went to finish the job his bullets had started.

Chapter Three – Revelations

Nika spent the rest of the evening overseeing the building crew as they carefully removed the artifacts from the shattered gallery. With the floor perforated and the ceiling open to the air, there was no way that she would allow those priceless materials to remain at risk.

Sigurdsdottir hovered near her, observing as she responsibly cared for the loaned treasures. The woman said virtually nothing, but she watched with icy eyes, silently appraising and judging everything that Nika did.

When the last of the artifacts were packed away, Sigurdsdottir finally spoke. There was something heavy and meaningful in her tone. "You look very Nordic, Miss Graves. Do you have any Scandinavian ancestry?"

She ran a hand over her red hair. "Most people say I look Irish."

The other woman smiled tightly. "Red hair is a Norse trait. If the Irish have it, it is because the Vikings owned Dublin for a very long time. But you haven't answered my question."

Nika shrugged. "I don't honestly know. I was adopted when I was very small, so I have no clue what my birth family's heritage might be."

"Too bad." Sigurdsdottir picked up her purse, a sleek black number with a tiny padlock on the zipper. "Everyone should know where they come from. Good night, Miss Graves."

She smiled. "Good night."

When the icy chill of Sigurdsdottir's presence finally left the blasted gallery, Nika let out a sigh of relief. Something about the woman made her profoundly uncomfortable, like a mouse pinned in the gaze of a raptor. It was unsettling.

She walked slowly through the mess that remained in her museum. The case that had held the sword was completely smashed, and everything else had been rolled away on dollies and stored in the archives under lock and key. This was not the way she had wanted this exhibit to end. So much for her hopes of success.

Her morose contemplation was broken by a soft green shimmer that caught her eye. Something in the bottom of the sword case was glowing, the illumination throbbing in her view. She moved closer, subconsciously holding her breath, and the glow intensified as she approached. Moving the shattered glass aside, she peered into the case.

A tiny green cabochon jewel, unfaceted and smooth, lay on the green felt. It was glowing, just like the sword had glowed in the hands of the thief. She remembered Erik's hand burning like meat on a grill when he'd grabbed that sword, and she was reluctant to touch the jewel. She looked over her shoulder, not sure what she was watching for, and steeled herself to the deed.

Against her expectation, the jewel was cool in her palm. It continued to glow, pulsing in rhythm with her heartbeat, which was quickening with excitement and wonder. She touched the little bauble with the index finger of her other hand, stroking it. It seemed to welcome her touch. She could almost hear a voice in the back of her mind, whispering.

She shook her head abruptly, breaking herself out of the strange reverie. This jewel belonged to the sword, and therefore to the Royal Museum of Stockholm. She would give it to Sigurdsdottir in the morning.

For now, she slipped it into her skirt pocket, where it settled with a hum.

**

Astrid went to her temporary office, a loan from the museum while she was there shepherding the exhibit. It was small and cramped, with one window, a desk, and one chair for visitors. A bookcase stood to the side of the room, beside the visitor chair and between the desk and the wall. "You failed me twice," she said without preamble. "Some special forces soldiers you turned out to be."

"We did our best," Gunnar began, but Erik silenced him with a look. He fell quiet.

"Two of the brothers are dead," he told her. "Sigrunn has the sword."

"Which two?" She took out her smartphone to make notes.

"Bjorn and Arne."

"Truly dead?"

He looked insulted. "I took their heads. They are as dead as it gets."

"Good." She sat back. "I don't need to tell you what this means. For the Draugr to have the Rune Sword while Hakon's body is here, unguarded –"

"My men are standing watch over it. They won't be able to get near enough to it to start a ritual without my knowing."

She sneered. "Like you knew that they were going to take the sword today?"

"I was expecting a night raid," he told her, his tone hard. "I did not anticipate that they would be so brazen."

Astrid looked at Gunnar. "Go get some dreyri," she told him. "Both of you."

Erik shook his head. "You know my vow." He nodded to his partner. "Go ahead."

Gunnar left them, and once the door was closed, Astrid leaned forward. "If you would take the dreyri, you wouldn't be reduced to bullets and automobiles."

He set his jaw. "I swore that I would abstain from drinking blood until I found her again. I swore to the Aesir. Would you have me break my oath?"

"Why not? You've broken countless others." Her tone was biting as acid.

"Only one."

"The only one that ever mattered to me."

He looked like he wanted to scream. "Time and place, kona. This is neither."

She smiled thinly at his use of the word for 'wife.' "So at least you remember making the vow, even if you chose not to keep it."

"That was hundreds of years ago."

"We are immortal. What are a hundred years to us?"

He scowled. "Long enough for you to get over yourself." Erik ran a hand over his face. "Sigrunn used the sword. That's how Gunnar was hurt."

She looked surprised, their argument forgotten. "He wasn't burned."

"No," he agreed. "He wasn't. That means that the Sálsteinn is missing."

Astrid's eyes widened. "You have to find that stone. Everything depends on it."

"I'll check by the display and backtrack. Maybe, if we're lucky, it just fell off somewhere between here and our little urban battleground."

"Wait." He stopped halfway to the door, and she said, "The curator."

"Miss Graves?"

"Yes. I left her alone in the gallery." She looked up at him, her eyes stormy. "She may have it."

He nodded. "Then I'll find the curator, and I'll have Magnus and Rolf do the backtracking. If we know the stone is missing, you can bet for damn sure that they do, too."

Against her better judgment, Astrid told him, "Find the curator and stay with her, even if she doesn't have the stone. She is one of the Valtaeigr."

Erik was surprised. "Descended from the vala?"

"No." She curled her lip as she said it. "The vala reborn."

****

She took the bus from the museum to her apartment building, just like she did every night. The driver was the same as always. She smiled at him as she climbed the steps into the vehicle.

"Evening, Sam," Nika greeted.

"Evening, Nika," he returned. He waited for her to scan her bus pass, and then held the bus while she found a seat halfway to the back, just past the benches that faced the center aisle. She sat and held her purse on her lap.

A young man got on the bus after her. He was small but muscular, wearing a leather jacket and motorcycle boots with his faded jeans. She watched him as he made his way slowly through the bus and took up a position on the seat across from her.

He had a handsome face, and his eyes were the bluest she had ever seen, but there was something disturbing about him. The other passengers made room for him, either because he willed them to do so or because they were made too uncomfortable by his presence to stay too close. He was staring at her.

She looked out the window. Darkness was falling heavily outside, bringing a touch of chill wind. It would be winter soon. She put her hand into her pocket and fiddled with the stone, wishing Sam would stop being quite so cautious and put on some speed.

The bus stopped, and there was a general exodus as a majority of the riders got out at one of the busier subway stations. Sam closed the door, and she was alone beside the man in the leather jacket.

As the bus rumbled forward, he moved to sit beside her. He put one arm across the back of the seat and grasped the upright rail in front of him. She was three-quarters contained by his body, and she started to panic.

"Hello," he said, his accent lilting. "And who might you be?"

She looked away from him. "I'm sorry... I'm just trying to get home."

"Alone?"

There was something obscene insinuated in his voice. Her heart was pounding, and she pulled her purse closer. He reached out with one hand and tucked a stray hair back behind her ear.

She pulled away and glared at him. "Yes. Alone."

"No," he smiled. "I don't think so."

His eyes flashed, a speck of green light igniting in the center of his pupil. She tried to recoil, to look away, but something in that gaze held her fast. She could feel all of her will draining away the longer she looked into those deep blue pools.

He reached over and took her purse away. Her hands fell uselessly to her sides, and she let it go. Without breaking eye contact, he turned her purse upside down, spilling the contents across the bus floor. Wallet, makeup mirror, mascara and lipstick rolled away from her, and she could not find the will to reach for them. She could not bring herself to even look away.

The young man reached into her purse and tore out the lining with his fingers, feeling through the wrecked bag. She realized that he was looking for the jewel, and cold fear dripped down her spine like ice water. He abandoned the purse with a grin.

"I guess you have it on you," he said softly, his voice a nasty purr. He slid closer. "How lucky for me."

The bus driver slammed on the brakes. The folding door whipped open, propelled by a push from the outside, and Erik Thorvald sprang into the vehicle. The man with Nika's purse growled and threw it at him, though Erik easily batted it out of his way. He stalked forward.

The hold over Nika's mind shattered, and she could move again. She grabbed her keys and held them between her fingers like claws, rising to her feet and pressing her back against the windows.

Erik grabbed the young thug by his shoulders and gave him a solid shake. "You tell her," he hissed, "that this one is off limits. Do you understand?"

The man snorted. "What? Do you choose her?"

The words seemed to mortally insult Erik, who retaliated with a fist to the other man's face. The smaller man staggered backward, tripping over the seat and falling onto his back on the black rubber of the aisle. Thorvald leaned over him, grabbing him by the jacket. He pounded him once more, striking him so solidly that Nika thought she could hear bones cracking.

Sam came out of his seat with a blackjack in his hand. He swung wildly and brought it down on Erik's head. The man winced but did not fall. Instead, he turned to face the driver with a furious growl. He pulled the weapon out of the driver's hand and flung it across the bus.

The man in the leather jacket took advantage of Erik's distraction and bolted, running to the door and leaping out onto the street. He raced away down the sidewalk with all the speed of an Olympic sprinter and was gone.

Sam put his arms out and stepped between Nika and the angry Swede. "Don't you hurt her," he warned. "I already called the cops."

Erik rose to his full impressive height. "I am not going to hurt you. I came to protect her. Are you all right, Miss Graves?"

She nodded. "Yes. Yes, I'm fine. Sam, it's all right. I know Mr. Thorvald. He was just defending me."

Sam looked unconvinced, but she smiled for him encouragingly. Erik took her elbow in his hand, not ungently, and guided her out of the bus. She went with him.

"I don't know who that man was, or how you managed to get here at just the right moment, but thank you."

He pulled her down the sidewalk, moving rapidly. Apparently, the wound in his leg was causing him no trouble.

He escorted her along the path to her home without asking for directions. Erik was watchful the whole time, turning his head to watch the street and looking up at the sky and the roofs over their heads. His discomfort was making her paranoid, and she disliked the feeling.

When they got to her building, she unlocked the outer door and held it open for him. He took it in his hand and hesitated on the threshold for a moment, taking stock of the entrance as well as the street behind him.

"Come in," she said.

He nodded. "Thank you." He stepped through, and she locked the door behind him.

They took the stairs in silence. For a big man, he was light on his feet, not stomping up the stairs the way her neighbors sometimes did. That wary look was still on his face, and he frequently turned to look back the way they'd come.

Her apartment was on the fourth floor, taking up the southwestern corner of the building. She hurried to her door and put her key in the keyhole. Erik stood close beside her, watching as she fumbled with the lock. She took a deep breath and squeezed her fists, trying to will her fingers to stop shaking.

Erik caught her hands in his. His skin was cool to the touch, his knuckles showing no scuffs or bruises from the fight on the bus. She could detect no sign of burns or cuts on the hand that had caught the sword. She looked up into his eyes, and he promptly looked away.

"It'll be all right," he told her softly. "I will keep you safe, my lady."

It was a strangely archaic thing to say, but she took comfort from it. She reluctantly removed her hands from his grasp and returned to the door. She managed to open the lock this time, and she pushed open the door.

"Am I invited?" he asked.

"Of course."

"Of your own free will?"

Nika was confused. "Yes," she said, perhaps a little more sharply than she intended. "Of my own free will."

He took a breath. "Thank you."

She held the door as Erik walked into her foyer. He turned to face her, and she closed the door and set the chain.

"I am glad that you have numerous locks," he said. "You live alone. You need to be safe."

She tossed her keys into a china dish on the console table beside the door. "Yes, I live alone... but you sound like you already know that."

Erik nodded, a lock of his blond hair brushing his forehead. "Yes. I know."

"And you knew exactly where I live."

"Yes."

She pushed past him, going into the kitchen. Her butcher block sat in the back corner of the counter top, and she put her hand near it. "That's a little creepy, you know."

He had the good grace to look embarrassed. "I... I know. My apologies. It's my duty to know the people who come in contact with the Rune Sword."

Erik seemed to realize that he was making her nervous, so he backed away from her, putting more space between them. He put his hands behind his back and stood almost up against the wall.

"You're not the average security guard," she said, shaking her head. "Would you like a drink?"

"No, thank you. But don't let me stop you."

She opened the refrigerator and chose a bottle of water. She would have liked something stronger, but she didn't want to risk having her mind dulled. There would be time enough for that when Thorvald left.

She swigged her water. "Who are you, really?"

A startled expression crossed his face. "I am Erik Thorvald."

"Yes. I remember your name from the museum. But who are you?" She faced him, leaning her hips against the dishwasher. "Why were you assigned to guard a sword?"

"The Rune Sword is incredibly valuable."

"Did Stockholm know that someone was going to try to steal it?"

"Well, we suspected that they would try to take the sword," he admitted.

"Who is 'they?' And was that creep on the bus part of 'them?'"

He considered her for a moment, his jaw muscles twitching. Finally, he spoke. "Perhaps we should sit down for this part."

She followed him into the living room, where he sat on the edge of the sofa, his hands clasped on his knees. She perched on an armchair, safely out of his reach and with the coffee table between them, just in case.

"So... tell me. Who are you, who are they, and why do they want the sword so badly?"

He sighed. "I am an operative with the Swedish Special Operations Task Group. They call themselves the Draugr. And the sword... the sword belongs to them."

Nika frowned. "The sword was excavated by a team from Stockholm University," she reminded him. "It belongs to the museum in Stockholm, if it belongs to anyone."

"No." He ran a hand over his head, mussing his carefully-combed blond hair. "Not exactly. It's much more complicated than that."

She rose. "I don't know how that woman tore my museum apart today. I don't know how I saw what I saw, but I know I saw it. Those teeth! I've heard of some weird body modification stuff that people do, but that was... extreme."

She took a deep breath and began to pace.

"And then I was almost assaulted on the bus, and you came out of nowhere to save my bacon from some weird group that calls themselves the Draugr, which means that they either play too much Skyrim or they think they're undead."

She heard her own words, and an unwelcome thought dawned upon her. She wrapped her arms around herself. Thorvald simply watched her silently.

"My God. That woman who stole the sword - she really was a Draugr, wasn't she? A revenant."

"Not revenant," he corrected. "Vampire."

Chapter Four – The Draugr

She blinked once, then narrowed her eyes. "There are no such things as vampires."

Thorvald rose from his own seat and walked to her, closing the space between him with one stride. He ended up only inches away from her. He pulled his lips back, displaying his long, white teeth.

"Yes," he said softly. "There are."

She should have backed away. She should have thrown him out of her apartment right then, called the cops, started screaming. There were a hundred things she should have done other than what she did.

She did nothing.

He took her silence as an invitation to explain. "The Draugr are a very ancient race. We are vampires, but not in the sense of your Hollywood vampires. We were created by very dark magic in very dark days, centuries ago.

"When mankind was young and savage, there was a man named Hakon. He was brutal. He was subject to the worst excesses, the worst vices, the worst violence. He had no sense of honor. He killed for the joy of killing.

"When Odin, the All-Father, saw this, he sent the vala to confront him. The vala are the wise women, the priestesses and the keepers of ancient lore. They are sorceresses. Very powerful."

He watched her carefully for a reaction. When there was none, he continued his story.

"The vala went to Hakon and told him that he had earned the enmity of the gods, and that if he did not amend his ways and become a proper king instead of just a butcher, he would be punished. He did not listen.

"So one night, when he was in a drunken orgy in his longhouse, the vala, and the Aesir – the old gods of the Norse – visited their wrath upon him. Through blood magic, they cursed him and his followers to be immortal, to be the Draugr, but not as a reward.

"For all time, they would be driven by a need for blood, a constant thirst that would consume them and drive many of them mad. They would live forever until they worked off the gods' anger through enough good deeds.

"Hakon, instead of being chastised, took his immortality as a challenge and a license. He became ten times worse than he was before, but now he had the strength and the supernatural abilities to visit death and destruction not just on his own kingdom, but on all of Scandinavia.

"It had to stop. The vala came together at the Temple at Uppsala, and they called those Draugr who wished to serve the Aesir instead of Hakon. These Draugr were enchanted to calm their thirst, and while we were somewhat weakened in body, we were purer in spirit. That was the birth of the Veithimathr – the Huntsmen.

"The Veithimathr and the vala had the greatest blacksmith in Uppsala create a sword. When that was done, the goddess Ithunn herself came down from Asgard and placed a curse upon it. The Veithimathr sealed the curse with blót, or blood sacrifice.

"From that day, the Veithimathr and the Draugr were sworn enemies, and the Huntsmen pursued them until they found Hakon and his inner circle. They slew many and took Hakon captive. He was given to the vala."

He leaned toward her again, emphasizing his words with the seriousness in his gaze. Nika's throat tightened.

"Hakon was the one buried in that ship. The Rune Sword contains the only magic that could keep him underground. When the archaeologists dug him up and moved the sword, he was freed... partially."

"You're crazy."

"Believe me; I wish I was." He reached into the pocket of her skirt with his fingers, fishing the jewel out and into the light. It flared between them, casting their faces in the green glow. "This piece... this is the Sálsteinn."

"Soul Stone."

"Yes." He held the jewel between his thumb and forefinger, bringing it up in front of her eyes. "When he was chained to the boat, and when the sword was put on top of him to keep him trapped, this stone was in the hilt. It was enchanted. As he lost physical power, the magic in this stone drew him in, trapping his essence."

She could hardly believe she was asking the question. "So... is his spirit trapped in there?"

Erik nodded gravely. "Yes."

"How did you know I had it, or which pocket it was in?"

"I am drawn to the sword and to everything about it. I can feel this stone, wherever it is. And so can they." He wrapped his hand around the jewel, hiding it in his palm. "They will be coming for this."

Nika shivered.

He continued to explain. "The Draugr want the sword and the Soul Stone so that they can reunite their chieftain's spirit with his body. Once they do that, he will rise again, and they will be a force of ruin in this world."

"Then we can't let them have it. We have to destroy it. Crush it, or hide it, or -"

"No." Erik shook his head. "If we destroy the jewel, he will be released. His spirit will go straight back to his body, but he will be unable to enter it. We would be creating a powerful and unquiet ghost, almost a demon. And if we hide it, they will find it, because they are drawn to it, as I said."

She backed away from him. "Take it. I don't want anything to do with it."

"It's not that easy." He watched her sorrowfully.

"Why not?"

He stepped closer to her again. She didn't know why he insisted on being so close, or why she felt so comforted to have him there when she should have been afraid.

"The stone called to you. That means that you are part of this, whether you want to be or not."

She backed up again, and the backs of her knees bumped the chair she'd been sitting in. She nearly fell, but he caught her, his hand around her wrist.

"What does that mean?" she asked. "Why does it call to me?"

"It calls to you because it recognizes its own."

She sat heavily. When she spoke, her voice was very, very small. "What?"

He crouched in front of her and weighed his words carefully. "It recognizes someone with immortal blood in their veins."

Nika didn't know whether she wanted to laugh or cry, so, to her embarrassment, she did both.

"Many people are descended from the immortals," he said, trying to reassure her. "They are part of the histories of many, many families in Sweden and Norway. It's not unusual, and it doesn't make you a monster."

"No, no. Only a partial monster." She wiped the moisture from her face angrily. "So, when the man on the bus asked you if you had chosen me, what did he mean?"

Erik rose and went back to the couch. His sudden absence from her personal space left her light-headed.

"It was nothing. Just foolishness."

"Are you one of the Draugr?"

He looked down and opened his hand, showing her the jewel resting on his upturned palm. The green light was pulsing. He raised his eyes to hers. "What do you think?"

"I think... I think you're Veithimathr."

He nodded. "Yes. I am."

"And the man on the bus?"

"He is Draugr."

She propped her elbow on the arm of the chair and rested her head in her hand. "Oh, my God," she sighed. "I can't believe this."

Erik closed his hand and tucked the gem into his own pocket. "I'm so sorry."

She had a million questions whirling in her mind, but she could only give voice to one. "Why are you telling me all of this?"

He sighed. "I wish I didn't have to. Unfortunately, you have come to the Draugrs' attention. Their agent saw you in the museum and knew you for what you are, and Astrid... Astrid knows, too."

"Is Astrid a Draugr?"

"Not exactly."

"What does that mean?"

"It means it's complicated."

"Like the rest of this is simple?"

He sighed. "Astrid is Valtaeigr, which means the arm on which the falcon rests. She is dedicated to Odin. She is one of the vala.

"The vala are the wise women, as I told you before. They're also known among the Draugr. They are the only vampires who can use magic."

Nika tried to wrap her head around what he was telling her. It was all too much. "So she's a vampire, too?"

"Yes."

She shook her head. "Of course she is."

He shifted slightly. "Now that they know you, they will be coming for you."

She covered her eyes with her hand. This cannot be happening, she thought miserably. "Coming for me for what reason?"

"To take you to him. To use your blood to complete the ritual that will bring him back to life." His voice was flat, but his eyes were bright with conflicting emotions that she could not identify.

"I think they want to sacrifice you, because only the blood of the Valtaeigr will complete the spell."

Nika thought back to Astrid's questions about her origins, and the loaded tone in the Swedish woman's voice made much more sense to her now. "And Astrid, what is her part in all of this?"

"It is her job to keep him from rising, just as it's my job to protect - and now retrieve - the Rune Sword. And now, my lady, my job is to protect you as well."

She wanted to object, to say that she didn't need protecting, but all evidence pointed to the fact that she did. She had never been a fighter. If the Draugr came for her, she would have no ability to fight them off, and the fate she could expect if they caught her was profoundly unappealing.

She closed her eyes and put her head back against the chair. "Ugh. I have such a headache now."

Erik looked down at his hands. "I've just given you a lot of information to process. I would think that a headache is to be expected at this point."

Nika opened her eyes again and considered the man on her sofa. She should have been terrified. A self-professed vampire was sitting in her apartment, and one that she had carefully invited inside, which meant that he could probably kill her any time he wished. Now she understood why he had been so particular about her invitation to come in.

He was sitting so quietly, though, and he seemed to solid. He seemed honorable. She knew that appearances could be deceptive.

Against her better judgment, she decided that she would trust him... for now.

"So are you my bodyguard, then?"

He smiled. "Yes, my lady, if you will have me."

"Why do you call me that?"

Erik frowned, confused. "What?"

"'My lady.' Why do you call me that? This isn't medieval Europe."

He chuckled. "Ah. Well, it's a mark of respect. You are descended from royalty, after all."

"Draugr royalty?"

"Something like that."

"Well, that's a mixed blessing." She smiled at him, and he smiled back. He had a lovely smile.

"It is, indeed."

"And you? Are you descended from royalty?"

His expression turned serious. "I am no royal. I am only a Huntsman, your faithful servant, my lady."

She considered everything he had told her about himself. "So... Special Operations Task Group. That's Swedish special forces?"

"Yes."

"And your special operation is to hunt the Draugr?"

He nodded. "Among other things."

"What other things?"

"I'm sorry," he said, sounding genuinely regretful. "I can't tell you that."

"Need to know basis, and I don't need to know?" she asked.

"Exactly."

"So you're telling me that you're a vampire with a day job?"

He shrugged. "The sword has been buried for centuries. I needed to do something with my time. The government of Sweden knows who we are and what we are called to do. That's why all of the men in my squad are Veithimathr, as well."

"Convenient."

He smiled and rose. "Tonight, I can tell you that my special operation is to keep you safe while you sleep. If you will consent to keeping your door open, I will stand guard just outside your bedroom."

She hated to admit it, but the thought of having a very capable man watching over her made her feel much more secure.

She nodded to him. "I would like that very much."

Chapter Five – Interlude (Erik)

He stood outside her room as she struggled to sleep. He knew that she was finding it difficult to relax, and it was no wonder - the life of a museum assistant curator was normally a quiet affair, where the greatest risk was a cut finger from the glass in a display case. She was completely unprepared for the message that he had brought to her last night, and for the ancient war that had come into her life.

She was actually sleeping now, and he took the opportunity to examine her. She was not what he had expected when he had first come to this place. He was not surprised at her physical frailty, given her bloodline - the women of the Valtaeigr were known for their delicacy. There had even been some who were physically disabled, their bodily forms overwhelmed by the spiritual gifts they had inherited.

He had just expected someone older.

To him, a curator should have been a woman of a certain age, with gray hair in a severe bun and sensible shoes. She should have been dour and dumpy, pudgy in the middle with stockings that wrinkled at the ankle. He was not expecting... her.

Nika Graves was none of those things.

He watched her now and took in the way her scarlet locks spilled over her pillow like the tributaries of some great fiery river. Her skin was porcelain white and flawless, her face unlined, her hands elegant and small like tiny birds. The stylish suit she had worn to work that day hung on a hanger, waiting to be taken to the dry cleaner, and her shoes with their ridiculous stiletto heels rested on the floor beside her bed. He remembered her running beside him, and he was amazed that anyone could even walk in such footwear.

She was beautiful. Unlike the last four women in her line that he had been able to find on his long journey out of Stockholm - or Agnafit, as he had known it in his youth - she was young and vibrant and full of potential. Her enemies had not yet found her, and she had not yet been made old and tired by her experiences at their hands.

She was still young as the Spring. It was appropriate.

She had clearly never been told about who she was, or about her bloodline. Being a Valtaeigr was both a blessing and a curse for her, as she was about to find out, just like being the Veithimathr was both blessing and curse for him. He would do his best to ensure that she only knew the blessing side of the equation. Let him take the curse from her this time.

She stirred in her sleep, and he looked away, worried that the weight of his stare had interrupted her hard-won slumber. He watched the living room clock and waited. When she fell quiet again, he returned back his contemplation.

He had known a Valtaeigr much like her once before, years ago. She had been the first of that family line that he had ever encountered, the first half-human, half-immortal he had ever known. He had loved her. Together, they had kept watch over Hakon's barrow. When she began to age, the mortality of her human mother dragging at her, she had begged him to choose her. He had refused.

Even now, he could remember the vivid green of her eyes and the scathing way she had castigated him for his decision, calling it a mistake. He had made enough mistakes to last a lifetime, even one as long as his, but not choosing her was not one of them.

Now, as he watched Nika sleeping, he vowed that things would be different.

Chapter Six – Interlude (Nika)

Her dreams were full of monsters, and the terror of being chased. In her dreams, she was running, always running, pursued by beasts with human faces and monstrous teeth that gnashed at her heels. She could feel them almost upon her, practically taste the fetid moisture of their breath as they bore down... and then she would wake.

In the quiet of her own room, with familiar shapes and scents around her, she would awake, and there he was. Erik Thorvald, standing like a sentinel at her bedroom door, his back to her, his face pointed out toward the enemy. She had never had enemies before, and it was still strange to have this man guarding her this way.

When she'd first retired that night, she'd found it difficult to get comfortable. It was alien and awkward having a stranger just outside her room. He was respectful, though, and as careful of her modesty and privacy as he was of her safety. Despite everything she'd ever heard warning her not to trust strange men at night, she had relaxed.

Now, in the sudden wakefulness following her escape from her nightmares, she was glad that he was there.

He was tall, much taller than any other man she'd known. Unlike some very tall men, though, he was broad as well, not gangly in the least. His shoulders were wide and even through his shirt, she could tell that his back was muscular and strong. His hair was thick and golden, ending just above his collar in a respectable businessman's haircut. If anyone gave him a second glance on the train, it would be because of his handsome face, not because he looked at all out of place.

When he was sitting still, there was nothing about him that seemed like anything other than a modern young executive. When he moved, though, that was when the mirage was shattered. He moved like a warrior, strong but controlled, with rapid reflexes and a fluid stride. She had seen him fight, and in retrospect she admired the economy of his motions. There had been no wasted energy in his struggle with the Draugr - the blows he had delivered had been precise, directed, purposeful.

She shuddered to remember the way that Draugr had looked at her, practically salivating like a wolf looking at a flock of lambs. He had captured her mind, paralyzed her against her will. He could have done anything to her. If vampires really were coming for her, she needed Erik's protection, because she was certainly not going to be able to protect herself.

She hated the feeling of weakness that the thought gave her, and the fear of being pursued in her waking hours made any hopes of going back to sleep evaporate. She sat up in bed and put her face into her hands.

Erik was beside her in an instant, sitting on the edge of the bed. "My lady?" he said, using that archaic phrase again. He put a hand onto her shoulder, alarmed by her tears. "What is it?"

In that moment, she was no longer the capable curator. She was no longer strong or independent. Instead, in the darkness, she felt small and vulnerable, and she took his hand and held it close to her chest.

Erik hesitated, then followed her lead. She pulled him down to the bed with her until he was lying behind her, his massive form curled around her back like a giant teddy bear. She clutched his hand in both of hers, holding it tightly. He pulled her into his arms and held her.

"I will keep you safe," he promised, his breath soft and warm against her ear. She shuddered, and he pulled her closer still. "I swear to you, I will not allow the Draugr to harm you."

Nika found herself crumbling, vulnerable in the mysterious mess her life had become, the pieces of the world she'd known lying scattered around her like so much rubble. She tried to speak, but in this dark moment, she could form no words.

Erik gently wiped her tears away and held her while she cried. He said nothing, and he did not pull away. There was nothing about him that was judging or disapproving. If anything, he was welcoming. He was safe.

She clung to him that way for a long while, and he held her the whole time. He said nothing, and he made no demands and passed no judgments. She needed him to lend her his strength, and he did so without comment or complaint.

He was everything she needed him to be, and soon, comforted by being in the safety of his arms, she slept.

Chapter Seven – Soul to Soul

When morning finally came, it found him in her kitchen, his suit jacket discarded. He had rolled up the sleeves of his white button-down shirt, and he was standing at the stove, beating a trio of eggs. His culinary preoccupation contrasted sharply with the shoulder holster and pistol that he was wearing, but somehow he made it look completely natural.

She wrapped herself in her robe and wandered out of the bedroom, a quizzical look on her face as she watched him puttering about. Erik looked up with a smile.

"Omelets," he announced. "And toast, and bacon if you want it."

"Wow. All this, and you cook, too."

"A man has to eat, and knowing how to cook is a good way to ensure that." He poured the eggs into the pan before him.

"Don't you... uh... Don't you drink blood?"

He paused in his busy work. "No. Not anymore." He glanced at her, looking almost embarrassed. "The Veithimathr are spared from the thirst, so we can go without... for a while."

She sat at the counter on one of the two stools that stood there. For the first time, she thought perhaps she should invest in a larger apartment, or at least in more furniture.

He turned from the stove and popped a cup into the Keurig. "You like expensive coffee," he commented. "And you're almost out."

She ran a hand through her hair. "Do you object?"

"Not at all. Whatever you like." He flipped the omelet in the pan, browning the other side. "I'm just more of an herbal tea guy, myself."

The image of him as an herbal tea swilling latter-day hippie made her smile. "Do you meditate?"

"Not if I can help it."

Erik put her mug into the right spot in the Keurig and turned it on, then plated up the omelet complete with a little vine of currants from her crisper. He put the plate in front of her and handed her a fork.

He smiled. "Bacon?"

"No, thanks. This is amazing." She took a bite. "You're hired."

"Glad to hear it." He retrieved her mug and provided her with her aromatic coffee, then took the bread out of the toaster and slathered it with butter. He put the toast onto a saucer and put it beside her plate.

"I'll say it again, wow..."

He smiled and made scrambled eggs for himself, which he piled onto a piece of toast he had already smothered in jam. She raised an eyebrow.

"That's different."

"I don't judge you for your hipster coffee," he teased. "Don't judge me for my Danish egg sandwich."

"No judging, I promise."

They ate together in companionable silence, and when they were finished, he cleared the dishes away. He had evidently made himself quite familiar with her kitchen and its contents. She wasn't sure if the end result was creepy or charming.

She retreated into the living room with a second mug of coffee and curled up on the couch. She had her feet tucked beneath her, the robe wrapped tightly closed. When he was done clearing up, he joined her, sitting at the other end, keeping a respectable distance between them. She was sorry that he hadn't sat closer.

She watched him as she sipped her coffee, and he sat placidly, allowing her to look and bearing the weight of her mild scrutiny. Finally, he smiled. "What?"

"Tell me about yourself," she said. "You know about me."

"I know about your ancestors. Not about you."

Maybe we can fix that, she thought. "No? Well... Tell me about this strange man I've invited into my apartment overnight."

Erik said, "Well, you know my name, Erik Thorvald. I'm the oldest of four brothers."

"All vampires?"

He looked surprised by the question. "Yes."

"Are you all soldiers?"

"Yes."

"Family tradition?"

"All Norse men are warriors," he said. "I thought you knew that."

"How long..."

"How long have I been alive? Centuries." He looked sad for a moment before he repeated, "Centuries."

"So you're a real Viking," she said.

"All Norse men who go out into the world in search of adventure and booty are Vikings, Nika," he said. "I know you know that."

She laughed, mildly uncomfortable and unable to say exactly why. "So you left Sweden to go a-viking."

"Exactly."

"And how's that working out for you?"

"Until last night? Not so well."

He looked into her eyes, and her mouth went dry. There were a million unspoken words in those blue depths.

"What made last night different?"

He closed the distance between them in less than a heartbeat, his hands on her face, turning her gently toward him. His lips grazed hers, then returned to steal a kiss that took her breath away. She put her mug aside and leaned into him, her hands sliding up his biceps to rest upon the rock-hard muscles of his shoulders. She pressed her lips to his, and for a long moment, there was nothing in the world but him.

He pulled away, his fingers soft as a whisper along the corner of her jaw. Her eyes were still closed when he sat back.

"I'm sorry," he began. "I shouldn't have done that."

She wanted to tell him not to apologize, that she wasn't offended, but words didn't come easily. Instead, she scooted forward, negating his retreat, and wrapped her arm around his neck, pulling him closer. He went willingly, bearing her gently down onto the couch.

He kissed her gently, as if she were a treasure. She delighted in him and his expert touch. Once she felt the tips of his teeth score her skin ever so slightly, just enough to make her skin tingle but not enough to make her bleed.

She put her hand in hair, holding his head to her throat. She knew she should not ask it of him, but she wanted so badly to experience the combination of his body and his teeth.

"Drink from me, Erik," she begged. "Please."

He kissed the throbbing vein at the corner of her jaw, and she could feel him quickening with the double desires that raged within him. Her spirit ached for him, reaching out, as if she had lifted ghostly arms around him as surely as she had wrapped him in her physical embrace.

She could feel a part of him stirring, his soul extending out toward her. His spirit, thrumming with life and with desire, seemed to reach out with invisible arms, wrapping around her and pulling her closer. She felt electrified and ecstatic.

She had never felt anything like this. It was as if he was loving her with his body and his soul at the same time. She was transported, and she ached for him to take more of her, to reach farther into the center of her being.

He lifted his head and opened his mouth, but at the last second, he turned away. The tendrils of his soul that had been pushing into her retreated, and though the physical pleasure was profound, she nearly wept with sorrow and frustration at the incomplete connection.

Erik pulled away reluctantly. He stroked her face. "I'm sorry," he whispered. "I can make love to you, but the rest... the rest I cannot do."

Nika tucked her head beneath his chin and simply held him.

Chapter Eight – The Calm Before the Storm

His cell phone ringing startled them both awake, and he located it with some difficulty among the pile of hastily-discarded clothes.

"Hello?"

She could hear another man's voice, and she was close enough to make out the words. "Rolf is inside."

"Good. Any reports?"

"Not yet," the other man said. "I'll let you know when he's gotten a good look around."

Erik nodded, though his conversation partner could not see him. "I hope to the gods that he avoids Astrid and Sigrunn. They both know his face."

"Trust him, Erik. He's the youngest, but he knows his job."

He looked unconvinced. Nika wondered if he had reason to worry, or if he was a professional control freak. She hoped that his need to control did not extend to his lovers.

"Well, keep me posted."

"Will do."

He hung up the call, then smiled at her apologetically. "Sorry about that."

"It's okay." She ran a hand through her hair. "I have a serious case of bed head. Or maybe couch head."

He chuckled. "I think you look beautiful."

"You'd better." She smiled at him, and he kissed the tip of her nose. "Who is Sigrunn?"

Erik deposited the phone onto the coffee table and cuddled up again. "She was the one who stole the sword."

Nika shuddered. "That's a face I won't forget…"

"Nor should you. It's important to know what your enemies look like. If she ever saw you again, she would try to kill you."

"That's not very comforting."

"Maybe not, but it's true."

She took a deep breath and suddenly felt awkward and uncomfortable. She slipped out of his arms and stood up, picking up her robe to hide her nakedness, although there was nothing of hers that he hadn't already seen.

He watched her, confusion making his eyebrows pucker. "Are you all right?"

"Fine," she lied. "I just... need to take a shower."

Silently, he watched her go.

***

The hot water cascading over her body was soothing, and she stood in the spray longer than was strictly necessary. Nika closed her eyes and let the heat wash over her.

She had never wanted to sleep with a man so soon after meeting him. She had certainly never felt that strange soul-to-soul connection that had almost formed. She was confused by the situation and by her own reactions.

Why was it so easy for her to accept his story about the vampires and the old Norse gods? She supposed it was because she had seen Sigrunn's teeth for herself, or perhaps because in the face of so much craziness, any explanation was better than more questions.

It just all felt so right.

She should have been horrified, not just for believing the unbelievable, but for actively trying to make him bring her into his strange world. She shook her head and ran her hands over her hair, sending excess water sluicing down over her shoulders.

'Please bite me?' What the hell was I thinking?

She knew that she should have been grateful that he had resisted temptation, but a part of her was so very disappointed.

She had never felt so completely out of her element.

***

Nika was still in the bathroom when Erik's phone rang again. It was Rolf.

"I'm inside," he said. "They've set up a hörgr."

That was bad news. If the Draugr had created a sacred stone table, then they were intending to use it for a sacrifice. "Do they have a sacrifice prepared?"

"No, although the pen is ready."

He nodded. "Well, that's one good thing, at least. Any sign of the sword?"

"No. I think Sigrunn is keeping it with her."

"That could make things complicated."

Rolf laughed softly. "My friend, when do we ever do anything without complications? I will call back when I know more."

The line went dead as Rolf ended the call in his usual abrupt manner. Erik rose and went to the window, contemplating the city below.

The world had changed so much in the years he had been alive. The sacred groves had all been replaced by high rises and parking lots, and nobody even seemed to remember the old gods at all.

As human attention passed and worship ended, the gods had lost their powers. They had finally been forced to take up residence within human hosts, binding themselves to lesser souls and riding along through incarnation after incarnation. Some had chosen to bind themselves to the Draugr, or to the Veithimathr. Others had chosen the Valtaeigr. A few had been forced to occupy humans, denied the more powerful vessels by those who had taken residence before them.

It had been on a dreary midwinter day when his time had come to take on a sacred passenger. He had agreed readily enough, though the ritual was painful in the extreme. He could still remember the feeling of liquid fire when the god Vidar had fused with his soul.

That was when Ithunn, goddess of the Spring, had taken Berit.

He closed his eyes as the memory rose. Berit, so small, so frail, the most delicate example of the Valtaeigr line. The princess, the priestess, his great love. He had come closer to choosing her than he had with any other woman.

He regretted every day that he had not done so in time. If their vampire selves had been linked, perhaps she could have gained enough strength from him to survive her transformation. Perhaps he could have experienced at least a little of that great happiness of living with a chosen mate before the ritual had taken her from him.

When she died, he vowed that he would find her again. He would know her soul anywhere, he was certain, and when the time was right, he would choose her after all. He had vowed to the gods that he would stop drinking blood, bypassing the life-saving healing that the dreyri could give, until he had found her again.

Three times before, he had re-encountered Berit, still bearing the companionship of Ithunn in her soul. Three times before, he had been too slow to choose her, and he had lost her. Three times, he had buried his beloved.

The last burial had left him grief-stricken and vulnerable, and when Astrid made him the offer of an alliance, he had rushed in, in too much pain to think about what he was doing. At the time, loneliness had been a bigger burden than the loss of his freedom. They were married at midsummer after the winter he had lost Berit the third time.

They had never been a good match. He had tried to be dutiful, to be a proper husband. Astrid was too cold, though, and too proud. She never stopped reminding him that she outranked him. She was the vessel of Freyja, the great goddess, and she never let him forget that the god who had joined with him was of a lower station.

They had never been equals, not even on their wedding day, and the situation only deteriorated from his perspective over the years. He was nothing more than a lackey to her, her prized possession, valuable as the chief of the Veithimathr and the vessel of the god who was destined to kill Fenrir at Ragnarok.

He doubted now if Ragnarok would ever come. The world had changed so much – if there was to be an apocalypse, it would be of humanity's own making. He very much doubted that there would be a giant immortal wolf for him to slay when that dark day came.

He heard the shower shut off, and he glanced back over his shoulder. Now was not the time to be lost in thought, he reminded himself. He turned back to his phone and dialed Gunnar.

"Go ahead," his old friend said.

"How's the arm?"

"Much improved. You should consider having at least a sip sometime... the dreyri is a remarkable thing."

Erik shook his head. "Someday you will stop trying to convince me."

"Only when you stop needing to be convinced."

It was an old conversation, and he abandoned it as quickly as he could. "How are things in the vault?"

"Hakon isn't much of a conversationalist."

"That's a good thing. If he starts talking, we have a problem."

Gunnar chuckled. "True enough. No, it's just me and the boys here around the box they have the old man's body in. Nobody is coming in, not even your wife."

"You know I hate it when you call her that."

"Would you prefer it if I called her your keeper?"

He groaned. "I like that even less."

"Then don't complain." He could hear Hrothgar's voice in the background, speaking to someone. Hrothgar seemed to be allergic to quiet. Gunnar responded quickly, his hand muffling the phone, and then he returned. "I'll call you if anything happens, but so far... nothing."

"Good. Be safe."

"Roger that."

He shut off the phone again and went back to staring out the window.

***

Erik was talking on his cellphone when Nika came out of the bathroom, fresh from the shower. He was standing by the window, not at all self-conscious in his nudity. His body was muscular perfection, and his skin was shining in the rays of the setting sun. She found herself staring at him while he talked, drinking in the beauty of the sight.

She didn't know where any of this was leading, but seeing him this way, she was happy to go anywhere, as long as he was going, too.

He ended the call and turned toward her, a smile on his face. "Look who's back," he said, coming to her and kissing her gently.

She returned the kiss and ran her hands over the hills and valleys of his rippling abdomen. "Look who's here," she returned. "Who was that?"

He tossed his phone onto the couch. "I was just checking in. One of our agents is on the inside now with the Draugr, and hopefully he'll be able to tell us where they took the Sword."

Nika wrapped her arms around his waist and looked up at him, her chin on his chest. "And until then?"

"Until then, we wait." He stroked her shoulders. "You stay here, and I stand guard."

"What about dinner?"

"I'll cook."

"Eggs again?"

He laughed. "Is there a problem with eggs?"

They sat together on the couch, Nika tucked up under his arm. She rested her head, her ear just above his heart. She could hear it beating, steady and strong.

"Are you really in the Swedish Special Forces, or is that just a cover?"

He chuckled. "I really am. I'm a captain in the Swedish army."

Nika listened to his heart for a moment more, her mind filling with questions. There would be no better time to give voice to them, so she decided to go ahead and ask.

"You said that the Draugr aren't like Hollywood. Obviously, the sun doesn't hurt you. And I don't think you're undead... are you?"

"No. Not undead. Immortal, more or less."

She frowned. "More or less? You can be killed?"

"Silver can hurt all Draugr. Fire can kill us. Having our hearts carved out, beheading, well... that will give anyone a bad day." He kissed her damp hair. "But those are the only things that can kill me."

"And what can hurt you?"

"Bullets hurt, but if they're only lead, they're just an inconvenience. If you drain out all of our blood, we're paralyzed. We can only come back from that by feeding."

She straightened. "What do you feed on?"

He looked almost embarrassed. "We're vampires, love. What do you think?"

"Blood."

"Yes. And the life force it contains."

"Animal blood?"

He shook his head. "It must be human."

She touched his lips, then pushed a fingertip into his mouth to feel the edges of his teeth. "You don't have fangs right now. I know I felt them earlier."

He kissed her finger, then said, "They grow when I need to feed, or when I'm badly hurt, or when I'm enraged."

She grinned. "Were you a berserker?"

He made a scoffing sound. "There are berserkers among the Draugr, make no mistake, but... no. Not me."

Nika settled back against his chest and took his hand between hers, interlacing their fingers. She was quiet for a long while, then said, "You've been alive for a very long time. You must have some amazing stories."

Erik shrugged. "Most of my stories are boring."

"I don't believe it for a minute."

"You would be very surprised. I go where my superiors tell me to go, and I do what they tell me to do."

"And today they told you to babysit me." She looked up at him. "Cushy job."

"Much preferable to anything else I can think of." He kissed her. "Rank has its privileges."

She grinned. "I should say so."

She was just about to suggest a way to pass the time when his phone rang again, and he answered it brusquely. "Thorvald."

Another male voice spoke over the line, hushed and rapid. She could not make out the words.

Erik responded, speaking that not-Swedish that she had heard him use with Astrid. She presumed now, given what she had learned about him, that he was speaking Old Norse. He and the man on the line spoke briefly, and then Erik hit the "end" button.

"They've found it." He rose. "I need to go and get that sword, and I need you to stay here."

She stood up as he gathered his discarded clothes and began to dress. He was moving rapidly, preparing to rush out into danger. She wouldn't have it.

"No."

He hesitated, his zipper halfway closed. "What?"

"I said no. I'm going with you."

Erik looked exasperated. "You can't do that."

"Why not? I can help."

He raised an eyebrow. "I doubt that. Not in a fight like this."

"How do you know you're going to fight?"

Now he looked insulted. "Nika, I have been a soldier for a millennium. I know when a fight is coming."

"And if they come for me in the meantime?"

"We'll keep them too busy to even think about it."

"But... how many of them are there?"

"Enough, but not that many. As long as you don't ask any of them inside, they can't hurt you. Just stay here behind your locks and you'll be safe."

He finished dressing and pulled the Sálsteinn out of his pocket. He put it in her palm and closed her hand over it. The stone was warm and pulsating against her skin.

"Keep hold of this. It's better if I don't take it into their den."

"So you trust me to keep this stone safe, but you don't trust me to go with you?"

He nodded. "Yep. That about covers it."

Erik kissed her soundly, then opened all of the locks on the door. "Lock this up after I leave," he told her.

The door closed on the rest of her arguments.

Chapter Nine – Enemies

Erik met Gunnar in a parking lot halfway across town. His partner was pacing when he arrived, ready for some action. Gunnar climbed into the car with him and they drove toward the Draugr's lair.

It was an old mansion on the outskirts of the city, standing on a steep hill and overlooking the town. The house had been some Victorian architect's triumph, and it still wore a certain weathered grace. There was a garage – probably formerly a carriage house – and a gardener's shed, a pond and a stable. Erik could smell the horses.

He stopped the car on the road, concealed from the house by a tall and unmanicured hedge. He and Gunnar conferred one last time.

"Hrothgar is standing over Hakon, but Magnus is already here. Rolf is inside, and he left the back door unlocked for us." Gunnar pulled out a hastily-drawn floor plan of the house. "This is the back door. It goes into the kitchen here. There's a mud room, with a landing that leads to stairs. Go up and you're on the first floor. Go down and it's the basement."

"Where is the sword?"

He tapped one of the rooms on the upper floor. "This is Sigrunn's room. Rolf says that she has it stowed in there."

"She's not carrying it anymore?"

"Apparently not. He said he saw her leave without it."

Erik nodded and went to the trunk of the car. It was loaded with weapons, both modern and ancient. He selected a Remington semi-automatic pistol and loaded it with a magazine of silver bullets. He donned a gear strap and attached three more magazines to it. Last, he took up a double-headed axe.

Gunnar smiled. "Ingrid is coming out to play."

"Stop naming my axes," he grumbled.

His partner armed himself, too, and then they crept up the hill to the back door of the house.

The grounds were suspiciously quiet, and Erik noticed as they reached the door that the silence was from a lack of birds. There should have been sparrows, or starlings, or at least an ant or two on the ground, but there was nothing. It was as if all evidence of animal life had been chased away.

"This is no ordinary hörgr," he told his partner in a whisper.

Gunnar nodded. "Hel."

He sincerely hoped that was not the case. Of all the gods he would like to encounter, the queen of the underworld was not high on the list. The last he had heard, the soul that Hel was tied to had been reborn, but far away, and very recently. There was no way that she and her vessel could be here.

At least, he hoped that was the case.

He turned the knob on the back door slowly, as silently as he could. It opened without so much as a click. The lock had been padded with shredded toilet paper, keeping the lock from engaging; Rolf had done his job well.

With Gunnar bringing up the rear, Erik entered the house cautiously. As described on the floor plan, the back door opened up into a recessed mud room area. A staircase led down to the left, leading into darkness that smelled of mildew and rotting onions. On the right, three steps led up into the kitchen.

Gunnar pointed down, and Erik nodded. They needed to find the Rune Sword, yes, but they also needed to find that altar.

Slowly, quietly, they crept down into the basement.

****

Nika paced through the apartment, feeling caged and ridiculous. Despite Erik's stories and his arch warning to stay behind closed doors, she was aching to go out. She felt as if she needed to be somewhere.

She sat on the sofa and held the Soul Stone in her hand. It was pretty, almost jade-green and smooth as glass. There were no flaws in the stone's surface that her fingertips could detect. It slowly pulsed, the light ebbing and flowing like the tide. It was somehow hypnotic.

She stared into the stone, watching the slow strobe of its light, and her mind began to drift.

She saw a stone altar, standing in the middle of a stand of giant oaks, occupying the central grove. She was standing beside it, dressed in a shapeless white robe. The grove was ringed by figures in brown robes.

They were chanting. It was an invocation of some kind. She looked to a woman who stood at the foot of the altar, a tall blonde with sea-blue eyes. The woman nodded to her, and she climbed up onto the altar, lying down.

She looked up and saw the sky, hints of black and starlight peeking down around the crowns of the ancient trees. She lay on her back on the cold stone altar.

She saw a robed man take a gem much like the Soul Stone and put it into a mortar. He ground it into powder while the other people continued their chant. When he was finished, he brought it to the woman, who poured an amber liquid into the bowl. They stirred the mixture with a sprig of mistletoe, and then the man came forward and bade her drink.

She took the cup and looked up into his eyes, looking beneath the hood of his robe.

It was Erik.

A sudden pounding sound shattered the vision, and she jumped back with a gasp, her hands flying down to grip the sofa cushions. The Soul Stone fell to the floor and skipped away beneath the couch.

The pounding came again, and she realized that someone was knocking.

The sound wasn't coming from the door.

Slowly, afraid of what she would see, Nika turned toward the window.

A man was standing there, the flat of his hand beating against the window frame. He saw her. She knew he saw her. He made eye contact with her and smiled.

He pounded on the window again. The glass pane shivered in the frame, but somehow it held.

Another sudden pounding erupted from the bedroom window, and she whirled to look. Through the open door, she could see the window beside her bed. Another man was standing there, grinning at her. When he saw her looking, he licked his lips obscenely.

They could not have been standing at her windows. She was on the fourth floor.

She ran to the window in the living room and pulled the curtain, as if that would make him go away. Another vampire appeared at the next window, and the next, until every window had a leering Draugr beating on the frame. She raced from window to window, pulling the shades and closing the curtains. At the last window, the Draugr laughed at her.

The pounding stopped, and a pregnant silence filled the room. She grabbed her purse and found the can of mace that she carried. She clung to it, although in truth she didn't know what good it would do her against a vampire. She backed into the bathroom, which had no windows, and closed the door.

The knocking resumed, deafening, shaking the building to its foundations. She could feel the floor vibrate with every beat of their impromptu drum. The Draugr were beating against the windows in unison, not just with each other, but with her heartbeat. They were showing her that she could hide, but they could still hear her pulse.

They were the hunters. She was the prey.

Nika dug through her purse and pulled out her cell phone, prepared to hit the pre-programmed panic button that would call 911. She hesitated just before she could send out the call. What was she supposed to tell them? That vampires were stalking her, please bring silver? They would send an ambulance to take her to the psychiatric hospital, not a cruiser full of officers prepared to do battle with the undead.

She hadn't gotten Erik's number, which had been a mistake on both of their parts. She could think of no one else to call.

Desperately, she pulled out Astrid Sigurdsdottir's business card and dialed her cellphone number. The phone rang twice, and then the other woman's voice came on the line, cool and collected.

"Hello?"

Nika fairly screamed, "You've got to help me! They're here. They're surrounding my apartment and they're trying to get in."

"Who is trying to get in?" Astrid asked. There was amusement in her tone.

"The Draugr!"

There was silence for a moment on the other end of the line. "What did you say?"

"I know. Erik told me everything. They're trying to get in." The pounding intensified. "Please, help me!"

This time when she spoke, any hint of mirth was gone. "Where is your apartment?" Astrid asked. "Quickly."

She rattled off the address and begged, "Hurry. Please, please hurry!"

"I'll be right there. Are you safe?"

"I'm locked into the bathroom," she said. "Please, I don't know what to do."

She could plainly hear the echoes of Astrid's heels on the museum floor. "Shall I come in when I get there?"

Nika nodded, "Yes. Yes, come in. Help me fight these things off!"

The phone went dead, and the pounding at the windows reached a frightful crescendo. Nika curled up in a fetal position in the shower, her arms covering her head.

***

Gunnar and Erik made their careful way down the stairs into the basement. There were no lights, but they were Veithimathr, so light was not all that necessary. The could see well enough without it.

Erik held his gun in front of him, carefully pointing the way, ready to open fire if any of the Draugr were to leap out at him. The musty smell was deeper here at the bottom of the stairs, and immediately ahead of him, a weathered wooden door stood closed. He pushed it open.

He should have predicted the whining of the hinges, the haunted-house sound effect that ripped the air around them. Gunnar froze, looking up the stairs toward the rest of the house. There was no sound of footsteps, and no indication of anyone approaching. Emboldened, Erik pushed the door open further and proceeded.

He stepped through the doorway and into a scene that took his breath away. Here in the basement of this modern house, in a room that took up the entire foundation, the Draugr had recreated the sacred grove at Uppsala. The hörgr stood in the center of a circle of papier-maché trees, molded in the form of giant oaks thickly hung with mistletoe and holly. The heavy branches, as false as the trunks, reached out over the altar and formed a protective canopy.

Between the trees, statutes stood, carved from real oak wood. The one in the center was Thor, the mighty god, his hammer in his hand. Flanking him were representations of Odin, his missing eye covered by a swath of homespun cloth. On the other side stood Freyr, god of joy. All three had been colored black with a combination of pitch and animal blood.

The smell of the blood was like a drug in their noses. Both men approached slowly, their weapons forgotten. Erik held out a hand and pressed it against Freyr's side. It came away coated with gore.

He smelled the blood on his hand. "Dogs and horses," he told Gunnar, speaking in their ancient native tongue.

"Then they have already begun the sacrifices." His partner sounded both awestruck and afraid. "What is the moon phase?"

He didn't need to look to know. He always knew. "Waning."

Behind Thor stood a stylized version of the World Tree, Yggdrasil. The bodies of the sacrificed animals hung from its branches, draining into vats beneath them.

"How long?"

He meant until the new moon, until the time for the darkest magic to be performed. "Three days."

Gunnar growled in his throat, and his voice was thick. "We need to desecrate this shrine. We need to stop them."

"First we need to find the Sword," Erik reminded him. "It isn't down here. Let's keep looking."

They abandoned the shrine and the echoes of the lives they'd led so long ago and so far away. Erik could not say that he didn't feel a little homesick. He also felt thirst, real vampire thirst, and he struggled to push it away. The sooner he left this blood-soaked room, the easier that would be.

***

The pounding outside Nika's apartment stopped abruptly, and the sudden silence was almost more unnerving than the noise had been. She clung to her mace and tried to stay hidden in the shower.

Someone knocked on her front door loudly, twice. "Miss Graves?"

It was Astrid. Nearly weeping in relief, Nika abandoned her hiding place and ran to the door, opening the locks and flinging it open wide.

The Valtaeigr looked concerned on the other side of the threshold. "Miss Graves!" She exclaimed. "I'm so grateful you aren't hurt!"

Nika grabbed her arm and pulled her inside, then slammed and locked the door again. "Are they gone? They were at every window..."

"They've gone." Astrid put her hands on the red-haired woman's shoulders. "Breathe. You're safe now. They've fled."

"Are you sure? Did you see them leave?"

"Calm down!"

The rattled woman hurried from window to window, looking out for signs of her unwelcome guests. They were nowhere to be found. Astrid watched her scurry for a while, then went to her, a gentle hand on her back.

"You are so terrified! I would not have expected someone of your bloodline to be so fearful."

She felt insulted. "They were going to kill me."

"No, they weren't." She pulled Nika to sit beside her on the couch. Beneath the furniture, the Soul Stone flickered once and went silent.

Nika felt the change in the jewel, and she looked from Astrid to the door. It was slowly dawning on her that she may have done a very bad thing.

"I asked you in," she breathed, more to herself than to Astrid.

The other woman smiled broadly, her long Draugr teeth descending into the light. "Yes, she nodded. You did."

She grabbed Nika's throat in one hand and squeezed. Nika struggled against the grip, kicking and clawing, but Astrid's strength was unbreakable. Astrid never stopped smiling.

She could not breathe, and her vision was darkening from the edges inward, sparkling with stars. She held on as long as she could, crying out in her mind for help, until finally the darkness overtook her and she fell still.

Chapter Ten – Flux

Erik and Gunnar searched the ground floor of the house, the upper floor with the bedrooms, and even the attic. There were signs everywhere of habitation, but the place was utterly vacant. There was no sign of Rolf or of the sword.

"Where is he?" Erik asked. Gunnar shook his head.

"I don't know. He was supposed to meet us here. They certainly all cleared out..."

"Suspicious, isn't it?"

Erik scanned the ceilings as he walked through the house, looking for the telltale signs of electronic surveillance. He could hear a soft whirring behind one door, but when he opened it, he found only a busily spinning clothes dryer on a timed cycle. He closed the door again.

"This feels all wrong," he told Gunnar. "Let's get out of here and regroup."

They retreated to their vehicle, keeping their eyes on the skies, watching for the airborne return of their immortal enemies. They made it to the car unmolested and climbed in, keeping their weapons with them instead of returning them to the trunk. Erik threw the car into gear while Gunnar fired up his radio.

"Unit one to unit two, do you copy?"

A long moment of white noise ensued, then a crackling voice replied, "Unit two, copy. Go ahead, unit one."

"Status?"

"All quiet. Dead man still dead." Hrothgar sounded bored.

"Any word from Rolf?"

"No. Didn't he make the rendezvous?"

"Negative. No contact."

Hrothgar cursed colorfully in Old Norse. Erik nodded and muttered, "That's what I'm sayin'."

A thought occurred to him, and he took the radio out of Gunnar's hand.

"Status on Diva?"

"She left here about an hour ago. Said she was going to lunch." Hrothgar hesitated. "You know. Lunch."

He meant that Astrid had gone to feed. Gunnar frowned. "In the middle of the day?"

Their colleague responded, "Hey, when the thirst hits..."

Erik frowned and handed the radio back to Gunnar, who told their friends, "Keep in touch with any changes."

"Roger that."

Gunnar put the radio away and looked at his partner. "Now what?"

He shook his head. "Everything feels wrong. This is... just..." He took a deep breath. "You don't think Rolf switched sides, do you?"

"No. Absolutely not. He'd die first. We all would."

"He said that the sword was there."

"Yeah, well, it's gone now..."

Erik scowled. "And so is he. Maybe he took it and ran when the house cleared out. But why wouldn't he contact us? And why did the house clear out?"

It wasn't unusual for a houseful of Draugr to empty at night, when they went out to hunt their human prey. During the day, though, they normally rested.

Gunnar fiddled with the dials on the radio and called out: "Unit one to unit three, over."

There was no response. Erik drove them out of the suburban neighborhood and back toward the city. His partner tried again.

"Unit three, do you copy?"

The radio tweeted, and Astrid's voice came through as steady and strong as if she were in the car. "Diva to unit one. Report."

"This is unit one." Erik shook his head sharply, and his companion amended what he had started to say. "Nothing to report. Heading out to the rendezvous site now."

Erik nodded approvingly, and Gunnar warmed to his own lie.

Astrid's response sounded very surprised. "You're going just now?"

"Encountered some delays in the city," he answered.

"Where are you now?"

Erik turned onto the eastbound lane of the local highway, and Gunnar said, "West bound to Hillsview. Three clicks to rendezvous."

"Very well." She sounded nonplussed. "Report back with what you encounter."

"Roger that." He turned the radio off. "She's gone over to them."

Erik nodded. "So it seems. She always was ambitious – I guess having the sword so close was more than she could stand. I'll bet she had Rolf bring the sword to her." He glanced at his partner. "Let's go check her hotel room."

***

Nika awoke to find herself bound at the ankles and wrists, lying on her side in the back seat of a limousine. Astrid was sitting on the seat facing her, her back to the driver, a wicked-looking dagger in her hand.

"Good morning, princess," she greeted coldly. "So good of you to join us."

In the rearview mirror, Nika could see that the woman Erik had called Sigrunn was driving the car. She tugged against her restraints but was held fast. She lay still again.

"You could have just invited me to take a drive with you," she said, her mouth dry. "You didn't have to choke me out."

"You were hysterical. You would never have come without making a huge scene," Astrid sniffed. "Honestly, I'm disappointed in you. I would have thought that a god's vessel would have more intestinal fortitude."

Nika scowled. "Well, pardon me. It was my first vampire attack."

Sigrunn chuckled. "Won't be your last."

"Hush." The reprimand was gently spoken, and it was received with a shrug. Astrid crossed her legs and leaned back, studying Nika. "He has had sex with you. I can smell it."

"Excuse me?"

"You heard me." She swung her foot idly. "I honestly don't care where my husband sows his seed."

She felt punched in the stomach. "Husband?"

"Yes," she smiled. "Didn't he tell you? Oh, well. I'm sure there's a great deal he hasn't told you yet. He's full of secrets, our Erik."

She should have known. It had been too good to be true. She closed her eyes. "Apparently."

"He's given your field a good plowing, but he hasn't chosen you. Odd, considering."

Her voice was flat. "Considering what?"

"Considering who you are to him."

"And what's that?"

Astrid chuckled. "Oh, my dear, if he hasn't told you, then I'm certainly not going to say a word. I'll leave that to you two love birds to sort out."

She looked away from the other woman's gloating expression, casting her gaze out the window. From her vantage point, she could see only electrical wires and the tops of trees. There were no buildings.

"We're not in the city any longer."

"No."

Sigrunn volunteered, "We're taking you someplace special."

Whatever that meant, Nika decided that it couldn't have been anything good. She pulled against her bonds again.

"It's no use," Astrid told her. "You're not going to break free. You might as well just enjoy the ride, little Valtaeigr."

"I thought you were Valtaeigr, too."

"Yes," she nodded, "but soon I'll be so much more. You'll help me with that, I hope."

Nika looked away and stayed silent.

***

The entire team from Stockholm was staying in the same hotel, with rooms on the same corridor. Erik and Gunnar went directly to Astrid's room.

"Do you have a key?" his partner asked.

Erik shook his head. "No. And I don't need one." He grasped the door handle and turned it with all of his strength. The mechanism within the lock shattered, and the door swung open.

He could sense the sword immediately. It took no time at all to find it, wrapped in a velvet cloth and tucked beneath the pillows of the bed. As soon as he picked it up, the runes in the blade flared and shifted, changing before their eyes.

The nonsense message that had been etched into the blade changed while they watched, the runes flowing together and changing until they spelled out a very legible message: What was lost has been found.

"By Odin," Gunnar breathed.

The spot on the cross piece where the Sálsteinn should have been was a dull spot in the middle of the green glow from the runes. The void was dark and foreboding, and Erik was suddenly filled with the conviction that Nika was in danger.

"Go to the vault," he told his partner. "They're going to come for Hakon, and we can't let them take him."

"Where are you going?"

"To get the Soul Stone." He tightened his grip on the sword. "May the gods smile on us all."

Chapter Eleven - Casualties

Nika was dumped unceremoniously in one of the bedrooms on the second floor, still hogtied. Sigrunn dropped her onto the bed and looked down at her with a sneer. She said nothing, but her opinion was clear to see in her expression. She left the room, locking the door behind her.

She worried at the ropes, tugging and twisting until her skin was rubbed raw, and finally one of the loops loosened enough that she freed one hand. After that, it was an easy thing to untie herself the rest of the way.

She tested the door, although she had seen Sigrunn lock it. There was no escape that way. There was only one window in the room, and it overlooked a sheer drop down to the driveway. The window itself had been painted shut, and though she tried, she could not open it.

She looked around the room and found nothing that she could use as a weapon that would hurt vampires. There was a brass candle holder, tall and ornate, but it would do nothing against her captors. The hinges on the door were on the inside, but the screws had been painted over, as well. She didn't have anything she could use as a screwdriver, anyway.

Nika went to the door and listened. She could hear no voices, and there was no indication of anyone moving around outside her room. If she was going to make a move, she would have to do it now.

She grabbed the candle holder and swung it like a baseball bat, shattering the window glass. The sound was startlingly loud. She grabbed the coverlet from the bed and put it over the broken shards, said a prayer for luck, and climbed out of the window.

She tried to grab the window frame and lower herself down, but the glass still bit through the coverlet, slashing her palms. She clenched her teeth to keep from crying out. Blood dripped down her wrists.

There was nothing to do but let go. She dropped to the ground and landed feet first. The impact was jarring but not as damaging as she would have expected. It was bad enough to jam both of her ankles, but she was not hobbled for long.

The limousine was gone, and there were no other cars in sight. She had no idea where she was. She only knew that she had to get away, and fast.

She ran across the yard to the stable, hoping she remembered how to ride a horse. She burst through the doors and looked around, taking stock of the seven stalls, each one occupied by a high-quality equine. She ran to the eighth stall, hoping to find something she could use.

When she saw the contents of the eighth stall, she stopped short, her blood turning to ice. There was a man hanging from the roof, naked and suspended by one ankle, his wrists bound and scraping the floor. He was surrounded by a pool of blood. His back was horribly mangled, the ribs shattered and his organs exposed. Horribly, she could see his heart, and it was beating.

He opened his eyes.

"Radio," he rasped.

She was in shock and did not respond immediately. After a moment, though, she searched the stall and found a heap of clothes and gear in the corner. There was no radio.

"I can't find one," she told him.

He struggled to breathe, barely able to inhale at all. He mouthed, "Phone."

She dug further into the pile, finding nothing. She was about to give up when she saw the edge of a smart phone sticking up out of the straw. She grabbed the phone and brought it to him.

He was silent, his eyes closed again. His heart was still beating, but it was ragged and irregular. She had no idea how to help him.

She turned on the phone and dialed 911. Before the operator could answer, she hung up, once again stymied by what she should say to the mortal authorities.

She was saved from her indecision by an incoming call. She answered it.

"We need help."

There was a pause on the line, and then a man spoke. "Who is this?"

"You've got to help me. Astrid kidnapped me and brought me out to this house – I don't even know where I am – and there's a man here whose back has been shredded and..."

"Who is this?" he repeated.

She took a deep breath. "Nika Graves."

"Why do you have Rolf's phone?"

"He... Rolf is injured. You have to help him."

"Stay where you are. I will get help to you."

The phone went dead, and she turned to look at the unfortunate man. "Rolf?"

He opened his eyes with some difficulty.

She tried to find a way to cut him down, but there was no way that she could reach the beam from which he was hanging. She went to him and knelt beside him, trying to offer him whatever comfort she could.

"Help is coming. Hold on."

***

Erik drove as quickly as he could to Nika's apartment. He parked in the alley and raced up the stairs to her door, the Rune Sword in his hand. His heart sank when he saw it standing open, the chains for the locks dangling down the frame.

He went inside, feeling a slight tingle at the threshold but having no trouble crossing over, since she had invited him inside. The sword began to shiver in his hand, pointing toward the couch, and in the shadows, he could see the Soul Stone glowing.

He knelt and reached under the couch, and the stone leaped into his hand as if someone had thrown it. It was burning hot, and he hissed in pain as he pulled it out. He heard a voice whispering in the back of his head.

Without taking a single moment to consider his action, he pushed the stone into the hole in the sword's cross piece. It melded into place with a burst of heat like an incendiary grenade that sent him tumbling across the floor. He rolled up unto his feet, his eyes wide.

The sword was hovering in mid-air, spinning slowly, point down. The Soul Stone was gleaming like the bulb in a flashlight, and the runes on the blade were shifting again. They moved and flowed like quicksilver. The whispering in his head grew louder, and he recognized the voice of Vidar, the deity who had melded with his soul so many years ago.

The runes on the blade coalesced so that on one side they said Ithunn, and Berit on the other side.

In his head, Vidar spoke. Nika.

Erik's mind filled with a vision of Nika in a stable, kneeling in bloody straw, tears on her cheeks. He knew without a doubt that she was in danger, and that he needed to go to her.

He also knew exactly where she was.

***

Hrothgar was just ending his phone call when Gunnar came into the vault. "Nika Graves answered Rolf's phone. She said he's hurt. I don't know where they are."

"Nika Graves?" the new arrival echoed. "Why would she... Oh." He got out his phone and dialed Erik.

There was no answer. The voice mail greeting played, and then he left a hurried message.

"Get to the house. Graves is out there with Rolf's phone. I don't know how we missed it."

Magnus was standing near the open-topped wooden box holding Hakon's remains. He was staring into the Draugr's face. "Do you think he can hear us?"

They never had a chance to answer. The door to the room burst open, shattered by a grenade. The three men were showered with shrapnel and tossed into the air by the force of the blast. A trio of men in black fatigues rushed in, and while one kept an assault rifle trained on the fallen Huntsmen, the other two stole the body.

Hrothgar drew his weapon and fired into the rifleman's chest, striking him squarely in the heart with a bullet made of silver and salt. The man dropped to the ground and disintegrated into a pile of ash. Gunnar appropriated the rifle and chased the retreating thieves into the hallway.

There were more Draugr outside, and as soon as he stepped foot out of the vault, he was riddled with silver bullets that tore through him. He managed to squeeze the trigger as he fell, but his shots hit the walls and ceiling.

Sigrunn stepped into view, standing over him while more Draugr rushed into the vault. He could hear gunfire as they raked his brothers in arms with bullets. He looked up at his enemy, and she smiled, raising her axe. The blade was the last thing he ever saw.

Chapter Twelve – Blood Eagle

Erik sped to the house on the hill, flouting every traffic law he encountered. The sword rested on the passenger seat, humming to itself like a distracted child. In his head, Vidar was still muttering, urging him onward. He thought he was going to go insane.

He drove right up to the house, abandoning stealth in favor of saving time. Without even turning off the engine, he grabbed the sword and climbed out of the car.

Night was coming. The sky was turning gray, and the wind was chillier than before. The Draugr were stronger in the dark. He had to hurry.

"Nika!" he shouted. "Nika!"

The sword tugged as if someone had grabbed it by the blade, and it pointed directly at the stable. He followed the sign, hoping that the Aesir would not lead him into any traps.

He burst into the stable. "Nika!"

She appeared in the door to the last stall on the right, her face streaked with tears, her legs coated with blood. He rushed to her and embraced her.

"Are you all right?"

She hugged him back, then stiffened. "Help him."

Rolf was dangling from the ceiling like Odin from Yggrasil. Erik's stomach turned when he saw his friend's back. They had given him the blothern – the blood eagle.

"Rolf," he said. "I've got you."

He launched himself into the air, indulging in Draugr flight. It was something that he rarely did, mostly because he rarely had the strength. His vow to stop drinking blood had left him weakened. He was strong enough to free his friend, though, cutting the rope that held him to the beam and lowering him gently to the bloody ground.

Rolf gasped for air, suffering greatly. He looked up at Erik with pleading eyes. Erik understood.

"Nika," he said softly. "Step outside."

She did not obey. She took a step back, but she stayed in the doorway, watching in horrified fascination.

Erik gently rolled Rolf onto his side and put him back together as best he could. He wasn't certain he could help his friend, and he blinked back tears. He held his hands over the horrible wounds in Rolf's back, and he closed his eyes. In Old Norse, he began to pray.

"Oh lords of Asgard, help me..."

His teeth descended, and he slashed his wrists deeply. His blood poured onto Rolf's injuries, but the power of his vampire blood could do nothing to help. He was too far gone for healing now.

Erik knew that he would not be able to save him, but he could not bring himself to abandon Rolf to his dark fate. He forced himself to continue bleeding, praying all the while, hoping against hope that his friend would begin to heal. His prayers went unanswered.

Nika saw the color draining from Erik's face, and she rushed forward. She grabbed his wrists in her hands and tried to seal the open gashes with her fingers.

"Stop," she said. "He's gone."

He leaned into her, his eyes closed, and he began to weep. "I failed him."

She held him silently, stroking his back. "It wasn't your fault. Come on...we need to get out of here."

She coaxed Erik to stand, and in his weakened condition, he depended on her for support. At their feet, Rolf's body shuddered once, then became a pile of soot and ashes amid the pool of red.

They went to the car and drove back to the city.

Chapter Thirteen – Choosing

They returned to his hotel room instead of to her apartment, since that was no longer safe. She helped him in, supporting him through the lobby and into the elevator. An older lady entered the elevator with them, smiling at them gently.

Nika supposed that she and Erik probably looked like young lovers coming back from an overly-indulgent night on the town. Luckily the Rune Sword was wrapped in Rolf's jacket and hidden between them. She smiled back and stayed silent.

They went to Erik's room, and he gave her the key. She swiped it through the lock, and then they were inside.

She put him on the bed and tucked the sword beneath the bedspread at his side. He looked up at her, but she could not meet his eyes. He sighed and turned away.

There were hundreds of things she wanted to say, but they all tried to come out at once, so she was unable to speak at all. Her emotions choked her, a bottle neck in the back of her throat that she could barely breathe around.

"Are you hurt?" he asked her, his voice barely above a whisper.

"No."

He closed his eyes, and she watched him. He was the most beautiful man she'd ever seen, and she yearned for him as she had never yearned for any man before. Something inside of her ached for him, and her spirit wanted to reach out to his once more. She needed him.

She wondered if his wife needed him, too.

Finally, she asked, "Why didn't you tell me you were married?"

Erik kept his eyes closed. "Because it doesn't matter."

"Doesn't matter? You made me think we had something special."

"We do. Astrid is nothing to me."

"She is your wife."

"She is my political obligation." He finally opened his eyes and looked at her again. "Marriage among the Draugr is not like marriage among mortals. Ours is an arrangement for political solidarity, nothing more."

"Solidarity?" she echoed, skeptical.

"The Veithimathr and the Valtaeigr must be united against the darkness. I am the chieftain of my kind, and she is one of the princesses of hers."

"I thought you said you weren't royalty."

"I'm not." He shook his head. "Huntsman rank is earned through battle, not by right of birth."

"Still..." She knew that the timing of this was all wrong, that he was grieving and shouldn't have to deal with this now. She couldn't stop herself. "I won't be anybody's mistress."

Erik ran a hand over his face in exasperation. "You aren't. Astrid and I have been separated for years and years."

"I think she still loves you."

"Astrid loves nobody but Astrid."

She stood and walked to the window, arms crossed. She stared out at the street, watching the traffic come and go like a mechanical tide.

"Nika," he pleaded, "don't turn away from me. Not now."

Erik rose from the bed and went to her, putting his arms around her. She shook free of him and took a step away. "What do we do now, with the sword and Astrid and all of this?"

"You're changing the subject, just like that?"

"There's nothing left to say."

"There is." He sat down. "Please... there's something I've been keeping from you, and you need to know."

"Something worse than the fact that you're married?"

"Something more powerful."

"I can hardly wait," she said, sarcastic. She sat on the other bed, facing him. "Fine. Talk."

"In all of my life, I have had only one great love. She was a princess of the Valtaeigr, and I was a lowly Huntsman. We never should have been together... but we were."

Nika's face was unreadable. He continued.

"Her name was Berit."

Something inside of her shook at the sound of the name, a strange combination of shock and elation. Her mouth opened in surprise.

It was the reaction that Erik had hoped to see. It confirmed all of his suspicions.

"Berit and I both were chosen to undergo a special ritual, one that would unite our souls with the gods of the Aesir. The gods were fading because the mortal people no longer believed in them, and they needed us so that they could continue to exist.

"I was chosen to house Vidar, the hunter. Berit was chosen to be the vessel of Ithunn, the goddess of youth and springtime, whose apples of immortality kept the Aesir alive. The ritual was painful and difficult, and while it was successful for me, Berit... she was not strong enough."

Nika breathed. "She died."

"Her body died. Her soul was fused with Ithunn, and souls are eternal. Do you understand?"

"I think so..."

"I knew that she would be reborn, so I swore that I would never stop looking for her. I swore that until I found her, I would no longer drink blood. It was a sacrifice, a way of begging the gods to bring her back to me."

"Did they?" Her head was buzzing, and she felt off balance.

"They did. She was reborn. Each time I found her, I lost her. I wasted chances, or she was taken from me too soon. Until now."

He leaned forward and took her hands in his.

"Nika, it's you."

She didn't know what to say, or how to react. Everything that she had been feeling since she met Erik, the visions and dreams and half-memories, coalesced. She knew that it was true.

"I... I was Berit."

"Yes."

She closed her eyes. More half-memories rose to the surface, images of times and places long gone. She again saw the altar and the robed figures, saw Erik handing her the potion to drink. She squeezed his hands.

"We were meant to be together in this life," he told her. "We are fated."

She kissed him, saying with actions what her words could not express. He wrapped her in his arms and pulled her to him. They tumbled onto the bed together, their embrace filled with urgency and desire. They undressed one another, punctuating every discarded item with kisses and caresses.

Their loving was deeper than skin to skin. It was soul-deep, and when he touched her, she felt as if she had known him forever. Something deep within her heart reached out for him, extending through a thousand years and a hundred lifetimes. She yearned for him, felt her soul crying out for him to take her and pull her into him, closing the gap between them once and for all.

He breathed her name and it sounded almost like a prayer. "Nika..."

She could feel his spirit reaching back to her, connecting, filling in all of the empty spaces she hadn't known were there. He rocked her in his arms, their bodies united as their souls entwined. She felt fire in her veins, and she looked up at him with wide eyes.

A power like nothing she had ever felt erupted between them, searing in its intensity but sweet to the touch. Tears sprang to her eyes as his spirit wrapped around hers, claiming her even as her own soul marked him as her own.

"I choose you," he gasped. "Nika, I choose you."

She didn't understand what was happening, but something inside her surged with elation. At last! The thought rose inside her mind, almost as if it belonged to someone else. In her mind's eye, she saw a cascade of memories from different places and different times, but all of them about him.

"I love you," she breathed, her arms tightening around his back. "I've always loved you."

"Lifetime after lifetime," he told her between kisses. "I have found you so many times."

"Don't let me go, Erik," she begged, her body aching for him even while they were still joined. She wanted all of him, as if she could open up her very soul and swallow him whole. "Please don't let me go."

He shivered, and then there was no more talking.

Chapter Fourteen – Transformation

They lay together in the silence after their loving, still entwined. She settled into the crook of his arm, her head once pillowed on his chest.

"You're still weak."

"Yes."

"You need to feed, don't you? I mean... since you've found me, you can feed again, right?"

He hesitated. "Yes."

"Would you feed from me?"

"No."

Surprised, she straightened again. "Why not?"

"Because I've chosen you. I can never feed from you, now."

"Why?"

He brushed a stray lock away from her eyes. "Because. I can't."

She shifted so that she was kneeling beside him. "What does it mean when you say you've chosen me?"

Erik looked taken aback. "Didn't you feel it?"

"I felt... something."

He took her hands, entwining his fingers with hers. "You felt my soul and your soul becoming one. We are now one spirit in two bodies. We can never be apart."

"Like being married?"

"Oh, no. Being chosen is so much more than that." He looked into her eyes. "Nika, I have looked for you across a hundred lifetimes. I have walked through a thousand years just to see your face. We are bound together, soul to soul."

"But I'm still human," she whispered.

"You are half Draugr."

"But I'll die someday..."

He stroked her hands with his thumbs. "As long as I am alive, you will live. Eternally young, eternally mine. And I will be eternally yours."

"And if you die?"

He kissed her. "Then I hope you will remember me."

She was strangely disappointed. "I won't die?"

"No... unless you want to. Some Draugr have pined away after their chosen mates died."

Nika understood. "Dying of a broken heart."

"Something like that."

She kissed him. "I don't want to live without you."

He pulled her back down to lie beside him again, his arms around her. "Let's not talk about dying. There's been too much of that today."

"I'm so sorry about Rolf. Were you very close?"

Erik's eyes grew moist, and he blinked the unshed tears away. "He was my brother."

His cell phone rang at that moment, startling them both. He hunted down the offending object and answered the call.

"Thorvald," he said.

"Your team is dead." It was Sigrunn's voice. She sounded smug. "I killed the three in the vault myself."

He closed his eyes. "Are you calling to gloat, or is there something you wanted?"

"I want your woman, and I want the sword."

"Well, that's just too damned bad."

"Don't make me come to get them."

"Make you? I wish you would." He ended the call, then told Nika, "Things are going to get very interesting, very soon."

"They're coming for the sword, aren't they?"

"Yes." He smirked. "Too bad they don't know where it is."

"They can find it. It will call to them."

"That's what I'm counting on." He gathered up his clothes. "We need to get into Hrothgar's room. He has the team's supply of dreyri."

"What is that?"

"It's the blood we drink. I need to recover my strength before they come."

They dressed again, and Erik collected the sword. He took Nika by the hand and took her with him into the hallway.

Hrothgar's room was across the hall, and he had the spare key, so entering was not a problem. They went inside and Nika applied the deadbolt while Erik went to an ornate wooden chest on the bedside table.

Inside the chest were dozens of vials of blood, each one stoppered with a cork. He opened one, and the scent dazzled him. He saluted her.

"Cheers."

She watched as he drank vial after vial. His long years of abstinence had created a deep need, and his attempt at healing Rolf had created an abiding thirst. After his fifth vial, he closed the chest. His pallor was gone.

"What would happen if I drank one of those?" she asked.

He was surprised by the question. "Why would you want to?"

"Would it make me stronger, so I could face them better when they come? You're not leaving me behind this time."

He considered her for a long moment, then said, "No. I'm not." He opened the chest again. "If you drink the dreyri, your mortal half will die. You will become all Draugr. Is that something that you are willing to do?"

Her answer was to step forward and pull a vial from the chest. She uncorked it and brought it to her lips. It was cold and congealed, deeply unpleasant and tasting of iron and salt. She swallowed it all.

Her stomach convulsed, and then she was filled with agony and ecstasy like she'd never known, a braid of conflicting sensations wrapping around her heart. She reeled backward, dropping the empty vial and staggering away from the chest. Erik went to her and caught her in his arms, holding her tight through her transformation.

Her mind was a violent sea of images, memories from a dozen lifetimes combined with the sudden awareness of the goddess within her soul. She shuddered and shook in her lover's arms, and then it was over.

She looked at Erik and saw him with new eyes. He was surrounded by a halo of light, golden and white, just barely visible but definitely there. It was an aura of power and magic, and she gasped when she saw it.

"Take it slow," he coached. "You'll adjust if you give it a moment."

She took a slow, steadying breath. Her senses were sharper than before, and she could sense the ebb and flow of magic emanating from the Rune Sword. She pulled out of Erik's embrace and went to the sword.

Slowly, as if she were sleepwalking, she pulled the sword free from its wrapping and held it in her hand. It seemed to throb in her grasp. The soul stone glimmered in its setting, and she could sense the seething rage of the entity trapped within it.

She remembered. She remembered everything.

"To reanimate Hakon, they need to sacrifice one of the Valtaeigr. Only our blood will be enough to power the ritual."

"The only Valtaeigr here are you and Astrid, and I can guarantee that she's not the one they're going to use."

"What is Sigrunn?"

"She's only Draugr."

She stroked the Soul Stone. "What does Astrid stand to gain from changing sides?"

"Honestly, I have no idea." He watched her warily. "Unless she means to ally the Valtaeigr with the Draugr instead of with the Huntsmen."

"Why would she do that?"

"I don't know." He ran a hand through his hair. "We need to get Hakon's body back and destroy it. That's the only thing that will end this nonsense."

She held the sword out to him. "All right, then. Let's go."

Chapter Fifteen – Destruction

They waited until daybreak, when the Draugr would be at their weakest. Erik drove while Nika held the sword in the passenger seat. All of his guns had been loaded with silver bullets, and he was ready to fight.

Nika was less secure, but she felt stronger now than she ever had in her entire life. She could feel the pulse of the earth beneath her feet, the radiating heat of the sun, and the watery flow of life all around her. Deep within her, she could feel the links that tied her spirit to Erik's, and when she began to feel too nervous, she would touch them for comfort.

The closer they got to the house, the more the Soul Stone hummed. She could practically feel its vibration traveling through the pommel of the sword, trembling in her hand. The soul inside the gem knew that they were approaching his body.

While he drove, she asked, "Tell me about the Valtaeigr."

"What do you want to know?"

"You said that they were magic users, right?"

"Yes."

"Do you think I can use magic?"

He considered it for a moment. "I'm sure you have the ability. You'd just need to be trained."

She liked the sound of it. "Do you know where I can get that training?"

"Yes. In Sweden. The queen of the Valtaeigr can teach you."

"Is that Astrid's mother?"

"Aunt."

She hesitated. "And is she my – Berit's – aunt, too?"

"No. She is your sister."

Nika looked down at the sword. "When we get there, what should I do?"

He clenched his jaw and turned onto the road leading to the house. "Stay behind me and watch your back. Can you shoot?"

Sheepishly, she replied: "I've never even held a gun."

"Well, I'll teach you. You should learn."

The house looked innocuous when they pulled into the driveway, but he knew that the inhabitants were waiting for them. He had long abandoned any thoughts of stealth or secrecy. He parked the car, and they both got out.

Erik armed himself with multiple guns, replacement clips, and the Rune Sword. As soon as he took it into his hand, it shimmered with the green light from the runes on the blade, which once again were shifting and reordering themselves.

He didn't take the time to read the runes, but Nika did. "It says 'beware betrayal.'" She looked up at him. "What's making it do that?"

"The power of the Valtaiegr," he answered, "in connection with the Aesir. It is responding to the fact that we are together now."

He handed her a canister of gasoline, matches, and an automatic pistol.

"Point it at the bad guys and squeeze the trigger. Just shoot. Even if you don't hit anything, you'll keep them guessing."

She took the weapon uneasily, but nodded to show that she understood. He spontaneously kissed her.

"May the gods be with us."

"They will be." She didn't know where her confidence on the point came from, but it was sincere.

They went into the house, Erik holding the sword ahead of him. Its glow filed the little mud room with a greenish light, making everything look surreal. He headed directly down into the basement.

The hörgr was still standing, but this time the ruined remains of Hakon were resting on its surface. Three robed Draugr stood between the altar and the statues of the gods, standing guard. They looked up in unison when Erik and Nika entered the chamber.

They were all male, and they all displayed their fangs in threatening grimaces. One of them spoke.

"You are the last Huntsman."

He twirled the sword at his side, limbering his wrist. "For now."

Nika pointed the gun at the Draugr and pulled the trigger. Her shots went wildly off the mark, but one of them ducked. The other two charged at Erik, arms raised, hand axes at the ready.

He swung the sword so quickly that the blade hummed through the air. When it touched the charging Draugr, it flared brilliantly. They screamed as they burst into flame, ignited by the power of the sword.

The two Draugr burned into ashes almost immediately, immolating like flash paper. The third attacked next, but Nika opened fire again. This time she hit him, and the silver bullet ripped into his arm. He shouted a virulent curse and threw his axe at Erik, but the Huntsman deflected it with the sword.

The sound of laughter filled the room, and they heard a scurrying sound above their heads. Nika looked up and saw Sigrunn, scampering across the ceiling like a spider. She dropped onto Erik and began wrestling with him for the sword.

Nika pointed the gun, but she was too afraid that she would hit her lover, so she held her fire.

"The body!" Erik shouted to her. "Destroy it!"

She ran to the altar and poured the gasoline over the corpse. In the sword, the Soul Stone flashed, momentarily blinding the two combatants. She emptied the can over the body, and just as she was about to light a match, someone grabbed her from behind.

"Don't even think it," Astrid hissed into her ear.

She gripped Nika's wrist like a vise, squeezing it until the bones ground together. She dropped the matches and screamed, "Erik!"

Her cry distracted him, and in that moment, Sigrunn was able to take the Rune Sword away from him. She kicked him in the face and moved back, standing over him with the point of the sword resting against his chest.

The magic in the sword hissed and burned, but Erik did not retreat. He glared up at his opponent and held his ground, even as she pressed the blade harder against him. It cut through the fabric of his shirt and punctured his skin, drawing blood to the surface.

Astrid chuckled. "What have we here? A little mortal Vataeigr and a useless Veithimathr, come to disrupt the return of our master?" She snarled at Erik. "Get up... husband."

She had one hand on Nika's throat, her fingers wrapped around her windpipe, ready to tear it free. Erik obeyed.

"Sigrunn, put him on the altar." She backed away, pulling Nika with her.

Sigrunn forced him onto the altar at sword point, prodding him to lie beside the ruined husk of Hakon's body. Once he was there, she bound him into place with chains at his hands and feet. He could have feinted for the sword, but Astrid's hold upon Nika was absolute. He couldn't risk it.

When she was confident that she had bound him securely, Sigrunn took the sword to Astrid. "The vessel is prepared," she said.

"No!" Nika cried. "You can't use him as a vessel. He's already carrying the Aesir!"

Astrid hissed in her ear. "Silence, you stupid cow. We are all carrying the Aesir. It's time that we stopped being their slaves and took our power in this world."

She struggled in the other Valtaeigr's grip, resisting as much as she could. Astrid tightened her fingers, driving them into her throat. Nika gagged, and Erik looked into Nika's eyes, shaking his head 'no.'

She fell still.

In her head, his voice whispered. Can you hear me, Chosen?

She took a deep breath. Yes.

Excellent. Do not be afraid. There is more to us than Astrid knows.

Sigrunn brought the sword to Astrid. "Shall I free the stone?"

"Yes."

"What are you doing?" Nika demanded. "This is insane!"

The female Draugrs ignored her. With the point of a dagger, Sigrunn pried the Sálsteinn loose, hissing as it burned her hand. She put it on the altar.

Astrid dragged Nika forward, forcing the wrist that she held toward the jewel. "Take up the stone," she commanded.

Erik closed his eyes and began to speak silently to himself, his lips moving rapidly though no sound was coming out.

Reluctantly, Nika did as she was told, gathering up the stone in her hand. It glowed fiercely, but there was no pain as she wrapped her fingers around it. Sigrunn stepped toward Erik's head and held him fast, prying open his jaws.

"Put it in his mouth," Astrid told her.

Nika clenched her fist around the stone. "No."

Astrid shook her. "You cannot protect him now. If you obey, you may still save yourself."

She did not want to live without Erik, and she fought against Astrid as the other Valtaeigr pushed her closer to the altar. She managed to slow the speed of their approach, but she could not stop it all together. Astrid brought her hand above her lover's mouth.

"Drop it in," she said.

Erik closed his eyes and stopped fighting Sigrunn. His body relaxed, as if he had accepted his fate. Nika began to weep.

"Drop it!"

Do not fear for me, Chosen, he whispered in her head.

Nika sobbed and opened her hand. The stone dropped onto Erik's tongue. Sigrunn forced his mouth shut, holding it closed with both hands.

"Swallow it, Huntsman," Astrid ordered him. "You are going to die anyway. At least die for something."

The smell of burning flesh filled the air, and Nika wailed in Astrid's grip. Erik's eyes flew open, and he began to convulse, his muscles shaking and rattling the chains against the altar.

The body of Hakon began to shiver.

The Draugr retreated, opening space around the hörgr. Erik's mouth and eyes flew open wide, and white light began to pour out of him, deepening the scent of burning. He began to scream, and Nika joined in, horrified by the scene.

Behind her, Astrid laughed.

Hakon sat up, his desiccated flesh creaking as he moved. His eyelids opened, revealing shriveled eyes that turned sightlessly toward the man beside him. He leaned over Erik until he was lying atop him, his mouth above his, and he began to suck in the light, channeling it all into his lifeless body.

Erik's body began to rise into the air, levitating above the stone slab of the altar. The chains at his wrists and ankles snapped.

"It's working!" Sigrunn exulted. "Now, quickly – the blood!"

Astrid's fingers tore into Nika's neck, and her blood sprayed onto Erik and the revivifying form of Hakon, the Lord of the Draugr. She screamed in agony and terror. The room began to shake.

Erik began to shout, "Odin! All-father! I call you – NOW!"

The statue of Odin, the most powerful Norse god, shuddered and exploded. A man's body made entirely of green light appeared where the statue had been, and he grasped Hakon in both hands.

The mighty form of Odin's avatar pulled Hakon off Erik's body, rending the Draugr king in two. Astrid and Sigrunn screamed and threw themselves onto the ground, prostrate before their deity. Nika fell to the dirt beside them. Her throat was wounded, but she was very much alive.

The light that Hakon had swallowed came rushing back out, and this time it filled Erik until he shone so brightly that none of them could look upon him. Odin's avatar shredded Hakon into pieces.

Nika pressed a hand to her throat and scrabbled up onto her feet. Astrid let her go. Beneath her fingers, she felt heat spreading through her injury.

Let me help you, child, a gentle female voice said in her head.

She could hardly have resisted. From a space deep within her, the same one that had exulted at becoming Erik's chosen mate, a power deeper than any she had ever felt radiated outward. She closed her eyes, unable to keep them open any longer, and then her body was no longer her own.

She felt her arms extending to the sides, palms up. That suffusing heat in her throat extended down into her solar plexus then through her entire body, filling her to overflowing.

She thought she could hear rain. Warm, salty droplets fell upon her upturned face, and she knew that what she was hearing was not rain at all, but blood. She could not open her eyes, could not even move. Her mouth opened.

The blood filled her mouth, and the newborn vampire within her swallowed eagerly. She felt power in the blood, felt it coursing through her veins. She felt her hands turning, slowly, until the palms were facing out flat.

The power pushed out of her then, and she could feel it connecting with a similar wall of might coming from Erik. Their soul passengers, Ithunn and Vidar, had broken free, and the two gods now entwined in that cellar room, disembodied lovers entwining. Everywhere they touched, they gained strength, and it pulsed back into Nika and into Erik.

She heard women screaming and knew that it was Astrid and Sigrunn. She could feel them bursting into flame on either side of her, blazing like giant torches, flailing as their deaths overtook them. Their fires rose and conjoined, becoming a giant pillar of flame, setting fire to the room and to the house above them.

The papier-maché oak trees burned. The statues of the gods lit, too, and the heat was stunning. She could not move, could not step away from the burning fire. The flames wrapped around her, but she found herself enclosed in an embrace that protected her from harm.

The house burned around them, and the as Draugr burned, too. The fire spread from the house, immolating everything around. The ground sizzled and the trees snapped and popped as they went up in smoke. Everything was burning, and she was in the center of the conflagration – though she was not harmed. The inferno raged, but she clung tightly to the arms that held her, recognizing Erik. They stood united against the firestorm, untouched, united.

Abruptly, it was gone, and Nika was standing beside the altar, wrapped in Erik's arms. The stones of the hörgr had cracked in the immense heat, but on the splintered slab, the Rune Sword rested, the Soul Stone back in place.

The house was gone, and they stood in the bottom of the hole that had once been the cellar. The ground was scorched around them in a perfect circle, the damage stopping just short of the stable on one side and the road on the other. Their car was a pile of melted scrap, and in the stable, the horses were frightened but unhurt.

Erik took her face into his hands. "Beloved, open your eyes."

She was almost too afraid to do it, but she obeyed. He was standing there, nearly glowing in the power that emanated from his soul, his body perfect and unmarred. His chest was adorned with a new tattoo, a giant, stylized owl with wings that spread from one shoulder to the other, talons clutching two runes.

She clung to him. Although their clothing had burned away, their skin was untouched, and they were complete.

"How... what..."

He did not answer. He bent down and claimed her mouth in a kiss. She leaned into him, accepting him, and in her mind, she could hear him say, I choose you, now and forever. I choose you for all time. My love, my love... do you choose me?

She said it aloud. "Yes. Oh, yes."

He took her into his arms and held her tight. She embraced him and, overwhelmed by everything she had experienced, she collapsed.

Chapter Sixteen – The Chosen

Nika woke up suddenly in her own bed, lying in Erik's arms. She sat up in confused disorientation and pressed a hand to her feverish brow.

Was it all a dream?

She looked at her sleeping lover, and the owl tattoo across his chest told her that it had all been real. She touched the two stones inked into his skin, reading the Elder Futhark runes that were written there. One was Uruz, the other Thurisaz.

She identified the meanings of the runes. Masculine energy. Sexual potency. Regeneration.

As she looked at him, she realized that she, too, had been marked by the sacred fire. Runes were tattooed into both of her inner arms, and she identified Perthro and Sowilo.

Female mystical power. The sacred sword of fire. Protection from evil.

Beside her, Erik opened his eyes. He looked up at her with such love on his face that she wanted to weep.

He touched her cheek and smiled, and she went into his arms for a tight embrace. Everywhere her skin touched his, she felt a tingling of power, as if she was filled with mystical fire that burned brighter when he was near.

"What happened? How did we get here? The last thing I remember, we were at the house, and everything had just burned up."

"We prevented the Draugr from raising Hakon," he said simply, as if that explained it all.

"But..." She touched the tattoos on his chest and on her arms. "I don't understand. What is this?"

He sat up and took her hands. "You remember me telling you about the old gods, how they could only continue for as long as they were melded with the souls of the Draugr. Right?"

She nodded.

"The gods with whom we were merged all those centuries ago rose up to help us, along with the All-Father."

"Odin."

"Yes."

"I don't understand."

He smiled. "You're still trying too hard to think with a modern mind. Not everything makes rational sense. In the world, remember, there is as much of the spirit as of the physical. Mortal minds cannot measure both."

Beside the bed, leaning on the wall with its point in the carpet, the Rune Sword sat placidly. The Soul Stone was quiet and dull, no light shining in its depths. She looked at it in confusion, then back at him.

"You, my darling, have taken a big step into a world you ever knew existed, but which has been waiting for you since you were reborn into this life." He smiled. "Do you believe me when I say that I love you?"

She smiled back, slowly. "Of course."

"Then believe me now when I say this: because you are Chosen, and because you have drunk the dreyri, you will never be the same."

Nika touched his arm, running her hands along the skin and the well-formed muscles beneath. He was distracting just by being there.

"Am I truly a Draugr?"

"Yes. You truly are."

She put her fingers to her teeth, but they felt no different than they had before. He chuckled.

"Some changes haven't taken hold yet, but they will do so as time goes on. The important thing is that your soul has been awakened, and the power that you have always had has been set free." He pressed his hand to her chest, resting his palm above her heart. "You and I, Nika... we are meant to be. We are soulmates."

"This is all so hard to understand," she said, shaking her head. Her scarlet hair fell over her shoulder, a curtain over her face that he brushed away, tucking it behind her ear.

"You need understand only this: we are immortal, and you are my love, and the gods have blessed us."

She pulled him into her arms, kissing him. He bore her gently down to the mattress, rolling her onto her back and leaning over her, his hand still cupping her head.

"I love you," she told him. "You are my Chosen."

"You are my life," he told her.

Her moved closer, and they were soon entangled in one another again, their physical loving echoed by the pulsing power in their breasts. Their souls united even while their bodies connected, making love on two levels.

As he moved within her, he breather, "You are my soul."

She wrapped her arms around his neck and pulled him as close as she could, giving herself to him, body, heart and spirit.

Against the wall, the Rune Sword glowed.

Epilogue

The museum workers finished putting glass panel into place, once more sealing the pressurized chamber that held the Rune Sword in place. The ancient Viking weapon gleamed in the light of the pinpoint spotlights that illuminated the runes on its blade.

"There," the curator said, satisfied. "Safe and sound, back where it belongs."

The representative of the Royal Stockholm Museum nodded. "I'm very grateful that the sword was found in one piece."

"Your agent, Mr. Thorvald, had a great deal to do with that."

"Ah, yes," the representative mused. "Mr. Thorvald. I shall have to find him to thank him personally."

"Oh, is he no longer in town, Mr....?"

"Sigurd," the man replied.

The curator admired the sword. "What do those runes say, anyway? My assistant used to read runes, but I'm afraid Latin is far more my style."

The Swede smiled, his narrow face an unlikely home for so friendly an expression. "It says 'united forever.' Strange, don't you think, for an ornamental weapon intended for a burial?"

"Well," the curator said, "perhaps it has a spiritual significance."

They walked away together, the Swede folding his hands behind his back. A runic tattoo peeked out beneath his shirt cuff.

"Most things do, my friend," he said. "Most things do."

*****

THE END

Rune Master

Rune Series Book 2

Contents

Prologue
    Chapter One
    Chapter Two
    Chapter Three
    Chapter Four
    Chapter Five
    Chapter Six
    Chapter Seven
    Chapter Eight
    Chapter Nine
    Chapter Ten
    Chapter Eleven
    Chapter Twelve
    Chapter Thirteen
    Chapter Fourteen
    Chapter Fifteen
    Chapter Sixteen
    Chapter Seventeen
    Chapter Eighteen
    Chapter Nineteen
    Chapter Twenty
    Chapter Twenty-One
    Chapter Twenty-Two
    Chapter Twenty-Three
    Chapter Twenty-Four
    Epilogue

Copyright © 2017 by Amelia Wilson/J.A. Cummings
All rights reserved.

In no way is it legal to reproduce, duplicate, or transmit any part of this document in either electronic means or in printed format. Recording of this publication is strictly prohibited, and any storage of this document is not allowed unless with written permission from the publisher. All rights reserved.

Respective authors own all copyrights not held by the publisher.

Prologue

Ingrid Nilsson knelt in her kitchen garden, pulling the weeds that grew around her herbs. On the other side of her stick fence, the hill ran down toward the rocky beach and the Baltic Sea, which glittered beneath the morning sun. The warming spring wind brought the scent of sea and salt to her nose, and she inhaled deeply.

She had lived on this hill forever. Her little house was tiny, but it was all that she needed. It was sturdy enough to withstand winter storms, and it was cozy and just the right size for a retired goddess living alone.

In centuries gone by, she had been called by another name, and the Norse had worshipped her in Uppsala and at *hörgrs* across Scandinavia. Then the Christians had come, the sacrifices ended, and there was nothing left for her to do but to meld with a human soul and consume Ithunn's Apples of Life.

The Vanir and the Aesir, the two tribes of Norse gods, had both chosen this uncomfortable way of continuing their immortality. The humans with whom they merged became the Draugr, continuing their lives by drinking the power in mortal blood. The Draugr were not truly immortal, though, not like the gods, and when they sometimes died, their souls went on to new incarnations. She herself had been reborn eighteen times. Her mortal identity changed with each new birth, but deep inside, she always knew who she really was. She was Frigg.

Now, though, she was content to live as Ingrid, the wise woman on the edge of Sweden, perched on a hill above the sea. She was the one to whom the Draugr came for advice, for she was the keeper of all wisdom and foreknowledge. She only spoke to whom she chose. Not everyone who petitioned for her aid was destined to receive it.

She sat back, with her hands on her thighs, and took another deep breath of sea air. This time, there was a curdled edge to the smell of the water, as if some hapless fisherman had left his catch to rot in the belly of his ship. It was the sweet-sour stench of death and decay. She turned toward the water, her heart uneasy.

At first, the bay looked calm and placid, rippled with tiny white caps and rolling beneath an untroubled sky. Then the clouds appeared in her mind's eye, glowering and dark in the distance. There were flashes of lightning, far away but coming closer, and she was filled with a sense of impending dread. She shuddered and felt herself falling into the vision.

There, on the horizon, was a drekar, one of the dragon boats of old. It was under full sail, headed rapidly toward the coast. She could see warriors on board, their heads just visible above the row of shields affixed to the sides. There was a single man standing near the figurehead, and she knew him immediately.

Loki had returned.

He and his warriors were bearing down on the coast, skimming over the water like a missile from Finland. Loki was standing in darkness, surrounded by a shifting cloud that revealed and concealed him at the same time. His men were just as shadowy, and she feared them all.

The boat and its stench vanished as quickly as they had appeared. She rose, abandoning her simple chores. There was important work to be done.

Chapter One

Nika Graves stretched languidly, enjoying a slow morning. Beside her in their rumpled bed, Erik Thorvald, her exquisite lover, was still sleeping. He was many things, but he was not an early riser. She smiled to herself and scooted closer to him, molding herself to his side as her arm wrapped around his waist. She kissed his shoulder.

"Morning," she said softly.

He made a sound somewhere between a grunt and a groan. She smiled more broadly and kissed him again.

"Erik," she cooed. "It's morning. Wake up. Up and at 'em."

He did not open his eyes, but the corner of his mouth curled upward.

She ran her fingernails lightly over his skin, eliciting a shiver. "Are you awake?"

Erik opened one eye to peek at her and then closed it again. "No."

Nika laughed and nipped him. He rolled over and grabbed her, pinning her in his arms and pulling her close. His blue eyes were bright when he spoke. "If you're going to bite me, do it like you mean it."

She grinned and let her new vampire fangs come down. She snapped at him playfully. He flipped her over onto her back and straddled her, his own fangs pressing to her throat. At the last moment, just before his teeth penetrated her skin, he closed his lips and blew a loud raspberry.

Nika squealed and squirmed in his grip, and Erik laughed, holding her tight. "That's what you get for being a tease."

She stopped struggling and grinned up at him. "Mercy, great Huntsman. I am your prisoner."

He kissed her deeply, and she was all too happy to return the embrace. He rolled onto his side and lay beside her, and she snuggled in, her head on his chest. He stroked her flame-red hair, feeling utterly content.

"Big day today," he said.

"Mm. Very."

The Viking exhibit at the museum where she worked as an assistant curator was ending. The artifacts, including the Rune Sword which had brought them together, were going to be packed up and sent back to Stockholm. Erik's work in America would be over, and he would be going back to Sweden. She had been devastated when she'd heard the news. Now, however, she was happy; she was going with him.

She was going to miss her museum and her friends in the city, but she was ready to move forward. Her life had changed completely in the short time she had known Erik and her old habits and the familiar places didn't suit her any longer. She was eager for a change, and was excited to see where Erik would lead her; she would follow him anywhere.

"The movers will be here at three to pack up the apartment," he said. "That gives us a few hours before we have to get out of bed."

She chuckled. "Why, Mr. Thorvald, whatever are you suggesting?"

He pulled her closer and kissed her tenderly, his lips barely grazing hers, just a tease of what was to come. His hand pressed gently against her flat stomach, then slid up to cup her breast. She put her arms around him and sighed happily.

She loved the feeling of his body pressed against her, of the hardness that pushed against her thigh, of the softness of his hair and the heat of his caress. She reached down and touched the evidence of his desire, stroking it. He moaned softly in the back of his throat and shifted so that he was hovering above her on his hands and knees, one hand holding him up while the other continued to explore her body.

He ran his fingers down her abdomen, slowly dragging them along her skin until he reached the welcoming moisture between her legs. She gasped when he touched her, electrified, her body tingling. She closed her eyes and arched into his touch, silently asking for more.

He put his knee between hers and gently eased her legs farther apart. She opened for him willingly, her hand on his heat moving faster, her other arm pulling him closer. He looked into her eyes, and she saw a glimmer of the green Draugr light in their blue depths. It was enchanting.

"Love me, Erik," she whispered.

He kissed her, this time hungrily, his mouth and tongue seizing possession of hers. He lowered himself down on top of her, sliding slowly inside of her. She moaned at the feeling, completely fulfilled, and he broke the kiss to throw his head back with a look of ecstasy on his face.

She gripped his shoulders as he began to move, feeling the hard muscles shifting beneath his skin, thrilled by his strength and his masculine scent. She was his.

He kissed her again, and then kissed his way down her jawline to the throbbing pulse point in her throat. His lips pressed against the vein, and she felt him harden even more inside of her. She brought a hand up to cup his head, burying her fingers in his golden hair, urging him to continue.

His sharp teeth extended and slowly, gently slid into her flesh. She shuddered with delight and moaned. The feeling of his mouth and tongue, soft and insistent, coupled with the penetration of his teeth was the most erotic thing she had ever felt, and it sent her over the edge.

He drank from her as she quaked in his arms, and her pleasure brought him to his climax. He trembled with the force of it, his eyes shut, his fangs still buried deep in her vein though he was no longer drinking. They stayed that way well into the afterglow, connected in every possible way. When he finally released his hold on her neck, he swiped his tongue over the wounds he'd left behind, healing them closed.

She clung to him as he shifted to lie beside her. He kissed her sweetly, his eyes filled with love.

Chosen, he said to her in her mind.

She smiled and responded with a telepathic voice of her own.

Chosen.

***

They were dressed and presentable by the time the movers arrived. The apartment was small and there were several people trying to pack up her belongings, so they needed to get out of the way. They went to the museum one last time.

The special gallery was still closed for repairs, but the exhibit itself had been moved to a side gallery, replacing the usual display. The replica dragon boat figureheads flanking the entrance were standing guard over the new location, and the last tour group was just heading inside. It was the last chance to see the archaeological wonders, rescued from their long rest in a Viking chieftain's grave.

Well... that was the story, anyway. What the public didn't know wouldn't hurt them.

They walked hand-in-hand through the display, following the boat-shaped path that was laid out on the floor. The path took them past ancient textiles, jewelry and pottery, ultimately leading to the main attraction, the Rune Sword.

The sword stood in its special case once again, quiet in the pinpoint spotlights the museum was using to highlight the runes etched into the blade. The ancient Norse markings were once again a mish-mash of meanings, saying nothing at all. The days of messages on the blade had come to an end.

Nika stood before the case and looked up at the Sálsteinn, the soul stone, set into the cross piece of the hilt. It was dull and lifeless, emptied of its dangerous cargo.

"Hardly looks like the same weapon, does it?" Erik asked, his own gaze on the stone.

"No, not really." She leaned into him. "Hard to believe."

He smiled. "What a difference a few weeks make, eh?"

It was dizzying when she thought about it. Less than a month ago, the Draugr, ancient Norse vampires, had attacked the exhibit and stolen the sword. The Soul Stone had once housed the soul of their fallen leader, and they were trying to get him back. Nika and Erik had found themselves united in stopping them, and in the process, they had encountered death and eternal life.

The public had been told that a group of daring thieves, led by the former curator from Stockholm, Astrid Sigurdsdottir, had cut through the floor and ceiling in broad daylight to steal the priceless artifact. Erik and his Special Forces unit were credited with recovering the sword, and Astrid was wanted as a fugitive. His brothers in arms had died as heroes.

Nika and Erik knew the truth. Astrid was no fugitive. She and the rest of the Draugr who had tried to resurrect their leader with dark magic had been destroyed. The authorities could search until the end of time, but they would never be found.

While they were studying the sword, Howard Rowan, the chief curator at the museum, came into the gallery. He let out a surprised sound when he saw the couple and walked directly to them.

"Miss Graves! Captain Thorvald!" He smiled broadly. "I am so glad to see you. I can't thank you enough for recovering this piece. It would have been a terrible tragedy if the thieves had been allowed to keep it." He sobered. "I'm... I'm so very sorry about your team, Captain Thorvald."

Erik offered a handshake, which the other man accepted. "Thank you. They will be sorely missed. They were good men."

"It just such a terrible thing that the thieves destroyed the chieftain's remains. I will never understand what would make someone do such horrible things."

Erik and Nika looked at each other, remembering well that the body in the boat had not been as dead as people believed. He spoke for them both. "Yes, it's too bad. It's hard to understand why people do the things they do. There's so much history that has been lost because of thieves and vandals."

Rowan turned to Nika. "Speaking of things we've lost, we'll be missing you when you leave. A good assistant curator is hard to find, but Central City's loss is the Royal Museum of Stockholm's gain."

She smiled. "Thank you, Mr. Rowan. It was an opportunity I couldn't pass up. I hope you understand."

Through a complex web of pulled strings, many of them originating with Erik's superiors in Stockholm, Nika had been hired to replace Astrid as curator. Her special assignment would be traveling with the Rune Sword and boat burial artifacts. Once she reached Sweden, she would be taking up where her predecessor had left off, in more ways than one. Astrid had been Erik's wife. Nika couldn't pretend that the irony didn't amuse her.

Rowan smiled. "I would be surprised if you didn't accept their offer, all things considered." He gave Erik a significant glance. "Have either of you seen Mr. Sigurd?"

"Who's Mr. Sigurd?"

"He came from Stockholm to help move the exhibit and confirm that the sword you retrieved is genuine. He was just here..."

She could feel Erik tense beside her. "I wasn't told that any Mr. Sigurd was being sent," he said. "How strange."

The curator shrugged. "Just an oversight, I'm sure. He fully verified the authenticity of the sword, which was good news. Well, must go... paperwork is never finished, it seems. Good day to you both."

When they were alone again, Nika spoke. "What was that all about? Who's Sigurd?"

"I have no idea. That's why I'm concerned." He looked at her grimly. "Remember Astrid's last name?"

"Sigurdsdottir..." Realization dawned. "Oh."

"Yes. Sigurdsdottir. Sigurd's daughter. It might just be a coincidence, but... I don't believe in coincidences." He shook his head. "This cannot be good."

She frowned. "Did you know her father?"

"We never met."

Nika wasn't sure she believed him. "That's odd, considering the two of you were married for, what, eight hundred years or so?"

"He was... absent."

"He couldn't even be bothered to see his own daughter's wedding?"

"There were reasons." He looked at her, and there were storms in his eyes. "Let's get out of here."

They left the museum at a quick pace. She remembered another time when he had walked so quickly and purposefully out of a gallery, and the similarity gave her pause. He was looking around as they walked, and her new Draugr senses told her that he was reaching out with vampire abilities of his own, trying to locate any immortal newcomers.

"He's a Draugr, too?" She already knew the answer. He wouldn't have been trying to find another Draugr's energy signature otherwise.

"I don't know. I just don't want to take the chance."

Chapter Two

They went to the Swedish consulate in Central City, where his military credentials bought them no-questions-asked admittance. He held Nika's hand tightly as he guided her through the gate and into the building. The architecture was Scandinavian in design, all clean lines and bright light, with a receptionist desk that looked straight from Ikea standing just inside the front door.

"God eftermiddag," the woman behind the desk greeted with a friendly smile. "Good afternoon. How may I help you?"

Erik produced his ID once more. "Captain Thorvald to see the Consul."

The Swedish woman turned to Nika. "And your identification, miss?"

Nika offered her driver's license. She hadn't thought to put her passport into her purse. "Nika Graves," she said. "I'm an American citizen."

The woman smiled. "Please, just a moment."

Erik looked around while the receptionist made a telephone call. Nika watched his eyes as they took in the door, the side entrances, and examined all of the people coming and going. She knew that he was attentive to every detail around him, always ready to act if necessary. It was part of his special forces training, but she suspected that his vigilance was an innate part of his warrior's soul.

The woman at the desk hung up the phone. "Consul Lindstrom will see you now. His office is – "

"I know the way."

They were given back their documents, and Erik took her through a side door that led to a stairwell. They climbed halfway up when he stopped and turned to her.

"Consul Lindstrom is also one of the Draugr. In fact, he's one of the few male Valtaeigr. He will recognize you as a sister. Be prepared for that."

"Valtaeigr means 'hawk's ground,' like the place on a falconer's arm where the hawk lands."

He nodded. "Yes. Why?"

"Why are we called that?"

"This is a strange time to ask."

"There are still a lot of things we don't know, and if he's Valtaeigr, I need to know what he might expect me to know. Right?"

Erik began leading her up the stairs again. "Hawks are known for their vision, for seeing everything on the ground. The falconer depends on his hawks to help him see small game, like rabbits and birds. So it is with the gods.

"The Draugr are the gods' eyes. In addition to keeping them alive, we help them to see their mortal enemies. The Valtaeigr are the wise ones, and you direct the Draugr. We are the hawks, the Valtaeigr are the falconers, and the gods are our keepers."

She smiled. "I like the idea of you being on my arm."

Erik smirked. "Does that make me arm candy?"

"If the shoe fits..." She looked up at his as he led the way. "How do the Valtaeigr know how to direct the Draugr?"

"They get visions," he answered. "The gods make their wishes known that way."

"Then why don't the gods speak to me?"

"You are melded with Ithunn, and she certainly spoke to you when we battled Hakon." He put his hand on the doorknob at the next landing. "As for the rest? You just haven't been introduced to them personally. They will speak to you in time." He gave her a naughty smile. "I seem to recall Vidar having a few things to say through me to Ithunn within you, if body language counts."

She laughed. "Oh, it counts. It counts a great deal. Is Lindstrom bonded with a god?"

He nodded. "He is one with Forseti, the god of justice, peace, and truth. He will know it if you lie to him."

"You should be careful, then."

Erik stopped short and looked at her. "What does that mean?"

"It means that you should be careful not to lie to him," she answered evenly. "You're not known for being one hundred percent forthcoming."

"I have never lied to you."

"You've never really told me the whole truth on anything, either." She was surprised by the sudden resentment and irritation she was feeling.

He searched her face, and she could almost feel that he was reading her. The muscle in his jaw twitched. "I have never withheld any information from you that you needed to know."

"So I'm being kept on a need to know basis?" She laughed, but it was an angry sound. "Very nice. I guess that's what I get for being with a special operator."

His voice was flat and hard. "I brought you here to share information with you. No, I don't tell you everything. Do you tell me everything about you? Don't play the victim. All I know from you is from your dossier. I have more reason to feel slighted than you."

He opened the door and held it for her, his body stiff.

"And not telling everything is not the same as lying. You have no right to accuse me of such things. This is a very strange time to start an argument." He glanced down the stairs as if he was looking for someone to blame for the abrupt shift in her mood. He gestured through the door. "After you, my lady."

She walked through, and he followed her, closing the door quietly behind them. They were in a corridor with highly-polished floors and white walls, hung with black and white photographs showing scenery in Sweden. One of the photos stood out to her immediately.

It showed a tiny house high on a hill. The photographer had been standing at the base of the hill, shooting upward, and the building loomed menacingly in the image.

Nika pointed at the photograph. "What is this?"

Erik looked and grumbled. "It appears to be a house."

"You don't recognize it? It seems... familiar."

He continued walking. "I recognize it."

"More secrets?"

He looked angry. "It is an old fishing cottage near the sea. There are hundreds of them."

"So you don't know this one in particular?" She didn't know why, but it felt important. Something in her head was buzzing.

He did not reply. Instead he opened a door and held it for her. She stepped through.

The room beyond was an elegantly furnished office with furniture of Scandinavian design. A young man with a shock of dark hair rose as soon as they came in, standing so rapidly that he nearly knocked over his mug of tea.

Nika looked at him and felt a shock run through her, emanating from the goddess melded with her soul. They stared at one another for a moment, both of them electrified, him with excitement, her with dread.

Erik closed the door. "This is Johan," he said. "He is melded with Bragi." Johan put out his hand and took Nika's, then brought her knuckles to his lips for a reverent and surprisingly passionate kiss. He looked into her eyes, and she realized that she had forgotten to breathe. Her head was swimming. Inside her soul, the part that was Ithunn began to shake.

Erik spoke again, his voice redolent with displeasure.

"Bragi is consort to Ithunn. In a manner of speaking, he is your husband."

Chapter Three

Johan and Nika were staring at each other as if they'd both been struck by one of Thor's lightning bolts. Erik set his jaw and waited for them. Behind the desk, the door to Consul Lindstrom's office was closed.

This day had very quickly gone entirely wrong.

He went to the door and knocked sharply. Lindstrom's voice responded. "Come in."

Erik took one last, resentful look over his shoulder, and then went inside, closing the door after himself.

Lindstrom looked up and smiled. He was an elegant older gentleman with silver hair, a kind face and bright blue eyes. He looked the way a diplomat of a friendly country should look. He offered a hand, and Erik accepted the handshake.

"Captain Thorvald," he greeted. "I'm happy you stopped in. I was hoping I would have a chance to say goodbye before you returned to Stockholm." He glanced at the door. "Is Miss Graves with you?"

"She is. She and Johan are getting acquainted. Or, rather, Ithunn and Bragi are having a moment."

Lindstrom's eyes flickered, but his placid expression remained the same. Erik knew he understood far more than he let on, which befit a diplomat, as well.

"I see. Please, sit down." He smiled. "What can I do for you?"

Erik sat in one of the visitor's chairs, occupying only the forward edge of the seat. He rested his hands on his knees. "I need to ask you something, sir."

"Of course, Captain."

"Who is Sigurd and why is he here?"

There was that knowing flicker again. Lindstrom folded his hands on the desk. His fingernails were immaculate, his hands free of calluses.

"I don't know whom you are speaking of," the Consul finally answered.

Erik narrowed his eyes. It had not occurred to him that the vessel of the god of truth might be a liar. It was an interesting combination.

"The curator at the museum said that Stockholm had sent a man named Mr. Sigurd to accompany the Rune Sword back home. I thought that you must know who he was, since any entry visas would be known to your office."

The diplomat smiled. "I cannot possibly be personally aware of every visa that our government approves, Captain."

"No, but when they're given for such a high-profile exhibit in the city where you reside, I would think you'd take a special interest."

They regarded each other squarely, each man keeping his own thoughts to himself. Finally, Lindstrom picked up his phone. Still watching Erik, he spoke into the handset. "Miss Andersson, please send me a listing of all visas associated with the Rune Sword exhibit."

On the other end of the line, the receptionist at the front door replied. "Yes, Mr. Lindstrom."

The Consul put the phone back in the cradle. "There. The list will arrive in a few minutes' time, but there will be a slight wait. May I offer you a refreshment?"

"No, thank you."

"Not even some dreyri? I heard you had begun drinking it again."

Dreyri. Bottled and enchanted human blood. Erik had gone many years without tasting its power, holding to the vow that he would not imbibe until he had found his lost lover again. She had been reborn at last, and now her spirit was inside Nika. He had permitted himself to taste the powerful drink again, and it had given back much of his vampire potency.

He thought of the strange confrontation in the stairwell and the meeting going on outside the office door. He needed to drink something a good deal stronger than blood.

"All right," he said, forcing a bland and civil smile. "That would be appreciated."

Lindstrom opened one of the bottom drawers of this desk and pulled out a black glass decanter. A silver dragon coiled around it, its head at the lip of the bottle where the stopper went in. The Consul brought out black glass stemware and pulled the stopper out of the bottle, releasing the dreyri's scent into the air. He poured a glass for Erik and one for himself, and then filled a third glass and handed it to the Huntsman with a smile.

"In case Ms. Graves wishes to join us," he said. "Terribly amusing about her last name, isn't it?"

"I suppose."

He put Nika's glass aside. Erik brought his own drink up to his mouth, hesitating while the intoxicating scent curled into his nostrils. He could feel the magic of the enchantment tingling against his lips.

Consul Lindstrom raised his glass. "Skål."

"Cheers."

They drank. The power in the dreyri coiled into his guts, penetrating into their bodies and souls with a thousand little tendrils. Erik could feel that power nudging at Vidar, prodding the sleeping god into something more like wakefulness. He swallowed the rest of the drink and put the glass aside.

"Would you like another?" Lindstrom offered. "I find that I can so rarely stop with only one."

Erik nodded. "Thank you."

He poured their glasses full of the ruby liquid, and they toasted one another again. They drank, their eyes locked, silently taking stock of each other.

***

Johan came around the desk, still holding her hand, his eyes boring into hers. She could feel the spirit of Ithunn in her heart, trembling in anticipation and fear. He pressed her fingers to his lips tenderly. Nika shook herself, trying to will away the overwhelming feelings that Ithunn was pouring through her. She did not know this man. She felt strange and off-balance.

Johan pulled her closer, putting his hand on his chest. In a deep baritone voice, he said, "Ithunn. You have returned to me."

She was worried that if he embraced her, she might never get away. There was menace there, and possessiveness, along with desire and dread. It was a heady combination. She pulled away gently.

"I... My name is Nika. Nika Graves."

He looked at her with confusion on his handsome face.

"But... Surely you remember me, my love?"

She met his eyes frankly. "I have never met you before today, sir."

He sighed and released his hold on her hand. He looked down. "Oh. You don't remember, of course. My apologies..." He cleared his throat and went back to his side of the desk.

"No harm done." She smiled. "May I... may I go in?"

Johan nodded. "Yes, ma'am."

She walked past him, feeling the portion of her heart that was Ithunn sag in relief and disappointment. She knocked on the door.

"Come in," the Consul beckoned.

She opened the door, and the scent of the dreyri made her pupils constrict. Her fangs tickled her bottom lip, begging for permission to come down. The power in that decanter very nearly glowed, and as a Draugr, she was still so young and still needed to feed so often. Usually, she drank from Erik, but the magic in the dreyri drew her in.

Erik rose to face her, though he said nothing. Instead, he picked up the still-untouched glass that Lindstrom had poured, and he handed it to her. She accepted it eagerly, her thirst making her abrupt.

"To your health," Lindstrom told her.

She drank it all in one gulp. She never drank anything that quickly. It only occurred to her to be embarrassed by her greediness after it was over.

The Consul smiled at her. "Welcome, Miss Graves."

"Th..." She cleared her throat. Erik took the glass out of her tingling fingers. "Thank you."

Lindstrom chuckled. "Still new to the dreyri, I see."

"That's only my second taste of it." She sat in the chair beside Erik's. He did not look at her, and she felt a stab of shame for the way she had acted in the stairwell. She looked at the Consul. "Thank you for seeing us on such short notice."

The gray-haired man smiled. "It is my pleasure." He gestured toward the decanter. "Would you like another glass?"

"Yes, very much." She sounded over-eager, even to her own ears, and she glanced at Erik in embarrassment. He showed no reaction.

There was a knock on the door, and Lindstrom called out. "Yes?"

The receptionist's voice spoke on the other side. "I have the list you requested, sir."

"Put it under the door, please, Miss Andersson."

"Yes, sir."

A manila folder slid beneath the door, and Erik bent to pick it up. Lindstrom finished pouring another glass for Nika and handed it to her with a smile.

"It's so gratifying to see another Valtaeigr coming into her power."

"Thank you. Everything is still so new to me."

"It takes some time to adjust to your new experience, especially if you've not died yet."

Nika's brow puckered. "Pardon me?"

Erik picked up the folder and leafed through the documents inside, not standing on ceremony and eager to change the subject. "There is nobody named Sigurd associated with the Rune Sword exhibit in any way. Whoever he is, he is here without official papers."

Nika put the glass aside, feeling slightly drunk, as if she'd been drinking hard liquor on an empty stomach. "Do you know this Sigurd?"

"Not at all," Lindstrom said.

He put the stopper back into the decanter, then stowed the glasses and the blood back into his desk. Nika was sorry to see it go. She turned to Erik. He was taut as a bowstring, and she felt anxious just looking at him.

"Was there anything else you needed?" the Consul asked. "Perhaps a bit of an explanation to Nika of what she can expect when..."

He shook his head. "No. We should get ready for the trip to Stockholm."

The consul smiled at her. "I trust that you've had no trouble with your visa or documentation for your relocation?"

"Not a bit. Thank you."

He looked at her, studying her intently for a moment. He began to speak, but Erik shook his head sharply. He nodded. "Well... I wish you well in your trip to Sweden. I think you will enjoy Stockholm immensely. It will be like coming home."

"Thank you, Mr. Lindstrom," she said. "I'm sure that it will be."

***

He let himself into the apartment, flashing a smile and a spell. The movers accepted the unspoken suggestion that he was a resident and continued their work, ignoring him as he came inside. Unlike the Draugr, he did not need to be properly invited.

Sigurd walked through the rooms, letting his senses tell him everything they could about the couple who lived there. Her scent was stronger, the imprint of her energy on the walls more complex. She had not been a Draugr for long.

The other scent, the one that was a newcomer to this place... He knew him. He and Thorvald had met before, centuries in the past. He could recall his face, his battle yell and especially his sword arm. Sigurd never forgot an enemy.

He picked up the pillows from the bed and brought them to his face, inhaling deeply. Yes, both Draugr, and both melded with lesser members of the Aesir. He could taste those gods on the outer edges of their energy traces. Ithunn, the goddess of spring and immortality, and Vidar, the god of forests and silence and revenge.

He had once attempted to make a pact with Vidar, back when the world was young. The Great Huntsman had rejected him then. He would not be given the opportunity to make the same mistake now.

Sigurd reached into his coat pocket and pulled out a playing card. It was the Jack of Spades. With a smile, he bent and tucked it, corner first, into the space between two floorboards. He was still smiling when he left the apartment behind.

Chapter Four

The drive back to the apartment was tense. Erik gripped the steering wheel until his knuckles were white. Nika watched his face for a long moment, then finally spoke.

"I'm sorry about how I acted at the consulate. I don't really understand why I started getting argumentative."

He did not look at her. "Apology accepted."

She sighed. "And as for Johan... If you're jealous, well, we're Chosen, remember? That's not something that I'd put aside so quickly. Besides, even if he was her husband, that doesn't change the fact that I'm with you."

This time, he glanced at her. "So that reaction you had. Was that you, or was it Ithunn?"

"I think it was her." She propped her elbow on the car door and leaned her head in her hand. "I was just as sideswiped by it as you were... or maybe more."

They were stopped in traffic and sat in silence, both of them staring at the red light above the street.

"You knew he was there, and who he was." It was not a question.

"Yes."

"Why didn't you tell me? I should have known."

"And what was I supposed to say?"

"You could have warned me."

The silence fell again, but at least the light changed and they could move forward. Neither of them spoke until they reached her apartment building and Erik parked in the underground garage. He turned off the car and took the keys out of the ignition, but he did not open his door. Instead, he twisted in the seat so that he could face her.

"There are a hundred things that you probably need to know, but I don't keep an exhaustive list in my head. I'm sorry I didn't prepare you to meet Johan. I'm sorry I haven't told you everything you think I should. I'm doing the best I can."

She studied his face, taking in the tension in his jaw and the conflicted emotions in his eyes.

"I just have one question." She faced him. "Do you love me, or do you love who I used to be? Am I just a vessel to you?"

He looked hurt, and she instantly regretted her words. "I loved Berit. I don't deny it. But now I love you. I was seeking you out, because I knew you had been reborn, and that we were meant to be together. My soul needs your soul to be complete."

He took her hand.

"You are not a vessel to me. You are my Chosen. You. I never chose Berit, even though she wanted me to. In all of your soul's other lifetimes, I never took this step. It needed to be you, this lifetime, this person. I chose Nika, not Berit. You."

Her eyes stung with tears, mystifying her. Her emotions were wildly out of control today, and she didn't recognize herself at all. "Is that how it works? Are souls always destined to be together?"

"Not all souls." He offered a weak smile. "Only ours."

"What about Ithunn and Bragi?"

"They're destined, too, but they don't have autonomy now. That was something they gave up so that they could live forever. Ithunn is not in control. You are. And Bragi is not living this life. Johan is."

He took a deep breath.

"Nika, be cautious about Bragi. He and Ithunn had... a stormy relationship, to say the least."

She looked down at their hands, at the intertwined fingers. "Was he cruel to her?" she asked quietly.

"In his own way, he loved her very much, but by modern standards, yes, you could say that he was cruel. They loved each other, but they hated each other just as much."

"What other gods are melded with the Draugr?"

He shrugged. "All of them."

"Are there any others that I need to know about?"

Erik released her hand, letting his fingers trail over her skin as he retreated. He slipped the car keys into a pocket and got out, moving around to open her door and offer her his hand. She accepted it.

"In time, you will know them all, but there are a few to be wary of," he told her as she rose to her feet. "Everyone wants to avoid Hel, but she's been reborn recently and is still just a baby. The rest are more or less scattered. There is one, though, that I'm going to introduce you to."

They walked together to the stairs. He held out his hand to her, and she took it, moving in to walk close beside him.

"Who?"

"Ithunn's big sister, the one who can teach you to use your Valtaeigr magic. Frigg."

They reached the correct floor and walked to her apartment. She had never given him a key, an oversight that seemed less in need of correction now. He waited while she unlocked the door, and then they walked inside together.

The movers had done their jobs well. Everything had been boxed and carted away. There wasn't even so much as a roll of toilet paper left in the bathroom. It had all been packed.

She walked through the empty living room, looking around with bittersweet nostalgia. This had been the first home she'd rented on her own, the first place that saw her living by herself. This was where she had grown from college girl to professional adult, and where she had weathered several relationships and a few bad break-ups.

She turned to face Erik, who was watching her quietly. "It's so... empty," she said.

He went to her and folded her into his arms. "Don't be sad, love. Think of all the wonderful things that are waiting for you."

She hugged him, her head on his shoulder. Her eyes caught a glimpse of something on the bedroom floor. "Looks like they missed something."

"What's that?"

Nika walked over to pick up a playing card, the Jack of Spades. "I've never seen this before. Is it yours?"

Erik came to see. The card was hand-drawn, painstakingly outlined in deep black and colored with carefully applied ink. The back was covered in intricate Nordic interweave depicting a dragon with a sword in its claws.

"No," he said, deliberately tearing the card in half, and then in half again. "This is not mine."

"What are you doing?" she cried. "That was beautiful."

He dropped the pieces onto the floor. "It has to be from this Sigurd, whoever he is. This is literally the calling card of the Bluffmakare. The Tricksters. Devotees of Loki who hunt the Valtaeigr and the Veithimathr, like we hunt the wild Draugr."

Nika picked up the pieces and looked at them in horror. "He was in our home."

"And he wanted us to know." He took her hand. "Let's go. I don't want to be here if he decides to come back."

She went with him, leaving the door unlocked in their haste. It hardly mattered now. "They hunt us? What are they?"

"Nøkken."

They raced down the steps and back to the car. He helped her into her seat while keeping a watchful eye on the parking garage. Once she was safely inside, he trotted around to the driver's side and got in.

Nika spoke as soon as he closed his door. "Help me understand. There are two groups of Draugr, the bad and the good, right? The good guys are the Valtaeigr and the Veithimathr. The bad guys are the Tricksters. Right?"

"The Tricksters serve the bad guys," he corrected mildly as he drove out of the parking garage. "The bad guys don't really have a name, other than Draugr. They don't need them. They're the majority. It's we who are small in numbers – smaller now that my men have died."

"But the Nøkken aren't Draugr?"

"No. They're tricksters. Shapeshifters. They serve Loki and the Draugr."

"Are you really the last Veithimathr?"

He nodded grimly. "Yes."

She was catching on. "Why do you hunt your own kind?"

"The Draugr are by nature evil. It's a consequence of who their chieftain was when they were made. Hakon and his people..." He stopped. "I never told you that part."

Nika clenched her fist, alarmed by his tone and prepared to hear something unpleasant. "Never told me what?"

He kept driving as he spoke, weaving through traffic and headed toward the airport. "When Hakon was punished by Odin for his rapacious and murdering ways, all of his band were with him. They all... we all... shared in his punishment. That was when we were made Draugr."

She let his words sink in. "You used to serve with Hakon?"

He nodded grimly. "I was in his raiding party. I was..." He took a deep breath. "I was his right hand."

"So you..."

"I murdered. I raped. I stole from innocent people and I put helpless priests to the sword. I did all of those things that Odin punished us for." He shook his head. "We all did. All of us."

Nika swallowed hard. "Those were different times," she said, trying to excuse his past offenses. "You were a different man then."

He laughed hollowly. "Oh, yes. Very different." He shook his head. "You would not have liked me very much if we had met back then."

"Didn't we?" she asked. "Didn't we meet back then? Wasn't that when Berit lived?"

"Not then. Berit was born later, after I had already become Veithimathr."

Nika put out a hand and touched his arm. "If the gods chose you to be their Huntsman, then they saw good in you. You said that the Veithimathr were purer of soul than the other Draugr. I believe that about you."

He looked at her and forced a smile. "Thank you, my love. You do me credit."

"I've never seen you do anything that would make me doubt you."

Abruptly, he pulled over into a parking lot and stopped the car. He turned to face her. "I was horrible when I was mortal," he told her. "I thought at the time that what I did was justified – might makes right. The strong take what they want and the weak have to give it. It was the way of things. It was the Norse way."

"It was a different time," she said again.

He continued as if she hadn't spoken. "Hakon was our jarl, and he wanted to be king. Anyone who stood against him had to die – even if they were only children. We murdered whole families. We slaughtered innocent children, just to prove Hakon's point that he was the strongest leader in all of Sweden."

He looked down and struggled with the words.

"Nika, I – I deserved what happened to me. I did."

She took his hand. "But something changed. Didn't it? I saw what happened with the Rune Sword. Odin favors you."

He nodded. "As time went on, I began to feel that I shouldn't just take whatever I wanted, just because I could. I suppose you could say that I developed a conscience.

"Hakon and our band went raiding one night, attacking a settlement in Denmark. It was defenseless. All of their men were out to sea, and it was only women and children and old people. Hakon was thrilled, because they had livestock, and there was gold there for him to take. And he took it. He took it all.

"I was with Gunnar – all of the Veithimathr were once Hakon's men - and we broke into a little house. Kicked the door down. Inside, there was just one maiden child and her siblings. She was barely a woman, just a tiny slip of a thing. She stood and faced us and told us she would do anything we wanted as long as we left her siblings alone.

"I was going to take her. Gods forgive me, I was going to do it. But I saw the look in her eye. The bravery. The honor. It stopped me cold. In that moment, I saw myself through her eyes, and I was ashamed."

His eyes were brimming with tears, and he wiped them away with the heel of his hand.

"We stayed in that house and we defended them from the rest of the band. We gave her the things we had stolen from her neighbors. We... we changed. When day came and Hakon called the retreat, we left her unharmed.

"We never went raiding with Hakon again. Oh, he raged about it, accused us of cowardice, made us laughing stocks in his longhouse. I just... I didn't have the heart for it anymore. That girl, she changed me. She changed me forever."

"Was that when Odin changed you and made you Veithimathr?"

"Yes."

Nika stroked his face. He turned into the touch and kissed her palm.

"I still see her face, how frightened she was, but how strong. I will never forget her."

She kissed him. "Only a good man can learn from his mistakes and start over. You've more than made up for what you've done in the past."

"I don't know if I can ever make up for all the things I've done."

"The fact that you even want to try means the world," she reassured him.

Erik looked at her searchingly. "Do you still trust me?"

She smiled. "More than ever. You've trusted me with your secret. How could I not trust you in return?"

He leaned in and kissed her gratefully. "I love you."

"And I love you. Forever and always."

They kissed again, lingering and sweet.

He pulled back and smiled at her. "Let's go. Stockholm is waiting. Hopefully we can make it back before Sigurd does."

Chapter Five

Nika giggled. Erik's hands were covering her eyes, and he was guiding her through the front doorway of his house in Stockholm.

"Okay. Take a look."

She opened her eyes. They were standing in a spacious living room with hardwood floors and a bank of floor-to-ceiling windows taking up one entire wall. The furnishings were elegant and understated, and although she didn't know what she'd been expecting, she knew it wasn't this.

"Erik! It's beautiful!"

He smiled. "Do you think you could get used to living here?"

She laughed. "I don't know. You'd better take me on a tour first."

He happily escorted her through the entire house. It was well laid out and airy, and much brighter than she had expected it to be. The main floor had the living room, the kitchen, a bathroom and a dining room. Upstairs, there were three bedrooms and a spacious master suite overlooking a green, tree-covered lot. The tour ended back in the living room, next to the fireplace.

"Nice," she said. "Apparently, the Swedish special forces pay well."

"Not so much. But when you've had a bank account open since the 1540s, interest tends to accumulate." He smiled. "Do you like it?"

"I love it." She put her arms around him. "It's perfect. Thank you for inviting me to live here with you."

He kissed her. "I couldn't bear the thought of you living somewhere else."

"When the movers come, where are we going to put my things?"

"Anywhere you'd like." He released her and sat on the couch. She joined him, curling up against his side. He put his arm around her. "This is your home, too, Chosen. I want you to be comfortable."

"I'm comfortable anywhere you are."

Their conversation was interrupted by Erik's cell phone. He answered it. "Thorvald."

She could hear a man's voice speak on the other end of the line. "Captain, this is Major Ulvaeus. Welcome back."

"Thank you, sir." He sat up, giving Nika an unreadable look.

"We need you to report to Karlsborg. In light of the casualties to your group, you've been assigned to a new unit."

"Yes, sir."

Ulvaeus continued. Nika frowned. "Be there at oh-seven hundred on Wednesday for further orders."

"Yes, sir."

The line went dead, and Erik put the phone aside. "Well, shit." He looked at her. "I know you heard. I'm so sorry."

"Do you know how long you'll be gone?"

"No. It could be a few days, or it could be a few weeks." He sat back with a scowl. "This is terrible timing."

She tried to be brave for him. "That's okay. I'll be busy getting acquainted with my new job and the staff and everything. You have to do what your bosses tell you."

He put a hand on her knee. "It still gives us a few days."

Nika smiled and scooted closer to him. "So let's not waste it."

***

They passed the time before his trip to Karlsborg by touring Stockholm. He showed her the sights of his home town – now hers, as well – and helped her learn her way around, at least well enough to get to the museum and back. He showed her where to shop, what to buy, and how to hail a cab. He got her added to his bank account and provided her with a copy of his credit and ATM cards so that she would have access to money even if he was somewhere far away.

She got to recognize the street names and the places, and she was picking up the odd Swedish phrase here and there. Luckily, many of the inhabitants of the city spoke English, so that made things easier. She was almost ready to be on her own.

On the last night before his departure, he took her by the hand. "I need to show you one more thing. It's very important."

"What?"

"I need to take you to the Draugr underground and show you how to get dreyri. When I'm gone, you'll need to drink from a bottle instead of from me... Obviously."

She could sense a wave of apprehension from him, and she squeezed his hand. "Should I be nervous?"

"When you're going to the underground, you should always be nervous. The Draugr there are a mixed lot ranging from the relatively good to the completely evil. They will be looking for a new vampire like you."

"Looking for me for what?"

"To dominate. To enslave. To seduce. Any number of things. Remember, Nika, Draugrs use power like a drug. When they have power over someone else, it's like an aphrodisiac."

She shuddered. "Maybe we should stock up a lot so I don't have to venture there without you."

"That was exactly my thought." He rose. "Shall we?"

They went to the street and walked south. The wind was cool tonight, and it smelled of distant snow. She pulled her jacket closer and looked at him. "Karlsborg is north of here, isn't it?"

He nodded. "Very far north."

"Don't freeze to death."

Erik chuckled. "There are many ways for a Veithimathr to die, but that is not one that I've heard of any of my brothers dying that way before."

"Well, don't be the first."

They walked until they reached a subway station. The ceilings of the station were vividly painted, and she was stunned by the impact of the bright colors in so dark a place. Erik smiled at her reaction.

"Stockholm loves its art," he told her.

They boarded a train and sat together. Another of the riders, a young woman with ice-white hair and equally pale skin, peered at them curiously over the top edge of her book. Nika offered her a nod and a smile, and the woman kept staring.

Erik noticed that they had a watcher, and he spoke to her in Swedish. "Is there something wrong?"

The woman laughed and answered in Old Norse, the language of the Draugr. "I just heard that all of the Huntsmen were dead."

"Sorry to disappoint."

"I'm not disappointed." She smiled. "I know someone else who'll be thrilled that you're here and alive."

"Oh? Who?"

She closed her book. "Follow me and find out."

The train stopped, and the woman rose. She looked pointedly at Erik and Nika, displaying the merest hint of her long and feral teeth, and he shook his head once. "No."

She laughed and said as she left the train. "Suit yourself. You will find out in due course."

She left the train. Nika turned to Erik. "What was that all about?"

"I don't know." He shrugged. "She was young. She was probably just flexing her muscles, trying to be intimidating."

"It sort of worked."

"Don't let them get to you, Chosen." He smiled. "You're stronger than they'll ever be."

"I don't feel strong..."

"Oh, but you are. And you have Ithunn with you, she won't let you fall." The train stopped at the next station, and he rose. "This is our stop."

They exited the train, and he took her hand. This station was adorned with statuary showing human figures soaring like wingless angels. She shook her head.

"Extraordinary."

"Many things in Stockholm are," he said proudly. He took her hand. "Stay close to me."

She smiled for him. "Gladly."

He took her up the stairs and out onto the street. There were people all around, and the streets were full of bars and restaurants. Music poured out of clubs, and everywhere mortal and Draugr mingled. She clung to his hand.

"There are so many here."

"This is the Draugr homeland," he explained. "This is where we were made... Literally right here, where this street now stands. A lot of us don't stray too far from home."

She looked around at the busy street with its riot of colors and neon. She tried to imagine what it must have been like all those years ago, back in Erik's youth, when the Draugr were first made.

He leaned close. "Don't imagine it. Remember it. You saw it then."

Nika had dreamed of the day when Ithunn was melded to her soul, had sat through half-memories of the event and the feelings it had caused. She knew that the process had been difficult, and that Berit had not survived. She remembered Erik bringing her – bringing Berit – the first and last cup of blood she ever drank. She wondered how the memory looked to him, and what happened after that first taste. She never saw anything past the moment she brought the cup up to her lips.

She had so many questions, and there was so little time. He was leaving in the morning, and suddenly her heart couldn't bear the thought of that imposed distance. Tears sprang into her eyes.

"You changed me then," she said, the sound vanishing into the noise of the crowd. She knew he could still hear her. "How many times have you changed me from a mortal into a Draugr?"

"Many," he admitted. He stepped to face her, his hand on her cheek. "I –"

He was interrupted by the noisy arrival of a band of young Draugr on roaring motorcycles. They were clad in leather and chains, their hair long and wild from the road, laughing too loudly and caring too little about the people in their paths. She wondered if this was how the Norse had seemed back in their day.

The motorcycle gang pulled up onto the sidewalk, indifferent to manmade laws, and they parked there. The man in the lead, a powerfully-built moving mountain with black hair that tumbled past his shoulders, looked at the two of them and smirked. He dismounted his Harley and pulled a blackjack from his back pocket, waving it like an old-time general with a riding crop. He sneered at Erik and approached them.

Erik pulled Nika closer to him, but his blue eyes went green with ancient power. The biker hesitated for barely a fraction of a heartbeat, but it was enough for Erik to see he had the advantage.

"Keep walking, child," he told the gang leader, his voice a feral growl.

"Keep your shirt on, old man," the man retorted. As he walked past, he bared his teeth in an unfriendly smile. "I'm just out for a good time here."

Nika could feel something inside of Erik coiling. The Draugr in biker leathers felt it too, and they wisely gave the ancient vampire a wide berth. He kept his eyes on them as they walked past and into a nearby club. The door opened to release a cloud of noise and human smells as they went in.

He did not relax until they were gone. Then, finally, he seemed to pull his rage back under control and locked it up again. She should have been afraid of how hot it burned so close beneath the surface, but she was convinced that Erik would never hurt her.

He turned to her, his eyes as blue as the summer sky again, and he smiled for her. "It's all posturing. These young ones puff and make a lot of noise, but as soon as they realize that you're too much for them to handle, they'll back down."

"Do they all have gods inside them?"

"No. They're too young. There are only so many gods to go around, after all." He pointed at another doorway, farther down the street. "That is where we're going – Snake Eyes. It's a stupid name, but there's a story to it. The current owner won the bar from the last one in a game of dice. You can guess the losing roll."

"So he named it in honor of how he won?"

Erik chuckled. "Yes. Just a little bit of spit in the face of the one who lost it."

He kept hold of her hand and they walked toward the door. It was darker than the others, and the neon lights were blue and purple. The glass of the windows and doors were tinted black, and the soundproofing was excellent. Even when they reached the threshold, she could not hear the noise inside.

"The current owner is a woman named Magda. She is the vessel of Sigyn. Have you heard of her?"

"No," She admitted. "The only Norse gods I know of are Odin, Thor, Loki, Freya, Freyr, Ithunn, Vidar, and now Bragi and Forseti."

"I told you of two others," he reminded. "Frigg is not to be forgotten, for she will be your greatest ally. And while you will not encounter her for many years, Hel is not to be ignored, either. She is the queen of the dead. Most of the Draugr worship her."

He put his hand on the door handle, and she could feel a wave of energy pulse beneath his touch. "What was that?" she asked.

"That was a ward. It tells the young ones that one of the First is coming."

"The First? You mean Hakon's band?"

"Yes." He smiled at her. "You'd be surprised how much respect a little fear can buy you."

They walked inside.

Chapter Six

The interior of Snake Eyes was darker than most clubs she had been to, but the blue lights set into the baseboards and the benefits of her new Draugr sight meant that she could still see. A human would have had a difficult time navigating the place, which might have been by design. The room was full of vampires, the power in their blood combining to give the atmosphere a heady buzz. She could smell the many open glasses of dreyri, and she could sense it in bottle after bottle behind the bar. She could also smell the regular alcohol that they were mixing with the blood, the smoke from cigarettes, and the warm, animal smell of the bodies pressed together on the dance floor.

When they came through the door, the others looked to watch them enter, alerted by the ward that Erik's arrival had activated. The vampires here were all centuries younger than him, and they instantly deferred, clearing a path for him all the way to the bar. He led her through, and she noticed that some of the young ones averted his eyes as he walked past, their fear hanging on them like perfume.

"I take it that the First come in here and bust some heads from time to time," she conjectured.

"You take it correctly. Many of my former brothers are dedicated to keeping the younger ones afraid of them. These children are cautious and respectful, as they should be."

They reached the bar, and a pair of stools were instantly vacated for them. He helped her settle onto one, but he did not sit upon the other. He turned his back toward the bar and leaned on his elbow, his eyes scanning the room. Slowly, the others resumed whatever activities his arrival had interrupted, and he nodded.

"Good," he told her. "The trouble makers haven't turned up yet. I'm the oldest one in the house."

She watched as the bartender approached, the friendly smile on her face belying the tension in her stance. "Good evening, Ancient One," she greeted. "What can I get for you?"

The bartender was making no effort to conceal her Draugr fangs. None of the vampires were. It was a bit unnerving to Nika. She felt surrounded and very, very grateful that Erik was there.

"Dreyri for us both," he requested. He put a gold coin on the bar, ancient currency that she accepted with a knowing nod. "Three rounds."

Nika raised an eyebrow. She had never had more than two glasses at a time. She wasn't certain what a third round would do to her.

"I don't know if I can handle that much," she told him quietly.

"You probably can't. I'll drink your third round along with mine."

She chuckled. "Once a Viking, always a Viking?"

"Something like that."

Two martini glasses filled with the scarlet elixir were brought forth, and they picked them up. He touched his drink to hers, the glass making a bell-like chiming sound as he clicked them together.

"Skål."

He drained his serving in one swallow, leaving not even a single drop behind. She tried to follow suit, but the enchantment on the blood was stronger than she was accustomed to, and it made her throat burn. She coughed on the first sip.

Erik chuckled. "It's a strong vintage. You'll get used to it."

He tapped the bar beside his glass, and the bartender filled it up again.

"There are vintages for blood?"

"Of course." He watched as a young Draugr female collected a tray full of glasses and turned back into the crowd to deliver them. "The stronger you are, the stronger the enchantment that you can handle. Not just that, but at some times, you'll need the stronger stuff to refill your energy, like when you're depleted from not drinking in a long time, or when you've just healed or are healing from an injury."

"The blood is the life," she said, quoting Bram Stoker.

He saluted her with his glass. "Exactly."

"You're building up your strength for Karlsborg." It wasn't a question.

"Yes. I don't know what to expect, so I'm preparing for the worst."

"You're just going to meet your new unit. How bad can it be?"

"When the army knows full well what I am, and they've handpicked the replacement for my team? When I don't know if I'll be in command or not? When I don't know who they've got waiting for me?" He shook his head. "I'm not going to take any chances."

The bartender came back with a folded piece of paper. "Magda sends her greetings."

He accepted the slip with a nod. He straightened and stepped away from the bar. Nika put her glass down. "Follow me, but bring your drink."

She obeyed. "Do vampires use roofies on each other like humans do?"

"Young ones with ambition will try to drink above their pay grade," he told her. "It gives them a rush of power and energy that makes them feel invincible. That almost always ends up with them doing stupid things, and I don't want to deal with that tonight."

"So it doesn't change them forever, like when a mortal drinks dreyri?"

He looked at her strangely. "No. Come along."

She followed him as he walked down another pathway opened by the respectful crowd. She kept her glass in one hand and Erik's hand in the other. The gazes of the vampires they passed were curious and wary, and she didn't overlook the fact that several of the onlookers gazed at Erik with open desire. Whether that was for his person or his power, she was uncertain. They looked at her with scrutiny and sometimes disapproval. One man looked her in the eye and licked his lips salaciously. She turned away.

Erik took her to a closed door at the back of the room. A woman stood there, and her body was obviously fit; her black jumpsuit was like the one Sigrunn had worn when she stole the Rune Sword back in Central City. He handed the woman the piece of paper the bartender had given him, and she glanced at it, then at the two of them. She flicked her gaze over Nika from foot to head, and then grunted to herself.

She opened the door. "Magda will see you now."

They went through, and the woman closed the door behind them.

The room they entered was a sumptuously appointed office, full of red velvet and black leather. There was a smoky scent lingering in the air, chased by the sweet smell of incense that was burning in a brass bowl in the back of the room. The walls were covered by red wall paper, and the artwork that hung upon them was dark and disturbing, showing battle and death. A massive wooden desk sat before them, with a black leather executive chair behind it. A less-impressive but equally expensive pair of chairs faced the desk.

The room was empty. Nika looked around. "I thought Magda would be in here."

"She will be. Patience, my love."

A hidden door to their right opened, and a woman spoke. "You are drinking again, Erik. This must be her."

He smiled. "Magda, this is Nika. Nika, Magda. Nika is my Chosen."

The other Draugr came into view, and if she had a reaction to his news, she did not display it. "Welcome, Nika. How does it feel to be home?"

She answered honestly. "Rather overwhelming, actually. I've only been here for a few days."

"I will be deployed soon," he told their hostess. "Nika needs a supply and a body guard. I was hoping maybe Sif…"

"Sif guards no one but me."

Magda sat behind her desk. She was tall and strong, with hair as red as Nika's but she had brown and knowing eyes. She was wearing a chic black dress, tight in all the right places, and expert make-up. Her scarlet tresses were bound up in a French twist, pinned with a trio of ebony pins. She looked like a fashion model.

She folded her hands on the desk. "I can offer you a supply, though. That's not a problem."

"Thank you."

"As for bodyguards, well… For that, you are on your own, Huntsman."

Nika caught the edge of a sneer on the word, and she glanced at Erik.

"No need to be unfriendly, Sigyn," he said.

The look she gave him was cold. "I respect you as an elder, Erik Thorvald, but I do not respect you as a warrior. You lost your team. You have not earned the right to come into my presence without shame."

Nika's jaw dropped.

Erik raised his chin. "I lost my team, but I did not lose the sword. Nor did I lose my fight with Hakon."

"True. And that is why I tolerate your presence at all." She sat back. "There are those among us who would happily have your head for destroying the chance for Hakon to return. You are a traitor, Huntsman. You have sided with the humans against the Draugr for too long. Your sins will catch up to you one day."

"That may be, if it is my fate," he answered evenly. "I fight according to my understanding, and I make no apologies. My brothers all died well in service to their beliefs."

"Even Rolf? Did he die well?"

Nika remembered the other Huntsman's terrible demise as a result of the Blood Eagle, and she shuddered.

"He died for what he felt was true. His soul was quiet."

Magda smiled thinly. "Ah, but I think those are not the same things. Did you not abandon him to Astrid Sigurdsdottir and her friends? Did you not fail to search the barn when you might have saved him?"

Erik's eyes were stormy but he did not quail. "Mistakes were made, for which the Norn will no doubt punish me in time. You, Magda and Sigyn, are not the Norns. You have no right to punish me."

"I am the goddess of victory and I find you wanting."

He made a show of looking around him. "Wanting? I do not see Hakon sitting here."

Nika spoke, but she startled herself. The words were not her own. "Just give us the dreyri and we will go."

Magda, or maybe Sigyn, ignored her. "I also do not see Gunnar or your other brothers."

"Men die."

"And their leaders take the blame."

"As it may be, in time." He tossed another gold coin to her. "I know your allegiances, and now I know your opinions. I did not request either. I came for –"

"The dreyri. Yes, I know." She looked at Nika, then back at the warrior. "Will you leave her as she is?"

Nika frowned, confused.

Erik answered. "That is not your concern."

"No." Magda stood. "Of course not."

At some silent signal, the hidden door opened again, and a bulky man emerged, a barrel in his hands. He put it down on the floor with a thud.

"This is what you came for. Take it and be gone."

The size of the barrel and the noise it had made when it hit the floor made Nika think it must weigh hundreds of pounds. Erik picked it up as if it were weightless, settling it onto his left shoulder. He kept his right hand free.

"My thanks."

He looked at Nika and told her with his expression that it was time to leave. She held the door for him, and they left the office.

They made it to the street without anyone stopping them. Erik hailed a cab, and when she got inside, he spoke to her. "There's no room in there for me and this, but I'll meet you at the house. Do you remember the address?"

She panicked briefly. "Don't leave me alone."

"I have to. I will meet you there in moments, I swear. Do you remember?"

She swallowed hard. "Yes."

"Good." He leaned down and kissed her. "I will see you soon."

The driver looked into the rearview mirror, and she gave him the address. He nodded and pulled away from the curb. Nika watched through the window as Erik walked away, bearing his burden back toward their home.

Chapter Seven

Nika kissed him good-bye at the door, and the vision of the tears in her eyes stayed with him throughout his long morning travels from Stockholm to Karlsborg. Now that he had reached the base, it was time to put emotional things aside.

A young soldier had been dispatched to pick him up from the train station. All during the trip to Karlsborg, the young man had watched him in the rear-view mirror, his eyes constantly leaving the road to study Erik's face. He had kept his visage scrupulously unreadable, but the observation made him cross. The new recruits were always over-awed when they encountered the SOG, and it was a compliment of a sort, but he was not in the mood for it today.

He knew what the soldier was thinking. Everyone here at Karlsborg knew what the Huntsmen were. For centuries, he and his brothers had been an unbreakable unit, untouched from the outside and largely autonomous, functioning with little oversight from the regular army brass. Their missions were always top secret, and their training was brutal. They were legends.

Now only one of the legends had returned, and that unbreakable unit had been shattered into pieces. He didn't know if the young human's look showed curiosity, pity, or fear, but he wagered it was a combination of all three.

He walked into the barracks and sought out the one open bunk, and he dropped his duffel onto the narrow mattress. The rest of his unit were elsewhere, probably in the mess or at liberty. He took the time to appropriately stow his gear in his foot locker and near his bunk, and then he went to HQ to check in.

Major Ulvaeus was in his office when he arrived, receiving reports from a young lieutenant. The younger officer watched Erik warily when he came in, sizing him up as he stood at attention, waiting to be recognized.

Finally, Ulvaeus spoke. "At ease, Captain." Erik dropped into parade rest. "Your unit is at physical conditioning right now, but they will be back in twenty minutes. I will introduce you then."

"Yes, sir."

"Walk with me."

The major led him out of the office and into his own private billet. There would be no interruptions here. Erik waited while the major shut the door and turned the bolt.

"First of all, let me say that the orders I am about to give you do not have my full support, and I would rather they were different, but sometimes orders from the Överbefälhavaren cannot be countermanded."

Erik nodded. "Yes, sir."

"Second, I do not approve of the men they have selected to be in your unit. They are not regular army."

"I would assume not, sir. We are a special forces group."

"They're not even soldiers," he said, clearly chafing at the orders he had been given, himself. "They're convicts. The worst of the worst. They're being assigned to Huntsman squad because of their special skill sets."

Erik took a guess. "They are murderers?"

"They are assassins, part of a secret society called the Red Hand."

"I've heard of them. I thought they'd been destroyed at the end of the Second World War."

Ulvaeus handed him a dossier. "I wish they had. They have powerful friends. I suspect that they, like you, have some very deep secrets, as well. Old secrets."

The implication surprised him. "You think they're immortal?"

"Or something very like it. We have reason to believe that they all took part in some sort of black magic ritual that stopped them from aging. I am unsure about their loyalties, and about their friends."

Erik opened the folder and read the information inside. Each of the men in the new Huntsman unit had been born in the twenties or thirties, during the darkest days of the years between the wars. They were assassins, and all were veterans of the heaviest maximum security prisons in Sweden. The list of their victims – both personal and political – was lengthy.

"And I'm to make these men into hunters."

"You're to teach them how to kill Draugr." He sighed. "They've been training for weeks. They're very excited about the chance to kill with official sanction."

Erik closed the folder. "I will do the best I can with them."

"That's all I can ask." He looked at his watch. "I'd suggest that you get back to the barracks to meet them. They're going to be back any minute."

"Yes, sir." He handed the folder back to Ulvaeus. "Thank you for your candor."

"It's the least I can do."

He saluted the major and was dismissed with a nod. He made his way back to the barracks. If they were not Draugr, what were they? It concerned him, to put it mildly, that he was being presented with the dregs of society, but in truth, he was once one of those dregs, himself. He understood the type from personal experience.

He reached the barracks before the unit arrived. With his vampire senses, he could hear them approaching, loud and raucous. Barbarians are barbarians no matter the century, he thought. He stood at the end of his bunk, crossed his arms over his chest, and waited.

The first man to enter the room was small and wiry, his blond hair in a military-style buzz cut. He had a nasty scar that ran from the corner of his right eye down to the point of his chin. Erik took note of it; either the scar had been from a wound prior to whatever had extended his life, or increased healing was not part of the bargain he had made.

The man strolled into the room, his eyes locked onto Erik. He called over his shoulder. "Ulf. The vampire is here."

The next man to enter, presumably Ulf, was also blond, but his hair was an unkempt mess, completely at odds with his putative position in the Special Forces and the uniform he wore. It was long and lank, swept back from his forehead to reveal a widow's peak that pointed down to a prominent and beak-like nose. His eyes were dark, and he narrowed them when he saw the Huntsman.

Erik looked at them with his Draugr senses. They were definitely not vampires. If he were pressed, he would have to say that they were nothing but human. Whatever had extended their lives did not involve his kind or the drinking of blood.

Ulf nodded to him. "Captain," he greeted.

"Sergeant," Erik responded.

Two others joined them, talking and laughing at some private joke. They looked like twins, with the same unfortunate orange hair color and the same freckles over their faces. They stopped laughing when they saw him.

"Gents, this is our vampire," the first man told the newcomers.

"Your captain," Erik corrected. "Captain Erik Thorvald." He offered a handshake to Ulf, who stared at his hand as if it might bite him. None of the others seemed eager to accept the greeting, either. He dropped his hand to his side.

"Too bad you got your other unit killed," the first man said.

"What is your name, Sergeant?"

The man raised his chin and crossed his arms over his chest. "Jan Stenmark."

"Well, Mr. Stenmark, let's get one thing clear. Your opinions about my late team are irrelevant. I am your commanding officer, and I expect to be treated as such. Do you understand?"

Stenmark laughed. "Sure. Whatever."

The twins looked at one another, and then the one on the right spoke up. "Aron Jansen. This is my brother Sven."

"A pleasure," Erik said. He turned to the last man. "And your name?"

"Ulf Magnusson."

He nodded in greeting. "Sergeant."

They stood and stared at him, no doubt taking stock of him, his physique and his apparent human-ness. To a man, they looked unimpressed. He didn't really care what they thought. He was doing some evaluating of his own.

It was clear that Stenmark was the ringleader of this little gang of thieves, and that he was the one Erik would have to win over if he intended to form any sort of cohesive team. Ulf and the twins Aron and

Sven were pure followers, but the most dangerous kind. He suspected that where Aron and Sven were concerned, all loyalties to anyone but family would evaporate the moment one twin was in danger. That made them a very weak link.

Ulf was a cipher. He had the look and air of the sort of brute who enjoyed kicking homeless people, but he was also strangely diffident. Erik wondered if he was a person who had a long fuse but huge and violent explosions. He supposed he would soon find out.

"I read your dossiers," he told them. "I know that you're not actually soldiers, and that until recently you've been guests of His Majesty at Kumla Prison in supermax. You know why you're here. I know why you're here."

Stenmark chortled. "We're here to kill vampires! You'd better watch out."

"I have no fear of you."

"Maybe you should."

Erik called on his Draugr speed and crossed the room like a blur. Before any of the members of the unit could react, he had his hand around Stenmark's throat. The man's eyes bulged in shock and fear. Erik leaned close to him so that he could see the green light in his eyes, and when he spoke, his fangs were fully extended.

"I will never have any fear of you."

He released Stenmark immediately, his point made. The others shifted uncomfortably, looking at each other in anxiety. Erik returned to his bunk.

"First, if you're going to hunt Draugr, you need to know that as humans, even as extended or amplified humans or whatever it is that you are, you will never, ever be a vampire's physical equal. Draugr are faster and stronger than you could ever hope to be."

Stenmark rubbed his neck and glared petulantly.

"Second – and I want you all to listen very closely to this – I am in command here. I and I alone can tell you how things look through a Draugr's eyes, and only I can help you learn the techniques you'll need. I expect to be given respect. You can give it freely, or I will extract it from you. But I will be respected."

Ulf swallowed hard. "Extract it from us? What do you mean?"

Erik turned his glowing eyes to him. "Pray you never find out." An uneasy silence filled the room. Finally, he gave them orders. "Hit the showers. You all stink."

Sullenly, they obeyed.

Chapter Eight

Nika reported for work the same morning that Erik left for Karlsborg. The Royal Museum of Stockholm was much, much larger than the one she'd left behind in Central City, and she was a little overawed when she first stepped through the doors.

She paused in the foyer and looked up at the cathedral ceiling soaring high over her head, through the sky light and out into the sunny day beyond. Sculptures hung suspended from the girders, floating above her head as if they had been frozen in mid-flight. On either side of the main entrance, twin banners hung from the ceiling to the floor, advertising the return of the Rune Sword and the ship burial display. The picture of the sword had been taken while the Soul Stone still held its unhappy occupant. She could see the little glimmer of green in the jewel in the image.

She shook her head. The place was fantastic, and this was just the front hall.

Nika walked to the information desk. "Nika Graves to see Director Blomgren."

The woman at the desk smiled and responded in perfect British English. "Of course, ma'am. I'll ring him."

She looked around more while she waited. The crowd was of a good size, especially for mid-week. She could sense no Draugr in the area, which was a source of great relief to her. She sincerely hoped that the only other vampire she saw for a very long time was Erik.

Thinking of him gave her a pang of loneliness, and she wished she could call him. She knew that he had his duties to fulfill, and that what he was doing in Karlsborg was very important to him. She also knew that she ached whenever she thought about going to bed without him that night.

"Ma'am? Mr. Blomgren is on his way."

"Thank you."

A man in an impeccably tailored suit stepped up to the desk beside her and spoke to the clerk in Swedish. She intended to make a concerted effort to learn the language as quickly as possible. It was a lovely language, she thought, very expressive, and it sounded beautiful rolling off of this man's tongue.

To her surprise, the man turned to her with a smile. "God morgon," he greeted.

"God morgon," she responded.

His smile widened. It was a beautiful smile. Unlike most of the men she had seen in Stockholm thus far, he was dark, blessed with a golden-brown complexion, wavy black hair and dancing dark eyes. "Or should I say good morning?"

Her pronunciation must have given her away. "Good morning works better if you want me to actually reply," she chuckled.

"Welcome to Sweden, then, Mrs –"

"Miss. Nika Graves." She offered her his hand. To her surprise, he brought it to his lips and kissed her knuckles.

"A pleasure, Miss Graves. I am Rahim Amari."

"It's very nice to meet you. That's not a very Swedish name," she teased. She instantly regretted her choice of words and hoped she had not offended him.

To her relief, he only smiled again. His teeth were white and perfect, an orthodontist's dream. "No, it is not. I am from Iraq originally." The clerk at the desk handed him a visitor's pass, and he accepted it politely. Switching back to English, he continued. "May I ask what brings you here to Stockholm all the way from America?"

"Work." She smiled back. "Today is my first day as assistant curator of the historical collection."

"Wonderful! Then we may cross paths again. I am doing research for a paper on Viking trade with the Middle East. I'm here on sabbatical from the University of Baghdad." He took a step back from the counter. "Enjoy your new job, Miss Graves. I hope to see you again."

"Enjoy your research," she replied.

He grinned. "Oh, I shall."

She watched Amari walk away, and then resumed waiting patiently for Blomgren. It seemed to take forever for the man to appear, but he did finally come hurrying down a side corridor, headed for the information desk.

"Miss Graves, I am so sorry to keep you waiting. I was preparing your employee badge and the laminator malfunctioned." He handed her the badge on an official RMS lanyard. "Welcome aboard."

They shook hands, and she put her new identification around her neck. "Thank you so much. I can hardly wait to begin."

He smiled. "Won't you come with me? I'll show you to your office." He led her back down that side corridor and into a stairwell. "The staff offices are in the basement, along with the storage and our restoration department." He held the door for her at the bottom of the stairs. "My office is right next to yours, and the employee lunch room and restrooms are down here, too."

She followed him to the office that would be hers. It was spacious, with elegant furnishings and a subtle pattern in the carpet. The walls were a soft rose, and she was happy to find a light table in the back corner. Blomgren smiled at her reaction.

"We encourage our curators to pursue research, if they are so inclined, and to help our professors and academic guests with their work. A light table is very helpful for examining old documents, as you know. You will be happy to know that the light it uses is free of UV rays, so it will not damage the artifacts."

She shook her head, unable to keep from grinning. "That's... amazing. Thank you."

"Naturally, you will have full access to the restoration laboratory and the storage area. I will provide you with the electronic codes for the locks to those areas."

"Terrific." She hesitated. "I met one of your – our – academic guests this morning. Rahim Amari."

"Ah, yes. Our Iraqi friend."

"He said that he was studying Viking trade with the Middle East. It sounds like a fascinating topic."

Blomgren agreed. "It certainly is. Did you know that there are gold coins from the Abbasid Empire among the goods excavated from the most recent ship burial? That's Iraq, eighth century, right at the very beginning of the Viking era. It's the earliest demonstrable contact between Scandinavia and Western Asia."

"Amazing," she said. "The exhibit that came to Central City didn't have any such coins with it, and none of the literature you send mentioned it."

"We have to keep our secrets," he said, jesting.

"How many coins?"

"Five. They were in a box marked with runes that translate to, 'payment for the hunters.'"

"Hunters? Or huntsmen?" When he frowned, not entirely understanding what she meant, she refined her question. "Jägare or veithimathr?"

"Veithimathr," he answered, smiling. "I will leave you to get settled, and I'll send in Inga from HR to explain the benefits and salary package."

"Thank you."

She sat at the desk, and after he left, she took up a pen and notepad from the drawer. She wrote down the names of the fallen huntsmen from Erik's team. Rolf. Magnus. Gunnar. Hrothgar. She froze.

Erik. That's five.

Who was paying for the veithimathr, and why? She made a mental note to tell Erik about this as soon as she spoke to him again. That missing-him pang returned, and she sighed. She had no idea when she would hear from him.

This is terrible. He's only been gone a few hours and it already hurts so bad...

Inga from HR arrived, and Nika pushed her sorrows away so that she could concentrate. She still had a job to do.

****

The next several hours were taken up with the mundanities of working life. There were forms to fill out, spiels to listen to, and then the docents requested a meeting with her. She was accustomed to the people at the Central City museum – relatively mild-mannered, sometimes obsessively possessive about their pet artifacts, and occasionally intellectual snobs and know-it-alls. It was a bit of a relief to realize that the docents in Stockholm were no different. It was the one known quantity in her new job, and she was grateful that this part of human behavior was a universal phenomenon.

The Director of the museum was at an all-day meeting with donors, so she was scheduled to meet him tomorrow. She met and talked with the registrar, the exhibit designers, and the conservation and restoration staff. By the time afternoon arrived, she felt as if she had walked for miles, and she still hadn't really seen the museum itself.

She had an hour to herself, which was meant to be used to eat lunch. Food was a strange subject for her these days. Her need for regular food was less than it had been before she had become a Draugr, but strangely, she still needed it. Erik never ate human food. She wondered if that was a factor of age.

The one thing that she did need every day, three times a day, was dreyri. Erik had been insistent that she should establish a regular schedule, taking the enchanted blood as if it were a prescription. Back in Central City, he would feed her himself, just a mouthful or so from his own veins.

It had been awkward and strange at first, and the first few times she tried to feed from him, her teeth weren't sharp enough and her technique was horrible. He had ended up with a shredded neck before she was able to get enough blood. Finally, he had just opened his blood to her himself, using his own teeth or a claw that he could grow or retract at will. Now that he was gone, she'd have to fend for herself.

She was grateful that he hadn't told her to start hunting humans or anything like she'd seen in the movies. It was bad enough that she was a parasite on her lover; she didn't want to drink from a stranger.

She had brought a little flask filled with dreyri from the cask in their house. She sat in her office with the door closed, seated at her bare desk – she really needed to bring in a picture or a desk calendar or something – and pulled the flask from her purse. As she unscrewed the top, she chuckled at the image of herself that rose in her mind. Swigging her liquid lunch like this, she looked like some movie version of an alcoholic.

Nika drank the dreyri and felt it tingle down her throat, the magic coursing into her. It was still so strange to drink blood. The thickness of it, and the salty copper taste, were things she still needed to adjust to. The way the dreyri warmed her from the inside out, and the power that she could feel filling her from her stomach outward, were delicious sensations, like drinking hot tea on a cold day. It made up for whatever psychological stumbling blocks she had toward the act of drinking blood.

She never expected to have become a vampire. Naturally, she had never even believed that they existed. At the time she had taken her first taste of dreyri, it had been what she needed to do, driven by their circumstances and her need to keep up with Erik and fight Astrid for the Rune Sword. She wondered, now that she was alone, if she would have taken that first drink if she'd had time to think it through.

Did she want to be with Erik? Of course, without question. Did she want to be immortal? That was harder to answer. She had family in St. Louis, and friends that she still cared about. She wasn't prepared to outlive them all. She wasn't prepared to stop being human, to become some sort of monster who lived off of another person's life force.

Well, she thought dourly, draining the flask, too late now.

With the rest of her lunch to kill, she thought she would venture into the museum proper for the first time. Her first destination was a natural, given the turn her life had recently taken, and considering that the gallery in question was to be her responsibility in her new job. She went to the ship burial gallery to see the Rune Sword.

The floor was covered a graphic depiction of the ship as it was when it was new, loaded with its cargo. The glass case that had once held Hakon's remains had been filled with an artist's recreation based on the extensive photographs the archaeologists had taken. The realism was striking. Nika shuddered when she looked at it, remembering that withered body opening its eyes and turning on Erik.

"We all react to the dead differently, don't we?"

She turned to face the speaker. It was Amari, the visiting professor from Baghdad. He was looking down at the artificial corpse on display.

"Some people, like your archaeologists, see them as curiosities, something to be poked at and examined. Others believe that human remains are sacred and should be treated as such. And some, like the thieves who stole this body in America... Who knows what they think?"

She smiled amiably. "Who knows, indeed? Maybe they thought he had precious stones or metals in his body, like the ancient Egyptians who put charms into the mummy wrappings."

"Perhaps. Or perhaps it was something darker." He looked up. "We shall never know, since they've not been caught and probably never will be. At least the Rune Sword was saved."

He walked to the display case at the head of Hakon's replacement body. She followed him.

"It's beautiful, isn't it?" she asked. "Such intricate interweave design on the hilt and pommel. It's a piece of art more than a weapon."

"Ah, but many weapons are works of art, are they not? And in some eyes, they damage they create is just as beautiful." A dark look fluttered across his face. "Forgive me. I do not mean to talk about sad things on such a beautiful day."

"We're standing in the middle of someone's plundered grave," she said softly. "If that doesn't lend itself to sad thoughts, I don't know what does."

"Indeed."

He accompanied her as she walked around the rest of the exhibit. Many of these objects had been too delicate to make the trip to Central City, and this was the first time she had seen them. One of the artifacts, a leather pouch, lay on its side in a little square display case, the coins it had held scattered around it, raised on acrylic stands.

"These are the Abbasid coins," she said, pointing. "That's what you're here to study, yes?"

He looked flattered. "Those, and some other artifacts in the collection that are not on display. You inquired about my work?"

"You mentioned it when we met, and I remembered. I did my Master's Thesis on Norse art and history, so it was right up my alley."

Amari looked delighted. "We should talk more," he said. "Perhaps we can compare notes on Norse travels in the eighth century."

She smiled as she considered someone else who could probably provide better information than she could, but she did not mention Erik to the professor. Instead, she said, "I would like that."

"Maybe over dinner?" She hesitated, and he hastily amended, "Purely platonic, of course."

"Maybe," she allowed.

"Tomorrow night? Perhaps you could bring your thesis. I would like to read it."

"I doubt it would interest you, but I'll see if I can find it. I just moved, and the house is a disaster. At least cleaning it up will give me something to do until my partner comes home."

Amari's face fell. "Ah. Your partner. Of course. No woman as exquisite as you would be without a mate." He brightened, and she could tell that it was by force. "Well, my offer was platonic, as I said. Perhaps your partner...?"

"He's indisposed," she said, shaking her head. "He was recently deployed."

"Ah! A soldier. American?"

"Swedish." She gestured toward the Rune Sword. "We met because of this exhibit, actually."

"Then he was one of the Special Forces men who retrieved the artifact. Only one survived – Captain Thorvald, was it?"

"Yes."

"It must have been very hard on him, losing his comrades that way."

She looked down at the coin purse again. "I'm sure it was."

"You don't know?"

"He doesn't grieve in front of me. He keeps his vulnerabilities closely guarded."

"A pity." She looked up into his handsome face, and his smile turned gentle. "A man should always be open with the woman he loves."

The conversation was making her uncomfortable, so she changed it back to something more professional. "I was told that the Abbasid coins were actually found in a box that had markings on it."

"Yes, that's right. The box is still being conserved, I was told."

"Ah." She continued to stroll among the displays, and Amari kept up. "What is it that the inscription said, again?"

"'In payment for the huntsmen,'" he replied. "It was difficult to translate, but luckily the Arabic was also written on the box."

"You've seen it?"

"Yes. The interesting thing was the implication of the word used in Arabic. In English, the meaning would be more like, 'in payment for the future delivery of the huntsmen.'" He sighed. "Presumably, the man who received the box was going to send some men back to the Caliphate, which at the time had its capital in Damascus. Did you know, in the middle of the eighth century, the Caliphate spread all the way across northern Africa and even included Spain?"

"The moors," she nodded. "They were from the caliphate."

"Yes, and at the same time, the Viking raiders were making inroads into Spain. They are known to have attacked Spain in 844, around the same time that the Abbasid dynasty was in control of the Caliphate. It would not have been unheard of for them to have trade contact, or even more." He winked at her. "There are some Iraqis born today with blue eyes."

She laughed. "That's a recessive trait. I doubt it would have lasted from 844."

"Well, that's the story I like to tell myself."

They continued into the general Viking gallery, stopping to admire a particularly well-preserved wooden shield. "The Norse king in 844 was Horik," she said, almost to herself. "And there was a powerful raiding band led by someone named Hakon."

He did not react to the name, which disappointed her. Instead, he shrugged. "Well, nobody knows who led which raid, really, unless they took the time to identify themselves to their opponents. The one who led the raid into Portugal and Spain was never identified in the chronicles of the time."

She was willing to bet that she knew who it had been.

The owner of the ship burial had not been identified by name, at least not to the knowledge of the human world. She glanced back at the recreated corpse. "Maybe the occupant of this ship burial was Hakon."

"Maybe. Maybe he was someone entirely different. It is strange that there were no inscriptions on any of his grave goods to identify him." He motioned vaguely back toward the exhibit. "The writing on the Rune Sword is nonsensical, as if someone who did not actually speak Norse tried to copy it. Perhaps he was a foreigner. We may never know. Such are the mysteries we are left with." His dark eyes searched her face. "Do you like mysteries, Miss Graves?"

There was something unspoken in his tone, something that hovered on the edges of her awareness like a threat. She cleared her throat. . "Thank you for your company, professor. I need to get back to work now. Perhaps we can talk more about it at dinner tomorrow."

"I would like that very much."

With her head full of information and just as many questions as before, she headed back to her office.

Chapter Nine

Against her better judgment, when she got home from work that night, Nika searched through the boxes stacked around the house. In the box labeled "böcker", Swedish for "books," she found her Master's thesis, which bore the entirely uninspiring title of The Poetic Edda, Norse Art and the Culture of Viking Age Scandinavia: An Exploration. She remembered hours and hours spent slaving over books and primary sources while she was composing the thesis, and of the gallons of coffee she had poured down her throat to make it through a hundred all-nighters. Little had she known that she'd end up with a boyfriend she could have just interviewed for the same effect.

She picked up her cell phone and pondered it for a moment, debating whether she should call him. The house felt so empty without him, and she truly hated the thought of sleeping in their bed alone. She decided that she needed to hear his voice, even if was only his voice mail greeting. She dialed.

To her great surprise, he picked up almost immediately. "Thorvald," he said, his voice all business.

"Hi," she responded, almost shy.

When he spoke again, she could hear him smiling. "Hey, love," he said. "What's going on? Is everything all right?"

"Oh, it's fine... I just needed to hear your voice."

He chuckled, and the sound was warm and welcome in her ear. "I miss you, too, beloved."

"How is Karlsborg?"

She could hear him walking, then the opening and closing of a door. He had gone somewhere to speak more privately. "About the same as it was last time I was here. Nothing much changes."

"And your team?"

"Ugh." He sighed. "The less I say about them, the better. They're not Special Forces, and they're not even regular army. They're...impossible."

She frowned. "Oh, that sounds horrible. Do you think you'll be able to train them?"

"I can train anyone, if they listen." He sighed. "I just don't think this lot will be listening to me. They're pretty argumentative, especially their leader."

"I thought you were their leader."

"I'm their commanding officer, but I'm not their leader yet. We'll see how it goes after we really get to work. Speaking of, how is the new job?"

She launched into a retelling of her day, keeping the awkwardness of her encounter with Amari from the tale. She talked about her office, about the HR executive and about the docents at the museum. She told him about the wonders of the collection she was curating now, and about the things she wanted to show him when he came home. He listened with interest, or at least he feigned interest by commenting at the right moments. When she stopped to take a breath, he chuckled again.

"My Chosen, you sound as if you've found your soul's true home." His voice was a sexy, masculine whisper, and it made her shiver.

"I have, but then my soul's true home went to Karlsborg."

He made a breathy sound, something like a cross between a laugh and a sigh. It was like having his lips against her ear, and she missed him keenly. "I will come home to you as soon as I can."

"You'd better."

This time, he did laugh. "I will, I swear. Listen, I have to go. I can't give leave these idiots unsupervised for long. I'll miss you every day."

Her eyes stung with unshed tears, and she looked down at the carpet. "I already do. I love you."

"And I love you, from this lifetime to the next and the one after that."

"I'll hold you to that."

"Please do."

They said their reluctant goodbyes, and then she hung up the phone. The house was still empty, but now that she had spoken to him, she felt a little less alone. She hoped that he felt the same way.

***

Erik returned to the barracks, his phone in his hand. Stenmark was lounging on his own bunk, leafing through a skin magazine and ogling the picture of naked women with unnatural physical proportions. The twins sat together on Sven's bunk, heads close together, reading a book together. Ulf, who was the only one actually doing something useful, looked up from cleaning his sidearm.

"Woman?" he asked Erik.

"Yes."

"She hot?"

Erik shot him a hard look, warning him not to get too familiar. He did not answer.

Stenmark replied for him. "She's probably just a blood bag on legs to him."

The vampire turned off his phone and tucked it into his foot locker. Stenmark was trying to goad him into losing his composure. "She is beautiful, and she's my woman, not my meal."

"So how many people do you eat a day?" Ulf asked. "Just curious."

"Yes," Stenmark agreed. "How many people can you murder in their sleep? Asking for a friend."

Erik lay down on his bunk, staying fully clothed. He put his left arm behind his head and rested his right hand on his pistol, which he put on the mattress beside his hip. "Why don't you go to sleep and find out?"

Ulf chuckled, and he earned a half a point in Erik's reckoning. It was an improvement. The big man saw his captain looking at him, and he asked, "Do you, like, sleep in a coffin?"

"That's Hollywood," Erik said, shaking his head. "I've never been in a coffin in my entire life."

"That's good," the man said, nodding. "That would be creepy."

Stenmark tossed a wadded-up sock at Ulf, who caught it and threw it back. They made eye contact, and Stenmark shook his head once, no. Ulf went silent.

"Let him talk," Erik told Stenmark. "He's not hurting anything."

"Maybe I'm sick of hearing his voice."

"Maybe we're all sick of hearing yours."

Ulf laughed. Stenmark glowered. "Shut up."

Erik closed his eyes. "I sleep in a bed like everybody else." He took a breath. "Let's address the big misconceptions here. Yes, I can move around in the daylight. No, sunlight doesn't make me burst into flame. I have a reflection. I actually like garlic. As for the rest, you'll find out tomorrow how a vampire can be killed and what we can do. For now, I'm sleeping."

"Sounds like," Sven said.

"-you're talking," his twin, Aron, finished.

"Okay," Erik said, opening an eye. "That's creepy. Don't do that anymore."

"What?" Aron asked. "Finish each other's sentences?"

"Yes. Exactly that."

Sven shrugged and went back to his reading. Aron looked at Erik for a long while, almost as if he was really seeing him for the first time. Then he nodded and returned to the book, as well.

Erik rested with his eyes closed, but he did not sleep. He tracked each of the members of his team as they carried on with their night. One by one, they took to their beds, with Stenmark being the last to go. His bed was closest to Erik, directly across the narrow room from him so that they lying with their feet toward each other. He listened to their breathing slow and deepen, and from a lifetime of hunting humans, he was able to detect the moment when they all descended deep into their dreams.

He rose when they were all fast asleep, and he extended his supernatural Draugr abilities to keep them there. It wouldn't do to have them wake up at an inopportune moment, and the effect of his hold would be nothing more than a deep dive into R.E.M. He solidified his hold and watched them in the darkness to ensure that they were not resisting. They lay like stones.

He went to Stenmark's foot locker and opened it. Inside he found a stack of pornography, underwear, socks, a shaving kit, and some average toiletries. Beneath the porno magazines, though, he found a copy of the man's release record from Kumla Prison. The release had been under the order of a Kommendör Nicklas Holm of Special Forces Command. He did not recognize the name. He had made it a point to have a passing familiarity with at least the names of his commanding officers. This name he did not know.

A check of the foot lockers of the other men revealed the same contents, minus the pornography. The twins had a stack of fantasy novels, dog-eared and smudged from repeated reading. Ulf had a pile of gun and ammunition catalogs. They all had release papers signed by Kommendör Holm.

Well, now he knew who was behind this scheme. Now he had to figure out who this Holm person was. He'd like to break into the office of Major Ulvaeus, but he knew that the officers' quarters and offices were regularly patrolled, and he would prefer to avoid beating down any soldiers in his own army. He had known Ulvaeus for years, and he had never steered him wrong. He was one officer that Erik trusted.

He returned to his bunk and settled in to get some sleep, letting his hold on his unit seep away with his consciousness.

***

When morning came, it came early.

The morning revelj, the Swedish Army's version of reveille, blasted into over the post through loudspeakers, jerking them all into wakefulness. They scrambled into their boots and uniforms and mustered in the yard. Erik stood at attention at the front of his men, who, to their credit, managed to mimic a proper military formation.

Major Ulvaeus walked past, reviewing the troops as he did every morning. He ignored Erik's group, which was probably for the best. He spared a quick order to Erik before he moved on to the regular army troops.

"Make something of them, Captain."

"Yes, sir."

Then the muster was released after roll call, Erik gathered his new unit.

"Listen up," he told them. "First PT, then breakfast, then it's the range for instruction."

"I already know how to shoot a gun," Stenmark complained.

"But you don't know what it takes to shoot the targets you'll be going after. I know you all know how to murder human beings. I'm here to train you how to hunt the Draugr."

"Maybe we'll end up hunting you," the mortal said.

"I heard this threat yesterday. It didn't impress me then, either. One more threat and you'll be on report."

Stenmark smirked. "Yes, sir."

"Ten miles!" Erik barked. "Let's go!"

He led the way, and his reluctant team followed, running in their combat boots like real soldiers. He wondered just how much training they had actually received.

He supposed he was about to learn.

***

Nika dressed in a dark green skirt suit and matching pumps, then pinned up her hair into a passable French knot. She had slept poorly, full of dreams of Erik and starting at every random noise in the garden. She hated to admit how vulnerable she felt, living in a strange country with her man so far away.

The Stockholm subway system was meticulous and prompt, and she arrived at the station in front of the museum with plenty of time to spare. The other riders had been polite and contained, not troubling her in the least, unlike the subway back at home, where she could be guaranteed at least one cat call a day. It was a relief to make it to work unmolested.

When she reached her office, she found a bouquet of wildflowers and a card waiting on her desk. The arrangement was simple but beautiful, all sunny colors in a cut crystal vase. She took the card and read it.

Welcome home. All my love, Erik

She smiled and touched the card to her lips, touched by his thoughtfulness. It had been years since anyone had sent her flowers.

There was a light knock on the door, and she looked up to see Dr. Amari standing there, a smile on his handsome face. "Am I intruding?" he asked.

"No, not at all." She tucked the card back into the bouquet and put down her briefcase. "I found my thesis last night. If you're having trouble sleeping, I'm sure it'll be just the thing."

Amari chuckled and came inside. "My own thesis would probably serve the same for you...but I doubt that I would find your writing at all boring."

"Well, you haven't read it yet." She pulled it out of her bag and offered it to him. "Enjoy."

"Thank you. I shall." He tucked it under his arm. "The archaeologist, Dr. Mansson, has brought a new case of artifacts for us to catalog. I thought we might look at them together. We are colleagues, after all."

She smiled. "It sounds exciting. Where is Dr. Mansson digging?"

"He's working on a new grave field outside Jordbro. Viking age burials, mostly. Very exciting. The graves he's working on belonged to a young man of some standing, he said."

Nika was intrigued. "Wonderful! I can't wait to see what he's discovered. What was the condition of the remains?"

Amari grinned and opened the door. "Why don't you come with me and see?"

She couldn't resist that invitation. Together they walked into the workshop, where the artifacts were being prepared for entry into the collection. The skeletal remains of a tall man lay in on the bench, the bones being sorted into place by a technician. They went closer for a better look.

It was clear that this man had not met with an easy end. Even now, with his skeleton completely disarticulated, she could see cut marks and unhealed fractures. She shook his head.

"What a way to go. It looks like he was hacked to death."

Amari nodded. "Ancient warfare was a bloody thing, brutal in the extreme." He peered more closely at the skull, which had two close-set punctures through the cranium. "It looks almost like someone stabbed him with a meat fork."

She wondered how far apart a Draugr's fangs might be, and if they could punch through a skull. "Seems like an odd weapon to use," she said, keeping her supposition to herself.

The technician looked up from her work sorting the carpal bones. "Take a look at his dentition," she said in English, slightly flavored with a lilting Swedish accent. "I've never seen anything like it."

Nika and Amari looked closer. The skull sported a row of pockets above the top teeth. Inside the pockets, the tips of sharp teeth showed through. She straightened in surprise. *I thought Draugr turned into dust when they died.*

"Extraordinary," Amari said. "What an unusual malformation."

"It's fascinating," the tech agreed.

They moved on to the grave goods, which stood on another workbench. A double-headed axe, corroded and pitted with time, sat amid a set of rusted chains. Other artifacts included a brass torc and a stone carved with stylized wolves howling at the moon. One stone was carved with runes, and both Nika and Amari bent closer to look at it.

"Leithr svik ulfr," Amari read. "Loathsome treason wolf."

"Sounds like someone was unpopular," she said.

Amari chuckled and gestured toward the brutalized skeleton. "Obviously."

She slipped on a pair of white cotton gloves and picked up the torc. It was engraved with more stylized wolves, and the ends were capped with snarling wolf heads. "This is beautiful," she said. "The torc was primarily a Celtic ornament, but it was also used by other Bronze Age groups. They were popular here during the Viking age, and this looks like the Viking style. This man obviously identified very strongly with wolves."

Her companion also donned gloves, and she handed him the torc. He examined it closely. "Maybe we should call this gentleman Fenrir, after the great wolf of Norse myth."

The technician nodded. "I like that."

Nika looked down at the dead man's remains and said, "I wonder what battle he was in that was so fierce."

"If only the dead could speak," Amari sighed. He glanced at his watch. "I am so sorry, Miss Graves. I have a meeting to get to. Will you have dinner with me tonight? You haven't accepted my invitation yet."

She hesitated, then nodded. "That would be lovely."

He broke into a brilliant smile. "Wonderful. I'll make reservations and we'll go directly after the museum closes."

"Sounds good," she said. "Thank you."

He left them alone with the newly-dubbed Fenrir. The technician smiled at her. "He fancies you, I think."

"I don't know," she demurred. "I'm not sure this is anything but collegial."

She snickered. "You may tell yourself that."

Nika stripped off her gloves. "Thank you for letting us poke into your work."

"No problem." As Nika walked away, the technician called after her, "Enjoy your date tonight."

She stopped and was about to protest that it wasn't a date, but she couldn't get the words to come. She wondered what Erik would say if he knew.

Chapter Ten

The team assembled on the shooting range, and Erik passed out a clip to each man on the firing line.

"Look at the rounds in these clips," he instructed. "See anything different?"

Stenmark spoke first, as he could have predicted. "Looks normal to me."

"Anyone?"

Ulf and the twins examined their ammunition, and all of them shook their heads, looking confused.

Erik explained, "What you're holding in your hands are anti-vampire rounds. They also work on werewolves and other shape shifters. They're steel jacketed, like normal rounds, but instead of a lead slug, they're filled with solid silver. "

Ulf grinned and laughed. "Honest to God? Silver bullets?"

"Honest to God."

"Who makes these?" Stenmark sounded interested in something other than himself for the first time in ages. It was a good sign.

"There's a specialty ammunition manufacturer in Lisbon who supplies them." He put a clip of silver bullets into his pistol. "In all ways, they act just like any other bullet. They're high caliber, intended for high-velocity shooting. They'll kill any human just as dead as any other bullet. But unlike lead, these things can actually hurt a Draugr."

"Lead don't work?" Sven asked, squinting.

"The impact will leave a bruise, but that's about it. The wound will heal immediately, and your target will keep running." He aimed at a target down field and fired – bull's eye. "But if you hit a Draugr with one of these, you'll hurt him, badly. The silver will burn, and it will bury itself in soft tissue. They actually burrow through muscle, gut and tendon if they hit a supernatural target. Once they're in the body, they emit a poison that sickens the target and retards Draugr or shifter healing. Until these babies are cut out, the vamp will be perforated and bleeding."

"Shit," Stenmark commented. "Awesome."

"These bullets give you an advantage. They slow a Draugr down so you can catch them. If you fill the vamp with enough bullets, or if you hit them in the head, you'll paralyze them. Then you can finish the job with one of these."

He held up his double-bladed axe. It gleamed in the sunlight, lethal and beautiful.

"What, you hack 'em to death?" Ulf asked.

"That's one way to slow them down, but no. You decapitate them." He put his axe into the holster on his back in one practiced move, seating it without fumbling for the loops. He had been doing this for years. "A stake to the heart will paralyze them, too, but it has to be wood. Metal – unless it's silver or silver-coated – won't do the trick. Stone won't do the job. Wood only. Any kind of wood."

Aron scratched his chin. "Holy water?"

"That'll only make him wet."

"Wolf's bane?"

Erik shook his head. "That's a good poison for werewolves and shifters, but not Draugr." He crossed his arms over his chest. "There are only three ways to kill a Draugr: wood through the heart, decapitation, and immolation."

"Immo... what?" Ulf asked.

"Immolation. It's a fancy word for burning them to death."

Stenmark loaded his silver bullets into his pistol and sighted down the barrel, almost but not quite at Erik. His captain glowered.

"Remember your fire discipline, and – I can't believe I have to tell professional assassins this – don't point a gun at someone unless you're ready to use it."

Stenmark smiled at him over the sights. "I'm not."

Ulf kicked his comrade in the ankle, and Stenmark put the gun down. Erik walked over to him and got up in his face, their noses only inches apart.

"I don't know where you came from or why you of all people were selected for this job. I don't know why Kommendör Holm thought using the Red Hand was a good idea. Let me tell you this: if you disrespect me one more time, or point that gun at me, or make one more threat, I will not hesitate to beat the shit out of you. Do you understand me?"

Infuriatingly, Stenmark laughed in Erik's face. The Draugr brought out his fangs and the green vampire lights in his eyes, and he grabbed the man's throat in a hand bristling with claws. Stenmark blinked and scrabbled at Erik's hand, choking. Aron took a step toward him, but Erik pointed a warning finger at him with his free hand, and the twin stopped short.

"Do you understand me?"

"Yes!" he managed to gasp out.

Erik released him with a shove. "You're on notice, Stenmark."

The ex-con stumbled and glared at Erik, massaging the bruises on his throat. "Yes, sir."

They stared at each other with withering spite for a long moment, and then Erik said to the team in general, gesturing to the targets on the range, "All right. Now show me what you've got."

***

Just after the museum closed for the night, Nika met Amari in the vestibule. He greeted her with a warm smile and offered her his arm.

"Shall we?"

She accepted his offer, and they walked together to the professor's car. It was a shiny new Mercedes, equipped with all of the very best bells and whistles. She settled into the passenger seat and told him, "Nice car."

He grinned. "Thank you." As he drove, he said, "I managed to get us reservations at a very exclusive restaurant tonight. A friend had reservations that he couldn't use, so he's allowing us to take them instead."

"That's very kind of him," she said.

Amari chucked. "Well, he owes me."

There was something ominous about that comment, but she chose to let it go.

"I've been thinking about our friend Fenrir," she said.

"Oh?"

"I wonder if perhaps his deformity marked him as spiritually significant. Maybe that was why he was accorded such a rich burial."

He considered for a moment, and then said, "It's certainly possible. It wouldn't be the first time that something like that happened. The only problem with that theory is that there were no artifacts of a spiritual nature with him. If he'd been marked as chosen by the gods, there should have been some sort of priestly accoutrements." He glanced at her and smirked. "Actually, I have a different theory."

"What's that?"

"I think he was a werewolf."

Nika laughed. "A werewolf? Seriously?"

He chuckled. "They might have thought he was one. There are numerous tales of wolf shifters called the Ulfen. Have you heard them?"

"No," she confessed. "I'm not really well informed about the region's folklore. I just concentrated on the history and mythology."

They arrived at the restaurant, a busy and manifestly trendy place. Amari left his car with the valet and escorted her to the greeting stand, where he gave his friend's name. "Sigurd Odinsson," he said, smiling his most charming smile.

The hostess consulted her reservation book and nodded. "Excellent. Welcome, Mr. and Mrs. Odinsson. Please come this way."

Nika glanced at Amari, and he chuckled at the assumption. "After you."

They were shown to a lovely corner booth, one obviously designed for couples. There was only one bench, and they were obliged to sit side by side. He sat close to her, his shoulder brushing hers. She shifted slightly and opened more space between them.

The menu was filled with self-consciously artistic dishes and Swedish specialties, including horse tartar, which horrified her. She could not imagine eating horse meat. When the server came, Amari ordered wine and an appetizer of fruit and cheese.

"You're very sure of yourself," she said, smiling. "What if I don't want to drink with dinner?"

"You're a sophisticated woman, Miss Graves. I can hardly imagine you drinking anything but wine with dinner."

The wine steward brought a bottle of a fine, old vintage, and Amari smelled the proffered cork. He nodded his acceptance, and the steward poured two glasses of deep burgundy red. Amari held up his glass.

"To new friends and old things made new," he said.

"Cheers."

They clicked their glasses together, then drank. The wine was very fine, and it tingled on her tongue. She liked the slight burn of it against her throat.

"Delicious," she said, smiling.

He sipped his own drink, and then put it aside. "I noticed that you had flowers in your office. A gift from your beau?"

"Yes."

"How thoughtful of him."

She smiled. "He's a bit of a romantic."

"I find that romance is one of the requirements in life," he said. "Without it, life is meaningless."

"You sound like you might be in love with love."

He nodded. "I do believe in love. I believe in its power, and I believe that it should be shared openly...with no limitations."

Their eyes met, and she was suddenly all too aware of the warmth of his body next to hers. There was a look in his eye that she could not describe, but it made her feel both threatened and enticed at the same time. She felt a tingle in her mind.

"No limitations?" she echoed.

"None. If we have desires, we should submit to them. We should allow them to conquer us and overcome our rational objections." He was still looking into her eyes, and she could not look away. "There is no need to be wanting just because your partner of choice is out of range. Friends can love as well as lovers."

Her palms were sweating. She was convinced that he was doing something to her will. It was difficult to resist him, with his perfectly kissable lips and dark, intelligent eyes. He was everything Erik was not. She found herself leaning closer, acting without knowing why.

"Well, how lovely to see you again."

The intrusion of a familiar female voice shattered the spell, and Nika sat back, perplexed. Magda stood beside their table, her cell phone in her hand.

"I got a really lovely photograph of the two of you just now," she said. "You're such a beautiful pair. I sent the photograph to Erik... I know how much he misses you."

Nika cleared her throat. "Hello, Magda."

Amari rose and offered his hand. "Rahim Amari," he said by way of introduction.

Magda looked at his hand and made no move to accept it. Behind her, Sif drifted into view, dressed in a black minidress accented with leather. She was a total contrast to Magda, who was all in white.

Magda looked into Amari's eyes, and one corner of her mouth turned down. She turned to Nika. "Careful, young one," she said. "You are swimming in dangerous waters."

She turned and left their table, and Sif trailed along behind her. Amari sat down again, shaking his head. "What an odd woman."

Nika took a deep breath. She owed Magda a huge thank you. "She's an associate of my partner's," she said. Her hands were shaking, and she gathered up her purse. "Thank you for the wine and the invitation, but I have to go."

He rose. "Miss Graves... Nika..."

She hurried away, putting distance between them. She didn't know what was happening to her.

Chapter Eleven

Erik hadn't hunted in a long time.

During his long wait for Berit's return, he would stay behind while his men went out into the night to find companions and the blood that kept them whole. He had developed a system whereby every few days, he would take a pint of blood from the infirmary, warm it in a pan of water on the stove, and then drink it. It was stale, but there was still some latent life force there, and he found that if he did this every night, he stayed alive, even if he was not as strong as he could have been.

The others drank dreyri at least once a day, as well, feeding on the magic in the enchantment as much as the blood. He had missed that power, and now that he had Berit back and could taste it again, he enjoyed it immensely. Still, he had not yet resumed hunting, even though he had his love back in his life, or perhaps because she was back in his life.

When he was with Nika, he would wait until she was asleep, and then he would boil his bags of blood when she wouldn't see. He disposed of the evidence carefully every time, careful that she wouldn't find out. They hadn't been together very long, so he had been able to hide his behavior, which was seen as shameful in Draugr circles. Not even Gunnar, his best friend and his true brother, had known how he fed.

In the time when he and his team were in America, the base had begun a new computer cataloging system for their blood supply, no doubt because they had been misplacing so many pints along the way. The blood was now carefully monitored, and any theft he committed would be noticed immediately. His one avenue of harmlessness had been taken away.

In a way, he was relieved. He had not enjoyed living like a thief. Indeed, thievery and heresy were the only two sins that his people had ever believed would gain him special punishment in the Halls of Hel. He was not looking forward to the pain that awaited him in the underworld after he finally died completely, at least until his soul was reborn to continue Vidar's existence... Unless Vidar convinced Hel to allow him to attach to some other soul and leave Erik to his suffering. He supposed that was a possibility, too.

The base hospital had the only blood bank in Karlsborg. His orders were that he could take liberty at night as far as the town, but that he had to be back in the barracks by dawn. His curfew ran several hours later than his team, who, by virtue of their prior occupations, had extremely limited freedoms.

His team hated him, and he returned the sentiment. In the two weeks they had been training, he had learned that they were able enough with weapons, but their ability to work together was seriously impaired. He wasn't certain he would be able to teach them enough about small group tactics to make them effective as a fighting force. He also wasn't certain he would ever trust them at his back.

He went to the exit from the based and showed his ID to the gate patrol. They waved him through, and he walked off of base property, headed toward town. His SOG insignia was clear to see, marking him as Special Forces, and the men at the gate had nothing to say about him until they thought he was out of earshot.

"Freaking special forces," one of them complained. "So many privileges."

"Well, that one's a captain, so, yeah. He gets a lot of liberty that we don't. It's all about rank."

The third guard commented. "Honestly, with the risks those special ops guys take? They're entitled to all the liberties they can get. I don't mind."

The first spoke up, bitterly. "Sure, Lars. Be reasonable. I hate you."

Erik smirked and kept walking.

The foot path to the town from the base wasn't long, but it was well-traveled. The grass had been worn down to nothing, and the weather had turned the path into a muddy slog. He walked beside the path, familiar well enough with where he was going that he didn't really need it to show him the way.

He passed through the fence that marked the outer edge of base territory and continued down a hill toward the town. The lights in the houses and bars were glowing, and from where he was, he could sense that most the inhabitants were gathered in three distinct bars. The rest were scattered through the various dwellings, safe and off limits from the likes of him.

Vampires, even the ones like him with supposedly good intentions, weren't allowed into people's homes without express invitations. It was why so much of their hunting and feeding took place in bars and taverns, in hotels and sometimes out in the open. In the old days, he had fed in places like livery stables and under piers. In the old days... Well, in the old days he hadn't been quite as interested in asking permission as he was now.

The first bar he came to was mostly filled with older folks. It was a working man's drinking hole, with regular customers and people who knew one another. This was the sort of place where a serviceman was barely welcome, and where a vampire would go hungry. He skipped it in favor of greener pastures.

He passed a brown house with a neatly terraced flower garden in the side yard. Inside, he could hear the television playing the evening news. Someone was cooking, and someone else was talking. It was all so normal, a glimpse into a life that had never been his and never would be. It was the life he was denying Nika.

Sadness pressed in at him, and he pushed it away. There would be time to brood later. Nobody would be interested in feeding a sullen Draugr.

The next bar was pulsing with hip hop music, and the lights were flashing like a kaleidoscope, spilling ever-shifting colors over the pavement when the door opened and closed. He wiped his boots on the sidewalk to rid himself of any excess mud from the footpath and went inside.

Nobody turned to look when he came in. The room was packed full to bursting with young, bored people desperate for fun: soldiers from the base, young women from the town, and lost souls of every other description. There were no other Draugr in the house, and for that he was thankful. He wasn't in the mood for a fight.

Erik went to the bar and ordered an aquavit. The bartender, a middle-aged woman who had clearly seen plenty of nonsense in her day, poured it for him.

"Here you go, Captain," she said. "First one's on the house."

He smiled at her. "Thank you."

"Don't mention it. Least I can do for SOG."

He raised the shot glass to her in salute, and then downed it in one swallow. It burned and twisted in his gut, but he kept it down without betraying his nausea. The things I do for my cover, he thought.

A young blonde in a revealing blue dress sidled up to him. "Hej," she greeted.

"Hej," he responded.

"I'm Lina," she said. "What's your name?"

"Erik."

"You alone?"

He looked around the room, and then turned back to her with his most charming smile. "Looks like it."

She slipped her arm through his. "Lucky me."

"What are you drinking?"

"Whatever you are."

I doubt that. He signaled the bartender for another round, and she supplied it. This time, she waited for him to pay up before she moved down the line. He handed her more cash than he needed. "Set up a tab," he requested.

"Sure thing, Captain."

Lina made a flirtatious move with her shoulder and wrinkled her pert nose at him. "Captain? Wow. That's above the pay grade that usually comes in here."

"Pay grade?" He shook his head. "I'm not paying for anything but drinks tonight."

She scowled. "Fine." In a huff, she stalked off in search of another customer.

"Hey, Lina," he called after her. She turned. "Don't forget your drink."

She took the glass and cocked her elbow back, preparing to throw it in his face. He met her gaze and his eyes flared. "Don't do that."

She hesitated, and then put the glass on the bar. "I won't do that."

"Thank you." He released the hold he had taken over her mind. He gestured toward the bar stool beside him. "Please don't leave. I may not be buying the whole thing, but I wouldn't mind some company."

Lina slid onto the stool and favored him with a smile. "You married?"

"Yes." Sort of.

"Where is she?"

"Back home in Stockholm."

"Must get lonely."

He nodded. "Yes, it does."

"If you ever need…"

Erik smiled at her. What he needed she could provide, certainly, but it wasn't what she was thinking. Still, one thing led to the other, and sex was often a means to an end. He doubted if Nika would understand that, though.

"Thank you."

He was so bad at this. The years had left him rusty and awkward. Back in the old days, he would have just waited for someone to be walking alone in the dark. He would grab them, take them, and that would be it. Now it was so complicated.

"Do you have kids?"

He started to answer honestly, but switched it at the last minute. "No."

"Do you have any pictures of your wife?"

He pulled out his cell phone and flipped through the images until he came up with a picture of Nika he'd taken in Central City. She was sitting on the couch, wreathed in sunlight like a halo, smiling at him with love in her eyes. He wanted to always remember her like that.

He showed Lina, and she nodded. "She's beautiful."

"Yes, she is."

"That's interesting."

Erik raised an eyebrow. "What is?"

"Most men say 'thank you' when you say their wives are beautiful."

"You're not complimenting me. Why should I thank you?"

She laughed. "You don't think it's a compliment that someone noticed that you have a hot wife? It's like a checkmark in the stud column for you."

He put his phone away. "If I have to measure my worth by the value of those around me, I'm not much of a man, am I? There are only two things that make a man valuable: his fame and his wealth. The beauty of my wife is a reflection on her, not on me."

Nina looked impressed. "That's pretty progressive."

He had to laugh. "No, actually, it's not. It's a very old attitude."

"I haven't encountered it before."

"Well, you haven't encountered anyone like me before."

She gave him a look that could have burned down houses. "That's for sure."

This was getting easier. He looked into her eyes. "Let's go someplace quieter."

"I thought you'd never ask."

They walked out of the bar together, and she took his hand when they reached the sidewalk outside. He squeezed her fingers gently. Without a word, she led him into the alley behind the bar.

The alley was cleaner and smelled better than similar alleys in Stockholm, but it was still filthy. She went to the back wall of the bar and leaned against it, her back pressed flat against the brick, her hands slowly drawing her skirt up her thigh.

Erik stepped up to her, one hand cupping her face. She smiled and leaned into his touch. He made eye contact with her again, and it took only a small exertion of his Draugr powers to make her his completely. He gently kissed her neck and turned her face away from him, his hand holding her chin and lifting it slightly. His other hand gripped her hip and held her fast against the wall.

She sighed as he pressed his body against hers. She melted into him, and he took that opportunity to bring his fangs to bear. They emerged from their sockets above his human teeth, extending their wicked points toward her soft and yielding flesh. It was easy, so very easy, to penetrate her skin, thrusting his fangs gently into her vein.

She sighed again as he began to drink. He took no more than he needed, and although the vampire in him cried for him to take everything she had, he released her. He licked the puncture wounds on her neck, and they healed immediately, not even a pink spot showing where they had been. He pulled back and looked into her eyes again.

"Wait ten minutes," he told her, "then go back into the bar. You will not remember this."

Lina nodded. He held her until she was steady on her feet. When he was certain she wouldn't fall, he released his hold on her hip and went back to the barracks.

Chapter Twelve

Two weeks passed in a blur, each day filled with work followed by coming home to an empty house and missing Erik all night long. She sent him letters, and he responded twice. She tried texting him, but he had never activated that function on his cell phone, which amused her to no end. Sometimes his antiquity showed itself.

She was in her office, working on labels for a new exhibit, when Professor Amari came in without knocking. He leaned on her desk with both hands, a look of annoyance on his face that was belied by a twinkle in his eyes.

"You are avoiding me."

Nika was surprised enough that words failed her. "I – what?"

"If you won't have dinner with me, then at least have lunch. Today. We can go to the cafeteria."

"I..."

"I won't take no for an answer."

She glanced at the time and sighed. "Well, all right, then. Lunch it is."

He smiled. "Excellent."

They went upstairs to the cafeteria that served the public. They stood in line, made their selections, and then stood in line again to pay. Amari insisted on paying for her lunch, and she allowed it. They managed to find a table in the atrium and sat down to eat.

"I should be very cross with you," he told her.

"I'm sorry, Professor. I'm just so busy, getting used to the way things are done here..."

"Excuses." He grinned. "I'm playing with you. And please, call me Rahim."

She looked down at her plate and toyed with her salad. "How is your research going?"

"Very well. In fact, I've almost finished." He gestured with his fork. "Now I just have to do the writing."

"I'm sure you'll do a fine job," she said, smiling.

The conversation was strained. She could tell that he was trying to be charming, and she was trying to be friendly, but it was clear that he had more on his mind than research papers.

"Thank you. I have news, by the way."

"Oh?"

"I have accepted a position at Stockholm University."

"That's wonderful! I'm very happy for you." It was a lie. She felt a sinking in the pit of her stomach. He wasn't leaving. She was beginning to feel hunted.

"Thank you." He looked down at his plate. "Have you heard from your boyfriend recently?"

"Not in a few days. I'm sure he's very busy."

"I would never be too busy for a woman like you."

That's enough. Nika pushed her plate aside. "Professor, this is becoming inappropriate. I am not interested in pursuing any sort of relationship with you outside of the professional arena." She rose. "Thank you for lunch."

She turned and began to walk away, but his next words stopped her in her tracks.

"I know about the Veithimathr."

She turned. "What did you say?"

"The inscription that you were asking about. I learned something about the Veithimathr."

Against her better judgment, she returned to the table and sat again. "What did you learn?"

He grinned. "What, here? In front of all of these witnesses? Do you really want me to tell everyone about the Draugr?"

Her mouth dropped open. "How..."

"I have my ways." He leaned forward. "Now I have your attention, I think."

"We should go to my office," she said. "We can talk more there."

"I couldn't agree more."

They left the cafeteria for the privacy her office could provide, and once they were there, she closed the door. Amari looked immensely pleased with himself. She sat down behind her desk while he occupied a chair in front of it.

"What do you know about the Draugr?"

"I know everything... Ithunn."

As he spoke, his face began to change. The features shifted, and his skin faded from swarthy to pale. His grin remained undimmed as his appearance changed completely. Now muscular and tall with long blond hair and dancing green eyes, he was as strikingly handsome as he was frightening. Watching the transformation took her breath away.

"You..."

"I am not Rahim Amari, no. The good professor met with an... unfortunate accident while he was still in Baghdad." He smiled, and she suddenly felt overcome by a wave of energy flowing out from him. He smiled more widely when he saw her reaction. "I am not Draugr, but I am older than they."

"What are you?"

"A rude question, but at least I know the answer. I wonder, could you say the same?"

She reached down toward her purse. She still had a can of mace in it from Central City. "What do you mean?"

"Your Captain Thorvald has told you that you are Draugr, just because he gave you dreyri. That is not true."

She reached her purse and unzipped it. His eyebrow twitched, but he showed no other reaction. She repeated, "What do you mean?"

"I mean, my dear, you are not a Draugr yet. And to answer your question, I am called by many names. Shifter. Trickster. Nøkken. But you may call me Loki... or Sigurd, if you would prefer."

She grabbed her mace and sprayed it into his face. He recoiled, and she bolted from the room. She ran as fast as her legs could carry her to the security desk on the first floor. When she arrived, panting, the officer behind the counter looked up in alarm.

"In my office," she said. "Someone attacked me. I sprayed him with mace, but..."

The officer frowned and called for one of his companions in Swedish. Nika nearly screamed in frustration. Of all times to have a language barrier!

Someone put a gentle hand on her shoulder, and she spun to see an old woman with kind eyes and thick white hair in a single braid down her back. The woman smiled softly.

"These people cannot help you," she said. "I am Ingrid. Come with me, Nika, vessel of Ithunn."

Shocked, she swallowed hard and obeyed.

Ingrid walked her quickly out of the building and to a car parked directly across the street. She got behind the wheel while Nika quickly occupied the passenger seat. Almost as soon as Nika's door was closed, Ingrid pulled into traffic and sped away.

"How do you know who I am?" Nika asked, trying desperately to stave off panic. "Who are you?"

"I am Ingrid. In other lifetimes, I was called Frigg."

She gasped. "Erik said I needed to speak to you!"

"He was correct. I was waiting for him to bring you to me, but I realized when I sensed Loki's arrival that it was too late for waiting." She careened through the street, cutting off other drivers and nearly causing a dozen accidents. Nika gripped the seat tightly.

"What is going on? I don't understand anything."

Ingrid smiled sweetly. "Oh, my dear. You have so much to learn, and Thorvald has never been a very good teacher. He does his best, poor man, but he has his limitations. Men of action are seldom good at words."

She skidded around a corner and got onto an expressway headed north. Nika closed her eyes when a lane change took them a little too close for comfort to a massive truck. Ingrid chuckled.

"We have a long drive ahead of us, Nika. Now is a good time to ask questions."

She had so many that they were like a logjam in her throat. She took a deep breath. "He said he was Loki, and that he was a Nøkken. How can that be? I thought all the gods were melded with Draugr." She put a hand to her head. "I'm so confused."

"What confuses you, dear one?"

"The Draugr were created as punishment by Odin. But then the gods were melded with the Draugr. Was that at the same time? Where do the Valtaeigr fit into this mess? Are all Valtaeigr vampires, or what? He tells me stories, but they're so hard to follow!"

Ingrid chuckled. "The first Draugr were Hakon and his band of raiders, turned into the undead by Odin as a punishment. Those fifteen men were the First. They were forced to live forever, which is actually a horrible curse for the hearts of men. They became unclean, doomed to exist only by swallowing the life force in human blood, marked by human hunters who wanted to destroy them because they were predators. They learned how to perpetuate their kind, using the secrets of death and blood and dark magic, and more Draugr were made. Then the gods fell out of favor and began to fade, and the best-hearted among the Draugr were selected to be Huntsmen. A few of the First were included in that number, like your Erik.

"The Huntsmen carried on a rebellion against the Draugr kings. They served only the Aesir, and they stood as protectors of humanity against the worst Draugr excesses. Those were bloody days.

"In time, the people stopped worshipping the old gods, switching instead to the veneration of the Nazarene. The gods became pale and weak, and they began to fade. They decided that they needed to meld with the undying into order to stay alive. They needed vessels.

"A few Valtaeigr were also selected to be vessels. We are immortal, but only some of us – those who have been turned – are Draugr as well. We were created separately. We can use magic that the Draugr cannot."

Nika's head was pounding. Every time she talked about this, she got a headache. "So all Valtaeigr are immortal, but not all of them are vampires. The Veithimathr are Draugr, but not all Draugr are Veithimathr, and not all Draugr are vessels."

"Exactly."

"So why isn't Loki in a Draugr vessel?"

"Well, that's complicated."

"What isn't?"

Ingrid chuckled. "Loki was not in favor with Odin. In fact, he rarely ever was. He was prevented from melding with a Draugr soul for this reason. Loki is clever, though, and he found his own way to maintain his immortality."

She changed lanes abruptly. Nika was tempted to close her eyes. Ingrid kept talking while she drove.

"He had long been worshipped and served by the Nøkken, who are shape shifters who used to live in waterways and lure people to untimely deaths. They are tricksters, like Loki himself, and usually up to no good. He went to them and they selected one of their number – I believe he was their chieftain's son – to undergo the melding ritual. It worked.

"The Nøkken can appear as anything in the world that they want to, and as anyone. Their native form is as a beautiful young man, the better to lure women to their deaths. They are not to be trusted, not at all. They consume humans, body and spirit. They are dangerous creatures.

"Loki was banished from these lands by Odin after the melding rituals took place, and ever since then he has wandered the world. He wants nothing more than to reduce the Aesir and take his position on Odin's throne, to take all of the gods' power for himself. He wants to be king of the universe. He is ambitious, but he is not stupid. Odin watches and opposes him, and sometimes in the past that has been dire and painful for Loki. He would not have come back unless he had a very good reason to risk defying the All-Father."

"What do you think the reason is?"

"I couldn't begin to guess. But there is a way to find out."

"How?"

She winked. "Magic."

"What kind of magic?"

"I told you, the Valtaeigr can perform all kinds of sorcery," Ingrid assured her. "You have much to learn."

They drove along in silence for a few minutes. "Where are we going?" Nika finally asked.

"To my house. We'll be safe there. Not even Loki would dare invade my space."

"I'll take your word on it."

"Wise woman." Ingrid smiled. "I like you already."

Chapter Thirteen

Things were starting to come together.

Stenmark still hated him, of course, but that was unimportant. The important thing was that he was listening to Erik now, obeying his orders and accepting his instruction. The team behaved more like a cohesive unit, with the four humans falling into complementary roles that made the team stronger as a whole. He was proud of them.

Major Ulvaeus called him to his office right after physical training. Erik took a fast shower and changed into a proper uniform before reporting to his commanding officer. When he arrived, another officer he did not know was in attendance.

He came to attention and saluted. "Captain Thorvald as requested, sir."

Ulvaeus nodded. "At ease, captain. This is Kommendör Holm from Special Forces Command."

The commander was studying Erik with open curiosity and just a hint of hostility.

"A pleasure, Kommendör," Erik said.

"Likewise," replied Holm. "I've never met a Draugr face to face."

"Then that's one thing you can strike off your bucket list, sir."

Ulvaeus chuckled. "Kommendör Holm, you will learn that Captain Thorvald has a very dry sense of humor."

Holm did not reply. Instead, he kept looking at Erik like a scientist with a new lab specimen. He was appraising the Draugr soldier, making judgments about his capabilities and his intentions. Erik had been studied like this before. Humans of power were always a bit askance when they first encountered one of their kind. The powerful disliked being introduced to someone more powerful than they. Erik bore the scrutiny with decorum, never breaking out of his parade rest.

An awkward silence fell for a moment, and then Ulvaeus picked up the reins again.

"As you know, we have been preparing your team to resume hunting rogue Draugr. According to your reports, they're coming along well. Do you think they're ready to go into the field for a live test?"

Erik considered. "Well, sir, they've learned as much as they can here on the base. A live field test would be the logical next step."

Holm finally spoke up. "In two weeks' time, the G8 will be having a summit in Stockholm. We absolutely must get all potential rogue vampires eliminated before the dignitaries arrive. I cannot stress enough the importance of this."

He was familiar with the G8, a political entity created from the eight largest economies in the world. The attendees at the G8 summits were generally the heads of state for the various countries. He could only imagine the damage that a Draugr with a bad attitude could do if he were able to kill or turn a sitting president or prime minister.

"Yes, sir."

"SOG will be handling the security for the summit, along with the protective services from each of the different countries involved. It will be a logistical nightmare." Holm already looked as if he'd been losing sleep. Erik was certain he'd be losing more before this event was over. "We cannot have any Draugr interfering."

"Sir," Erik asked, "is there a particular Draugr that you were concerned about?"

"Possibly."

Ulvaeus provided him with a dossier. Erik opened the folder and looked inside. The face in the photograph was lupine, with amber-brown eyes and a messy shock of red hair. The expression in his eyes was purely predatory.

Erik thought the Draugr looked somewhat familiar, but he could not place any particular memories of him. Perhaps he had seen him in passing at some gathering. It was entirely possible they had encountered one another once before. The Draugr community was not as large as the human population, obviously. Predators were always outnumbered by the herds they hunted.

Ulvaeus continued his briefing. "His name, or the name he goes by now, is Lorgan. He was last seen in Gothenburg. He's been hunting."

"I presume he kills his prey?"

Holm looked ill. "Yes. And he flagrantly discards the bodies. We've kept this quiet for now, but people will start asking questions. The United States has already requested murder and disappearance numbers from us and I don't need him creating an anomaly that will draw their attention. He's already done too much. I need you and your team to find him and eliminate him before he kills anyone else."

Erik closed the dossier. "Yes, sir. It will be done."

"Excellent. Brief your men, and then have them all come here for a formal briefing with Kommendör Holm," Ulvaeus directed. "Dismissed, Captain."

Erik saluted and then turned on his heel to leave.

He went to the barracks, where the team was relaxing after their hard workouts. Stenmark looked up with a sneer, and Sven nudged his brother. Ulf was lying on his bunk, eyes closed.

"Okay, men, listen up," he announced. "Magnusson, get up."

Reluctantly, the sergeant obeyed. When he was certain he had their attention, he continued.

"Training is over. It's time to go live."

The Jansen brothers high-fived each other. Stenmark pumped his fist. "Yes!"

Erik opened the dossier and displayed the photograph of Lorgan so they could see him. "This is our target. His name is Lorgan. He is Draugr, and he is killing in Gothenburg. We are going to stop him."

Stenmark snorted. "Friend of yours?"

Erik narrowed his eyes. "I don't know him." He closed the dossier. "We are going immediately to Major Ulvaeus's office for a formal briefing by Kommendör Holm from Special Forces Command. This touches upon a very important event coming up in Stockholm, the G8 Summit."

Magnusson rubbed his chin. "I used to have good luck with political summits. There was always someone to shoot."

He was well aware of Magnusson's past as a hired killer. "Well, there still is, but this time it's a vampire. Let's go."

He led them back to Ulvaeus's office, where they stood in a respectable version of parade rest before the major's desk. Erik fell in beside them.

"Huntsman Team One reporting for briefing, sir."

Holm nodded to Ulvaeus, who closed the door and locked it. The Jansen twins exchanged nervous glances, and Erik growled softly at them. They returned their eyes to the front. Their superior officer began to speak.

"What you hear now is not to leave this room. We have reason to believe that the Draugr are planning an offensive on the G8 Summit. They are led by this man..."

He held up a grainy photograph of a dark-haired man in a suit, his facial features difficult to discern due to the quality of the image.

"His name is Rahim Amari, a professor of history from Baghdad. We believe he may be linked to terrorist cells operating in Europe."

Erik knew that name. He had read it in Nika's letters. His heart sank.

Holm passed the photograph around for the team to see.

"Three days ago, he was observed meeting with these three known Draugr." He produced another photograph, and this time it was easier to see the people in question. "The three Draugr here have until recently been residing in St. Petersburg in Russia. Why they are here, meeting with this Iraqi national, we do not know. Given the timing, we suspect that they may have designs upon the Russian president."

"That guy's an asshole," Stenmark commented. "Let 'em eat him."

"Sergeant, you are out of order," Erik snapped.

The former convict sullenly fell silent.

Holm scowled at the outspoken man. "I trust that I do not have to tell you the damage that would be done to Sweden's standing in the European Union if we fail to keep our esteemed guests safe. We do not want an international incident taking place in our country. Do you understand, Mr. Stenmark?"

The man grumbled. "Yes, sir."

"You are all on probation from His Majesty's prisons, with the exception of Captain Thorvald. You are all here out of the crown's mercy and good graces. If you can hunt down Lorgan, the vampire in Gothenburg, then we will consider you ready to protect the G8. If you fail, you will be returned to your former cells with no hope of any sort of parole - if you survive." His harsh gaze fell on each of the men in turn. "Do you understand?"

"Yes, sir," they answered in unison.

"Excellent. Consider the hunt for Lorgan your final exam. If you pass, then we will assign you to protect the summit. Any questions?"

Erik spoke up. "If the team should fail, who will be assigned to protect the summit?"

"There are other groups in the SOG, Captain. They will be fully briefed and assigned."

"So the existence of Draugr is to become an open secret."

"Only to those with the highest security clearances."

The last thing that Erik wanted was for the existence of vampires to become common knowledge. Once the rest of the army was informed, it was only a matter of time before the whole country knew. He did not wish to see what would happen if all of the mortals rose up against his people again. It had been nearly disastrous when it happened before.

Ulvaeus took over. "We have a confirmed sighting of Lorgan in Gothenburg within the last six hours. You will be going by helicopter to an insertion point near the building where we believe he is living. The schematic of the building is in your dossier. Examine it well. You will go in, find Lorgan, eliminate him, and bring proof of death. You have twenty minutes to accomplish this. If you are any later than that, your helicopter will be gone."

Twenty minutes was not a lot of time. Erik hoped that the intel they were being given was sound.

"Your bird flies in ten minutes. Suit up and get going. Dismissed!"

They scrambled back to the barracks, where they got into their tactical gear and gathered their weapons. Erik distributed clips of silver bullets and silver-edged daggers, both of which he normally kept locked in his footlocker. He was proud of his team's development, but he didn't trust them not to shank him in his sleep.

"Remember to shoot for the head. Decapitation is the only sure way to kill a Draugr, but a head shot will keep him down. So will a shot to the heart or lungs. Any other shot is still useful, since the silver will poison him. Aim for the gut and thicker muscles so the bullet will lodge." He tucked his cell phone into one of his pockets. He could use the camera to film the execution as proof of death. "Remember that he's faster than you, and stronger, and probably smarter. Stay together."

"We're not stupid," Stenmark grumbled.

"When we get back, I'm going to adjust your attitude," Erik warned. The human scoffed. Erik checked his watch. "All right - let's go."

***

North of Stockholm, overlooking the Bay of Bothnia where it met the Baltic Sea, Ingrid finally stopped the car. They were on the top of a hill that cut away steeply on its way to the beach, giving an excellent view of the water. The hill was crowned by a modest little house with a welcoming herb garden delineated by hand-woven stick fences. It looked idyllic, like something from a tourist postcard.

Nika got out of the car and took a deep breath. The sea air smelled clean and was refreshingly brisk, cooling her still-jangled nerves. Ingrid joined her and looked up at the house with a smile.

"My late husband and I built this house together in 1823," she said. "It's held up very well, don't you think?"

She hooked her arm through Nika's and ushered her inside. The door opened into a tiny kitchen, only ten feet square, with a tub sink, a water pump and an old cast iron cook stove. A trestle table stood in the middle of the room with two chairs on either side, and the entire room smelled like apples. A ladder led up through a square opening in the ceiling, presumably into a loft where Ingrid slept.

"It's lovely," Nika said with a smile.

"Thank you." She gestured toward one of the chairs and grabbed a kettle from a hook above the sink. "Tea?"

"Thank you."

She sat and watched while her hostess busily puttered about the little kitchen. She pumped water into the kettle from an ancient rig by the sink, then lined a basket with cheerfully-embroidered cloths and filled it with fruit and homemade muffins. Nika felt like she was in some house beautiful magazine spread, or maybe she was dreaming.

"I know you have more questions," Ingrid said. "Ask anything."

She took a breath and considered. "Erik said that you and Berit were sisters."

"Not Berit. Ithunn." She smiled. "And not me, but Frigg. Our goddesses are sisters."

"He said you could teach me magic."

"Ah! But that's like teaching someone how to breathe. It can't be done." She put the kettle on the stove and filled the belly with firewood. She tossed kindling on top and lit it with flint and steel. There was nothing modern in this place.

"Can't be done?" Nika echoed, disappointed.

"No. You can't teach someone how to do what comes naturally. You just have to help them get out of their own way." She sat in the chair opposite Nika, still wearing a kindly smile. "You are Valtaeigr, and not yet a Draugr... although you will be, once he finishes changing you."

"What do you mean?"

"I mean you're still mortal. I can see he's been feeding you dreyri, my darling. That prolongs your life and amplifies your senses, but it doesn't make you a vampire. Not even if you drink blood from him." She patted her hand. "You have to die first."

She stared at her. "But I... I felt a change. A transformation. When I drank the dreyri for the first time, I became something different than I was before."

"Yes. You became an elevated and extended human. But you are no Draugr yet."

"How will I know when it happens? And what... how do I have to die?"

Ingrid smiled. "Those are answers you will find when you come to them."

***

The helicopter hovered over the roof of the apartment block that Lorgan was reportedly occupying. Erik and his team fast-roped to the flat area behind the satellite dish and water tank, taking up position at the door to the interior. Ulf tried the knob. "Locked."

Erik was not impressed. He gripped the knob and twisted, his grip punching divots into the metal. The lock broke with a snap, and the door swung open.

"Not anymore," he told his team. "Let's go."

He had studied the schematics for the building during the flight from Karlsborg to Gothenburg. The stairway led down the entire southwest corner with portals to each floor. The electrical box was just to the south of where the stairs ended in the basement, and that was their first objective.

The apartment that was supposedly Lorgan's was on the second floor, fourth door to the left from the stairwell. An informer in the Gothenburg police department had advised that he and a brunette were in for the night. Erik wondered if the woman was even still alive.

They descended the stairs. At the second floor, Erik called a halt and reached out with his Draugr senses. He could feel the other vampire, his energy muddled and muted. He was sleeping off a big feed, which told Erik that his brunette companion was no longer among the living. He nodded to Sven, who trotted down to the electrical box. Aron shifted his grip on his rifle, nervously watching as his twin headed down the stairs.

Stenmark looked at Erik, and the vampire captain motioned for the team to put on their night vision goggles. He had no need for such paraphernalia. At the bottom of the stairs, Sven tapped the wall, a quiet signal that only Erik would hear. At the count of three, the power would be cut, and hopefully that would keep the human residents from seeing more than they should.

Three... two... one...

Right on cue, the electricity in the building stopped buzzing with a whimper. Ulf opened the door and they swarmed out into the hallway. They rapidly advanced on Lorgan's room. Inside, the sleepy vampire was stirring, but slowly. So far everything was going according to plan, which made Erik nervous. Nothing ever really went according to plan.

Ulf went past the door and flattened himself against the wall, his rifle held at the ready. The apartments around them were filled with chatter as people reacted to the electrical failure. Stenmark mimicked Ulf's posture on the near side of the door, and Aron took up position across the hall from the vampire's door, his gun trained on the opening, ready to blast if their quarry burst into view.

Erik raised his leg and kicked the door off of its hinges. Lorgan was in the middle of the living room floor, his brunette companion dead at his side, white as paper. The startled vampire leaped up onto his feet like a martial artist, snarling.

"Veithimathr!"

Stenmark opened fire. Lorgan was no fledgling, though, and he leaped up above the bullets before they could reach him, moving in a blur of black and green. Ulf threw a silver dagger toward the vampire, and it went over his shoulder and embedded itself in the ceiling. Lorgan laughed.

Sven joined them, pounding up from the basement with a wild grin on his face. As soon as he arrived, Aron lost his hesitation and waded into the room, spraying the room with silver bullets. Erik could hear screams in the neighboring apartments, and he shouted an order. "Precision fire only!"

Aron glared at him but stopped shooting so indiscriminately. Lorgan ran for the window, hitting it feet first and flying out into the night. Erik cursed. If Gunnar and his boys had been here, that vampire would have been dead by now. He followed him out the window, leaving his team behind. He could hear Stenmark ordering them to the roof.

Lorgan soared ahead of him, and then turned, facing him with a wide grin on his face, his cheeks ruddy with the life he'd stolen from the woman on his carpet. He was no vessel. "You missed," he taunted.

Erik gathered his power. He had never been much for flying. He called upon the god within him, and Vidar woke, his divine force pouring into his vessel's limbs. He launched like a missile, aiming straight at Lorgan's midsection. The younger vampire's smile died as he realized that he was facing off against one of the First.

Erik pulled his axe from its sheath on his back and swung it as he swooped by, decapitating Lorgan in one shot. His body was dust before it ever hit the ground. He circled back toward the building and dropped onto the roof beside Sven.

"Did you record it?" he asked.

The Jansen twin nodded and indicated the infrared camera that he was holding. "Proof of death, right here."

Erik nodded, satisfied. Stenmark pulled a cell phone out of his pocket and dialed the police station. Their contact answered. "It's done," he informed him. "There's a body in the apartment."

"We'll clean it up. Good work."

Stenmark shut off the call and cast a resentful look at Erik. "That was a little too easy."

The vampire locked eyes with his subordinate and issued an order without breaking his gaze. "Ulf, take the twins and check the neighboring apartments. Make sure we didn't shoot anybody through the walls."

The two of them were left alone, staring at one another with pure spite. Stenmark spoke first.

"Had to be the hero, didn't you, captain?"

"We were sent to stop him," he said, his tone flat and dangerous. "So I stopped him."

"Yeah, I saw."

"You have something to say?"

Stenmark shook his head. The sarcasm was rolling off of him in waves. "No. Not at all. Why would I?"

Erik narrowed his eyes.

The mortal reconsidered. "Actually, I do have something to say. This is our training mission, right? Our final exam?"

"I suppose."

"So how come you didn't let us make the kill? You know that our futures depended on this raid."

The Veithimathr frowned. "I did what needed to be done."

"You made us look like idiots."

"I accomplished our objective. Whether you looked foolish or not is on you."

Stenmark took a step toward him, glowering dangerously. Erik was not impressed. "Our freedom depended on this raid. We're going to be sent back to prison because of you."

His patience with this man had come to an end. The helicopter appeared in the distance, and he spoke. "The mission was a success, so I doubt that's the case. But I'm fine with that if that's what command choose to do." He put his axe back into its strap on his back. "It's where you belong, anyway."

He turned his back on Stenmark, showing him utter contempt. The man crossed the roof quickly, rushing up on Erik. The vampire didn't even have to look to know that there was a knife in Stenmark's hand. He stepped aside and turned, catching the man's wrist in an iron grip and squeezing. He dragged Stenmark to his knees and held him there, his blue eyes cold as ice chips as they bored into the man's face.

"I have no respect for assassins," he ground out.

Stenmark spat in his face. Erik backhanded him and sent him sprawling. He grasped the man's shirt and hauled him up, his long teeth bared.

"The Red Hand," he growled, "means nothing to me. I don't care how many political enemies you've eliminated, or how many contracts you've fulfilled. I am not impressed by cowards."

Stenmark gripped Erik's wrist with his right hand and squeezed, trying to make the vampire release his grip. "You will be," he swore.

He tried to strike with the silver dagger still in his left hand. Erik knocked it away.

"Is that the best you can do?"

The others came back onto roof, stopping short in shock when they saw their leaders locked in a wrestling match. Erik released Stenmark with a shove.

"Pick up your fucking knife," he snarled. "If you ever point it at me again, I will gut you with it."

Aron stepped forward and came between Erik and Stenmark. "What's going on? I thought we were a unit."

"We are a unit," Stenmark spat. "He's just a vampire."

Sven looked from his twin to Stenmark and back. "Jan?" he asked the mortal. "Is it now?"

Aron looked confused. "Has the order been given?"

Ulf answered for him. "The helicopter is almost here. Now isn't the time."

"What order?" Erik demanded.

Stenmark stood up, his automatic pistol in his hand. "Now is the perfect time."

He raised the gun and fired at Erik. The Veithimathr was able to dodge the first two bullets, but the third struck him solidly in the stomach, the silver burning deep into his body, just the way he'd taught them to shoot. Erik doubled over. Emboldened by their companion, the Jansen twins opened fire on him, as well. Erik took two more bullets, one in the leg and one in the shoulder, before he was able to take cover behind a ventilation stack.

Holm's voice came through the loudspeakers on the helicopter. "Finish the job!"

More bullets ripped into the roof and the metal he was hiding behind. Erik was bleeding heavily, and the silver lodged in his body was like a living thing, the burning and twisting pain making his vision swim. He ground his teeth and took a chance. Rising to his feet, he ran to the side of the building and jumped off.

The silver was poisoning him, and its disruptive power prevented him from taking flight. He plummeted nine stories to the pavement, where he landed on his side. Bones snapped on impact, and he groaned.

In his mind, he heard Nika's a voice. *Erik!*

Stay where you are, Chosen, he told her. He managed to drag himself to a nearby car. The door was locked, but he still retained enough strength to wrest it off of its hinges. The helicopter crested the roof of the building, a spotlight on its underside searching the alley for him. He hauled himself into the driver's seat and reached under the steering column as the helicopter passed by overhead. After a few clumsy attempts, made more difficult by the way his hands were trembling, he hot-wired the car. The ignition roared into life, and he straightened in the seat.

The helicopter got halfway down the street before it reversed directions. It bore down on him and the spotlight shone through the windshield, lighting him up. He swore every vile curse he could think of and slammed the car into reverse. The guns on the chopper opened up, scoring the street and his stolen car with heavy ammunition. This time, the slugs were only lead. It would hurt if they hit, but they would not kill him... not like the silver that was already inside of him.

He swung the car around a corner and then pushed it into forward gear. He floored the accelerator and roared through the narrow streets of Gothenburg. The helicopter followed, but it stopped shooting. Erik hoped that he could count on Holm to have an aversion to killing civilians.

Sickness twisted inside him, and he could feel the bullets burning their way deeper into him, digging channels through his flesh. The pain was excruciating.

Nika spoke to him again. Erik, what's happening?

I was betrayed, he told her. His mental voice sounded anguished even to his own ears. He could not prevent it - it was impossible to lie mind-to-mind.

A spasm gripped him, and he nearly went off the road. He took a wrong turn onto a one-way street. The headlights of onrushing vehicles looked unreal, dazzling his eyes like Christmas lights in the fog. He avoided one collision, then another, clinging to the steering wheel in desperation. His consciousness was slipping away.

He found the entrance to a parking structure and drove inside. The helicopter's pursuit was frustrated by the masses of concrete that now shielded his escape. He drove around the structure's tight turns, headed toward the lowest level. His vision was beginning to fade.

His foot slipped off of the accelerator, and he twisted the steering wheel, avoiding a concrete pillar by less than an inch. He tried to clear his eyes, but the fog in his head was spreading, and he was growing weak.

One bullet worked its way out of his leg, starting in his calf and burning all the way out on the other side, creating an agonizing through-and-through injury. It fell onto the floor with a thud. There was less silver inside him now, and he sagged with relief. It helped.

He parked the car and struggled out onto his feet. There was a roaring in his ears like the sound of the sea raging against a wooden hull, and he swayed, unsteady. For a moment, he saw himself as he used to be, standing on the deck of his drekar with his brothers around him. He shook his head to clear it, but the vision refused to budge.

Dark clouds. Angry lightning. The judgment of the gods. It was all around him now.

A spasm of pain shook him, and he fell onto his knees. In his vision, the warrior beside him turned his head, his face wet with sea spray, his beard stained with blood. It was Gunnar. Erik reached a hand toward him, but his best friend refused to accept it, shaking his head.

"No, brother," Gunnar said. "It's not yet time."

"Gunnar…" he groaned.

The silver twisted inside of him again, and he groaned in agony. In his vision, the ship rocked, and he pitched forward onto the ground, landing face down on the asphalt. His last conscious awareness was of strong hands that grasped him under the arms and hauled him away.

Chapter Fourteen

Nika leaped to her feet when she felt the first bullet rip into Erik's body. Ingrid watched her calmly. The young woman paced in the tiny house, her hands gripping each other in anxiety. She could feel his pain, could feel the way the silver was sapping his strength.

Erik!

Stay where you are, Chosen.

She was marginally relieved to hear him respond to her so quickly, and his mental voice sounded strong, but she knew he was in horrible pain. It brought tears to her eyes. She spoke without looking at her companion. "Ingrid, he's hurt."

"Do you know where he is, child?"

"No."

"Can you help him with your tears?"

Nika turned to face her. "No."

"Then dry them and sit here again. Calm yourself. You have much you need to learn, and you will help him more by learning it than by airing a woman's grief."

It took everything she had, but she swallowed hard and sat back down facing the old woman.

Ingrid smiled at her. "Good. Now put him from your mind so that you can concentrate."

"Put him from my mind!" she exclaimed, scandalized. "How can I do that? He's my Chosen!"

"No, darling. You are his. Until you are a vampire, too, you can't Choose anybody."

She reached out to him. *Erik, what's happening?*

She heard Erik's words, *I was betrayed*, and it was so full of hurt and physical agony that she could not contain her sorrow and fear. Nika buried her face in her hands and wept. Ingrid allowed her a moment, and then put another cup of tea in front of her.

"Now, now, that's enough." She offered Nika a handkerchief and waited for her to pull herself together. "Your man is strong. He's survived centuries. You don't get to be that old without being very smart, and very tough, and very lucky."

Nika balled the cloth up in her hand. "How do you know him?"

"Of course I know Erik Thorvald, Chieftain of the First, Champion of Odin, vessel of the Forest King. All Valtaeigr know him."

"Champion of Odin…?"

"Yes. When the time comes, he will be fighting at Odin's side."

She took a deep breath and reached out for him, but she could not sense him anymore. Tears welled up in her eyes, but she blinked them away. "You're talking about Ragnarök."

"And other things."

She was finding it difficult to sit still. Somewhere out there, Erik was hurt, possibly dying, maybe already dead. She fidgeted. "Do you have some sort of magic that can find him?"

"Yes, but I won't use it."

Nika looked at her, aghast. "Why not?"

Ingrid smiled like a saint in some Renaissance painting, distantly unreal and serene. "He's where he needs to be right now."

"How do you know?" She clenched her fist around the handkerchief and shifted in the chair, ready to bolt. "How do you know any of the things…"

"I know because I have the gift of Seeing, and I have the gift of Foresight." She looked unmoved by her guest's emotional upset. "I know that he will not die this day, if that is what you fear the most. I also know that there are worse things than death."

She asked the obvious question. "What is happening with him?"

"What needs to happen. There are consequences for every action. When we lay down with dogs, sometimes we get up with fleas."

"I don't understand."

"He has kept bad company, and now he pays the price. Den som ger sig in i leken, får leken tåla. He who enters the game must endure it." She waved a hand. "Enough about him. He is on his own path, and now you must see to yours."

Nika stilled herself. Ingrid was right. Having hysterics here and now would do nothing to help Erik, and it wasted time. She clenched her hands in her lap.

"You have things you need to teach me." It wasn't a question.

Ingrid nodded. "Yes. Are you prepared to learn?"

"I must."

The old woman smiled. "I know. Now... I know you have questions. I have answers. The sooner we get you caught up to speed, the sooner we can get on with the work at hand. Ask me anything, Nika, and I'll answer you if it's relevant."

"How old are you?"

"Seventy-six. Irrelevant. Try again."

"Who was Berit?"

"She was your former self."

"I know that," Nika said, beginning to feel irritable. "But who was she?"

Ingrid took a deep breath. "She was King Magnus Barefoot's daughter by a druid priestess from the Orkney Islands, which at that time belonged to the Norse. She was a princess, and she was beloved by her father. One day, the Draugr came to raid old Barefoot's longhouse, and the Veithimathr came to help defend the humans against them. Berit was in the longhouse, and that was when she met Erik.

"If you reach very far back into your mind, you no doubt will be able to remember. But that will be a story for another time. The important thing is that Berit became his love, and everyone could see it. They were a beautiful pair – the strong Veithimathr chieftain and the delicate Valtaeigr princess."

She studied Nika's face, her head tilted to the side as she considered her. "You resemble her, you know. Berit. But you are stronger. She was never a healthy woman."

"Is that why the vessel ritual killed her?"

Ingrid nodded. "Yes. Do you remember it?"

"No. I remember the altar, and the chanting, and I remember Erik bringing me the cup that the priestess had prepared. The rest is gone."

"That is a blessing," the old woman told her. "Berit did not die well."

That was an unsettling thing to hear. She shifted slightly in her seat. "Erik told me that I have the blood of immortals in my veins. Am I descended from the Draugr?"

"No, dear. The Draugr are dead. They cannot create offspring in that way. You are Valtaeigr, descended from the line of priestesses called the vala. If you were full-blooded, you would be immortal, as the pure Valtaeigr are."

"But not Draugr?"

"No. Our immortality comes from a different source. We were not cursed by Odin. We were blessed by Hel."

Nika's stomach soured. "By Hel? The Goddess of the underworld?"

"Yes. She who is half alive and half dead, the light and the dark. She will be the source of Ragnarök one day. We Valtaeigr are the workers of the light half of her spirit – the seers, the magic users, the healers."

"I'm almost afraid to ask, but is there a group who represent her dark half?"

Ingrid nodded. "Yes. Immaterial for now."

"Are you sure?"

The old woman laughed. "Child, I am Frigg. I see all. Of course I am sure."

She reached out for Erik again, almost reflexively, and received nothing but an echo. She sighed. "Do the Valtaeigr predate the Draugr?"

"Yes. We go back into the mists of time, so far that the sagas cannot tell us when we began."

"What magic can the Valtaeigr do?"

Ingrid smiled broadly. "Ah! At last, one of the questions I have been waiting for you to ask."

She went up the ladder to the loft and came back down a few moments later with a massive leather-bound book. It was girded with iron, with locking clasps holding the covers shut. Ingrid put the book on the table in front of Nika.

"Open it, child."

She looked at the book carefully without touching it, trying to gauge its antiquity and fragility. The leather was both clearly old and in pristine condition. It appeared to be from the skin of a cow. The iron bands that secured the cover were speckled with oxidation, but someone had cared for it, keeping the metal oiled and rubbed. She hesitantly reached out a finger to touch one of the locks.

Before she even made contact with it, the lock sprang open, and the book flipped onto its spine. The boards fell to the side and the pages flipped rapidly like leaves in the wind, riffling through from back to front until finally the book fell open. The pages that were now displayed were covered with a painted rendering of destruction. A wooden palisade at the top of a hill was burning, and men were tied to the posts, caught in the inferno. In the foreground, a trio of women stood, books in their hands. Their mouths were open in the painting.

"I've seen before," she breathed, "In a dream."

"Tell me your dream."

"I had it several times when I was a teenager, but I haven't had it for years. I don't remember all of the details now. But... in the dream, I was standing with my sisters and we were praying. Chanting. And we were burning people alive as sacrifices."

Ingrid nodded and pointed to the trio of women in the picture. "This is Frigg. This is Ithunn. This... this one is Hel." She nodded into Nika's look of surprise. "This is when the gods walked the earth. This is when the Valtaeigr were created."

"Those poor people in that fire..."

"They were killers and thieves. Do not waste your tears on them." She pushed the book toward her. "You wanted to know what magic we can do. It is all in there, but until you relearn Old Norse, the writings won't be of any use to you. I can tell you that we can heal. We have the gift of prophecy. And we have the gift of rune casting."

"Rune casting?"

She smiled. "Yes. It's the art of reading the future in the runes, and some Valtaeigr have the ability to scribe runes and imbue them with great power."

They were interrupted by the sound of tires on the gravel drive. Ingrid frowned and stood. Nika looked up at her. "Were you expecting someone?"

"No."

The old woman went to the front window and looked out. When she parted the curtain, Nika could see a gleaming black sedan. A tall blonde woman exited the vehicle, her smart suit and high heels making her look out of place. She was wearing dark glasses and leather gloves, and her hair was swept up into an immaculate bun.

Ingrid opened the door. "Angrboda."

The visitor removed her sunglasses. "Frigg. May I come in? I have business with Ithunn."

"Ithunn isn't here."

Angrboda's eyes narrowed. "Don't lie to me, old woman, or you'll be preparing for your next incarnation."

"I do not lie. Ithunn is not here, but her vessel is."

Nika, tired of being spoken of in the third person, went to the door. "What do you want?"

The newcomer smiled tightly. "I have a message for you. My lord would like to meet with you, alone, to discuss a business proposition." She held out a business card. When neither Nika nor Ingrid moved to take it, she tucked it into the fence. "The time and place are written there."

"What if I don't show?"

"Then my master will kill Erik Thorvald."

Nika's stomach lurched. "And who is your master?"

"I am Angrboda," the woman said archly. "Work it out."

She climbed back into her car and drove away. Ingrid stayed in the doorway with her arms crossed until the car was out of sight.

"Loki," Nika said. "Angrboda was his wife."

Ingrid nodded. She took the card and handed it to Nika. "You will not be seeing him alone, not until you're ready."

"When will that be?"

She put her hand on Nika's arm and guided her back into the house. "That all depends on how quickly you can learn."

Chapter Fifteen

He woke to pain hanging over him like a blanket. He was blindfolded and manacled, lying on a hard, cold surface that he assumed was a floor. His body was still burning from the silver bullets that remained lodged inside of him, and the bones he had broken in his fall had not healed. He groaned.

"You're awake." It was a man's voice, completely unfamiliar. He was speaking Old Norse.

"So it seems," he replied, using the same tongue. He struggled to sit upright, but when he tried to move, his body refused to obey. The effort made his suffering close over him, and he fell still, trying not to lose consciousness again. "Where am I?"

The man chuckled. "Somewhere safe from the mortals who were trying to kill you."

Every breath Erik took was a fiery misery. He stayed silent.

His captor spoke again. "Why do you think they were trying to shoot you, Thorvald?"

"I don't know," he admitted.

He heard footsteps approaching, with the crunch of hard soles on pavement. There was an echo of the sound, and he guessed that he must be in a basement or some sort of concrete bunker. He wished he could see.

The man crouched down beside him and stuck a probing finger into the bullet wound in his gut. Erik groaned in agony and tried unsuccessfully to evade the intrusion. The man clicked his tongue.

"You realize, of course, that this is what happens when you teach humans how to kill your own kind. Eventually they turn on you. Seems fitting for a traitor like you."

The man pulled his finger away, and he could hear soft, wet sounds. He could imagine that the man was licking the blood off of his finger. He opened his senses and confirmed that his keeper was a Draugr, and an old one, to boot.

"I'm no traitor," he murmured. Even as he said it, he knew it was a lie. He had betrayed Hakon to become Veithimathr, and in the eyes of many of the Draugr, he and his brothers had all become traitors for defending humanity against their own kind.

His captor snorted. Erik could hear him walk away. A door opened and closed, and a key turned in a lock. He was alone. Worse, he was helpless.

He could taste the silver in the back of his throat, cloying and toxic. It galled him that after everything he had overcome, he would be consigned to slow death by poison, shackled in some concrete prison cell.

There was still so much left undone.

***

He spent hours drifting in and out of consciousness. It felt like swimming in a vast internal ocean, trapped within the confines of his own soul and struggling to reach the surface. He was drowning in his own blood.

He was startled awake by the press of cold steel into his shoulder, cutting the flesh. He hissed at the new pain, unable to make any other protest. Someone was cutting the bullet out of him. The silver slug had been burrowing, and it took some time for his unkind physician to locate it. Erik's fangs extended, called down by his extremity, and he gnashed them in agony and rage.

"Quiet," a woman's voice said. She reached into the wound with her fingers, digging and probing, and she finally pulled the bullet free. His body convulsed as she withdrew her hand.

He could suddenly smell dreyri, and if he'd had a voice, he would have begged. His thirst roared within him, more powerful than it had been since he'd been made veithimathr.

"Open your mouth," she commanded.

He obeyed. A single drop of the enchanted blood fell upon his tongue, electrifying him. When no more drops followed, he moaned in protest. His unsatisfied thirst raged.

His torturer walked away, leaving him alone again.

***

Nika sat in Ingrid's house, contemplating the card that Angrboda had left for her. It was the same as the card that Sigurd had left in her apartment in Central City, with the same hand-rendered interweave decoration on the back. On the front, in an elegant hand, it said: One week from today, 11 am. Snake Eyes.

Her hostess looked up from the cook stove, where she was busily preparing the evening meal. "We will keep that appointment, young one, but we have a lot of work to do before then. You must be prepared."

"I understand."

She ran a hand over her forehead. She had a splitting headache, caused partially by tension and partially by the fact that she was several hours overdue for her next dose of dreyri. She wondered if she was in some form of withdrawal.

Ingrid put dinner on two plates and placed them on the table. "Come and eat, child."

Nika had no taste for food, but she obeyed. She felt dulled and diminished. She sat at the table but did not take up her fork.

"The need will pass soon," Ingrid promised her. "Then you will be clear-headed and your training can begin."

"So I'm feeling this way because of the dreyri?"

"Because of the lack of it, yes." She sipped from her cup, then said, "Tomorrow morning we will start with simple things, like feeling your power. Depending on how quickly you master it, we will move on from there."

Nika picked up her fork and listlessly pushed some food around on the plate. "What does Loki want with me?"

Ingrid hesitated, clearly weighing her words carefully. "You are a special person. You are the seventh incarnation of Ithunn. That gives you power beyond that of normal valtaeigr. You can wield more magic than others, and you are more susceptible to others' magic than others, as well. It is a double-edged sword."

"He wants my power?" she asked dubiously. She didn't feel very powerful.

"Yes. I'm sure of it."

She fell silent again. Thoughts of Erik crossed her mind, and she felt the sting of unshed tears pricking her eyes. She pushed her plate away.

"I'm sorry. I'm just not hungry."

She went out into the herb garden, standing in the wind and the clean salt air. The water was steel grey and choppy, speckled with white caps and attended by seabirds. The house and the hill on which it stood felt timeless, as if she were in a pocket of unreality that left her disconnected from everything and everyone she had ever known. A raven flew down and landed on the fence, watching her with bright, intelligent eyes. It was joined by a second raven, and the two of them regarded her closely. She looked back at them.

"Are you hungry?" she asked the birds. The first raven tilted its head as if it was considering the question. "Let me see if Ingrid knows what to feed you."

She turned to go back inside, and the birds flew away, taking to the air in unison. They were out of sight before she could even process that they'd gone.

Ingrid came out of the house and leaned against the doorjamb. "Hugin and Munin," she said. "They are the companions of Odin."

Nika had heard of the myth. Hugin and Munin were Odin's eyes and ears in Midgard, the world of men, and each day they gathered information that they gave to their god each night. She wondered what they would be telling Odin about her.

***

Days passed.

His body was a riot of pain. His unknown torturer returned each day to bestow one drop of dreyri upon his tongue, but it was not enough to heal him or to address the horrid pain that still rolled in his midsection. The bullet was still there, deep inside of him, and when he was quiet and still, he could swear he felt it spinning.

His broken bones prevented him from moving, and he was gripped by silver sickness. He was still blindfolded and bound, still held captive by people he never saw. He was giving up hope that he would escape this place.

The door to his lonely prison opened, and the click of high heels announced the woman's return. She walked right up to him, her feet stopping just shy of his head.

"Thorvald," she said. "Are you awake?"

He managed to answer weakly. "Yes."

"My master has a gift for you."

Erik was almost afraid to ask. "A gift?"

Abruptly, she pulled the blindfold from his head, and he blinked in the sudden brightness. There were electric lights blazing down from the ceiling. He was lying on a gray concrete floor that was bounded by four gray concrete walls. The door was iron and heavily reinforced, with a spinning wheel in the center like the opening of a vault.

Before him, a tall blonde woman was standing, her black patent stiletto heels nearly touching his face. She was wearing a business suit, which surprised him. He had been expecting something more military. He looked up at her. He did not recognize her face.

"Bring her in."

Two guards dragged in a struggling woman with scarlet hair. For a breathless moment, he thought that they had captured Nika. They flung her down onto the floor beside him. The woman in the suit pressed her foot against the prone woman's back, leaning on her and forcing her to stay on the ground. The guards came forward and held her down, as well. She began to weep.

"Do you want the pain to stop, Thorvald?" She waited for him to answer, but when he did not, she continued. "You only need to feed from her."

He tried to turn his head away. As weakened as he was, and as powerfully as his thirst was howling inside of him, he would not be able to stop himself from killing her.

The woman in heels leaned down and grabbed Erik's jaw, turning his face back toward her. She growled at him. "Such pretty scruples. Always choosing the humans before your own kind," she spat in his face. She turned to the guards. "Cut her."

The woman shrieked. "No!"

Her objections were useless. One of the guards produced a knife and cut a notch into the side of her neck, bringing blood bubbling to the surface. It was a serious wound but not a fatal one, and she howled.

The scent of her blood made Erik's stomach spasm, and he could feel the green Draugr lights ignite inside his eyes. His teeth, which had already been extended because of his pain, grew even longer. He needed to feed.

They pulled the woman closer to him, so close that he could smell the salt in her tears. She was begging for mercy, but he heard none of her words. Her fear was intoxicating, a reminder of his mortal days when power was at his beck and call and came on the backs of the frightened.

He tried to move closer to her, but the pain from his injuries stilled the motion before it began. He winced, but the vampire within him would not be denied. Over the anguished protest of his broken body, he inched closer to her, dragging himself along the floor.

The woman looked at him with terror in her brown eyes. She was like a cow at a sacrifice, seeing her doom and unable to prevent it. No longer able to think of anything but the blood, he attacked. His fangs sank into the soft flesh of her neck, his mouth wrapped around the bleeding wound the guard had opened. He drank greedily, swallow after swallow, frustrated by the manacles that prevented him from pulled her closer to him.

He drank until there was nothing left to take. The guards pulled the woman's dead body away, and the woman in the suit smiled down at him triumphantly.

"Where are your scruples now, Huntsman?"

They dropped the woman's corpse in the corner and left him to struggle with his shame.

Chapter Sixteen

Nika sat cross-legged in the garden, facing Ingrid with a white cloth on the ground between them. On the cloth was a set of runes, carved from a single oak branch, the symbols burned into the wood. After five days and nights of constant tutelage, she was about to attempt magic for the first time.

Ingrid nodded to her. "Cast away."

She held her hands out over the wooden pieces and concentrated. A pulse of energy shot from her palms and scattered the runes in all directions.

"Try to control it," Ingrid coached, putting the runes back where they'd started. "Keep the flow of your energy constant."

Nika took a deep breath and tried again. This time, the power seeped slowly out of her palms, creeping down to encompass the runes with a barely-visible shimmer. The wooden pieces began to vibrate, and the runes inscribed upon them began to glow a soft white.

"Good," her teacher approved. "Now cast."

She focused her mind on the question she was supposed to ask, but another question rose to the fore instead. Where is Erik?

The glowing runes sorted themselves until only three remained in the center of the cloth. Nika read the symbols. "Hagalaz reversed. Pain and loss, suffering and sickness. Nauthiz. Recognizing your fate. Endurance and survival." She took a deep breath. "And Algiz reversed. Consumption by divine forces and loss of a divine connection."

"A dire reading, to be sure," Ingrid said quietly. "I am sorry for your Huntsman's suffering, but this is not about him. You must clear your mind if you are to face Loki and survive. This constant worry about Thorvald will be your undoing."

"I have two more days," she whispered.

"You have only two more days. There is little time to prepare." She put the runes back in their original positions. "Now... try again. Ask what I told you to ask."

She took a deep breath and closed her eyes. How can I protect myself against Loki?

Again, the power poured out of her soul and through her hands, and again the runes glowed and sorted themselves. She looked to see what message they gave.

"Kenaz. The power of light. Revelation and creativity. Transformation and the use of power. Perthro. Precognition and knowing your own fate. Initiation and secret matters. Algiz. Protection, or a shield. A higher connection with the gods." She looked up at Ingrid, her eyes intense. "I think I know what shield it's talking about."

***

Erik sat on the cold concrete floor with one knee bent and his other leg extended out in front of him. His hands were still bound behind his back, forcing him to slouch against the wall. His bones had finally healed, fueled by the blood and the life he had taken, and the relief from that pain had allowed him to clear his mind somewhat. The silver bullet still burned inside his body. The blood had healed the wound around it so that he no longer bled, but the toxic pellet was still encapsulated in his flesh, still flooding his system with poison.

The electric lights continued to glare down on him and the body of his victim, which was still lying across the room like an oversized rag doll. He could smell the first tainted whiff of decay coming from the corpse.

He had been staring at the body for hours, too sick to feel much of anything. He supposed that his captors had left her there to try to demoralize him, but he had seen too much of death and had killed too many times to be so affected by a single dead woman. They had underestimated him, and he intended to use that to his advantage.

He pushed himself up to his feet. His head swam dangerously, and he fell back against the wall for support. He had to get that bullet out. It was killing him.

He looked around the room, but it was utterly featureless. There was nothing he could use as a weapon or as a tool. It was frustrating.

He bent brought his manacled hands down, forcing them under his hips so that he was bent double. With some difficulty, he managed to step first one foot, then the other through the circle his bound wrists created. His balance failed him and he toppled onto the floor, landing hard. Perversely, the fall helped him gain the last inch of clearance that he needed, and he brought his hands up to the front of his body.

He pressed one of his palms to his abdomen, feeling the silver bullet lodged deep beneath his hand. He extended his claws, letting his Draugr nature take the forefront. He clenched his teeth, steeled himself to the task and began to dig.

The pain was excruciating. He groaned in anguish as he thrust his fingers into his own stomach, ripping through the flesh in search of the bullet. Blood poured out of his self-inflicted wound, forming a spreading pool on the concrete floor. He nearly lost consciousness from the intensity of the agony. Finally, his fingers found the offensive object, and he pulled the bullet out of his body. As soon as it was freed, he collapsed.

***

Night was falling over the little house on the hill. Nika no longer felt any of the augmentation that the dreyri had given her, and its absence was a source of both sorrow and relief. She sat on the rug in front of Ingrid's hearth, the ancient tome in her hands. Ingrid sat beside her.

"Feel with your spirit, not with your hands," she instructed. "You have held this book before. You have read this book before. Remember."

Nika closed her eyes and concentrated. The book felt warm against her skin and almost welcoming.

"Go within," Ingrid coached. "Go back into the lives you led before."

She felt sleepy and awake at the same time, as if her mind was wandering but she was exquisitely aware of every detail that she saw. She saw sailing ships and wood fires. She heard the babble of voices in a distant marketplace. She saw Erik.

"Yes," her teacher said. "He has known you many times."

"How do you know what I'm seeing?"

"I am Frigg, child. I see all. Now concentrate."

She saw the book she was holding, but in her mind's eye, it was sitting on a shelf, open to the image of the burning men. She saw hands - her hands - reaching out to turn the page. She looked at the words written on the vellum sheet, the letters carefully scribed. Between the words, in the open spaces between and within the letters, she could see pinpricks of light shimmering.

"Can you read it?" Ingrid asked.

She opened her mouth to answer, but no sound came out. She was lost in the vision. In the physical world, her hands opened the book to the page that she saw in her mind. The vellum was twinkling with a thousand tiny stars.

Nika looked closer. The little glowing specks were not specks at all. They were runes. They glimmered and shone, and as she watched, they shifted like the engraving on the Rune Sword until words were formed.

Destiny cannot be cheated.

She put her hand on the page, and the glowing runes sparked like lightning, fingers of energy racing up her arm and into her chest. She gasped as the light plunged into her body. It was terrifying and exhilarating at the same time, like plunging down the steepest hill on a roller coaster. Her entire body tingled with the messy, uncontainable feeling.

The runes on the page vanished, and they appeared on her skin, dancing like fireflies. They moved up from her hand to her arm, shining as they went, forming and breaking apart and forming again. The words destiny and transformation appeared and disappeared as the glowing runes raced up toward her heart. Like the first tendrils of energy had done, they plunged into the very center of her soul.

She opened her eyes, and they were glowing with an unearthly golden light. The scent of apples filled the tiny house, and Ingrid smiled broadly.

"Ithunn," she said with a smile. "Welcome back."

The goddess spoke in Old Norse, her voice musical and terrifying at the same time. "Why have you called me forth?"

"Loki has returned to Sweden," Ingrid said. "He brings the Nøkken."

Nika's nose wrinkled, though the expression was Ithuun's own. "Why the Nøkken? Have they not been destroyed?"

Ingrid's eyes began to glow a pale violet as the goddess within her fully woke, and Frigg spoke through her. "They still exist, as they always have, but now they do not stay to the bogs and lakes. They walk freely among mankind, working their mischief."

Nika's hand stroked the page of the book on her lap. "This is Odin's book."

"Yes."

"Why?"

"The Veithimathr are almost destroyed. The last Huntsman, the only one who can defeat Loki, is captured and may be dying... or dead."

Nika's head shook sharply. "No. Not dead." She turned slightly, as if she were listening to something. "Bragi is awakened."

"His vessel has encountered yours."

"We cannot get involved in this, sister. We sacrificed our right to act except in self-preservation when we took these vessels." She stroked the book again. "Otherwise, it would have been too easy for us all to proclaim ourselves kings and queens over all mankind."

"Is it not self-protection, my sister, to prevent Loki from causing mischief? I fear Loki has some plan."

Her voice was heavy with disapproval. "Loki always has a plan, and if he is destroying the Huntsmen, then he is no doubt preparing to attack humanity."

"There are more humans now than ever before," Frigg told her. "If we – if our Draugr and Valtaeigr hosts – are exposed, then they will destroy us. We are as nothing before the weapons and science that mankind has created. Our vessels are still fragile."

Nika put her hands to her face, covering her glowing eyes. She felt the other personality within her, the goddess who hid inside her soul, and every part of her rebelled. She would not be controlled. "Stop it," Nika whispered, pushing against the powerful soul that was Ithunn. "Let go."

Frigg looked on through Ingrid's eyes, surprised. "Do not resist her, child. She needs to come to the forefront. Let her work."

"No!" Nika shoved, hard, with all of her psychic energy, pushing Ithunn back into the back of her mind where she belonged. The goddess did not resist, and Nika had the impression of a smile of amusement on Ithunn's incorporeal face. "This is my life, and I will do what needs to be done."

Ingrid's eyes burned brighter. "You do not know how. You are not a Rune Master, and only Rune Masters can contain Loki."

Nika looked up into her teacher's face, and she said, "I will learn."

The goddess in the old woman laughed at her, but then fell silent, considering. "Yes... perhaps you can. You are not fully goddess, not fully Valtaeigr, no fully Draugr. You are a mix of all three things."

Ithunn's voice spoke in both of their heads. *They will not expect her. She can combine all three. It will make her powerful.*

Frigg looked at Nika, but spoke to Ithunn. "You are speaking of a true melding. Do you really intend to lose yourself forever that way? Do you really mean to subjugate yourself to this human soul?"

Ithunn sounded contemplative when she spoke again. *It may be that the time has passed for the gods. If the humans have become as powerful as you say, and if we have all been only sleeping, then the time of humans it upon us. Ragnarök cannot be far behind.* She shuddered, and Nika's body shook. *I would avoid seeing that calamity. I would avoid seeing the end of all things.*

"Vidar can still be awakened and brought out of the Draugr," Frigg suggested.

Vidar, son of Odin, is destined to kill Fenrir, not Loki, Ithunn objected. *That honor falls to Heimdallr.*

"Heimdallr is deceased," Frigg told her. "The Veithimathr who carried him, Gunnar, has been slain and his soul has not yet been reborn."

Nika took a deep breath. "Stop." She pressed her hands against the book and looked down. The runes and the words suddenly took on meaning to her, and she realized that she could read the writing. "It's not time for Ragnarök yet. It's just time to stop Loki from... whatever he's doing. And to do that, we need Vidar. And to do that, we need to find Erik." She fixed Ingrid, and the goddess inside her, with a hard look. "You said that you could find him. Do it. Now."

Chapter Seventeen

Erik opened his eyes slowly. He was lying in the pool of blood had created, but it was dry now, telling him that time had passed in increments of hours rather than minutes. The silver bullet was on the floor beside his manacled, gore-stained hand, no longer capable of harming him. The terrible pain in his midsection was gone, and though he was weak from lack of blood and the urge to feed, he felt like himself again.

He went to the door and examined it closely, looking for a way that he could force it open. The hinges were on the other side, and there was no knob or handle that he could see or reach. The steel was reinforced with more metal that was welded into place. At his best, and with a full day of feeding behind him, he might have been able to force that door, but not today.

It was time to get creative.

He went to the body in the corner. With a snarl of distaste, he used his long, sharp teeth to gnaw through the dead flesh until he was able to disarticulate one leg enough to steal the femur. When the bone was free, he hefted it in his hands like a club and took up a position next to the door, waiting.

It took longer for him to receive a visitor than he had expected. Finally, he heard the click-click of high heels approaching in the hallway outside, and he prepared his attack.

The door opened, and he heard a woman gasp when she saw the bloody mess on the floor before her. Before she could react in any other way, he stepped out into the doorway and swung the club. The ball joint connected with her head, and she crumpled to the ground, her skull caved in. He grabbed her by the hair and pulled her up, sinking his fangs into her neck. She was dying and he needed her blood more than she did, now.

He drank every drop, and he could feel her spirit struggling against him. She was powerless, her brain too destroyed to allow her frantic messages to get through to her body. He pulled at her vein until that spirit snapped, severed from the world of the living and shuttling off to her fate.

Erik dropped the body and searched it quickly. He found a key ring in one pocket and a holster at the small of her back containing a Glock 26 with a 12-round magazine filled with silver bullets. He appropriated the weapon with a grim smile.

His last act was to toss the body into his cell and shut the door. No casual passers-by, if there were any, would see the corpse from the hallway and sound the alarm. It also pleased him to jail his jailer, even if she was already dead. It appealed to his sense of spite.

He flipped through the key ring, hoping for a key to his manacles. His luck did not extend that far, however, and he cursed.

The hallway extended straight ahead for thirty yards, and then to the right for another ten before it ended in a blind right turn. The way ahead led to a heavy steel door like the one on his prison, but with a tiny barred window. He crept rapidly to the door, leaning his shoulder against it and peering cautiously through the window. There was a control room on the other side, with rows of monitors, their screens still and dark. The room was empty.

He pushed the door open and slid into the room, closing it behind himself again. He had no idea how many people were in this compound, but he remembered that there had been at least two guards. The longer it took for them to notice that he was free, the better.

There was a desk off to the side, and sitting on top of its was another set of keys and the key fob for a Volvo. This time, the key ring gave him the way to open his manacles, and he happily freed himself of the annoyance. He grabbed the car keys.

Another door stood behind the desk, this one wooden and featureless. He listened carefully for any movement on the other side, but he heard none. He closed his eyes. His Draugr senses, fully activated now by the blood he had consumed and the adrenaline in his system, scanned the room for human heartbeats.

There were two. Both hearts were beating steadily, calmly, completely oblivious to his presence on the other side of the door. There were two people sitting in the other room, one nearer than the other, both on the left side of the doorway, sitting about four feet apart. He could smell antiseptic and metal oil, along with the faint tang of sweat and musty cloth. He decided that the room on the other side of the door was a locker room or a changing area. The two people were probably sitting on a bench, getting ready to come through into the control room and take up position at the monitors.

Not today.

They were only humans, and they didn't stand a chance when he kicked down the door. He grabbed the first one around the throat with his left hand, and with his fully extended right hand, he fired point-blank into the second one's face. He was dead before the hit the ground. Erik snapped the neck of the one he held, then drained his body dry, his Veithimathr's reticence for blood completely overcome.

He had been right about this room being a locker room. Even better, it was a partial armory. He found another pistol, three more clips of silver bullets, and an AK-47, which he happily appropriated. Now fully armed and fully sated, he opened the door on the far side of the locker room and slipped outside.

Since he had discharged his weapon, the need for stealth was less important than the need for speed. He held his rifle in his hands, pointed ahead of him, ready for combat. The door opened onto a corridor with three closed doors along one side and two glass doors at the end. Through those doors, he could see daylight and freedom. He ran for it, found the doors unlocked, and burst out into the open air.

Sirens were going off inside the building, which was a low brick affair with a series of tiny windows on the side facing the parking lot. A chain link fence butted up against the building and enclosed the parking lot, which was filled with Jeeps and other military vehicles. There were a few sedans, as well, and when he hit the button on the car key fob, Volvo in question beeped and blinked its headlights like a flirting barmaid.

Erik sprinted for the car and jumped inside it as armed men poured out another building within the enclosure, standing on the other side of the pavement. They wore the uniforms of the SOG. They fired upon him, and he threw the car into drive. There were five heavily-armed SOG soldiers at a gate, leveling their rifles at him. He snarled at them and laid on the horn, giving them fair warning before he gunned the engine and crashed the gate. He didn't want to hurt other members of his unit, but if they tried to stop him, he would kill them all.

As he raced out of the enclosure, he passed an incoming truck that disgorged Stenmark and his mates. Erik flipped them off as he drove past. Stenmark shot after him, but he missed, only one bullet dinging into the driver's side tail lights.

Jeeps roared out of the ruined gate in pursuit of him, each one full to bursting with special operation forces. He had trained many of them and had worked with others during his time with the army, and he knew their tactics better than they did, themselves. He regretted not stealing a vehicle with better off-roading capabilities, but the sedan would have to do. He turned a sharp right and left the paved road, driving over a bumpy field until he reached a dirt road headed due west.

A glance into the rearview mirror showed him that his former cohort were following closely, not thrown off at all – as he had expected. It would take more than a little stupid driving to shake the SOG. He wrestled with the car, spinning it on the dirt and taking it on another sharp turn, this time running on turf. The changing weather had frozen the ground, so there was no mud to contend with, and it made the running easier.

He was reminded of another time he had been chased this way, but that time he had been astride a horse, racing away from a Draugr encampment in Finland. He and Gunnar had made a mess of them that day. He missed his brother with a sudden, poorly-timed pain that made his chest hurt. He pushed the rogue emotion aside and kept driving.

He played with the SOG for miles, dragging them further and further from their base. He had no idea where he was, but he could feel the pull of magnetic north, and he put it at his back. He would reach either Stockholm or the sea this way, and both were acceptable choices to him.

The fifty-caliber gun mounted in the back of the Jeep behind him opened up, and it tore open the back half of his Volvo, the massive rounds shattering metal and ripping through the interior of the car. He swerved to destroy their targeting, but he knew these men. They were good. They would hit him soon if he didn't shake them.

His car began to whine and shake. One of the bullets had penetrated the gas tank, and he was losing fuel rapidly. He had made it back onto the paved road, and a little town was just ahead of him. He didn't want to bring a firefight to an innocent village, but they were leaving him little choice. He accelerated and roared into town.

It was a small town, with one large central road and several side streets winding off of it like glorified cow paths. He turned down the first side street he came to, turned again, and then crossed to the next block. He turned once more, and then careened around a building to park in someone's lawn. He abandoned the car, grabbed his weapons, and ran.

Without an invitation from a homeowner, he could not enter any of the houses, but he found what he was looking for less than half a block away. An automotive service center stood here, its bay doors open, a single vehicle in the lot waiting to be serviced. He could see two other vehicles inside up on the hoists, and a trio of humans working on a third. He ran into the garage and climbed up to conceal himself within the ceiling joists.

The soldiers would be duty-bound to check the car he'd left behind, but that wouldn't take all of them. If they knew anything about the Draugr, and he wagered that they did, they would know that he would only be able to enter a public space. In a village like this one, that gave them a very narrow set of possible locations for him to be. They would be here soon.

"Soon" came far sooner than he would have liked, and he had to give grudging respect to the men on his tail. A quartet of SOG soldiers, walking with great caution and showing excellent discipline, entered the garage and ordered the civilians out of the building. He watched his former comrades as they began their sweep.

He recognized the leader. He was a man called Lars Bengstrom, and Erik had worked with him in the past. They had shared a particularly harrowing mission in Afghanistan, and he had liked and respected the man. Now he was being hunted by him. Fate was a strange thing.

Bengstrom scanned the garage while his men carefully poked into the corners. His green eyes flicked up to the ceiling, taking in the jumble of cables and gears, and for one heart-stopping moment, his gaze locked with Erik. The Huntsman looked back. They sized one another up silently, and the human slowly, deliberately nodded.

"Nothing, Sir," one of the other men reported.

Bengstrom looked away. "Clear. Let's go to the next one."

The operators left the building, and Erik said a grateful prayer to Odin, asking for a little extra luck to be sent in Bengstrom's direction.

He waited until he was certain that his pursuers had completely moved out. He climbed down from the ceiling girders and helped himself to a car from the parking lot, then headed out of town and onto the road to Stockholm.

***

It was well after midnight when he reached their house. There were no lights shining through the windows. He no longer had his keys, but he knew the way in without them. He climbed the side of the house and went in through the bedroom window.

He was surprised to find the bedroom empty and cold. Nika's scent was faded. She had not been here in days. A cold finger of panic brushed his spine, and he hurried down the stairs, hoping that he would find her asleep on the couch. She wasn't there.

Chosen? He called out to her through their connection, but only silence answered. *Nika?*

She was gone.

He resisted the urge to scream in frustration. He didn't have time for an emotional scene. The army was hunting him, and they knew where he lived. Hunkering down in the first place they'd search for him was a foolish thing to do.

He showered, washing off the blood from his self-inflicted gut surgery, and then quickly dressed. He filled a flask with dreyri from the cask in the kitchen and collected his double-headed axe. He had to find Nika, and he had to find a way to stop whatever the Draugr and their contact Rahim Amari were planning for the political summit. He knew now that he was on his own.

He left the house and headed out into the night.

Chapter Eighteen

She woke from fitful sleep in the quiet hours between midnight and dawn with an echoing head and an aching heart. She could not remember her dreams, but the first thought she had was of Erik out there somewhere. She wondered who had betrayed him, why, and how. She supposed she would never know for as long as she stayed her in Ingrid's little seaside house, hiding from the world.

She rose from her makeshift bed in front of the fire and dressed. Ingrid had produced a few changes of clothing for her from a chest in the loft, including a sturdy pair of hiking boots. She pulled them on and laced them in the dying light of the fire. She grabbed her coat and went out the door.

Outside the moon was hiding behind a screen of clouds, hiding her face from the earth, and the night was the darkest she had ever seen. There were no street lights out here, and no other buildings stood nearby to shed their illumination through their windows. There was only the darkness and the sea and the sky.

She walked as far to the edge of the hill as she dared. Nika crossed her arms over her chest and listened to the distant rush of the sea. She supposed that this was how it had been back when the Draugr were first created – utter darkness, and the stark loneliness of being the only person awake for miles.

She sat down cross-legged on the grass, ignoring the way the cold seeped up from the ground and into her bones. She held out her hands and looked at them, remembering the dancing runes that had surged up from the book and into her body. She was not a stupid woman, but she had difficulty understanding all of the things that were happening.

She wasn't certain she had quite reconciled herself to being a mere vessel for a nearly dead goddess. It seemed so inglorious, in a way, reducing her to the level of a clay pitcher. She knew it also made her special, but to what end? She had heard Ithunn talking about melding with her completely instead of just riding piggy back. She wasn't certain if that would be better or worse than how things were now.

Out on the water, she saw a glimmer of light. It was just a flash at first, the merest spark like the flickering of a firefly. Then the light expanded, grew and separated into two shining dots, just barely peeking above the waterline. A wave washed over the lights but did not extinguish them.

She peered out into the darkness, trying to see what was causing that glow. A tug seemed to pull at her, urging her to move closer to investigate. She started to rise.

Do not go to those lights, child, the voice of Ithunn said in her head.

Nika hesitated. Why not?

It will be the death of us.

She frowned. It's just lights.

No. It is the Nøkken.

She saw it rising from beneath the waves, a horrible figure of mottled skin and sparse black hair hanging in lank strips around its toothy maw. Its eyes were large, protuberant, and glowing. Its arms were too long and its torso potbellied and misshapen.

Before it reached the strand, it began to shift, and before her eyes, the creature changed. Its height increased, and its body became more graceful, more beautifully made. Its face transformed into the face of an angel, the visage of the most handsome of men emerging from the sea like a gift of the gods. It went from monster to man in heartbeat.

What does it want? Nika asked the goddess with her.

To kill you.

She retreated into the house, locking and barring the door. Why does it want to kill me? she asked. What did I do?

It felt your power when you awoke the book. Ithunn sounded almost apologetic. It was called when I was summoned forth.

Nika dragged a cedar chest across the door and closed and locked the windows, pulling the curtains closed as if that would do anything to keep the monster out.

You must listen to me, Ithunn told her. You are the seventh incarnation of this soul since I bonded with it. More than that, you are the seventh daughter of a seventh daughter.

Nika had never known her family. She had been adopted by the only parents that she knew, plucked out of some orphanage in St. Louis. "This makes no sense," she objected aloud.

Listen. Seven, three times. That is a powerful number.

"Powerful numbers won't help me if I can't keep that thing out of the house."

Upstairs, Ingrid was rising, attracted by the sound of her voice. "Nika?"

"There's a Nøkken coming!" she shouted. "I don't know what to do!"

Ingrid came down from the loft like a firefighter, sliding down the ladder with her feet on either side of the supports. She hurried to the fire and grabbed the poker.

"It is a faery creature, so cold iron will injure it. And it is a water creature, so we turn to fire." She pressed the poker into Nika's hand, and then set about filling a bottle with lighter fluid from the fireplace. She tore a strip from her nightgown and shoved it into the neck of the bottle.

Nika, listen, Ithunn urged. The runes have chosen you. Only you have the power to wield them. I had hoped you would have time to learn, but time is coming to an end, and you must know what you are. You must become a Rune Master.

She could hear the crunch of the creature's feet on the driveway outside. A smooth masculine voice, musical and seductive, called out in perfect American English.

"Nika, come out."

What do I have to do?

Swing that poker when it breaks down the door, and do what I tell you to do.

They prepared themselves for the crash to come, but instead, there was a very polite knock.

"Nika?"

"Go away!" Ingrid shouted.

There was a moment of silence, and then the Nøkken replied. "I wasn't speaking to you, old woman."

Nika went to the door and slowly, carefully opened it.

The creature standing there was nothing like she had expected. He looked like a tall human man, perfectly shaped in every detail and perfectly naked. His magnificent body shone beneath the water droplets still clinging to his golden skin. His hair was blond and thick, falling in damp waves around his handsome face. He looked at her with the greenest eyes she had ever seen and smiled, revealing teeth that were white as pearls and perfectly even.

She gaped.

"Nika," he said warmly. "May I speak with you? My master has a message."

She looked over her shoulder at Ingrid, who was shaking her head furiously, a lighter in her hand preparing to set the Molotov cocktail ablaze. Within her, Ithunn had gone still. She faced him again.

"All right."

He unleashed that smile again, and something inside of her went watery. She put the poker down and joined him in the front yard.

As she faced him, she realized that her hands were shaking. She crossed her arms to hide them. "What's the message?"

"He would like to move up the date of your rendezvous from next week to tomorrow night. Snake Eyes, midnight. Will you come?" The look he gave her was very persuasive, and somehow very intimate. It as an unspoken promise of carnal delights on offer. "Please?"

She took a deep breath. "Yes. I'll be there."

His smile grew wider, and he looked delighted. "My master will be so pleased." He bowed to her slightly, the motion making his manhood sway. She realized that she'd been staring at it. "Until tomorrow night, then."

Against all expectation, he simply turned and walked back to the sea, displaying two perfect little dimples in the small of his back. It was only when he reached the water that the hold he had on her snapped, and she felt herself released from the lustful feelings rushing through her.

She backed up into the house and closed the door, sliding the bolt into place. Ingrid put the Molotov cocktail aside, unlit.

"What. The fuck. Was that?" Nika asked her.

"The Nøkken are very seductive. That's how they lure their victims to the water."

She shook her head and put her hand to her cheek. It was hot. "I would have followed him anywhere."

We know, Ithunn replied. He knows. And he knows what your weakness is.

Hot blond men?

No. Your weakness is surprise. If you can be taken off guard, all of your defenses fall.

"Well," she whispered. "That's not very good, is it?"

No, Ithunn agreed. That's not very good at all.

Ingrid tossed the lighter onto the kitchen table. "If you're meeting him at midnight, then we had better get to work."

***

Erik got a hotel room in Stockholm and paid in cash. He wasn't stupid enough to use a credit card when the army was busy looking for him, eager to put a silver bullet into his brain. When he got into the room, he bolted the door and tossed his gear onto one bed before flopping down onto the other.

He didn't understand why his superiors had turned on him. He had always done an impeccable job for them, always did his duty – he had never had so much as one discipline in his entire time as an army officer. The Huntsman unit had always been highly prized, their special abilities making them good choices for many covert operations in many different lands.

Clearly, something had changed.

He buried his face in the pillow and clasped his hands behind his head. And where was Nika, and why was she not answering when he called? The dreyri cask had barely been tapped, and that was probably his answer. She wasn't consuming the blood anymore, and without its enchantment, her nascent Draugr abilities were weakened or had disappeared completely. He hoped that she was all right.

He had no idea where to find her, but he knew how to start looking. In the morning, he would go to the museum and pay a call to Rahim Amari. The man's involvement with the Russian Draugr and with Nika was a double concern, and he intended to get to the bottom of it.

For now, though, he needed sleep to stay sharp. Otherwise, the only thing he'd get to the bottom of would be a hole six feet deep.

***

Ingrid sat with Nika at the kitchen table, the Book of Odin open between them. Nika put her hands onto the printed page, and she felt the burning of power deep within her body, as if a match had been lit just beneath her heart. She imagined opening a window in her chest and pulling in air to stoke the flame.

The power flared, and on the page, the inscribed runes began to glow and dance. Ingrid spoke.

"These runes were written by Odin's own hand, and they contain all of the knowledge he gained while hanging from Yggdrasil, the Tree of Life. This is the knowledge for which the All-Father suffered, the things he saw with the vision he gained by sacrificing his eye. You are the heiress to all of this. You, seventh incarnation and seventh daughter of a seventh daughter, are destined to be the Rune Master."

Nika turned her hands over so that the palms were facing up. Runes danced in the air above them, golden and glowing, slowly rotating as she looked at them. They were the runes from the new tattoos on her inner arms, the ones that had appeared there after the sacred fire that had destroyed Hakon. Perthro and Sowilo.

Nika looked at them and announced their meanings. "Female spiritual power. The sword of fire. Protection from evil."

As she spoke, the two runes spun faster, emitting light into the room that bathed them both in its golden glare. A shaft of light connected them, lengthening, forming a sword made of light and air and spiritual power. It pointed to the left, its hilt over her right hand. It rotated like a drill bit, spinning silently but with increasing speed. The blade burst into flame.

She dismissed it. It vanished as if it had never been.

She clenched her fists, then opened her hands again, palms upright as before. This time, the runes from Erik's tattoo appeared, spinning as the ones before them, this time glowing the green of the Draugr lights that shone in his eyes. Uruz and Thurisaz.

She announced these runes, too. "Masculine energy and male sexual potency. Regeneration."

Again the runes spun and glowed, and again a bar of energy connected them. Instead of forming a weapon, though, they formed flat plane of energy like a sheet of glass, or a mirror. Images raced along its surface, forming and changing and reforming too quickly for her to recognize anything they showed. Finally, she saw a darkened room and a figure lying on a bed.

She saw Erik. Her heart surged, and the image shattered, the runes vanishing and all of the light they had created extinguished in a moment.

Ingrid nodded. "You must learn control. Try again."

She summoned Uruz and Thurisaz out of the book and repeated the exercise. This time when the green sheet of light displayed her lover, she studied him carefully. He looked exhausted. He was lying face down on a hotel bed, sleeping. She could not see him breathing at first, but then, the Draugr did not breathe like mortal men. She watched him for a moment.

"He is alive," Ingrid told her. "And he looks unharmed. That should put your mind at ease."

She concentrated, and the image changed, widening out the view so that she could see the rest of the hotel room. His gear bag lay on the bed opposite the one where he was sleeping, and beside it was a double-headed axe, the blade gleaming in the light, honed and ready for a fight.

He was alone. She was ashamed that a part of her was relieved by this, when she had been considering giving it up to the Nøkken. The image wavered, and she stilled her mind, pushing the guilty thought away. There would be time to think about that later.

"Good," Ingrid said with a smile. "Good. Now call another. Show me what you would use to counter Loki when he tries to beguile you."

She closed and opened her palms again. "I call Elhaz for protection and to connect me to the power of Asgard. I call Isa to know and maintain mastery over myself. I call Kenaz for truth."

The three runes appeared as the others had done, glowing on the page before traveling up to hover above her hands. They spun together and their shared light created a dagger. She grasped it in her hand, and it changed from air and fire to solid steel. The runes were etched into the blade, dancing in gold along the fuller, one part decoration, one part enchantment.

Nika held up the dagger for Ingrid to see. Her teacher nodded in approval.

"You are ready."

Chapter Nineteen

Erik rose in the morning, feeling stiff and tired. He shouldn't have felt this unwell, not after all of the damage he had done and all of the blood he had swallowed yesterday. Perhaps his hurts had been more severe than he had believed.

In any case, there was no time to think about it now. He put his pistols in their holsters, one at the small of his back, one under his left arm and another on his ankle, and he strapped on the leather scabbard that held his axe with its head flat against his shoulder blades. He drew a leather jacket over the arsenal and a black cap over his head, and he made his way to the Royal Stockholm Museum.

The entry had not yet been made unfriendly by metal detectors at the doors, not the way the gates at other museums had. He was grateful for this one piece of luck as he was able to enter the place without attack and unimpeded.

The lobby was wide and brightly lit, with smooth marble tiles that reflected the incandescent glow back upward into his eyes. In the center was the ticket sales and information booth, three desks wide, and to the left and right were open arches that led off into galleries. The merchandise store was ahead and to his left, with a narrow corridor beside it that led off behind a pair of drinking fountains. Directly past that was the banner announcing the ship burial exhibit and the Viking history collection beyond it.

Nika was here to work with the ship burial and the Viking history collection, and she had said in her letters that Rahim Amari was interested in the same subject matter. He hoped that he might find them both by starting his search there. It nagged at him that he was risking finding them together. He shrugged off the sting of the thought, reasoning that his Chosen alive and unfaithful was better than dead and true.

He passed by a cloth banner screen-printed with the image of the Rune Sword. He would have been happy to die without ever seeing that particular weapon again, but that was not to be his luck. One of the docents, a studious-looking young man in a blue button-down sweater, started to pass him, and Erik stopped him with a hand on his arm.

"Excuse me. Have you seen Assistant Curator Graves?"

The man stopped for him, mildly taking no offense to the uninvited touch. "No, not for days."

Erik felt his stomach go sour. "What about Dr. Amani?"

"He's in the second room of the history gallery, with the St. Olaf Collection."

Erik let him go with murmured thanks, wondering if he was supposed to know what the St. Olaf Collection was. He went into the history gallery.

The scent reached him before anything else. It was the stench of salty musk and decaying fish, and it carried an undertint of power that he disliked immensely. It made his teeth itch. He walked more quickly, limbering his shoulders as he did, hoping against hope that there might be a fight.

The gallery was full of the detritus of another Viking ship burial, including old, corroded swords and armor and lots of less interesting objects. There was also a figure in the room, bent over a particular display and scribbling notes in a wire-bound notebook, a stubby pencil scratching away at the paper.

It was a Nøkken dressed as a man. Erik knew it from its smell. The Nøkken was not just dressed as a man – he was dressed as Rahim Amari. He recognized him from the photo at the briefing in Karlsborg. Erik wondered if Rahim had ever been Rahim since his arrival in Sweden, or if perhaps this shape shifter had adopted his face after he'd started work in Stockholm. It hardly mattered. Wherever it had happened, for the Nøkken to be wearing his face now, it meant that the real Amari was dead and Erik had a faery to kill.

Silver bullets wouldn't work. Neither would his axe, which had been forged in the traditional manner. He needed fire or cold iron, neither of which he had to hand. He backed out of the gallery and into the side hall with the drinking fountains. As he had hoped, there was a janitor's closet there – they were usually to be found near plumbing – and it was an easy thing to spring the lock. Once inside, he found a nearly-full can of aerosol furniture polish. All he needed was a lighter, and he always carried one of those. You never knew when fire would be needed.

He returned to the gallery, the can in his left hand and the lighter in his right. The Nøkken looked up briefly, turned back to his scribbling, and then looked up again. The first glance had been one of annoyance at an interruption, but the second brought the wary recognition that a heavily-armed Veithimathr deserved.

The false professor put down his notebook and backed away from the display. He clearly knew what Erik was, and Erik just as clearly saw through his disguise.

"What do you want?" the Nøkken asked, nervously.

"To talk, to start," Erik answered honestly. "I have questions, and I was hoping you'd have answers."

The man raised his chin pugnaciously. "I have nothing to say to you."

"Maybe not yet. Maybe in a while you will. Who knows?" He tucked the lighter into his jeans and shrugged his jacket down on his shoulders. He drew his axe. "Let's find out."

The Nøkken turned and fled. Erik pursued as quickly as he could. No faery could compete with a Draugr in a footrace, and the fleeing creature resorted to flinging trashcans and furniture in his wake as Erik followed. He jumped over the obstacles like a hurdler, his axe in his hand, and when the Nøkken burst into the employees-only area, he was right behind him.

They raced around a corner, and the false Amari shoved open a door. Erik was on him before he could close it again, and a swing from the axe, striking him with the flat of the head, sent the Nøkken tumbling head over heels down a short set of steps. Erik leaped over the steps and onto the landing, his feet on either side of the creature's head. He dropped his axe, pointed the furniture polish, and pulled the lighter back out of his jeans pocket.

"Don't move," Erik said firmly. "I'm warning you."

The Nøkken put up his hands in a protective gesture, guarding his face. "Don't do it," the creature begged. Now that he was this close to it, he could detect no whiff of a god riding shotgun on the monster's spirit. This, despite his expectation, was not Loki. It was one of the Bluffmakare, though, and that was reason enough for him to have pursued this creature.

"I won't, if you tell me where to find Nika Graves."

"I don't know."

"You're lying." He sparked up the lighter.

"No! Stop!" It was panting now, clinging to its composure on the brink of a full-out panic attack. "Don't do that! You're going to kill me!"

"That's the idea," Erik admitted, "unless you give me a reason not to."

To the Veithimathr's surprise, the shifter started to laugh. He moved as if he was preparing to stand, and Erik put his foot down hard on the creature's chest.

"What's so funny?" he asked.

"You. You really think that you can do this? You think that you can kill me?"

He pressed with his boot, letting it slide closer to the monster's throat. "I know I can."

"I can never die. I will outlive even you."

"Not likely, unless you start talking."

The Nøkken shifted slightly, and then a second mouth opened in its chest, grasping teeth reaching for Erik's leg. The Huntsman pointed the furniture polish through the flame of the cigarette lighter. A jet of fire whooshed out, striking the supine creature where a human head should have been. The fire caught immediately, and Erik jumped back as the Nøkken burst into flame, screaming and flailing. He tossed the can into the corner and reclaimed his axe.

The Nøkken writhed on the floor of the stairwell, emitting a greasy black smoke that smelled as foul as anything Erik had ever encountered. He gagged on the stench as the fire alarm went off. Sprinklers overhead doused them both with water, coldly expunging the suffering monster's fire.

Erik pressed the edge of his axe to the monster's fore head, ignoring for a moment the second set of jaws that still gnashed beside his calf.

"Where is she?"

"I don't know."

"When did you see her last?"

"Days ago." It writhed and tried to bite him, but he kept his leg out of range. "I've answered you. Let me go."

"Do you know where she might have gone?"

"I don't know."

A thought occurred to him, and he asked, "Did she go to Ingrid?"

"I don't know!"

The next question rose in his head from a source he could not identify, but which was probably Vidar. "Where is Loki?"

The monster lunged at him, and out of reflex, Erik recoiled. His axe came up in an arc, then whistled on its way back down. The Nøkken lunged out of the way and avoided a direct blow, but the blade bit into its shoulder. It screamed again.

"Those are woman sounds," Erik mocked. He wrestled the axe back out of its body.

The Nøkken wrapped its hands, long and amphibian-looking, around the vampire's ankles and pulled. Erik landed hard on the steps, his tailbone taking the brunt of his fall and snapping beneath him. He hit it again, and this time the axe head was buried between the creature's eyes. It transformed into sea water and rolled away, dripping down the steps to the basement.

Erik wiped the axe on his jeans leg and returned it to the scabbard on his back. This had not exactly gone according to plan.

***

He found his way to Snake Eyes, the last place he wanted to go today, but the first place he probably should have gone after all was said and done. If you needed to find a lost Valtaeigr, you went to a Valtaeigr for help. Too bad this particular Valtaeigr hated him.

Even at this time of the morning, the club was occupied with Draugr. The music was no longer pumping as it would be after dark – Stockholm's human ordinances on noise pollution had to be respected, after all – but there were still patrons scattered around the room. The blue lights in the floor lowlighted their ghastly pallor, these immortal barflies, clinging to their hightops and swigging their dreyri straight.

Immortal dissolutes, all of them.

Erik went to the bar, aware that his presence had once again set off the ward at the door. Whatever little alarm system Magda had installed was already telling her that one of the First was here. The closed-circuit cameras behind the bar would tell her which one of them it was. As far as he knew, there were still eight of the First alive and kicking. He wondered if any of them would be less welcome than he was.

The elegant blonde in the black jumpsuit came into view, leaving the private offices in the back of the building to meet him at the bar. She put her hands on the counter top in front of him.

"What?" she asked him.

"Counsel," he replied.

Sif snorted. "We'll see." To the bartender, she nodded toward him with a desultory jerk of her chin. "Serve him."

A glass of dreyri appeared at his elbow, and he drank it without looking. The glass went back to the countertop with a click. "Another."

"Easy," the bartender advised him. "It's a good vintage. This one has been specially brewed."

The so-called brewing of dreyri was a complicated process, and it involved no actual brewing at all. It was herbs, and blood, and enchantments cast by the Valtaeigr in their hidden temple somewhere under Stockholm. Depending on whose blood it was, and which of the vala was doing the spell casting, the drink could be mild and spicy to hair-raising. The more power, the better the vintage was said to be.

"A good vintage," he allowed, "but I've had better. Another."

She poured the glass with a hint of a pout. Erik was amused in spite of himself.

"Leave the bottle," he directed.

Sif returned. "Magda will see you... if she must. Huntsman."

He picked up the bottle and his glass and followed Sif back into the proprietor's office. Magda was sitting at her desk, not as put together as she had been the last time he'd laid eyes on her. Her hair was down around her face, a little messy as if she'd just left her pillow. She was wrapped in a red silk kimono, the flaring sleeves a stark contrast to her slender white forearms.

He sat before her desk. She looked at him with a scowl.

"What do you need, Huntsman?"

"My Chosen has gone missing. She is Valtaeigr. I need for you to cast an enchantment and find her."

Magda laughed. It was a short, harsh sound. "Oh, really? And why would I cast such a thing for you?"

"Because I asked nicely."

"You know that I hate you."

"Yes."

"I say that she is better off without you. You haven't turned her yet, anyway."

"No," he admitted, finishing his glass. "Not yet."

"You won't. You always let your fear rule you when you try to turn the ones you care about. Ever since Berit."

She sneered the name. He poured another glass full and put the bottle on her desk.

"What makes you think she hasn't run away?" Magda challenged him.

"I don't know. Maybe she has." He pulled his pistol out of his shoulder holster and rested it on the desktop. "Maybe that's not your concern."

She looked at him in disbelief. "Are you seriously threatening me with that contraption?"

"No, not with the gun." He drained his glass. "With the silver bullets inside of it."

She narrowed her dark eyes. "You wouldn't dare."

He sat back and trained the gun onto her pretty face. "You would be surprised at some of the things I would dare to do."

"Desperation makes you unpleasant," she snarled. Her Draugr teeth were descending. He could smell that she was afraid.

"And why would I be desperate?" he asked. His manner and voice were calm. When lying to the vala, it was important to always lie convincingly.

She leaned back in her chair and crossed her legs. "Because you can't find your Nika, and Loki is looking for her. Because the squad of Draugr pets you trained are out hunting you."

Draugr pets. Well, that certainly explains their longevity. "They won't find me."

"Are you so sure? They know where my bar is. They know where all of the Draugr hot spots are." She smiled. "What makes you think that Sif hasn't already called them to tell them that you're here?"

"Because Sif is loyal to her own kind, and loyal to you above all else. And she knows that I have you in here, and that I am never unarmed. She wouldn't risk you that way." He cocked the gun. "Now... about that spell?"

She frowned. "You were more fun before you decided to have a conscience."

"We all have our challenges in life."

Magda rose. "May I go to my cabinet without you shooting me in the back?"

He smiled. "If I were to shoot you, it would be between your eyes, not between your shoulder blades."

She turned her back on him and walked to a locked cabinet in the corner of the room. "I had to ask. It's so difficult to predict what traitors like you will do."

He watched in silence as she entered the combination into the lock and opened the cabinet doors. A rush of scents from the old days reached him, earthy and moist, smelling of herbs and wood fires. The feeling of raw power rolled out into the room, as well, and he breathed it in.

Magda did not turn. "Do you like that, Thorvald? Or perhaps it is Vidar that breathes so deeply."

"Perhaps it is both of us."

She made a noncommittal noise and began to pull out the components of her spell. An earthen brazier, then a small wooden tray went onto the desk. She added sprigs of herbs and a pinch of sulfur and mixed them all together in an earthenware mug. She brought it to him and held up a silvered dagger.

"I need blood," she said. "And I will not bleed for you."

The corner of his mouth turned up sardonically and he extended his wrist. She slashed his flesh with the dagger, the silver burning and keeping the wound from closing right away. His blood dripped into the concoction she was making.

First she heated it over the brazier. Then, when it began to smoke, she added mead and stirred it with her finger. With her eyes closed, she chanted over it in the ancient tongue of the vala, and then consumed the potion. It hit her fast, like a drug, and he watched her with curiosity, pressing his fingers to the wound in his wrist.

Magda tipped her head back, her eyes closed. She continued to chant. With her right hand, she began inscribing lines and swirls in the air, her finger leaving behind a white trace almost like the condensation trail from a jet plane. She began to rock in place, her voice growing louder. He could hear a rushing in his ears as power gathered in the room, filling the space between them until it was difficult to breathe.

Her eyes flashed open, and she spoke in a voice like a hundred women speaking at once. He was in the presence of the spirits of all Valtaeigr who had ever lived and who were not currently clothed in flesh.

"What do you seek?" she – they – demanded.

"Nika Graves and the god Loki."

Her eyes flashed white. The goddess Sigyn had come forward. "Why do you seek Loki?"

"For my own reasons."

"Answer."

He felt his own eyes flip to the same iris-less glow. Vidar responded. "Not to you."

"I will not help you seek my husband!"

Vidar took control of his limbs and walked him to her body. His hands went to her throat. "You are compelled. You consumed the drink."

She pulled away, but he followed, his hand clutching her still, propelling her backward. They crashed into the wall at the back of the room, dislodging a painting from the wall. It crashed to the ground and the glass in the frame shattered.

"Nika Graves is coming," she hissed, speech difficult around the pressure of his thumb on her windpipe. "She seeks you."

"And Loki?"

"He comes."

"Where. Is. He?"

"In Agnafit!" It was the Old Norse name for Stockholm. "He sleeps in Stadsholmen."

He nodded. Stadsholmen, also known as Gamla stan, was Stockholm's Old Town, built on the island in the center of the city where the first settlement had sprung up all those years ago. The buildings there were relatively new by his reckoning – they'd been built in the thirteen hundreds. He had known it then, and he knew it now. "Where?"

Her only response was to spit in his face. He laughed and released her. The white glow in his eyes retreated, leaving only the green Draugr spark behind.

"How far is Nika? Where, exactly?"

She stepped away from the wall and side stepped him, her own eyes returning to their usual brown. "Find her yourself."

Magda left the room through her private door, locking it behind her.

Chapter Twenty

Snake Eyes was busy, as it probably always was. The Draugr likely had no jobs to concern themselves with, and no need to wait or weekends to do their clubbing. Every night was a party and every day just a chance to catch their breath.

Nika slowly drove past Snake Eyes in Ingrid's car, judging the place and the stream of vampires coming and going. She was hesitant to go in without Erik, but while she was driving down from the coast, she had seen a vision of him in Magda's office. Maybe it had been the wishful thinking of an exhausted mind, or maybe it had been a true moment of clairvoyance, but it was the only thing she had to go on.

Her stomach burned with the power of the runes she had absorbed, and the Book of Odin sat on the passenger seat, sleeping like a child. She had come to realize that some inanimate objects were not as inanimate as she might have believed.

She pulled into a parking garage down the street. She had a messenger satchel that she'd liberated from Ingrid's loft, and she slid the Book into it, keeping it close. She pulled the strap over her head so that it hung across her body, the leather snug between her breasts, weighted by the heavy book in the bag. It felt good. It felt real.

Nothing else did.

She had gone to the house first, and she had swallowed as much dreyri as she could bear. It combined with the rune power in her gut to make her hot, just this side of feeling sick. Her forehead was slick with a fine sheen of sweat. The power was gathering.

***

Erik sat in the corner of Snake Eyes, slowly drinking his way to the bottom of another bottle of enchanted blood, keeping his attention on the door. After his audience with Magda, something inside of him had shifted from active to watchful. Both Nika and Loki were in Stockholm. He was certain that one or both of them would end up here.

The chance that Stenmark and his fellows, or possibly the entire SOG, might also arrive here was not lost on him. He chose to take that chance.

To the other vampires in the bar, the presence of one of the First sitting in the corner and loading up on the strongest dreyri in the house was intimidating. They left him to his own devices and gave his table a wide berth. Some of them went so far as to studiously and respectfully avert their eyes from him, eager not to attract his attention.

These young ones had nothing to fear from him. He cared nothing for them or their petty little concerns. He had his own agenda, and they did not feature into it.

One of the middling-aged Draugr in the bar was sitting a few tables away, his smart phone flickering as he flipped through his Facebook newsfeed. Erik turned and looked at him, and the younger vampire, feeling the sudden weight of his gaze, looked back, startled.

"Your phone," Erik said. "Bring it here."

The man obeyed immediately, putting it on the tabletop. Erik pulled it over and opened a news site, where he searched on the G8 summit. After a moment, the tiny screen lit up with a video showing the arrival of the American President, surrounded by his Secret Service operatives and members of Swedish security on loan from SOG. In the background of the shot, while the President was waving to the crowd at the airport and getting into his limousine, he recognized Stenmark, shaved and suited. He was with the SOG contingent.

Apparently, his little group of wanna-be huntsmen had landed the G8 gig after all.

He tossed the phone back to the other Draugr. "Thanks." The man retreated in relief.

Erik poured himself another glass of dreyri, even though his head was already buzzing from it. Loki was a powerful god, and if he was inhabiting one of the Nøkken, he would be a difficult adversary. He needed to be prepared and to have his own power level as high as he could get it. Vidar was the son of Odin, but he had never been one of the strongest gods in Asgard. He was never supposed to face Loki, and Erik certainly was never meant to take him on.

He sipped his drink. The next twenty-four hours would be interesting.

When they hit the wards, the power echoed through the entire establishment. Draugr looked up, startled and wary, as the alarm told them by the flavor of its magic that three of the First and an ancient faery were entering. Erik pinned the door with a fixed stare as the Nøkken and his three companions entered the room.

"Loki," he said aloud.

The Nøkken heard him, as he had been meant to do. The fact that he was wearing the face of a man Erik had already killed meant nothing. Every one of the Nøkken could wear any face they wanted, and they could walk in here together, thirty-one Rahim Amaris wide. They were shape shifters and could appear to be anyone at all.

What they could not do was disguise the singular energy of an ancient god riding one of their souls like a jockey.

The Nøkken looked at him, and the appearance of the Iraqi professor fell away, replaced by the face of the most singularly beautiful man Erik had ever seen. This, too, was a deception. There was nothing beautiful about the Nøkken or about Loki himself. There never had been.

The quartet walked to Erik's table while the rest of the occupants made room for them to pass. Several of the younger Draugr took this opportunity to leave the bar, abandoning ship in favor of safer spaces.

"Huntsman," Loki said. "You are very brave to face me here this way."

"I do not fear you," he said. He waved to an empty chair. "Sit. Drink with me."

Loki raised on impeccable blond eyebrow and nodded to his escort. Erik remembered these men. They had been brothers in arms once, a millennium ago.

The nearest, Brevik, had his wild red hair pulled back at the nape of his neck. His broad body was encased in motorcycle leathers, and his beard still bore the little braids and pewter charms that he had always favored. He no longer carried an axe, but Erik could clearly see the handle of a pistol at his belt.

Beside him was Agnar, blond and blue-eyed and built like a walking mountain. Back in the day, he'd had a prodigious appetite for women and for violence. Erik was willing to bet that nothing much had changed. Agnar pulled a chair from a nearby table and sat on it backwards, straddling the back and folding his arms on top. He appeared to be unarmed, but the chances of this being true were slim to nil.

The last of the trio accompanying Loki was Dag, who had once been Erik's friend. Smaller and lither than the others, he hovered in the background, his eyes warily fixed on the seated Huntsman. Erik nodded to him, but Dag did not respond.

Loki sat across from Erik and took the bottle of dreyri from the table. He examined it with amusement, and then put it aside. "It will take more than a fine vintage to defeat me, Thorvald."

"Perhaps," he allowed. "Perhaps that's not why I'm drinking it."

Loki produced a cigarette and lit it. He took a deep lungful of smoke and exhaled it back out into Erik's face. The huntsman did not react. Loki smiled.

"You know why I am here."

"No. Why don't you educate me?"

The Nøkken smiled thinly. "Don't lie to me, boy."

Erik retrieved his bottle and emptied it. "It's not a lie. I know it has to do with the G8 summit, but that doesn't seem like your style."

"And what would you know about my style?"

"More than you might think."

The door opened, and Nika stepped into the bar. Erik's heart flipped in his chest, and he was unable to keep the spark of joy and relief from his face. Loki turned and saw her, and an oily smirk crossed his handsome face.

"Ah. My rendezvous has arrived."

Nika stopped short as soon as she entered the room, her eyes falling immediately onto Erik's face. He rose to his feet, and she flushed. Her hand went to her chest, pressing against the flesh over her heart.

Chosen, he greeted.

Her face lit up. Erik. Are you all right?

Better now that I see you.

She crossed the room at a trot. Before she could reach him, Loki stood and neatly interposed himself between the lovers. She stopped short.

"Miss Graves," he said. "So good to see you again. I trust this time your mace will remain in your purse."

She stepped back, out of reach. "You wanted to see me."

"I did. We have much to discuss." He gestured toward Magda's office. "Shall we?"

Reluctantly, with a conflicted expression on her face, Nika nodded. "All right."

Erik attempted to follow, but Loki's Draugr escort stopped him. Agnar said, "Let them talk alone. No harm will come to her."

"Loki," the huntsman called after him. The god in the Nøkken vessel turned to face him. "If you touch one hair on her head, I will destroy you."

Loki laughed and walked away, leading Nika into the quiet of the office.

Erik considered his options, including the logistics of a silver-bullet shootout in this Draugr bar. He decided, much to his dismay, that discretion was called for. He sat back down.

***

Nika followed the Nøkken into the office, her hand gripping the strap of the messenger bag. The Book was vibrating against her hip, responding to the proximity of the god inside the shape shifter.

Loki sat behind the desk as if the office was his own. Nika sat across from him.

"Has Ingrid told you how special you are?" he asked.

"She's told me who I am. Why did you want to meet with me?"

He looked at her intently, his green eyes bright. Sensuality rolled from him in waves, something she had not been prepared to face. She could feel her face flushing in response to it, an inadvertent physical betrayal. She did not want to want him.

"I believe that we can help one another."

"Help one another with what?"

He smiled. "You must know that the mortal world is completely out of control. It's chaos. People cannot be trusted to run their affairs appropriately. They're backstabbing, lying, frightened children in need of a keeper. It is time for the gods to return to our ascendancy and to take control of mankind, once and for all."

She frowned but did not respond.

"These are harrowing days, Nika and Ithunn. The Asatru movement is resuming our worship, and we are gaining strength. I have gained immeasurably from the fascination caused by popular culture – did you know that a movie series exists where I, or someone with my name, plays a prominent part? I am remembered." He smiled, just shy of gloating. "The more they speak my name, the stronger I become, and I am certain that the time has come for mankind to welcome its new king."

"No."

He raised his eyebrow again. "No?"

"No, I won't help you enslave humanity."

"Who said anything about enslavement?"

"You did," she retorted, "without actually saying the word."

"You object?"

Her voice was hard. "Strenuously."

Loki chuckled. "You Valtaeigr are so alike. Always so concerned about the way things should be done instead of with the way things need to be done."

"I fail to see the problem."

He gestured toward the bag she was holding so tightly. "And what do you have there? A present for me?"

"No. Not for you. This is mine."

"Tell me what it is."

She could feel a tendril of energy snaking out from him, reaching into her mind. He was trying to force her obedience. She raised her chin.

"I said no."

He grinned, delighted. "You have a strong will." He rose and walked around the desk. "I wonder how strong it would be under actual duress."

She raised her hand toward him, her palm facing him. A glowing rune appeared there, white and gold shining brightly. "Do you want to roll those dice?"

He stopped short, surprised. "So you have found your power."

"Found it, learned it, harnessed it." The rune began to spin. "I'm ready for you."

Loki looked uncertain for just a moment, and then he forced a laugh. "I look forward to a duel at a later date." He stepped back and bowed to her, half mocking, half sincere. "Since you will not join me, I will allow you to leave. Our parting will be less civil the next time we meet."

She rose and retreated toward the main area of the bar. "We'll see."

Chapter Twenty-One

Nika emerged from the office and was almost instantly met by Erik. She embraced him tightly.

"I was so worried!" she gasped.

"I couldn't find you anywhere. I called but you didn't hear." He pulled back and cupped her face in his hands. "Are you all right?"

She nodded and covered his hands with her own. "Let's get out of here."

He was happy to comply with her request. Taking her by the hand, he led the way out through the delivery entrance and into the street. She looked at him quizzically as he took them on a circuitous retreat through back alleys until they reached the subway station.

"We have a lot to catch up on," he told her once they were safely underground. "We can't go back to the house."

"Why not?"

He looked around, and then pulled her after him into a service tunnel. When he was certain they had not been followed, he opened a maintenance closet door and pulled her inside with him.

"Erik, what is going on?"

"The army is trying to kill me."

Her eyes widened. "So that's what you meant when you said you'd been betrayed."

He nodded. "I'm thinking they don't like having vampires on their payroll anymore."

"What about the team you were training?"

"They're not vampires. They're mortals who've been fed dreyri."

Her face clouded and she felt her heart sinking with disappointment that she had been resolutely refusing to acknowledge. "Like me. Were you going to tell me?"

He hesitated, clearly not wanting to discuss this, but also clearly aware that he had no choice. "I couldn't risk losing you."

"So you lied to me instead?"

"It wasn't lying."

"Yes, it was. You told me that I was Draugr once I drank the blood."

"You were." He ran a hand through his hair. "Nika, once you taste dreyri, you belong to us. You are Draugr then by allegiance."

"But not in fact," she pressed. "For that, you would have to turn me."

He looked miserable. "Yes."

"You weren't going to turn me, were you?"

"Nika..."

She felt her neck tighten. "Tell me."

Erik sighed. "No. Every time I have tried to make you in the past, with your past incarnations, it has failed. I can't fail again, not when failing means watching you die." His eyes glittered, suddenly moist. "I can't bury you again."

Anger flared in her. "So you're telling me that you're a liar and a coward."

He turned from her, and then turned back. His jaw muscles twitched. "Yes. Are you happy? Yes. I am afraid of losing you and never finding you again. But I am no coward."

"But you don't dispute the part about being a liar?"

He spread his hands at his sides, helpless. "I can't."

It was Nika who turned away, turning her back on him in the narrow confine of the maintenance room he'd dragged her into. She fell the Book in her satchel begin to hum again. *It's responding to my emotions,* she thought.

She stayed facing away from him. "Loki asked me to help him subjugate mankind."

"What did you say?"

She turned back to him, stung. "How can you even ask me that question?"

"It's a valid one."

She spat, "I told him no."

"Just no, or did you elaborate?"

Nika wanted to hit him. "What does it matter?"

"Because when you deal with Loki, you are dealing with the devil. Every word you speak is a contract." He put his hands on her upper arms, holding her gently. She did not pull free. "What did you say?"

"I said, 'No, I will not help you to enslave humanity.'"

"That was all? No elaborations?"

This time, she did pull out of his grasp. "Jesus Christ, Erik, give me some credit. It's not like it was hours ago."

"I'm sorry."

His apology had a cavernous air to it, as if he was sorry for a hundred things she didn't even know. She thought about how he had admitted to a past of rape and murder, and she wondered how much she really knew about him, and how much people could really change.

She raised her right hand toward him, palm out. A rune began to glow there, spinning, transforming into a dagger of fire. She gripped it and pointed the tip at him.

"We're done here. I don't even know who you are."

"Nika," he pleaded. "I'm the man who loves you."

She almost wavered at the sight of the pain in his eyes, but she steeled herself to what she had to do. "Get out of my way."

The dagger was now fully solid, made of silvered steel that still glowed red-hot. He shook his head.

"If Loki wants you involved in his plans, he will stop at nothing to make you join him. I can't risk that you'll be captured by him, or worse."

She stepped forward and pressed the point of the blade against the zipper in his jacket. "Move."

Reluctantly, he stepped aside. "You may have become a Rune Master, but you don't know what you're walking into." She opened the door, and he continued. "I know what he's planning."

She hesitated. "What?"

"He's going to either subjugate or murder one of the dignitaries at the G8 conference."

Nika shook her head. "That's ridiculous. He'd never get close enough."

"He is a shape shifter vessel for the trickster god. I'd say that if anyone could walk through security without being noticed, it would be him."

She closed the door and stayed inside with him. Her hand holding the dagger dropped, and the weapon itself returned to the form of energy and dissipated. She felt torn. On one hand, she was angry with him for his lies and half-truths. On the other, he was the only person in all of Sweden that she felt she could depend upon if the chips were down. She decided to give him a chance, at least on the level of this current crisis. She would decide later if she would give him a chance in a more personal arena.

"So what's your plan?"

"I can't go openly to the G8, not when SOG and every other security force known to man will be standing guard."

"And I can?"

He sighed, looking exasperated. "Neither of us can. But... we can keep watch outside."

"Just the two of us?" She shook her head. "You know these things always take place at really large venues. How are we supposed to be keeping an eye on a hundred different entry and exit points?"

"We're not." He hazarded a smile, and it brightened his eyes. "We're going to let regular security handle those. Since you've mastered the power of the runes, I assume that you've been to see Ingrid."

"Yes." She was confused. "What has she got to do with anything?"

He didn't answer, which was an infuriating habit of his. He said, "She has a book of magic..."

"Had." She opened the flap on her bag and showed him her humming, magical cargo. "Now it belongs to me."

Erik looked suddenly delighted. "Perfect. Because that book will tell us how to set faery wards on the conference."

She thought of the ward on the door at Snake Eyes, the one that told the house that a First was entering the bar. It made sense. "So if I set a ward on the building, as soon as the Nøkken steps foot on site, we'll know."

He smiled. "Exactly."

"That's a pretty big ward, Erik. I'm new at this. I don't know if I can create something that big."

The look he gave her was skeptical. "You're a Rune Master and the seventh incarnation. Of course you can create something that big. You could probably set a ward over the entirety of Europe."

"I doubt that."

"I don't."

He took a deep breath. "I know you're angry with me, and you have the right. I should have been more open with you. I don't know how happy you would be with me risking your life without taking the time to have a detailed discussion about turning you, either. We were going to have that talk, but after I got back from deployment. It's not the sort of thing you can get through over texts.

"That being said, we have to work together to stop Loki. He cannot be allowed to do whatever he's going to do – which is probably to take the form of one of the sitting heads of state, either of Russia or the United States. Once we've beaten him, we can have the long conversations we need to have."

She knew he was right. "I was going to stop him," she told him. "After I left that office, I was going to stop him. I just didn't know how."

"Let me work with you." He took a cautious step forward. "After that... after that, I will let you go, if that's what you want me to do. But let me work with you on this threat. There's too much at stake."

Nika sighed. "I'm not going to let humanity suffer because I'm having a fight with my boyfriend."

He grinned. "I didn't think so, but it's good to hear."

Nika put her hands on her hips. "So where do we go now? This closet is a little small, and we have to someplace where I can study the book. The house is off limits because of your bosses, and I'm willing to bet that every hotel room in the city is booked because of the summit."

He considered. "I know just the place."

***

He took her to a little house outside the city. It was non-descript, just a white house on a block of other white houses in a tidy little suburban neighborhood. There was a planter shaped like a frog on the front porch, and the house key was beneath it. He retrieved it and opened the door.

The inside was nothing like the outside. Whereas the exterior of the house was nondescript and everyday, the interior was like stepping back in time. The only walls were the ones bearing the weight of the structure; the others had been cleared away, leaving only support pillars in their place. The center of the single room had a pit dug into the floor, and it was ringed with stones and filled with cold ashes. The ceiling was blackened from the smoke of bygone fires. The walls were covered with wooden planks, all elaborately carved and painted with Norse interweave figures. Round shields with steel bosses were hung on the walls, and between the shields were weapons of every description, from the medieval to the modern, running from a double-headed axe like the kind Erik favored all the way to an actual grenade launcher in the corner. The floors were covered in dirt, and the only furniture was benches, a trestle table, a trio of chairs and a bed against the far wall, mounded with furs.

Nika walked in while Erik shut and locked the door behind them, her eyes taking in the ancient style of the place. She could sense the echoes of a powerful Draugr here, and she turned to Erik, an unspoken question in her expression.

"This was Gunnar's house," he told her.

"It's…"

"Weird?"

"Nice."

She sat on one of the benches and pulled the Book of Odin out of its bag. It seemed to be feeling content, if a book could feel anything. She put it on the bench beside her.

He sat in one of the chairs, watching her. She could feel his eyes upon her. He was thinking a hundred things; she wondered what they were. To forestall any uncomfortable topics, she spoke. "Have you ever seen this book before?"

He shook his head. "No. I've heard of it, though." She stroked the cover, and the book purred audibly. Erik looked startled. "It's alive?"

She chuckled at his reaction. "It seems to be. It's sort of like having a book that's part cat."

"That's extraordinary."

"Says the Viking vampire."

He smiled. "Touché."

She stroked the book again, trying to leech some of its contentment. Her stomach was in knots. "You were hurt, weren't you?"

Erik shrugged. "I had a bad day or two. I'm all right now."

"You can't even answer that question directly?" She could not keep the disappointment from her voice. Erik lowered his eyes.

"I'm sorry. Yes, I was hurt. Badly. I was shot with silver bullets, and I fell from a building, and I was captured and held in chains."

"My God…" She shook her head. "It's a miracle you weren't killed."

"I almost was."

Nika warred with herself, with her irritation and pride, and with her need to touch him and reassure herself that he was as healthy as he seemed. Her desire and love won out, and she went to him. He looked up at her, his blue eyes searching her face, and she embraced him, holding him to her breast. He put his hands on her waist, and then encircled her with his arms.

She kissed the top of his head and stroked his soft blond hair. "No more getting shot. That's an order."

"Yes, ma'am."

He pressed a kiss to her chest, his lips above her heart. She pulled back and looked into his eyes, seeing no lies there and no threat.

"I'm still angry with you for lying to me about the dreyri."

"Okay."

She kissed him, deeply and passionately. The tip of his tongue flickered against her lips, and she opened her mouth to allow him to explore her. He groaned softly, pulling her tighter. She ran her hands through his hair, encouraging him to continue. She had missed this.

His hands skimmed over her body, moving from her waist up over her ribs, and then gently cupping her breasts. She arched into his touch, and he slid one hand down her flat abdomen to slide under the bottom edge of her shirt. The feeling of his skin on hers sent a shock of excitement through her, and she shivered. Beneath his touch, the rune power flared, and she knew that he could feel it, too.

Chosen, he whispered in her head. He pulled away from the kiss and moved his lips to the corner of her jaw, then to the hollow behind her earlobe.

"I love you," she responded, breathing the words like a sigh.

He rose and gathered her up in his arms. He carried her to the bed and put her down gently on the pile of furs. Their eyes met and held as he knelt above her. She ran her hands over his strong shoulders, down the hills and valleys of his muscular arms. His strength was an aphrodisiac, his pure masculinity fueling her desire.

"Make love to me," she whispered.

He dipped down to take her lips in another burning kiss. She opened the button on his jeans and pulled the zipper down, feeling the evidence of his desire straining for freedom. He groaned softly in the back of his throat when her fingers brushed against him.

He broke the kiss and straightened, pulling his shirt off over his head and flinging it aside. She loved the way his muscles rippled beneath his skin. She pulled off her own top and opened the button on her own jeans. He grasped her waistband and slid the confining garment down and off, baring her long legs.

"Erik," she said, reaching out to him.

He stepped back and divested himself of his clothing. She smiled when she saw the evidence of his arousal, proudly jutting forward. She took it in her hand and stroked slowly. He smiled at her, his eyes thick with desire, and he slid her panties down. She lifted her hips to help him with his task, and he smiled. It was the most entrancing smile she had ever seen.

He knelt at the side of the bed and pulled her closer, his hands beneath her hips. She shivered at the first touch of his tongue, and she buried her hands in his hair, urging him on. He complied eagerly, his mouth warm and wet against her sensitive flesh. She moaned and writhed, but his hands held her hips steady.

He took her to the edge and then tipped her over, sending her into a pleasure-drunk free fall. She cried out in ecstasy, and he stayed with her, pushing her into climax after climax. When she could bear no more, she pulled him up to lie beside her.

His desire was still straining for release, hot and hard against her thigh as he pulled her close. She looked into his eyes and touched his face, her hand resting on the strong line of his jaw. He kissed her palm and smiled at her, his eyes warm with love. Nika reached down and touched him, and he shivered.

She held him in her hand, her thumb playing gently over his sensitive flesh, enjoying the way he responded to her touch. His hand skimmed over her skin, light and teasing as a feather, leaving a trail of goose bumps in its wake. She pressed against him, signaling for him to lie on his back. He obeyed, a smile on his handsome face.

He was burning in her hand, and she was burning for him. She straddled him, sinking down onto his length and taking him in as far as he could go. She rocked against him, and he gasped, his hands falling onto her hips. She ran her fingernails lightly down his chest and over the washboard of his abdomen, and he shivered. When she touched his tattoo, the runes emblazoned in his skin flashed in response. He moaned.

She rode him slowly, deliberately, transporter by the feeling of him deep inside of her. He met her downward motions with upward thrusts, gentle but insistent. Their speed increased, and neither of them were going to last much longer. He took her hands in his, and their eyes locked as they neared the apex of their loving. He tipped his head back with a groan and found his release. She was not long behind him.

She collapsed onto him, and he wrapped his arms around her, holding her tight. There were no words, and no need for any. The moment and the feeling was enough.

Chapter Twenty-Two

They spent the day in preparation. Erik cleaned his guns and made sure his clips were full, taking ammunition from the ample stockpile Gunnar had left behind. Nika studied the Book of Odin. She read everything that it had to say about faery wards in general and the Nøkken in particular. She had much to learn.

After hours of silently being preoccupied with their own pursuits, Nika closed the book and sat back, rubbing her eyes. Erik gave her a tender look and asked, "Tired, my love?"

"Yes." She sighed. "There's something that's bothering me."

"About what?"

"About you."

He hesitated and put aside the gun he had been reassembling. "I will answer any question you ask me, with total honesty," he said in an even voice.

"You said that you were one of Hakon's men."

"Yes."

"How many women have you raped?"

A muscle in his jaw twitched. "I don't remember."

"Too many?"

"Too long ago."

She frowned. "I would think that's the sort of thing a person would remember."

"It would be, if it were an uncommon occurrence." He looked away. "The gods punished me for a reason."

She pulled her knees up to her chest, her heels on the seat of her chair. "When was the last time you did it?"

He considered. "Almost fourteen hundred years ago."

"Not since?"

"Not since. And it will not happen again." He faced her again. "I told you the story of the girl who changed me. That was my last raid in the old style. I am not the man I once was, Nika, I promise you."

"Would you ever rape me?"

Erik looked horrified. "Never!"

She put her elbow on her knee and rested her head in her hand. "Were you really going to tell me that you needed to turn me?"

"Yes. I just didn't want to drop the information on you, or worse, turn you, and then have to leave immediately for Karlsborg. That wouldn't have been fair."

"Are you going to turn me?"

"Do you want me to?"

She looked away, conflicted. "I don't know."

He went back to his gun and continued to reassemble it. "Then there's no reason for you to be angry with me for not telling you, because it's apparently immaterial."

They were silent for a long while. Finally, she said, "If I said yes, would you do it?"

He made eye contact, steady and unswerving. "Yes."

Nika spoke without thinking. "Then do it."

Erik put the gun aside and rose. He walked to where she was sitting and crouched in front of her, his hands on her feet. "Are you certain? Once we start this process, there is no turning back."

She looked into his eyes and considered what she was asking. It was immortality, but an eternal need to feed on the blood of the living. It would mean an eternity to be with Erik, to enjoy him, to love him...and to be worried for him and about him. It would mean a farewell to family and friends, but she had already said those goodbyes before she'd moved to Sweden. She felt the gentle pressure of his hands, smelled the scent of his skin, and the answer became clear.

"I'm certain."

"Do you want to wait until after we stop Loki? Being turned may change your powers."

"It won't. I don't know how I know, but I do."

He rose and offered her his hand. She took it. Gently, he led her to the bed. "There will be pain," he warned.

"A lot?"

"Enough to notice."

She swallowed. "I can take it. Let's go."

With his silent direction, she lay down on her back, her hands at her sides. He reclined beside her, his hand on her stomach, then on her chest. He looked both excited and sorrowful, and she could see a hint of fear in his eyes, as well.

"You tried to turn Berit."

"No. She died from the ceremony melding her to Ithunn. I never had a chance."

"But the other incarnations... you turned them."

"I tried." He sighed. "I failed."

She could see him faltering, and she took his hand. "That was then. This is now."

He bent to kiss her, and she kissed him back. Then he shifted to lie closer to her, his face next to hers. He kissed her neck, and then licked the skin above her vein. She trembled, but tried to hold still. She felt a sting, and then his teeth were in her throat.

He had fed from her before, but not like this. Those had been taps, tiny sips, compared to this aggressive taking. She could feel herself going pale, and her head began to spin. She gripped his shoulder to steady herself. He took more, and more, and then the world went black.

***

Erik drank.

He took Nika's blood by the mouthful, gulping instead of sipping, draining her with a purpose. She was going cold beneath him, her skin ashen. Her hand, which had been gripping his shoulder, fell aside as she lost consciousness. He continued to drink until her heart began to flutter.

He pulled back then, and he ripped open his wrist with his fangs. The blood dripped onto her lips, and he forced her mouth open so that he could get the first few drops down into her throat. To his relief, she swallowed.

He listened to her heart shudder. He heard it stop.

As soon as her pulse went quiet, he pressed his bleeding wrist against her mouth, forcing the blood to flow onto her tongue. At first there was no reaction, and he felt the first frisson of fear course through him. It had happened exactly this way, so many times before. He prayed to Odin that this time would be different.

There was a skittering sound, and then her heartbeat resumed. It was uneven and weak. He poured more blood into her mouth. She swallowed again, and this time she moaned softly, a needy sound. Her pulse grew stronger and more regular. He began to pull away, but she grabbed his arm, holding his wrist to her lips. She began to actively draw at his open wound, sucking down the blood he offered her, replacing the blood he had taken.

She released him just before he was going to push her away. She fell back onto the pillow, her red-stained lips parted, breathing heavily. Her eyes were closed.

He touched her face. "Nika?"

***

There had never been so many colors. She saw light and shadow, dark colors and brilliant hues, all swirling in her mind's eye. She saw runes floating and dancing like cells on a biologist's slide. They glowed and combined, separated and mixed. She was dizzy.

She felt the fur beneath her fingers, aware of every separate hair. She could feel Erik beside her, and could see his power through her closed eyes. She could see the white kernel in his soul that was Vidar, and the white spot in hers that was Ithunn. She could see all of time, into the mists of the past all the way to the mechanical glare of the future. She was everything and nothing all at once.

Slowly, the hallucinogenic high began to dissolve, and in its place she felt wracking pain. Her muscles began to spasm, pushing and pulling her against her will into herky-jerky movements like a marionette with tangled strings. Erik grasped her in his arms and held her tight, and the cramping in her body fought against him. She heard growling, and she realized with a start that it was coming from her.

Pain rose around her like a black sheet, and she wanted to rage at it. She pushed at Erik with her hands and with her runes, sending glowing symbols to sear into his skin. He did not let go.

She convulsed. She felt herself dying.

She heard Erik as if from a very great distance. "Hold on, my love. It will pass."

Her mouth hurt. Her eyes hurt. Everything hurt. She writhed in agony as her body rebelled. The growl became a scream, and still he held her tight. In anger, she bared her newly-sharp teeth and buried them in his arm. He did not flinch.

As quickly as it had come on, the pain departed, leaving her gasping and disoriented. She released the bite hold she had on Erik's arm and licked away the blood that welled to the surface. It tingled on her tongue.

She opened her eyes and closed them again. The light was too bright, the outlines of things too stark. She could hear music playing in the house next door, a song about diamond rings. She could hear people talking in the house on the other side of them, and in another house, and another. The noise crashed in on her, deafening, each sound canceling out the other until she had no idea what she was hearing. She put her hands to her ears and whimpered.

Easy, Erik said, his voice quiet and soothing in her head. This will pass, too.

She pulled him into her arms and held him tight, drawing comfort from the security of his embrace. He lay beside her and held her until the storm passed.

***

It was after midnight when her quaking finally stopped. When he was sure the worst was over, Erik left her sleeping. She would be asleep for hours, possibly even until dawn. That left him time to get to the house and retrieve the case of dreyri. He packed two pistols and a knife and slipped out into the darkness.

He hired a van and drove it back to his house, careful to drive past to be sure that there were no cars or watchers. He saw no surveillance units, but he decided to be careful. He parked around the block and walked through his neighbors' yards to his back door.

He had lost his keys when he'd been taken captive, along with his cell phone and his dignity, so he had no choice but to break in. He had developed a habit recently of twisting door locks into oblivion, and he applied the same technique now. The door swung open.

He could smell the scent of a mortal man. He ducked out of the doorway and peered around the jamb into the kitchen. All of the lights in the house were extinguished, but he knew that there was someone in there. His visitor was not in the kitchen, so he crept in and checked the pantry, then the laundry room, where the scent faded.

He followed his nose and walked carefully forward. At the door to the living room, he peered inside and saw a man in fatigues, night-vision goggles on his head and an AK-47 cradled in his arms. He could smell silver. Whoever it was, he had come prepared.

Erik grabbed a wooden spoon from the rack near the stove, and he let his Draugr nature come to the forefront. He climbed up the wall like a spider and clung to the ceiling. The man in the living room did not react. From his upside-down perch, Erik flung the spoon at the back door, and the clatter brought his unwelcome visitor to his feet, the rifle pointed in the direction of the door. Erik flattened himself against the ceiling and waited.

The soldier stepped cautiously forward, gun trained on the back door. Like everyone everywhere, he failed to look up. He passed directly under Erik without noticing him at all. The soldier did see the spoon, though, and he was clearly puzzled about how it had ended up against the door. He took a step forward.

Erik dropped from the ceiling and landed behind him, wrapping his arm around the man's throat. He put pressure on the man's carotid arteries and squeezed until he stopped struggling. Erik laid him down on the ground and retrieved the cask.

He had been careless. As he was picking up the cask in the dining room, a gun cocked behind his back. He froze.

"Hands up. Turn around."

He knew that voice. He turned around to face Ulf Magnusson, one of his convict huntsmen. Ulf grinned like a happy monster.

"Caught me the big fish," he said. He pointed a pistol at Erik's face. "If I kill you, the Master will make me a king."

A Draugr could move faster than any human. A Draugr pet, like his convict friends, fed on enchanted blood and given infusions of power, could move faster than a human, and almost as quickly as a true vampire. Erik was tired and weakened from turning Nika, so he would be slower than normal. They might be evenly matched.

Then again, they might not. There was only one way to find out.

Erik lunged at Magnusson and knocked the gun out of his hand. The big man grappled him, and they went down with a crash, shattering the dining room table. Magnusson was larger than Erik, and he had reach, but Erik was meaner and had hundreds of years of experience that the Draugr pet could not begin to replicate. Soon Magnusson was on his face in the table splinters with Erik on his back, his arms wrenched high up to his shoulder blades.

"The Master?" Erik echoed his earlier words. "You serve Loki now?"

"I always did." He bucked, trying to dislodge his captor. Erik kept his seat.

"Where is Loki?"

The man twisted and tried to spit at Erik, but there was no way he could get the trajectory right. His spittle landed on the carpet. It was almost laughable. "I'll never tell you."

He shook the man beneath him, rattling his teeth together. "He's in Stockholm. Where?"

"You're the huntsman," Magnusson snarled. "Find him yourself."

It was clear that he would be getting nothing helpful from this man. He considered snapping his neck, but he choked him out instead. There was a better use for him.

When Magnusson went limp, Erik zip tied his wrists and ankles. He gathered up the cask of dreyri and hauled it to his rented van, then retrieved Magnusson and dumped him in beside it. He covered both with a tarp and drove away.

Chapter Twenty-Three

Nika woke in a fever of thirst. It clawed at her throat, choking her with its desperation. She clutched at the furs on which she lay, bunching them up in her hands, puncturing them with the claws that had sprouted at the ends of her fingers. Her long Draugr teeth gnashed together, and as she woke completely, she found the energy to stand.

Erik was beside her then, his arm around her shoulders, guiding her toward a huddled shape that smelled of blood. She pushed Erik aside and lurched toward that intoxicating scent. The man on the floor cried out when he saw her, and he tried to scoot away from her on his backside, his bound feet churning against the tarp that lay beneath him.

His efforts to flee magnified her thirst, and she fell on him, seizing his head in her hands and forcing him to lift his chin, exposing the tender throat beneath. Her teeth were in his vein before he could scream.

***

Erik watched dispassionately. The first feeding of any Draugr was a messy affair. It could not be helped. Nika clutched Magnusson, her fangs buried in his neck, her hands holding him like vises. He died with a scream on his lips, his eyes bugging in terror. Erik knew from experience that his fear had flavored his blood like a chef's spices flavored a stew.

When the corpse was dry, Nika dropped it and tipped her head back, caught in the ecstasy of feeding. It could be as gratifying and pleasurable as sex in its own way, he knew, and he let her revel in her first kill. Every vampire needed to have this moment.

When her body relaxed and her Draugr claws had vanished once more into her human hands, he brought her a mug filled with dreyri. She took it, her eyes still glowing green in the last throes of her feeding frenzy. With a gentle arm around her shoulders, he led her to a bench beside the fire pit and left her there to drink.

There was a basement in Gunnar's house where he used to bury his "empties," at least until he could drag them out to sea. He dumped Magnusson's body there, intending to finish the job later. He had a fledgling to attend.

***

Nika slowly returned to herself, clutching the mug of dreyri as if it were hot chocolate on a cold day. She huddled around the drink, blinking, feeling her head begin to clear. Everything seemed so strange.

The runes in her belly burned. She shook her head and held up her left hand, palm up. The rune Kenaz appeared there, hovering, burning with golden fire... phoenix fire, transformative fire. Rising from ashes.

Rising from the dead.

Erik came back into the room, and she looked up at him, extinguishing the rune. He was beautiful in her new vision, colors swirling around him in an active aura, spinning in and out of the brilliant white in his center that was the god Vidar. There was a layer of yellow around Vidar's white, the color of Erik's own soul, and then the green power of the Draugr a whirling cloud around the whole. His body was outlined in Draugr green, while sparks of white and yellow danced irregularly around him.

She realized that she was staring, mouth open, at him. He smiled at her.

"Blink a few times and you will master it," he told her. His voice was more resonant than ever before, deep and strong and achingly masculine. She did as he told her, and after a moment, the colors were still there but she was no longer dazzled.

"I..." She choked on the word, her own voice failing her. She tried again. "I feel so strange."

"In an hour or two, you will be steady." He sat down beside her. "Drink. It will help."

She drained the mug in her hands. She was aware of him watching her, still smiling, relief and delight evident in his expression. She looked back at him when she had swallowed the last of the dreyri.

"It worked," she said.

He nodded happily. "Yes." He took her hand. "And you can still cast your runes."

"Yes." She put the mug aside. "Erik... I... I shouldn't have pushed you. I shouldn't have forced your hand, but I don't regret it."

He kissed her, his hand gentle on her cheek. "Neither do I."

***

When morning came, they went to the Hotel Scandic Talk in Älvsjö, which was right next door to the Stockholmsmässen, where the G8 summit was to be held. Both buildings were in downtown Stockholm. The crowds grew thicker the closer they came, a mixture of protesters, media staff and the dozens of security and police officers attempting to keep the place from becoming a powder keg. Limousines flying the flags of the G8 member countries lined the street, taking turns disgorging their distinguished passengers according to the rigid diplomatic rules of engagement.

Erik took Nika by the hand. He had two large duffel bags, resplendent with Swedish flag patches and airline tags, hanging by straps over his broad shoulder. They were dressed casually, like young tourists visiting the sites in the capital, with sunglasses and baseball caps, blue jeans and hiking boots. They dodged around the milling people in the lobby, past photographers and a bored-looking television news correspondent, incongruously dressed in a suit only from the waist up.

They rode an elevator to the top floor, sharing the lift with several other people who all exited before them. One of their fellow lift passengers, a middle-aged man, was speaking in German on his cell phone. He glanced at them once to see if they were listening, and Erik gave him a pleasantly bland smile. The man went back to his conversation with a frown.

When the elevator stopped on their floor, Erik went to the doors on one side of the hallway, listening closely at each one. Nika watched him sniffing at each door, scenting for human occupation, but the smell of beating hearts was so strong to her that it was all she could smell. Finally he stopped at one door and nodded.

"This one's empty."

She stood beside him, keeping watch down the hallway, as he produced a tiny cylindrical object from one pocket. He inserted it into the bottom of the hotel room lock, and the red light above the card reader flipped to green. Erik grinned at her.

"SOG has the best toys."

He opened the door and held it for her, and they went into the room, closing it behind themselves. She flipped the deadbolt, and he went to the window. Through the curtains, they could see the Stockholmsmässen and its swarm of humanity.

While he took stock of the situation, Nika pulled the Book of Odin from one of the bags he carried. The book's boards began to shimmer with a cascade of golden runes, glowing and streaking from top to bottom and back again.

"That book gets excited when you touch it," Erik said. "I know how it feels."

Nika laughed and opened it, turning to the appropriate page. She looked out the window. "I think I can get the front door if I cast the faery ward from here, but not the rest of the building."

"Where would you have to be to cast it and get everything?"

She shook her head and closed the book. "Probably on the roof."

"I can arrange that."

"In broad daylight?"

"Trust me on this," he assured her. "Nobody ever looks up."

He got into one of his bags. Gunnar had accumulated a lot of SOG equipment over the years, even more than Erik had realized, and he gave silent thanks to his brother's kleptomaniacal spirit. He found what he was looking for and activated a hand-held laser.

"What's that for?"

"Window won't open any other way."

He used the laser to inscribe a line all around the central pane in the three-paned panoramic window, careful to pull the glass back into the room instead of letting it drop out into the street. Cold wind rushed into the room when the pane was removed, and he put away the laser.

"Nice," she commented. "Very handy."

He shuffled through the bag and came up with his axe and shoulder harness, which he strapped on over his jacket, and a pair of pistols. He kept one and offered the other to Nika, who waved it off.

"I don't like guns. They're too dangerous."

He looked at her in disbelief, and then roared with laughter. She raised an eyebrow at him, and when he could finally speak, he said, "My darling, you are the most powerful woman in the world today, and you say guns are too dangerous!"

"I'm not the most powerful," she protested. "Stop teasing."

He kissed her, and then pointed a spool gun out the window, firing it at the roof of the Stockholmsmässen. A cable extended, connecting them with the other building.

"Oh, hell, no," Nika objected.

"Just hold on to me, then, and I'll take us across."

"They're going to see!"

"Not if you use the right runes."

She shook her head into his grin. "Are you kidding?"

"I'm serious as a train wreck."

Nika opened the book and looked for a spell for invisibility, completely expecting to come up dry. Instead, she found three varieties of magical invisibility, and she shook her head.

"All right," she said. "Here goes nothing."

"No, no," Erik hastily corrected. "Not that attitude. Do it, or don't. We can't have any doubt in this today."

She considered his frank blue eyes, and then took a breath. She put the book back into its bag, and looped the bag around her body. He tied off and tested the cord, and when it was clear that it would hold, she wrapped her arms around his neck.

"Ready?" he asked.

"Ready."

She summoned a cloud of runes around them, surrounding them with spinning iterations of Thurisaz, Raidho and Eihwaz, calling on protection and success. Erik put gloves on his hands, then grasped the cord and began to slide. They flew over the heads of the people below, riding their zipline to the Stockholmsmässen roof.

She clung to his back, pressing her cheek against the cold metal of the double axe blade. She held her eyes squeezed shut, trying not to panic. She had never enjoyed heights.

Erik landed lightly and released his hold on the cable. He put her on her feet and swung his bag down onto the roof. He pulled out a few extra clips and a can of hairspray, which he tucked into a pocket of his tactical pants.

Nika knelt with the Book of Odin in front of her. She raised her hands to her sides, palms up and flat, channeling the power of the runes to flow out into the world. Erik kept his distance and a respectful silence as the spell went into motion.

Like a golden waterfall, the runes and their power poured out of Nika's body, rising in her heart and exiting through her palms. A pool of gold began around her knees, slowly at first, but with gathering speed it expanded to cover the entire wide expanse of the Stockholmsmässen. The power raced outward until it reached the edges of the roof in all directions, and then it tumbled over, coating the sides of the building until a new puddle, much larger than before, was formed around the base of all the walls. It sank through the ground, continuing to follow the foundations, then turned under the massive building, finally meeting in the middle.

Nika felt the runes burning, felt them spinning and careening out of her soul. She pushed it out, this silent power, until the building was completely warded against any faery creatures who might try to pass. Even now, the wards pinged quietly, notifying her that there were faery beasts nearby.

She realized that she had stopped breathing, and further, that breathing wasn't all that necessary for her anymore. It was a strange thing to have the in-out rhythm of air she had known since her birth suddenly go still. She was nearly distracted by the unwelcome novelty of it, but she forced herself to concentrate. Ingrid would have been pleased.

When it was done and the building was fully protected within her wards, she stopped pushing out the runes and instead set them into place. The energy sank into the stone and metal of the Stockholmsmässen, merging with it seamlessly, invisible to any without Valtaeigr sight. She looked up at Erik.

"You don't see it anymore, do you?"

He smiled softly. "My love, I never saw it at all. I could feel it, though, and I knew that you could do it. I've seen Valtaeigr ward buildings in the past, but never one as big as this."

She rose shakily and brushed off her knees. "I expected it to be harder."

"What did I tell you?" he teased. "Powerful."

She smiled at him, and he went to the edge of the roof on the side near the dignitaries' entrance. She joined him, and they both lay on their stomachs, keeping as low of a profile as they could.

"Are there any inside?" he asked.

"No. Not yet."

"Good. Then we beat him here." He nodded. "The SOG and the Secret Service and all of the other security players have closed down all of the doors but that front one. It makes it easier to have a checkpoint if you only have one way in or out." He inched back. "If Loki comes, it will be right through this door beneath us."

She watched him as he retrieved a sniper rifle, the last of the toys in his bag of tricks. He set it up quickly, professionally. She could imagine him doing this a hundred times on a hundred different missions in the past.

"Will the SOG stop hunting you if the summit ends without a problem?"

"I don't know," he admitted. "And there is going to be a problem – a big one."

"Why? Can't we just prevent him from going in?"

"Loki is one of the most powerful gods we have in our pantheon. He's also riding a shape shifter, and those are easier to kill than to dissuade. We're going to have to burn him to end him. So..." He shrugged. "This won't happen quietly."

"What will you do if they don't stop hunting you?"

Erik flashed her a smile. "Let's get through this mission before we worry about the next one."

She smiled back, sheepish. "Yes, Captain."

Chapter Twenty-Four

They waited on the roof for nearly an hour, watching the press corps jostle for position with the arrival of each new limousine. They watched as nearly all the dignitaries arrived, including their staffs and assistants. The only delegations missing were the ones from Russia and the United States. None of the Nøkken had appeared.

"You don't think we missed them, do you?" Nika asked. She was flushed from the heat due to the lack of shade over their position, and he could see that she was beginning to feel the naked edge of blood thirst again. It was making her restive.

"We'd know if they came around," he assured her. "Your wards will ping if they come within fifty feet of this place."

A large van with the insignia of the Swedish Army pulled in to the parking line, and Kommendör Holm from Special Forces Command stepped out into the light. Erik pointed him out and identified him to her.

"Is that the man who ordered them to shoot you?"

"Yes."

"I don't think I like him."

"I know I don't."

The remaining members of the Huntsman unit exited the vehicle behind him. Erik noted that Lars Bengstrom had the place of Ulf Magnusson for this afternoon's activities. The sight of a good man in the company of such thieves made him sorry. He wondered if Bengstrom was also serving Loki now, or if he'd just been unlucky in his assignments.

He brought his sniper rifle forward, just in case.

The Huntsman unit and their commander arrayed themselves out along the sidewalk, about a hundred feet outside the cordon in front of the building. They were joined by members of the Russian FSB, all of them standing watchfully as the SOG van pulled away and a limousine flying the flags of the Russian Federation pulled up.

Erik tensed. If Loki was going to make his move, this would be the time. He had to go in through that front door, and his target had just arrived. He resisted the urge to double-check his clip; he knew that it was loaded with incendiary rounds, and indulging in his nerves would only make him miss his shot because he was busy fiddling with his equipment.

"Get ready," he told Nika. "This is our guy."

She began chanting softly, her fingertips glowing and the Book of Odin on her lap.

An FSB officer opened the limousine door, and the Russian president emerged. He turned to wave to the crowd and the reporters, and the protesters began to boo. He gave no response. Kommendör Holm strode up to him and offered a handshake, which the president accepted. They stepped together toward the building.

The wards screamed. Nika's whispered chanting became a shout, and she rained rune fire down onto the assembly. The spell she had chosen was one that would sap her strength, but she had enough energy in her to power it. The light from the rune magic descended, and everybody froze.

It was as if time had stopped, but the spell had only paralyzed everyone in her target range. The circle of immobilized people extended out to fill the street and encompass the checkpoint. She shuddered as she fought to hold her targets.

"Go," she gasped. "This is only going to hold humans and faery…"

He thought of Loki's three Draugr companions, and he had no doubt that they were nearby. He stretched out his senses and found them, seated in a car across the street wearing ill-fitting uniforms stolen from some unfortunate security detail. He abandoned his rifle, which was poorly suited to close-quarters combat.

"Hold them," Erik said, and jumped off the roof.

Unlike the last time he'd done this, he was not poisoned with silver slugs in his guts, and he was able to fly again. He made a controlled landing on the sidewalk beside the Russian president. Now that he was closer, and now that he was seeing with his Draugr eyes, he realized that Holm was no human being at all.

"Loki," he said, seeing the hard, white kernel of energy in the center of the Nøkken host.

"Thorvald!"

Agnar, one of the three Draugr in the car, emerged with a pistol in his hand. A flash of rune fire from the roof struck him and knocked him backward, tumbling head over heels over the roofs of the parked vehicles. Erik smiled at Nika's aim. Brevik lurched out of the car next, an automatic rifle in his hands. He was struck with another bolt of runic energy, and he, too, spun away.

Erik pulled the hairspray from his pants pocket and grabbed a lighter with the other hand. He was just preparing to hit the false Holm with his makeshift flame thrower when a bullet crashed into his shoulder, knocking him sideways. It burned like silver.

Dag stepped out of the car and into the street. In the distance, Erik could hear sirens, and he remembered that the rest of Stockholm was not paralyzed. They had to move quickly. He turned his back onto his former friend and ignited the hairspray, shooting Loki's Nøkken vessel in the face.

The creature was paralyzed and could not shift or try to run. It could not even scream. Erik almost felt bad about the way it was unable to do anything but burn... almost.

Police cars entered the spell radius and swerved out of control as their drivers fell under the magic's effects.

Dag leaped on Erik, his feral teeth long and flashing. He buried them in the back of Erik's head, simultaneously stabbing him in both sides, a silver dagger in each hand.

Erik dropped the flame thrower and tried to grab Dag, but he was skewered too effectively to be able to twist or spin. Dag held on, pulling blood as fast as he could, intent on draining his former fellow. Erik reached his pistol, but with Dag holding on the way he was, there was no way he could shoot him without shooting himself, as well.

He went down, silver inside of him in three places, and landed with his face toward the burning shifter.

***

Nika saw the attack on Erik. She could practically feel it. She screamed, and her hold on the paralyzing spell wavered. The Draugr pets in the Huntsman unit broke free of its power and advanced on her fallen lover.

She flung rune power at them, hitting Stenmark and the twins with her only two remaining offensive spells. The rest of her energy had been taken up in the main spell, and now she had nothing left to throw. They staggered from the blows but continued to advance.

She bumped against Erik's sniper rifle.

She had never fired a gun in her life, let alone a powerful weapon like this one, but she was running out of options. She propped the muzzle up on its tripod and flung herself down onto her stomach the way she'd seen Erik doing. Below her, on the street, the Nøkken burned and Dag continued to drain Erik's life force away.

She shook with rage. She would not let him die.

Her first shots went wildly off target, and she nearly screamed with frustration. Grinding her teeth, she tried again. She found a switch on the side of the gun that changed the fire rate, and she held down the trigger, spraying bullets into the SOG van and the Huntsmen.

The bullets ripped into the Draugr pets, and spurts of blood erupted into the air. The bullets caught fire immediately, and one of the Jansen twins went down immediately, his forehead gone. The other twin abandoned his attack, wailing over his fallen brother. That left only Stenmark, who had pulled a silver-edged hatchet from somewhere and was advancing rapidly on Erik. She was just preparing to open fire again when Stenmark spun backward with a bullet in his brain that had come from behind him.

Bengstrom stepped into view, a pistol in his hand. He fired once more into Stenmark's head, then double-tapped the surviving Jansen twin. He stepped to Erik and put another bullet directly into Dag.

Nika tried to find more energy to send another paralyzing spell, but she had nothing left to give. She was still too weak and new as a Draugr to fly. There was no way she could reach Erik unless she simply jumped.

Given the choice between watching him die and a possible broken leg, she opted for breakage and jumped.

Bengstrom was ill prepared for her descent. She landed hard beside Erik and grabbed Bengstrom's arm, wrenching him away from her lover. She could hear a bone snap inside his shoulder, and it matched the one that had shattered in her leg. Her teeth were flashing and she flung him away.

"Nika," Erik managed to say. "The knives..."

She pulled the daggers out of Erik's sides, and he sagged in relief. Bengstrom approached cautiously, holding up his good hand.

"He called you Nika. Are you Nika Graves?"

She hissed at him, her human side completely subsumed by the vampire. He did not come closer.

"Nika, I am a friend."

She bent over Erik and helped him to his feet. Police officers and other humans were running in from the outer edges of the spell, and she was no longer maintaining it. The hold the magic had was beginning to weaken.

"We have to get out of here," she told Erik. He nodded.

Bengstrom came to her and helped her carry him. She growled warningly, but he ignored her. With a common effort, the three wounded Draugr made it to the SOG van, and Bengstrom drove away at top speed, roaring away from the conference center.

Epilogue

They ditched the van about two miles to the east and stole an unremarkable sedan. Bengstrom continued to drive until they reached Ingrid's little house by the shore. The old woman helped them inside and opened the root cellar, where a cask of dreyri waited. The three vampires settled down around it and drank it nearly dry, fueling their healing and recovery.

They stayed at Ingrid's house for days, waiting until the furor over the attack on the summit died away. Somehow, the old woman retrieved the Book of Odin and returned it to Nika. When she was asked how she had done it, she only smiled.

Nika cut the bullet out of Erik's shoulder while Ingrid splinted both Nika's leg and Bengstrom's arm. She left them to the dreyri and their conversation.

"When did you turn?" Erik asked his friend.

"Just after your team was killed," he said. "I was approached by a woman who said she was your friend, someone who said that you would need a proper team again. She offered me the power, and I took it."

"What was her name?"

"She said her name was Sif."

Nika's jaw dropped. "Magda's bodyguard?"

Bengstrom shrugged, and Erik chuckled. He raised the mug he was using to drink the dreyri and held it up.

"Here's to old friends and unexpected rescues," he said. He looked at Nika. "And to old loves made new."

Nika smiled. "Skål."

And then they kissed for a very long time.

*****

THE END

Rune Hunter

Rune Series Book 3

Amelia Wilson / J. A. Cummings

Contents

Prologue
- Chapter One
- Chapter Two
- Chapter Three
- Chapter Four
- Chapter Five
- Chapter Six
- Chapter Seven
- Chapter Eight
- Chapter Nine
- Chapter Ten
- Chapter Eleven
- Chapter Twelve
- Chapter Thirteen
- Chapter Fourteen
- Chapter Fifteen
- Chapter Sixteen

Copyright © 2017 by Amelia Wilson/J.A. Cummings
All rights reserved.

In no way is it legal to reproduce, duplicate, or transmit any part of this document in either electronic means or in printed format. Recording of this publication is strictly prohibited, and any storage of this document is not allowed unless with written permission from the publisher. All rights reserved.

Respective authors own all copyrights not held by the publisher.

Prologue

Summer had come to Sweden, bringing warmer days and the days of the midnight sun. The wildflowers bloomed and gave their scents to the warming breeze coming in from the sea, intertwining with the salt and the water to create a natural perfume. It was idyllic.

In the depths of the forest, a council was underway. A campsite that was normally used by humans had been reserved for the event, and a wall of illusion had been put up around it to conceal the happenings inside. The faery had gathered from all around Scandinavia, something they normally did not do, but the events of the winter had made it imperative.

Ardrik, the Ulfen chieftain, stood in the center of the meeting ground. Around him were arrayed trolls, with their hairy heads and hulking bodies, and the Nøkken, rightly angry. A trio of the Huldra sat together, their comely faces and shapely bodies nearly entwined, throwing sexual tension into the mix because they simply could not contain themselves. There were nisse and tomte, sensed more than seen, and a bevy of witches complaining bitterly to one another about the actions of their sister, the Aesir vessel and witch Ingrid Nilsson.

Ardrik believed that there had never been an assembly like this one, and for a good reason. The faery creatures were too chaotic to accept an order for long, something that made his people, the wolf shifters, eschew their company. It was best, he thought, to get this meeting underway before everything got out of control. Already there were hungry looks from one of the Vittra to the youngest of the Mara, and the mylings were beginning to cry. It was time to get started.

"My friends," he said, raising his voice as only an Ulfen could. The raucous gathering fell quiet, and he heard only the whisper of the wind in the trees. "We are gathered because of the affront of the Draugr to our kind."

The leader of the Nøkken rose. "They killed my brother! Our king, who carried the soul of Loki! They burned him!"

A chorus of anger and calls for retribution rose. Ardrik held up one of his hands and allowed a half-shift, his hand elongating and claws growing from his fingertips. "Yes. Your brother Sigurd was slain by the Draugr Rune Master and her Huntsman."

"Two Huntsmen," one of the Huldra objected, her cow's tail whipping in the open, crumpling her skirt. "We had been told that only one remained, but there were two."

One of the elves waved his hand dismissively. "The second one is of no concern. He is newly turned, and he is no vessel."

Ardrik asked, "Though the death of the Nøkken leader is a great pity, it is only one murder, and from what I have heard, he had it coming. Have there been other actions by the Draugr? Speak."

One of the Mara complained, "They have been harvesting our blood against our will." The crowd grumbled in anger. "They kidnap us and drain us for their evil tastes."

Ebba, the most powerful of the trollkona, rose. "They went into one of our villages and destroyed all of the trolls living there. Trolls, trollkona, even our children – all put to flame."

Again, there was a wild outcry of rage. In the midst of the cacophony, the Nøkken chieftain roared, "They have begun a war against the faery! I demand justice!"

The eldest Mara rose, her black hair wild around her emaciated shoulders, pooling like shadows on the white fabric of the nightgown that she wore. "The Ulfen are our soldiers. Will you rise? Will you protect us against these attacks by the vampires?"

Ardrik looked at his contingent, including his three eldest sons. They dropped to all fours and transformed, their huge wolf-forms quivering in anticipation of the order. He made his decision.

"We rise. Let this be war!"

Chapter One

Nika woke to the gentle sound of a summer rain against the window pane and the warm security of Erik's arm looped around her waist. She was lying on her back, and beside her, his head sharing her pillow, he was sleeping on his side, his arm flung across her with the sort of protective possession that he always showed.

She looked into his face, taking in the tousled blond hair and the pale perfection of his skin. He was the most beautiful man she had ever seen. His lips were ever so slightly pink and his nose was perfectly straight. With his eyes closed, his golden lashes spread out against his cheeks. His fine, high forehead was unlined, and he looked like an angel. Unable to resist, she kissed him.

The first kiss went unnoticed, but the second brought the barest opening of his lips and a sigh of contentment. She smiled and let him sleep.

The windows were speckled with moisture, and the morning light was filtered through rain clouds blowing in from the east. From where she was lying, she could look out the window and see the choppy grey sea, the whitecaps cresting toward the rocky shore. Sea birds wheeled overhead, and she could see boats on the water as the village fishermen went out in search of herring.

Their lives had been quiet since New Year's, when Erik had purchased this cottage on the island of Mellerstön, extending out into the Bay of Bothnia. Theirs was the only house on the island, and if they wanted to reach civilization, then they had to take a boat to the mainland. The nearest big town – if you could call a city of 23,000 people "big" – was Piteå, where they obtained their groceries and picked up the shipments of *dreyri* that Sif sent them from Stockholm. Their isolation was splendid and complete, leaving them with nothing but nature and each other.

In this quiet place, they lived as Erik might have lived before he was cursed, with a few exceptions. Nika was modern enough to require electricity and indoor plumbing, and he complied with her wishes. Their cottage was thoroughly modern in amenities, with a massive generator that Erik and Lars Bengstrom had hooked up in early January. There was a stable with two horses, a boat house and their boat, and a satellite dish so that Nika could still make contact with the world at large via cell phone and computer. It was perfection.

Ostensibly, she was here working on a book about Viking history. Her employers at the Royal Museum of Stockholm had given her a twelve-month sabbatical to do her research. She was halfway through that span of time and hadn't committed a single word to paper. She had been too busy enjoying her new life with her man.

Erik stirred beside her, pulling her closer, his hand cool against her stomach through the thin fabric of her night gown. She put her hand over his, marveling not for the first time how large his hands were compared to hers. Erik was a big man, strong and capable, but he was also loving and gentle. She had seen all sides of him in the time they had been together.

She held up her palm and brought forth rune power, something that came easier to her every day. She let a series of tiny runes dance along her skin. She pressed the runes to his hand, and he inhaled sharply at the unexpected prickly sensation as the glowing runes raced up his muscular arm. She grinned as he opened his eyes.

"No fair," he murmured, still half asleep.

Nika kissed him. "All's fair in love and war."

"Not runes. Runes aren't fair." She kissed the tip of his nose and ended her magical caress. He smiled and opened his bright blue eyes. "You didn't have to stop."

"I thought you said it wasn't fair."

"I did, but I didn't say I didn't like it."

There was mischief in his eyes, and she laughed. "You always wake up happy."

"Why shouldn't I?" He kissed her neck. "Look who I have in my bed."

"Hmm, and I thought I was the lucky one."

Erik smiled. "You can keep thinking that all you like. Don't stop on my account."

She snuggled in against him. "So...I was thinking maybe we could go into Piteå, do some shopping... maybe eat out..."

"We don't need anything, do we?"

"That's not the point."

"Bored?"

"No."

He sat up a bit and looked into her eyes, clearly puzzled. "Then what's the occasion?"

She put her arms around his neck. "Seven months ago today was the day we met in America."

He kissed her, then broke into a smile. "Our souls have known each other for over a thousand years, and you're excited about seven months?"

Unperturbed, she answered happily, "Yes."

He chuckled. "You're adorable."

They kissed again, and he moved away, sliding out from under the covers. The blankets fell away to reveal his well-built frame, the view unhindered by clothing. She wholeheartedly approved. As he walked toward the bathroom, she enjoyed the sight of his muscles flexing beneath his fair skin. He could make fitness models weep with envy.

As he walked, ignoring that fact that he was providing her with a feast for the eyes, he said, "When you get older as a Draugr, you'll have a completely different perspective on time."

"Maybe," she allowed, "but this is my perspective now."

She got out of bed and followed him into the bathroom. He was turning on the shower, testing the water temperature with one hand, facing the door with a grin. He'd known she would come in.

"Okay," he said. "We'll go celebrate our monthiversary."

"Monthiversary?"

"Well, it's not a year yet, so it can't be an anniversary, can it?"

She slipped her nightgown over her head and hung it on a peg on the bathroom wall. When she turned back to face him, his eyes were warm and he was smiling in appreciation of the view. She chuckled. "Were you just ogling me, Mr. Thorvald?"

"Why not? You were ogling me when I was on my way in here."

"I'm not ashamed."

He pulled her into his arms. "Neither am I."

They went together into the heat of the shower, the steam rising around them when he closed the shower door. He tipped his head back to wet his hair, then stepped aside so that she could wet down, too. They stood facing each other, the water running down their skin like searching fingers, warm and soothing.

He took her mouth in a deep kiss, his arms around her. She stepped into his embrace, her breasts pressing against the hard planes of his chest. He dropped one hand to cup the roundness of her buttocks, squeezing gently. She sighed into his mouth, and he moved his kiss to her cheek, then to the corner of her jaw.

Nika tightened her arms around his neck, and he slid both hands down to grab her, pulling her closer to him. She could feel the heated rod of his desire caught between their bellies, throbbing against her, almost as if it was pleading with her to let it in. She swayed, rubbing her body against it, pulling a low moan from his throat.

Nika pressed her lips to Erik's neck, feeling the power of his heartbeat just below the surface. She licked the smooth skin above his vein, savoring the feeling of his pulse against her tongue. He moved one of his hands farther down, his fingertip just brushing against the engorging lips of her sex. She shivered and pulled him closer, wrapping one leg around his, her heel rubbing against the rock-hard muscle of his calf.

He turned her so that her back was against the shower wall, and he pressed her against it. His hands supported her seat and brought her up into position, and she happily allowed it. In truth, he was so strong and in such control that she could not have prevented it, but the thought of resisting him never crossed her mind. He was all she wanted.

She stroked his pulse point with her tongue again, and he breathed, "Do it."

She felt the green Draugr lights ignite in her eyes, and her long teeth descended hungrily. He rubbed himself against her, the weeping head just skimming along her slit, and she needed more. She pushed her fangs into his vein.

He shuddered in pure pleasure at the onset of her feeding and arched against her, sliding home. He reached deep inside her, and as he began to move, she moaned against his neck. She sucked the blood to the surface and into her mouth, wet passes of her tongue mimicking the rhythm he was setting farther down. Erik held her up and rocked into her, impaling her along his thick length again and again. She clutched at his shoulders and urged him to go faster.

He complied, setting a fast pace that neither of them would be able to sustain for very long. She reached her climax first, pulling her mouth away from his neck to cry out, leaving the blood to run in two tiny rivulets down his body. She quaked, tightening around him like a fist, making him groan out her name in a voice thick with passion. She was still clenching in her orgasm when she felt him spill inside of her, his breath catching in his throat.

The wound in his neck had closed of its own volition, but she licked it anyway, lapping up the traces of blood that remained. It made her shudder and very nearly made her come again. The feeling of his hard heat still sliding back and forth inside of her completed the inspiration and she tumbled over the edge for the second time.

He held her tightly as they both regained their senses, their bodies shaking, their hearts full of each other and the love they shared. He kissed her, his tongue gentle against hers as he claimed her mouth. Gently, slowly, he lowered her down to her feet.

She kissed him, her hands running down his sculpted abdomen, memorizing every hill and valley with her fingertips. He ran his hands through her wet hair. When he cupped her head in his palms, she broke the kiss to look up into his eyes.

"I love you, Erik," she breathed.

His answer was in the form of a kiss. Sometimes he expressed himself best when he used no words at all.

***

They finished washing up, dried off, and adjourned to the bedroom for another round of lovemaking before they decided to finally go to Piteå.

They got clean and bundled up against the wind and rain and headed hand-in-hand to the boat house to begin the trek.

Lars' boat, a 50-foot Princess V48 yacht, almost identical to the boat Erik and Nika owned, was anchored in the open slip of the boathouse, and he had politely waited for them to come out of the house instead of charging up and disturbing them. When they entered the building, he stood up from the stool he'd been sitting on, a paperback novel in his hand. He smiled broadly. When he looked happy this way, Nika thought he was nearly as handsome as Erik.

Nearly.

"Well, good morning, lovebirds," he greeted. "Did we get enough sleep?"

"How long have you been sitting out here?" Erik asked him. "Nothing better to do with your time?"

"You might ask Nika what I'm doing here," Lars said. He turned to her. "Everything's loaded."

Erik looked from his lover to his friend and narrowed his eyes. "I haven't lived this long without being able to tell when someone's plotting against me," he warned.

"This is the very nicest of plots, I promise," Nika told him. She kissed him. "Get on the boat, Huntsman."

He looked from Nika to Lars, then back again. There were suitcases on the boat that he hadn't seen her pack. Nika grinned at him, delighted to have caught him off guard. "Fine," Erik relented. "But I'm prepared to defend myself if you try to take my honor."

Lars laughed. "What honor? Get in the damn boat."

Erik climbed on board and gave Nika a hand in, then Lars untied the vessel and climbed aboard. He got behind the wheel and piloted expertly out into the bay.

"There's some paperwork in the cabin you might want to look at," he told Erik.

Erik went into the cabin and found a manila envelope, marked with the emblem of the SOG, the Swedish Special Forces to which he and Lars had once belonged. Nika sat at the table while he opened the envelope and pulled out an official-looking letter signed by Supreme Commander of the Swedish Armed Forces, General Torsten Jung.

"What is it?" she asked.

"It's an apology for letting Holm and his Red Hand buddies fill me full of silver shot."

She frowned, unimpressed. "Nice of him."

"Keep reading," Lars coached.

He complied. "He's also inviting me and Lars back into the SOG as the new core of the Huntsman unit." He glanced up at his friend, who had turned around to watch him from the wheel. "What do you think of this?"

Lars grinned. "I think he can shove that invitation up his ass. We'll get more done to protect people from rogue Draugr if we work on our own terms."

Erik nodded. "I agree." He put the letter back into the envelope. "At least they're not going to hunt us anymore...unless that gets reinstated when we tell them no."

"That's not the Swedish way, is it?" she asked.

"Neither is shooting at their own operatives from helicopters, but they certainly did that," Erik shrugged. "I'll consider it."

"We should go out on our own. Hire some SOG retirees, maybe some mercenaries with Special Ops backgrounds. We'd have to fill them in, of course," Lars mused. "Maybe even turn them. Think you could get into that idea?"

He sat beside Nika and put his arm around her. She leaned into him with a smile. "I'm not interested in starting my own army."

Nika asked puckishly, "What about your own raiding party?"

He groaned. "I'm *really* not interested in that." He looked out the window. "We're not bearing toward the inlet."

Lars shook his head. "Nope."

"We aren't going to Piteå?"

"Nope."

He looked at Nika. "What are you up to?"

"You'll see," she said. "We're heading to Finland. Our passports are packed in the bags."

"Finland?" Erik echoed, surprised. "Why?"

"It's called a vacation, numbskull," Lars said. "Sif let me know that a certain VERY old man has a birthday this week, and we're going to celebrate."

He laughed. "I don't know when my birthday is. It's not like we kept track back in the day, and the calendar has changed so many times since then..."

"Sif said it was right about this time, and I trust her." He turned back to the wheel. "Anyway, she'll be meeting us in Oulu."

"Magda can't have agreed to that," Erik said.

"Magda can kiss my ass."

Nika chuckled. "Sif and Lars are a couple now. Magda isn't happy, but, well... she doesn't own Sif, now, does she?"

Erik snorted softly. "Someone needs to tell Magda that."

Lars looked sheepish. "Actually... Magda is coming, too. We're... well, the three of us are..." Erik laughed, and Lars defended, "Hey, she was angry about being left out, so we included her. Nothing wrong with that!"

"If you say so. I'd rather sleep with a snake than with Magda," Erik said. "Actually, it probably wouldn't be too different. She's just as cold-blooded as a snake, and just as likely to bite."

"She's immortal, not a vampire, and she doesn't do the biting in this relationship." He flashed his Draugr fangs, and they all laughed.

Nika reached into her purse and pulled out a brochure. "We're going to be staying at the Hotel Iso-Syöte, in one of their rental cabins. It's got three bedrooms, so Sif and Lars and Magda can mix and match however they want while we have our own place to sleep. It's got a beautiful view of a national forest, its own sauna, and it's away from the body of the hotel. Very nice. We've got it for a month."

"There are other cottages nearby, but if we keep the screaming to a minimum, it shouldn't be a problem," Lars teased.

He flipped through the brochure. "I've heard of this place. Very romantic."

She leaned her chin on his shoulder. "That's what I'm counting on." She smiled. "Happy birthday, my love."

He kissed her. "You're crazy, but I appreciate the gesture."

"So how many years do you have under your belt?" Lars asked.

Erik considered carefully. "One thousand one hundred and ninety-four, give or take."

"So, you basically fart dust."

He chuckled. "Basically."

Nika smirked. "I love older men…"

Chapter Two

A courtesy driver picked them up at the customs station at the dock and drove them to the hotel, where they registered and picked up their keys. The same driver then delivered them to their cottage, which was on a hill overlooking a dense evergreen forest. He helped carry their bags inside.

Magda and Sif were sitting together on the couch when they arrived. Magda's legs were drawn up onto the cushion beside her, and Sif was lying with her head in her lap. Magda had a glass of *dreyri* in one hand and was dropping the enchanted blood into Sif's mouth from her fingertips, one drop at a time. She put the glass aside when the mortal driver entered the room.

Lars walked to the two women and kissed them both soundly. Erik grinned at Nika and waggled his eyebrows, and she laughed, smacking him in the arm. Since the episode with the G8 summit, she had seen more of his relaxed, casual side, and she'd learned that he was actually blessed with a lively sense of humor. She enjoyed the moments when he let it show.

"Happy birthday, Huntsman," Magda said.

"Thank you." He sat in an armchair, and he pulled Nika onto his lap. She went happily. "I have to say, it's strange to see you outside of Stockholm. When was the last time you left?"

"1823," she replied. "I went to England."

Lars sat beside Magda, lifting Sif's legs so that he could slide beneath them. "Then it's high time you got away from that bar. All work and no play..."

Sif put a hand over his mouth with a twinkle in her eye. "Hush. You talk too much."

Their conversation was interrupted by a howl in the forest below. Sif said, "Strange to hear a wolf in daylight."

Magda's eyes softened for a moment as she focused her mind inward. She said softly, "That was no wolf. That was one of the Ulfen."

Nika asked, "Ulfen?"

"Werewolves."

"Are they common in Finland?"

Erik shrugged. "They're scattered all around the world, like vampires. They began here, like us, but they've expanded their territory."

Lars frowned. "If I'd known this was werewolf territory, I'd have picked a different hotel."

Magda waved her hand dismissively. "No Ulfen will attack a house with four Draugr and a *vala*. It would be suicide." She stroked Sif's hair. "Besides, we have one of the First with us, and four vessels. They'd never stand a chance."

"Do you think they know that?" Lars asked.

Nika asked a more pertinent question, to her way of thinking. "Do you think they care?"

Erik chuckled and put his arms around her. "We'll find out."

"Are we in danger?" she asked, worried.

He shook his head. "No. Magda is right. They wouldn't dream of attacking us here, not all of us together."

Sif said, "But you shouldn't go wandering in the woods alone."

"I wasn't planning to."

"Smart girl."

Erik smiled at her. "Would you like to take a tour of our new digs? See where everything is?"

She nodded. "Sure."

Magda spoke up. "We picked the second bedroom, so stay out of it."

Nika left Erik's lap and held out her hand to him. He stood up and took her hand, then told Magda, "Don't worry. I won't invade your inner sanctum."

They left the room together to explore.

In the kitchen, they found a large keg of old-vintage *dreyri*, and Erik patted it appreciatively. "Magda," he said with grudging admiration. "Nothing but the best."

Nika went to the window and looked out. There were other cottages on the hill, but none were really in her line of sight. It made the building feel private and secluded, as if it was just the five of them and no part of the world existed beyond the walls.

Erik wrapped his arms around her from behind and pressed against her back, his cheek against the side of her head. "Thank you for tricking me."

She chuckled. "You're welcome. I thought it would be a nice thing to have some time with friends, and to celebrate you for a while."

He kissed her ear. "You're very considerate."

"I try."

She loved the feeling of standing with him this way, his body against hers, the two of them fitting together as if they'd been born to do nothing else. She put her hands on his, holding them against her stomach. She was happy.

They stood that way for a long while, wrapped up in each other. Finally, Erik pulled away, leaving her with a kiss on the cheek.

"I'll get the bags and put them in a room."

"Not the second one," she reminded.

"Oh, no. Never."

***

He went back into the main room and collected their bags. They were heavier than he would have expected, and he found himself wondering what Nika had packed. She came out of the kitchen and followed him up the stairs. On the couch, the threesome were absorbed in each other and paid no attention to their passage. He wondered if they would even make it to a bed.

Erik took them to the farthest bedroom from the stairs, one with a window that looked out over the forested valley below. The view was breathtaking, and Nika stood in front of it, shaking her head in wonder.

"I had no idea that Finland was so beautiful."

"All of Scandinavia is like heaven," he said proudly. "We're very lucky to live here."

Another howl rose from the wood, and Erik frowned. "That was closer."

"Why do they howl?"

"They usually do it to gather their pack, or to let their packs know where they are. I'm only hearing one wolf, though, so it seems there's no pack nearby. If there were, they'd be answering."

She sat on the bed. "I guess I should feel reassured that he's alone."

"I do." He smiled at her and sat beside her on the bed. "Don't worry about them. Really. I'll keep you safe."

She leaned over and kissed him. "I know."

Another howl went up from the lonely Ulfen in the forest, and this time another howl sounded in the distance, followed by a third. Nika frowned. "Now there's three of them."

"And five of us." He ran a hand through her hair. "Relax."

"I packed your guns and your silver ammo."

"I'm glad." He smiled. "That would certainly explain why the bags are so heavy."

She rose and went to her own suitcase. She put it onto the mattress, something that was easier with her new Draugr strength, and unzipped it. With a smile, she pulled out the Book of Odin and dropped it on the bed.

"Brought some light reading, I see," Erik teased.

She opened the book, and the runes on the cover danced in response to her touch. She turned a few pages and looked up. "I'm wondering if Odin has anything to say about Ulfen."

"I'd be curious to know…"

Erik stretched out on the bed and relaxed while Nika flipped through the ancient pages. She found many things that distracted her, rune magic that she had not yet learned and secrets that were still hidden from her view. Some pages sorted themselves immediately into a form she could read, and some maintained a densely-packed runic jumble that might as well have been computerized encryption for all the sense she could make of it.

She went all the way to the backboard of the ancient tome, then shook her head. She looked up at Erik with a sigh.

"Nothing?" he asked gently.

"Nothing."

She put the book aside and laid down on the bed next to him, her head on his chest. He put his arm around her. It was familiar, habitual, and comfortable.

"Well, that's a book on magic, and Odin probably wouldn't have included the Ulfen in it, anyway. They're not magical. They just…are."

"Are they faery?"

He considered. "No, not really, although they serve them."

"Serve them how?"

"Some faery are pretty formidable, but the majority of them are easily killed or injured, especially with cold iron. The Ulfen are their bodyguards, I guess you'd say, and their army when they're on the march."

"Are the faery on the march?"

"No, not that I know of." He shook his head. "The Ulfen wander. They roam all through Europe and probably beyond. This call and answer thing, that's just them getting the band back together." He kissed her, then smiled. "Don't worry so much. You have nothing to fear."

She wasn't so certain, despite his repeated assurance, but she held her peace. She stroked his stomach through the fabric of his shirt, feeling the hard planes of his impossibly strong muscles. "If you say so."

"I do say so, and I'm right."

She chuckled. "That would be arrogant coming from anyone else."

He laughed softly. "No. It's still arrogant."

"Self-awareness is half of the battle."

From the outside of the house, a man's voice shouted, "Draugr!"

Erik leaped to his feet, dislodging Nika, who did not complain. He went to the window and looked down at the yard below. She followed him, peering out into the gathering darkness and falling rain.

A man stood there, naked to the waist, his magnificent body glistening with fallen water droplets. He had black hair, thick and wavy, that hung halfway down his back. His eyes glowed amber, and his massive fists curled at his sides.

"Draugr!" he shouted again.

From downstairs, Lars's voice responded. "Keep your shirt on – oh, too late."

Sif giggled.

Erik turned from the window and collected his pistol, checking to be sure that it was loaded with a full clip of silver bullets. Nika asked, "Ulfen?"

"Yes." He snapped the clip back into place. "Stay here."

"Hell, no. I'm coming with you."

He trotted down the stairs, not taking the time to argue. Nika was at his heels with the Book of Odin in her hand. Lars stood beside the door, his SOG training showing, his own pistol in his hand. He looked up at Erik as he appeared in the living room. Erik went to stand against the other side of the door. Sif pulled her own weapon and rose to stand in front of Magda, pulling the Valtaeigr *vala* under guard.

Nika came into the room. Sif pushed her onto the couch, making her sit beside Magda. The *vala* draped her long legs over Nika's, holding her in place.

"Stay here," Sif told her. "Let them handle this."

Nika wanted to protest, but a quick shake of the head from Erik quieted her. He looked to Lars, who opened the door. Erik stepped out, pistol first, with Lars right behind him.

***

Erik stepped off of the porch and took two strides toward the Ulfen male, the pistol trained on the creature's face. The shifter stared back, unmoved. Lars took up position on the porch, his own gun ready.

"What do you want?" Erik asked, speaking in Old Norse.

"Are you the leader of these Draugr?"

He claimed it, by virtue of age and power. "I am."

"Then I came to speak to you."

He nodded. "Then speak."

"The faery have declared war upon the Draugr, starting with the Rune Master and the last Huntsman."

He lifted his chin, and two more Ulfen emerged from the forest. These two were in their wolf forms, as large as ponies and snarling, their lips curled back from teeth that they licked in anticipation of biting.

Their black fur bristled, their hackles raised. They were spoiling for a fight.

Lars demanded, "Why?"

"You Draugr have raided Trollheim and attacked the Mara and the Huldra for your perverse use. You have slain the king of the Nøkken. You have burned and murdered and defiled faery people."

Erik shook his head. "I killed the Nøkken, but I deny the rest."

The Ulfen was unimpressed. "Take our message to your king. War has come, and the Ulfen fight on the side of faery. This is your only warning. From this moment on, it is a fight to the death."

"We have no king," Erik protested.

"Then take the message to yourself, for the fight will start with you." He unballed his fists, and then his body moved, flowing like water as it changed from human to wolf in less than a heartbeat. He put his head back and howled, and in the forest, a dozen answering calls replied. The Huntsmen stood their ground, and then the Ulfen turned and raced back into the woods from which they had come.

Erik backed up to the porch, not lowering his gun, and climbed up the steps until he and Lars stood shoulder to shoulder. Lars looked at him.

"Well," he said softly. "This should be fun."

Erik chuckled wryly. "There goes the neighborhood."

Chapter Three

The three women looked up expectantly when Lars and Erik came back inside. Lars shut and locked the door, and Erik tucked his pistol into the waistband of his blue jeans, snug against the small of his back. Magda released her hold on Nika, and she rose to meet him.

"What's this all about?" she asked, concerned.

"The faery have declared war on the Draugr," Lars answered for him. "Something about raids on Trollheim and kidnappings and such."

Erik looked at Magda. "Do you know anything about this?"

She crossed her legs and examined her fingernails. "Maybe."

"Damn it, woman, this is no time to be coy!" he snapped. "If you know who is behind this, tell me now."

"You do not order me, Erik Thorvald," she responded icily.

Lars interceded. "How about we all ask each other nicely? I know that you two tend to butt heads, but this is a bad time for dissension in our ranks. Right? We've got to hang together."

Sif put her hand the nape of Magda's neck, and a private telepathic conversation linked them for a moment. Finally, Magda softened, her own hand moving to rest on Sif's knee. She sighed.

"Of the original forty First Draugr, eight remain alive, including you. Three of them work as mercenaries and were in the employ of Loki, as you recall."

Erik nodded. "Brevik, Agnar and Dag."

"Yes. The remaining four – Bjorn, Halvar, Kjeld and Olaf – have formed a new raiding party."

Nika frowned. "And they're raiding the faery?"

"Apparently."

"Why?" Erik asked.

Magda shrugged. "For the joy of killing, or perhaps for the blood. Faery blood brings a magic all its own."

"How long have you known about this?"

She looked at Erik without expression and told him, "Since they began, two years ago."

He frowned. He wanted to ask why he had never been told, but he knew the disdain that Magda had for him. She would never volunteer anything for his benefit. To be fair, as well, he had to admit that his duties with the SOG had made him difficult to contact. Two years ago, he had been in Afghanistan. He sighed.

"First order of business is to get them to stop," Erik said. "So, we need to make contact with the Ulfen Alpha and arrange a parley before this gets out of control. Is the Alpha still Ardrik?"

Sif nodded. "Yes. And he now has three sons who are of age, ready to start packs of their own. The one who was just here? That was his oldest, Alaric."

"Who are the other two?"

She shook her head. "I don't know their names."

Erik nodded. "We also need to make contact with the remaining First."

Lars raised an eyebrow. "We?"

"All right, *I* need to make contact with them."

"Seems fitting," Magda said, "considering your place in Hakon's group."

Nika looked at her, curious. "What place is that?"

The *vala* smiled. "Didn't he tell you? Erik is Hakon's son and heir. He was his second in command. Now that Hakon is dead and gone, that makes Erik the king of the Draugr, if such a thing exists."

Erik looked uncomfortable. "I'm no king."

"Ah," Sif said, "but you could be."

Magda chuckled cynically. "Although it's hard to be king of people whom you've betrayed."

"I have betrayed nobody." He sounded weary. Nika suspected that this was an old argument, and that he was tired of repeating it.

"That all depends on whom you ask," Magda said. Sif squeezed her hand on the back on her lover's neck again, and the *vala* fell silent.

"Do you have a way to get in touch with the rest of the First?" Erik asked Magda. "I know you supply *dreyri* to all of them."

She went to her purse and retrieved her cell phone, then tossed it to him. He caught it and looked through the contacts. Magda walked to his side and plucked the phone out of his hand. She swiped her finger across the screen until she found what she was looking for, and she gave him back the phone.

He looked down and set his jaw. He glanced up at Magda, who stood over him and smirked in triumph. He glared at her. Nika wondered, not for the first time, about the things the two of them had been through together. She knew there had to be a story there.

Erik looked up at Nika briefly, and she saw the briefest flash of hurt in his eyes. She frowned. He went into the kitchen with the phone, and Magda sat beside Sif again, a look of supreme satisfaction on her face.

***

He stood with the phone in his hand, staring at the photograph it displayed. It was Nika and Rahim Amari, the false face of Loki's Nøkken vessel, leaning toward each other in a fancy restaurant. They were clearly seconds away from a kiss. He told himself that the Nøkken were seductive creatures, and that Nika could not be blamed for falling under its spell. His mind concurred with the assessment, but his heart still ached.

Damn you, Magda, he thought. *Why did you have to show me this?*

He angrily swiped his finger across the screen and dismissed the image. He heard someone approaching, and he caught Nika's delicate scent in the air. He tried to keep his body language and his voice casual as he greeted her.

"Hello, Chosen," he said. Despite his best efforts, he sounded tight.

She went to him and put a hand on his arm. "Is everything all right? What did she show you?"

He sighed. He went back to the photograph and showed it to her. "This."

Nika's mouth dropped open, and she stammered, "I can explain. It's not..."

"I don't care," he said softly. "It doesn't matter now. Loki's vessel is dead, and anyway, you were under his spell. I don't blame you."

She looked relieved. "I would never betray you, Erik."

He kissed her. "I know." He wished he were as certain as he sounded. Irritated with the situation and with himself, he dismissed the photograph and went to the list of contacts. "I need to make some calls. You're welcome to stay if you'd like, but it'll probably be boring."

Nika kissed him. "I'll be in the living room."

He smiled at her as she left, and then he scrolled through the list of names and numbers. He encountered an entry for the First named Bjorn, one of the four who had resumed his raiding ways. He dialed the number.

The phone rang several times, then Bjorn's deep voice came on the line. "Magda! To what do I owe the honor?"

"This is Erik Thorvald."

There was a stunned silence on the other end, and then Bjorn asked, "What happened to Magda?"

"Nothing. She let me borrow her phone so I could call you."

"She *let* you? She hates you."

"I know, but this is important."

Bjorn's tone turned hard. "What do you want, Thorvald?"

"I need to meet with all of the First."

The other vampire laughed. "Why would we meet with you? You and your Huntsmen betrayed the rest of our brothers. We won't walk into your trap."

The Huntsmen were the reason only eight of the First still survived. Everyone knew that there had been a time when Erik had hunted his former brethren, back when he had first become Veithimathr. It had been the only way to stop the massacres that were attracting too much human attention. Nobody in the Draugr community realized anymore how close they'd come to living the old trope of the mob with torches and pitchforks.

Erik scowled. "I assure you, if I was planning a trap for you, I would be much subtler. Gather the First, and we will meet in Snake Eyes. Neutral ground."

"When?"

"Three days, at sunset."

Bjorn grunted, "I'll tell them, but I can't guarantee that they'll show up."

"Be persuasive. I know you have it in you." He ended the call and returned to the living room. He tossed the phone back to Magda, then told the assembled immortals, "I'm going to be meeting with the First at Snake Eyes in three days."

Magda tucked the phone back into her purse. "If you destroy anything in my club, I'll take it out of your hide."

"We're not going to fight. We're going to talk."

She pursed her lips. "With the First, everything ends with fighting."

"Not this time." He turned to Nika. "Would you like to take a walk with me?"

She frowned. "With those werewolves out there? Is that safe?"

"We can't live under house arrest," he said, shrugging. "Besides, even the Ulfen are too smart to attack in the middle of a human settlement. Nobody wants to attract that kind of attention."

She looked uncertain, but she nodded. "All right."

They left the house hand in hand. The sun was high overhead, bright and cheerful. He probably would not have risked a walk in the darkness. He listened to the wind through the trees, straining to hear the telltale sounds of paws, but there were none. Apparently, the Ulfen had gone back to wherever they had come from.

They walked down the hill toward the body of the resort, where the sound and scent of people beckoned. He could feel her looking at him, curious, full of questions that for once she wasn't asking. He took a deep breath and stopped walking. She stopped, too, and turned to look at him.

"There's a lot I need to teach you," he said. "I haven't been giving you very good instruction on the ways to be a Draugr."

She smiled. "I'll learn as I go. I have time, right?"

"Perhaps." He stroked the soft skin of her hand with his thumb. "In case you ever need to be self-sufficient, though, there are things you need to know how to do."

"Like what?"

"Like hunt."

Her smile faltered. "Hunt? Can't I just drink *dreyri*?"

"*Dreyri* will keep you alive and keep the magic in your belly, but if you want to be truly strong, you need the life force in blood from a living human. If we are really at war, and if the Ulfen are going to attack, you will need to be as strong as you can be."

"But you drank strong *dreyri* when you needed to power up instead of human blood," she said, confused. "Why can't I do the same?"

"I am older than you, and as Veithimathr, I have been enchanted to allow me to live with less of the human life force than other Draugr. You haven't had the benefit of that spell and will need more life force than the *dreyri* can give you. Until now, I've been supplementing you with my own. You also may not always have access to *dreyri*, so you'll need to feed the old-fashioned way." He canted his head, considering her. "Are you uncomfortable with the idea?"

She shifted on her feet, her uneasiness plain in her face and in her body language. "I don't really relish the idea of being a parasite."

He bristled and corrected, "Predator. Not parasite."

She looked away. "Sorry."

He softened his face and his tone. "Sorry... I hate being called a parasite. I really fucking hate it." He took a deep breath. "Regardless, you will need to learn how to feed in case you're on your own, if we get separated, or if you can't get to *dreyri* when the thirst hits."

He knew that she had not really experienced the agony that true thirst could bring, and he hoped that she never would. It was an agony no Draugr ever wished to experience.

She met his gaze steadily, squaring her shoulders. "What do I need to do?"

"I'm going to show you," he said. "Learn from what I do. It will look and feel like cheating, but it's all about the blood."

A strange expression fluttered across her face, somewhere between ire and fear, and she asked, "Does feeding involve sex?"

He told her honestly, "Sometimes. Sometimes that's the only way they'll let you close enough. The sex, if it happens, is a means to an end."

She turned away and took a step or two down the hill. She turned back. "Are you seriously going to pick up another woman while I'm sitting there?"

"To drink her blood? Yes. To take her to bed? No." He walked down to her. "And then you're going to pick up a man and you're going to do the same."

"But... we're together," she protested. "I don't want to... I don't know how to..."

"That's where the learning comes in. I'll teach you how to attract prey, how to hold them and then how to release them. I won't turn you out on your own until you've gone through the process with me a few times."

Nika shook her head. "Why do I feel like we're talking about having a threesome?"

He smiled a little ruefully. "Because we sort of are." He held out his hand. "It's honestly just about the blood. If we can avoid sex, we will."

"And if we can't?"

"Then we enjoy it while it's happening, and we chalk it up to experience."

"I don't know if I like that."

He sighed. "Your life as a Draugr will be very different to your life as a human being. You have to be ready to change to meet that new life." He took her hand. "This is necessary, Nika. I don't want to share you with anyone, but I want you to know how to feed yourself if something should happen to me."

Her eyes widened. "What do you mean? What are you talking about?"

"The Ulfen and the faery are a formidable foe, and if they are truly on the march, then anything can happen. Even my luck might run out. We all can die, if it is our time."

Nika shook her head. "No. Don't talk about that."

"Not talking about it won't prevent it from happening, if that's what's meant to be." He squeezed her hand and kissed her. "It may even be that if we prepare for it, it will never happen. I just want to be certain that you'll be all right, if the worst should come."

They continued walking toward the main hotel. She had her head down. "I still don't like to talk about it."

"I'm sorry. I'll let it drop, then."

They walked in silence for a moment, and then she asked, "What do I do?"

"Just watch me, and listen."

The hotel bar was filled with guests and their visitors, many of them attractive and fit, all of them well-to-do. Erik walked into the room with Nika at his side, and he scanned the crowd for likely marks. A pretty but slightly heavy brunette sat at a corner table by herself, her face sad. A young man, probably on his gap year, was at the bar, sitting alone and watching the women, his face buried in a mug of beer. His eyes were somewhat glassy, and Erik thought he would be easy to take.

He asked Nika in her mind, *Do you see the college boy?*

Yes.

He's our mark.

She looked at him, startled. *I thought you'd want to feed on a woman.*

He smiled. *I've fed on men before, when the occasion warranted. It's not my preference. I love the taste of a woman, but this one is for you.*

She looked around. *What about her?*

He looked where she indicated. It was the sad brunette. *If we can't set the hook in this one, sure. We'll give her a try. Come on.*

They walked together to the bar. Erik nodded for Nika to get on one side of the young man, and he sat on the other. Erik gestured to the bartender, and he came to collect their drink orders.

"Aquavit," Erik requested. "Red wine for the lady, and another round for our friend, here."

He could feel Nika's eyes on him, studying every move and every word. He knew she had a quick mind; it wouldn't take her long to figure out the subtleties.

The human man looked at Erik. "Thanks, man," he said.

"No problem." He held out his hand. "My name is Erik, and this is my partner, Nika."

The man accepted the proffered handshake. "Valtteri."

"A pleasure to meet you," the vampire said, looking into the young Finn's eyes. He did not release his hand, and the man made no move to take it back. Pinpoints of green Draugr fire flared in Erik's eyes, and Valtteri's mouth dropped open. Erik was certain that Nika, especially with her Valtaeigr abilities, could see the waves of power transferring from him to the mortal man.

"Likewise," he said. When Erik finally released his hand, he turned to face Nika, his eyes raking her from head to toe and back again. He smiled. "Hello, there."

She smiled, and Erik nodded to her when he saw tiny green sparks in her eyes, too. She would be stronger and more certain with practice.

Her attempt at mesmerism may have been feeble, but Erik had primed the man's mind to be receptive. Valtteri smiled widely and took Nika's hand, kissing it.

"You are absolutely beautiful," he told her.

The bartender arrived with their drinks, and Erik paid with cash. He told him, "Put my friend's drinks on my tab."

"Yes, sir." The bartender glanced at Nika, then back at Erik, and he walked away.

Valtteri took a drink of his beer. "So...are you two here on holiday?"

"We are," Erik nodded. "We're just getting away from Sweden for a few days. It's my birthday, you see."

"Ah! Happy birthday."

"Thank you." He looked at Nika and nodded again. She took the signal.

"I've been promising him a special trip all year," she told Valtteri, her hand on his arm. A slight golden glow of runic magic pulsed under her palm, and the young man shivered. Erik approved of the unexpected improvisation. "I want to make it memorable for him."

"Mem – *Oh*."

Erik leaned closer and pushed a tendril of his Draugr power into the mortal's mind, a slick finger inserting itself into his thoughts, encouraging him to go down the avenue they wanted him to travel. "We thought maybe you might like to help with that."

Valtteri turned a surprised look toward Erik, and the Huntsman raised an eyebrow and nodded, smiling. The Finn looked at Nika next, and she sidled closer to him, as well.

"I want to make this trip...*very*... memorable."

She glanced at Erik and thought to him, *Am I coming on too strong?*

He's a twenty-something male and you're a beautiful woman, Erik replied. *There's no such thing as too strong.*

"Wow. Me? Uh...with... both of you?"

Erik smiled at him, his blue eyes twinkling, the faintest hint of Draugr fire dancing in his irises. "Is that a problem?"

The young man looked like he thought he'd just won the lottery. "Oh, no! Not at all. It's just... I'm not...."

"Neither am I."

"So, what...."

Nika leaned forward and kissed the young man, her hand cupping his face. He returned the touch eagerly. She broke the kiss and leaned back, whispering, "He likes to watch."

Valtteri's face nearly split in two from his grin. "Well... wow. I have a room here... Do you..."

Erik put his glass down, the alcohol untouched. "Let's go."

They rode up the elevator together, Valtteri standing between the two vampires. Nika ran her hand down his chest, her eyes locked with his, the Draugr lights shining. Erik smiled. She was a fast study, just like he knew she'd be.

When they reached the appropriate floor, the young man produced his key card and handed it to Erik. While Valtteri put his hands on Nika, kissing her and cupping her round buttocks, Erik opened the lock. The three of them went inside, and then Erik secured the door behind them.

I don't want to go to bed with him, Nika told him telepathically. *What do I do?*

You've got him on the hook. Now put him to sleep and make him forget all about us.

But... how? She sounded near panic.

I will do it. Watch from inside my mind.

He could feel her piggy backing onto him as he gently interceded between his woman and their prey. Valtteri looked up at Erik in confusion as the much bigger Draugr pushed him onto the mattress.

"I thought you said you weren't gay," he accused.

"I'm not." He smiled and brushed a hand across the mortal's forehead. The green lights danced in his eyes again. With a voice more mental than physical, he said, "Sleep..."

Valtteri fell back onto the bed, his head lolling. Erik followed him down, whispering in his ear.

"You will remember an incredible sexual experience with a beautiful woman, and that her boyfriend simply watched. It was erotic, and it was exciting, and it left you tired."

He pushed his power into the mortal's mind, conveying the words as it went. Valtteri moaned and gripped the bedclothes in his hands, lost in the fantasy his mind had been told to create.

Erik sat up and held out a hand to Nika. "Do you see?"

"I know what you did, but I don't know if I can," she admitted.

He smiled. "Practice makes perfect. Now he's ours. Open his vein."

Nika knelt beside the moaning Finn, and she looked up at Erik uncertainly. He smiled encouragement and nodded to her, letting his eyes gain the brightly glowing green of his full vampire self instead of just the sparks that had burned there until now. His teeth lengthened in his mouth. She followed his lead, and her Draugr came forward. She leaned over the young man's throat and sniffed delicately at the corner of his jaw.

"Here?" she asked.

Erik stroked her back with one hand. "Wherever you like."

He could sense her hesitation, but she mastered her nerves and pressed her mouth to the man's throat. He knew how it felt to have a pulse pounding against thirsty lips, and he knew that if she let it, the feeling would take her. She just needed to let her new nature take its course.

She pushed her fangs into the man's vein, and Erik could hear the soft puncturing sound of tooth penetrating skin. Then there was the scent of blood and the sound of Nika's mouth, her lips and tongue working at the bite. Her eyes were closed, and she was lost in the feeling of the feeding. It was the sexiest thing Erik had ever seen.

He took Valtteri's hand and sank his own fangs into the soft inside of his wrist. The Finn's blood splashed onto his tongue, and he shivered at the tingling pulse of it. He drew once, twice, then licked the bite wound, healing it shut.

Nika was clutching onto their prey, pressing her mouth harder into him, forcing her fangs deeper. She was still too young to have developed much in the way of blood control. He gently pulled her away, and though she fought him at first, she eventually obeyed.

He stroked her hair and kissed her, reveling in the combined tastes of blood and her. She clung to him, and her fang grazed his lip, bringing a scarlet drop to the surface. She sucked it away, her mouth and tongue doing great damage to his self-control.

Close his wound, he told her mentally, because his physical voice would have failed him. *Lick it and it will seal. Your saliva will heal it.*

She backed away from him, releasing his lip with great reluctance, and bent to obey. She crouched over the sleeping Finn like a cat and sealed the bite wound she had opened. She licked the last of the blood away, lapping all traces of it from the man's skin, her shoulders low and her hips high.

Erik put his hands on her hips with gentle pressure, bringing her back to herself. She rose, pulling away from their prey, and she turned in his arms. The kiss she gave him was full of passion and promises, and his body sprang to respond.

Not here, he told her, although he would have liked nothing better at that moment than to roll Valtteri onto the floor and to commandeer his bed. *Not now.*

She nodded her understanding and pulled away from him, glancing down once at the outward evidence of his excitement. She grinned, biting her lower lip.

"Hold that thought," she told him. "I'll race you back to the cottage."

"I'll win," he told her.

She grinned wider. "Prove it."

He took her by the hand and hauled her up into his arms. Proof would be easy to come by. He opened the door to Valtteri's balcony, and with his love clutched to his chest and his need aching for her, he took flight.

***

He brought her to a secluded park in the city, a place where darkness was deep. She smiled at him. "This isn't the cottage."

"It's better," he said, and kissed her.

His kiss was insistent and deep, his tongue probing into her mouth to dance with her own. She wrapped her arms around him, and they lay on the soft grass, intertwined. He broke the kiss long enough to pull her shirt over her head and to fling his own aside, and then he returned, his body on top of hers.

She moaned softly when she felt him hot and hard against her thigh, and she pulled him closer. Clothing was an obstacle that was easily overcome, and soon they were locked together, rocking in an endless rhythm. He was so strong and powerful, and his loving went so deep that she was breathless. She could feel him with every nerve ending in her body, and her spirit sang along, vibrating along their Chosen cord. They were connected in every way but one.

He pressed his face to her shoulder, and in that instant, his beautiful neck was bared. She called down her fangs and pushed them into him, piercing the vein and bringing his sweet blood to the surface. She licked and suckled the wound she was making, and he moaned, bucking against her as his excitement skyrocketed. She crashed around him like a wave, shuddering in her pleasure, and he followed right behind.

They stayed that way, utterly interconnected, for a long while. Finally, reluctantly, she pulled her teeth out of his salty flesh, and he sighed in contentment. He wrapped his arms around her and pulled her closer, lifting her off of the ground as he sat back on his heels. She put her hands on his shoulders and looked down into his rapture-moist eyes. He gave her a slow smile, and she kissed him, still feeling him deep inside of her.

"This is heaven," she whispered.

He shook his head. "No," he breathed. "It's better."

Chapter Four

They spent the next two days in the comfort and safety of their rental cottage, drinking their *dreyri*, the lovers enjoying one another at sensuous length. On the day he was to meet with the First, Erik rose early to begin his trip to Stockholm. He left Nika sleeping in their bed, her scarlet hair spread like a pool across her pillow, her naked back smooth and flawless. He was tempted to kiss that back, to touch her perfect, milky skin, but he didn't have time for such delightful distractions.

He had arranged a private flight to Stockholm, and he had a plane to catch. He packed his weapons and ammunition and headed down the stairs.

Magda was sitting on the living room floor, her eyes closed and her legs folded. She was meditating, and he tried to move through the room without disturbing her. Her eyes snapped open, though, and she stood in one fluid motion.

"I'm coming with you," she said.

He raised an eyebrow.

Magda scowled. "Don't argue. And don't think I'm coming because I have any loyalty to you. I want to make sure you idiots don't ruin my club."

"Fine. Come with, then."

She picked up her purse, and he held the door for her. The courtesy shuttle to the airport was already idling outside. The driver opened the door for them, and Erik waited while Magda slid into the back seat. He sat beside her, and the driver closed the door and returned to his seat.

"What will you do if they don't answer your summons?" Magda asked him.

He shrugged. "Hunt them down, I suppose. That is what I was made for."

She smirked. "Indeed. And you've been very good at it in the past."

"I know."

The driver glanced at them in the rear-view mirror, eavesdropping. Magda glared at him, and he turned his eyes back to the road. Erik chuckled.

She turned that glare onto him. "What are you laughing at, Thorvald?"

"You. You're so irascible."

Magda raised an eyebrow. "Irascible? That's an impressive word for a walking beefcake like you to use."

He laughed. "I'm full of surprises."

"You always are. And they're not always the good kind."

Erik considered her for a moment, a thousand years of memories running through his mind. Softly, he said, "It hasn't always been that bad, has it?"

She turned her green eyes onto his face, and something in her gaze softened for the first time in centuries. "Not always," she admitted. "When you're not in Sweden, it's much more tolerable."

He shook his head and turned away, looking out the window at the passing city lights. The airport was not far from the hotel, and from there it would be a short flight to Stockholm.

He wondered how many of his remaining comrades would be there for the meeting. He hoped that at least Bjorn would show up, since he was responsible for bringing the raiding party back into existence. He needed to talk to them about their attacks on faery settlements and the consequences for those actions.

If Magda was correct, they were raiding to obtain faery blood. He knew from past experience that the blood of the Huldra and the Mara was highly addictive. One of his late brothers, Ivar, had developed a fixation on those two races of faery women, nymphs who seduced mortal men to their demise in the wood. He had nearly caused a war with the faery in the late 1540s.

Blood had been the currency used by vampires in those days. Now they used regular money, but obviously blood still flowed, from the simple pints that he obtained from the blood bank to the bottles and kegs at Snake Eyes. The immortal Valtaeigr sitting in the seat beside him was the main supplier of enchanted blood, that vintage that gave the Draugr a little something extra in the form of magic.

Back in the day, when the curse had first been laid upon Hakon's band, the unadulterated blood from a human vein had been enough to make a Draugr powerful. Now, like in an arms race, they needed to drink the heavily-enchanted *dreyri* to remain strong enough to stay on top of the heap. The older the vampire, the stronger the blood had to be, and when the young ones obtained strong *dreyri* intended for their elders, they responded like humans with a system full of narcotics. They became temporarily strong but locked in the chains of addiction. So it had been with Ivar and the blood he stole from the Mara and the Huldra.

Now it sounded like the First had gone into business creating *dreyri* using faery blood as the base component. It would be like humans who manufactured street drugs like bath salts and krokodil – they were making something that was nearly too powerful to control. If they weren't stopped, not only would they be bringing the wrath of the faery down onto the Draugr community, they would be seducing their own younglings into a life of addiction and misery.

He wondered how many faery had been taken, and how much *dreyri* had been created. For that matter, he wondered how many humans had been bled to create the drink he himself imbibed on a regular basis. To skip his daily dose was to court headache and fatigue, and now that he was thinking about it, he supposed that was the first sign of withdrawal.

Such a slippery slope, he thought. *You fall and never realize it until you're at the bottom of the hill.*

"Magda," he said suddenly. "Where do you get the base material for the *dreyri* that you sell?"

He didn't say the word *blood* out loud, because the driver was still eavesdropping.

His companion looked at him, surprised and annoyed by the question. "From appropriate sources."

"What is an appropriate source? And how many of those 'appropriate sources' did you have to use to fill the keg back at the house?"

She gave him a hard look, and for a moment, he thought she wasn't going to answer. Finally, she said, "Don't worry your pretty head about it, Huntsman. Just keep drinking it like you always have and never mind my sources." She looked away. "You've never cared before."

He felt vaguely sickened. "It never occurred to me to ask before."

"Slow, aren't you?"

"Apparently."

They rode to the airport without another word, and when they boarded the plane, Magda curled up beneath a blanket and watched out the window instead of acknowledging him in the other seat. He fiddled with his phone, playing a mindless app while letting his mind wander.

The Ulfen were an enemy to take seriously, and he would have liked to have avoided their involvement. The faery must have been severely aggrieved to have involved them, since deals with the Ulfen always came at a high price. Their alpha, Ardrik, had a reputation as a shrewd negotiator, and he had an eye toward improving his pack like a general improved his stockpile. Erik wondered what price the canny wolf had asked for his pack's protection.

The landing in Stockholm was smooth and untroubled, and they found a cab easily. On the ride to Snake Eyes, Magda finally spoke again.

"Forty-seven humans are exsanguinated for each barrel of *dreyri* that I create. That means twenty-four for kegs the size of the one in the cabin. I get the blood from a supplier. I don't ask where it comes from before that."

"Who is your supplier?"

Magda pursed her lips. "Some secrets, Huntsman, are not for you to know."

He considered himself foolish for never having asked these questions before. He had always assumed that the blood came from willing donors, but the mathematics of scale begged the question of how many people would have been required, and how many human beings had died, creatures that he and the rest of the Veithimathr had been sworn to protect.

The Veithimathr had been created in the same year that the first *dreyri* began to circulate among the Draugr. The gods, and the *vala*, acted in mysterious ways.

Magda had been the apprentice to the *vala* who had bewitched Erik and his brothers, making them into Huntsmen. She had been at the elbow of Inga, the wise woman who had created the potion that allowed the old gods to take up residence in new bodies. She had seen and learned everything in her many centuries of existence, and she knew things that he would never hope to understand. The ways of the *vala* were the ways of women, and men were not to know them.

Nika, though, could learn.

He looked out the window and endeavored to keep his body language casual, despite the ringing of his own pulse in his ears. He was on to something important here.

"The Veithimathr have almost all been destroyed," he began.

"Yes, I know," Magda said sharply. "Good job, there."

He rankled but refused to rise to the bait. She knew how to push his buttons. "I was wondering... how have the Valtaeigr been doing? How are your numbers?"

She sighed. "Decreasing."

"Why?"

"Well, those of us who are immortal cannot bear children to normal men, and as you know, Draugr are infertile. That leaves us very few options as mates. Our numbers decrease the old-fashioned way – the old ones die, and not enough new ones are born. We are forced to rely on reincarnation and try to find the souls when they return. It is easier said than done."

He nodded. "The same is true of vessels. The gods' souls attach, but then scatter when rebirth happens. The vessels need to find one another again. They're not always reborn in the same place."

"Yes."

"When you find newborn Valtaeigr, what do you do?"

She shifted in her seat. "Not your business, Huntsman."

"Perhaps not, but my Chosen is Valtaeigr..."

Magda interrupted, "She will be trained."

"By whom?"

"Well, it started with Ingrid, didn't it? She just needs to go back, if you'll let her. You seem to be spending a lot of time distracting her."

Erik felt foolishly complimented by the comment. "Well...it's her choice."

"She needs to be trained. We need as many *valas* as we can get." She looked at him, finally, with a serious expression. "Sif is going to talk to her while we're gone. Your Chosen may be taken from you, Huntsman."

"I have no trouble with her being trained, but if you try to take her from me, you will have a fight on your hands," he warned.

Magda smiled and shrugged. "I'm not concerned."

The cab parked outside the club, and Erik paid the tab while Magda strolled to the doors. She punched the code into the electronic lock, then let it scan her thumbprint. The door lock opened with a click.

"Very high tech," he said, approving.

"It's a very modern facility," she said, opening the door. "Try not to break it."

"I can't promise anything."

He followed her inside and sat at the bar while she went through the process of turning on the lights and waking up the HVAC system. He helped himself to a bottle of her finest vintage of *dreyri,* one of the ones on the top shelf. She went by him with a click of her tongue as she went to check the back door.

"You're paying for that."

He took a gold piece from the reign of Harald Hardrada out of his jeans pocket and put it down on counter with a click. "Good enough for three bottles?"

"It'll do."

"Four?"

"Don't push me."

He laughed.

Sunset was a long way off, and there was money to be made. Magda opened the doors, and soon a few young Draugr trickled in. He moved from the bar to a corner table, where he could drink and watch the entire room without obstruction. A newly-turned Draugr male came in, stealing furtive glances at Erik when he sensed the power of one of the First. He was skinny and dark-haired, with a gaunt face and a hipster man bun. He carefully avoided making eye contact.

Erik shook his head and sipped his *dreyri.* That young one was not destined to last for long.

As the day wore on, more Draugr came and went. Some brought their mortal hangers-on, lovers or friends or possibly blood slaves. They came, danced, and drank, and all of them gave Erik's table a wide berth. He didn't mind.

He drank his way through all three bottles of ancient *dreyri*, enjoying the tingle of the magic on his tongue and the way it burned in his throat. He savored the taste, his mind turning back to the question of Magda's sources, and he tried to determine if there was any faery blood in the mix. He could not tell.

He looked at his watch. Still three hours to go until nightfall.

Chapter Five

Nika sat on her bed with the Book of Odin on her lap, reading through the pages she could decipher. Learning how to wield rune magic was an ongoing project, and she doubted she would ever be finished with her studies.

Sif knocked on the open door, and Nika greeted her with a smile.

"Come in," she said.

Sif sat beside her, curling her long legs up beneath her on the mattress. The statuesque blonde moved like a cat, all sinew and muscle beneath a beautiful exterior. Nika was intimidated by her, although she would never have admitted it.

"Are you learning much, young one?" Sif asked.

Nika turned a page. "This book is full of things to learn. I will be learning from it every day of my life, I think."

Sif chuckled. "That is a lot of days. You are immortal now, after all." She ran her hand through her own thick hair, pushing it back over her shoulder. She rarely wore it down. "Tell me, would you like to learn more than the things that are in that book?"

"I love learning," she answered honestly. "Of course I would. Are there other books like this?"

"Odin is not the only god to make a record of his magic," she said. "In fact, I know where there is a library full of books just like this. Would you like to know where it is? Perhaps you could visit it one day, when you are done playing with your Huntsman."

Nika raised an eyebrow and looked at her. Sif was sitting very close to her, almost uncomfortably so. "You have your own Huntsman to play with, I thought."

"Lars?" She chuckled. "He is a pleasant distraction, and I turned him, yes, but he is no Huntsman. Only one of those men remain. Only a Huntsman is worthy of a Valtaeigr. Lars is temporary at best. A hobby, if you will."

She closed the book and rose, putting a little distance between the two of them. "I'm sorry to tell you that the only remaining Huntsman is spoken for, then." She put the book on the dresser, then said, "No, actually, I'm not sorry to tell you that. Not sorry at all."

Sif laughed throatily. "You are an amusing child."

Nika rankled. "Thank you, I think."

"You haven't said whether you would want to see this library."

"I would be interested," she said warily, "If Erik were to bring me there."

"Erik doesn't know where it is. That is a Valtaeigr secret."

"And you'd be willing to show me, I take it?"

Sif chuckled again. "I would be happy to show you many things."

She felt hunted. Nika turned suspicious eyes onto the other Draugr woman and said, "What are you doing, Sif?"

Her response was a clear, bell-like laugh. She uncurled her body and rose from the mattress. "Just making conversation, little one. You are so untrusting."

Sif went back down the stairs, and Nika could hear Lars' voice in the living room, as clear as if he were in the room with her. There were benefits to having Draugr hearing. "Where have you been?"

"Chatting with Nika." She heard a shift of furniture cushions; either Lars had stood up, or Sif had sat down. "She's a bookworm."

She stopped eavesdropping and pulled on her boots. She was suddenly feeling very confined in this house and needed to get some fresh air. She went down the stairs and into the kitchen, intent upon getting a little *dreyri* to start her night.

The keg was missing. The counter where the thing had stood was bare, and there were no cupboards large enough to hold it. She went into the living room, where Sif and Lars were sitting, his head in her lap. They looked up at her when she came in.

"Where is the *dreyri*?" she asked.

"Oh, it's gone," Sif said. "We drank it all."

"All of it? But..."

She smiled, her teeth showing. "We've been very thirsty."

Lars said, "It was gone when I got up this morning. That's why Magda went with Erik - she's going to get more and bring it back."

Nika very much doubted the story. Even at their thirstiest, the five of them could not have consumed thirty-one gallons of blood in such a short amount of time. Even Erik, who was the heaviest drinker of them all, never had that much. She looked at Sif, who was smiling blandly and innocently at her.

"If you're thirsty," Sif said, her voice light, "I guess you'll have to go hunting."

Lars started to sit up, but Sif put her hand on his shoulder, pressing him back down. He looked surprised, as if this was the first time he'd realized that his girlfriend was physically stronger than him.

Nika put on her jacket. "Fine. I'll be back."

Lars objected, "There might be Ulfen."

"I guess I'll have to take that chance." She looked at Sif, the two of them measuring each other. Something very unpleasant was going on.

"Have fun," the other woman said, her tone airy and false.

"Sif -"

She silenced his burgeoning objection with a kiss, still holding him in place. Nika said, "Leave him alone, Sif. You're threatening him."

Sif looked up, surprised. "Why would I threaten my own lover?"

Lars said, "Let me up." She allowed it this time, and he sprang to his feet. To Nika, he said, "I'm going with you."

"Don't leave," Sif said, and her tone was one of command.

The former SOG officer looked at her without a word, then opened the door for Nika. She walked out, and he followed close behind, shutting the door on Sif's objections.

They walked down the path toward the hotel, keeping their silence for several moments. Finally, Nika said, "She's up to something."

"Yes. Both she and Magda. I don't trust them."

She looked at him, surprised. "But you sleep with them."

"Of course I do. Have you seen them?" He smiled. "That's just sex, Nika. Trust is something entirely different. I trust very few people in this world."

"Do you trust me?"

He looked at her, almost as if he were deciding on his answer. "Yes. I trust you. And I trust Erik. Those two? Not a chance."

They continued walking, and just before they reached the building, she said, "You must have found it difficult to believe what he was, when you were told."

He thought back. "Not really. You learn a lot of secrets when you're in Special Forces, and some of the things I've learned about certain elected officials pale when they're compared with being an honorable man who happens to drink blood to survive." He glanced at her. "It must have been harder for you."

"No," she admitted. "It was actually surprisingly easy."

"Well, you're one of the wise women, and a vessel to boot. You probably always knew, subconsciously." He opened the door to the hotel lobby and held it for her. "Ladies first."

They walked together to the bar, where Erik and Nika had encountered Valtteri. She glanced around to see if he was there, but the young Finn was nowhere to be seen. She was relieved.

Lars escorted her to a corner table, and they sat together, looking out over the assembled mortals. The night was still young, so there weren't many people yet, but there was enough of a crowd to make for interesting people-watching.

At the far side of the bar room, in the corner booth diametrically opposite their own, a dark-haired man with a high-planed face sat brooding, his large hands cupped around a mug of coffee. He was exotic and beautiful, with an air of other places and other times about him, a sort of cloud of mystery that clung to him. Nika had never seen a man like him before.

"Who is that?"

Lars looked. "I don't know. Some guy."

"Don't you think there's something...different... about him?"

Her companion looked, and shrugged. "He's a tourist, probably."

She fell silent, keeping her suppositions to herself. She could not deny the way this strange man shimmered in her mind. She wondered if she was seeing him with senses that Lars did not share, and that thought was strangely appealing. She rose.

"I'm going to go say hello."

Lars sat back. "If you want."

She walked across the room, aware that Lars was keeping an eye on her movements. He was acting as her bodyguard, she supposed, and the knowledge that he was there to keep her safe made her feel bold.

The man at the table looked up at her when she approached, his eyes an almost impossible golden-brown, rimmed with the longest, blackest lashes she had ever seen. His body, wrapped in tight denim and a black leather jacket, was the body of an athlete, and a tattoo sleeve peeked out from beneath his right cuff. She smiled at him, and he looked at her almost warily.

"Hi," she said in English. "Is this seat taken?"

He glanced at Lars, then responded in the same tongue, mildly accented. "No. Please sit down."

She slid into the booth with him, taking up a position across from him, her back to Lars. Her new companion could see the other Draugr over her shoulder, and he spent as much time looking at him as he spent looking at Nika. She wanted to change that.

"I'm Nika," she said, offering her hand.

"Dominic." He accepted the friendly greeting, albeit stiffly.

"You're not Finnish."

He shook his head. "Not entirely. My father is." He sipped his coffee, his movement slow and deliberate. "You're American."

"Yes." She crossed her legs and leaned back, letting one scarlet curl fall over her shoulder to land on her breast. He watched the motion of the fall, and his eyes stayed for a moment. She smiled. "What brings you to Oulu?"

He dragged his gaze back up to her face. She could feel its weight almost physically. "My family is visiting the resort," he told her. "My father wanted us to come, so here we are."

He smelled of fir trees and cold air. It was an enticing scent. Now that she was closer to him, she could get a better reading on the energy that swirled around him. He wasn't Draugr, but he certainly was no human. She reached out a tentative finger of energy, intending to stroke his aura to gain a better sense of him.

To her surprise, the seeking tendril was batted away by one of his own. She started at the snap of it, and he frowned.

"That was rude," he scolded her.

"I just... I wondered..."

"I am not your next meal, vampire," he growled. He rose and tossed some money onto the table.

She said, surprising herself, "You don't know what you're missing."

He pulled down the collar of his white T-shirt, exposing a keloid scar on the side of his neck, ragged and painful-looking. "Yes, I do." His eyes turned even more golden, and the hand holding his collar lengthened and changed before her eyes. His fingers were curled, but she could see a long claw growing on his thumb, and the dark hair sprouting on his skin confirmed her guess.

"You're Ulfen."

"Yes," he growled, his voice deepened by his partial change. "And you are my enemy."

She put out a hand and stopped him before he could leave, aware that he would not attack her with so many mortal witnesses. "Why am I your enemy? What have I done to you?"

He pulled away with a snarl. "Don't lie to me. You know exactly what it was...Rune Master."

She watched as he stalked away, his wolf aspect pulling back and hiding once more beneath the beautiful human veneer.

She was full of questions.

***

Nika and Lars found a mortal woman in the hotel lobby who was open to their suggestions, and they fed from her together in her room upstairs. The way Lars fed was less sexual than Erik's way, more animal and frightening. It left Nika feeling uncomfortable in the aftermath.

They walked back to their cottage in the silent darkness, neither of them speaking, the taste of the blood they'd stolen still coppery on their tongues. The only sound was the crunch of their boots on the gravel path and an occasional rustle in the forest as a night bird took flight. Once she thought she heard a fluttering overhead, like the wings of a bat, but when she looked, there was nothing there.

She wondered how Erik's talk with the First was going, and whether the others had come to Snake Eyes after all. He had admitted to her that there was a chance they would stand him up. Her mind flashed to dangerous scenarios of the First lying in wait for him outside the bar, ready to ambush him, and she worried that he might be walking into a trap. She clenched her hands in the pockets of her coat, trying to force down the fear. *Erik is strong and crafty*, she told herself. *He'll be fine.*

He had nearly died not long ago when the SOG had filled him full of silver bullets. She shivered at the thought of facing eternity without him.

Their path took them past the forest's edge, and in the gloom beneath the trees, Nika thought she saw two pinpoints of amber light. As quickly as she had seen them, they were gone.

"Lars," she said. "There's something in the woods."

He looked, but did not stop walking. He moved around her so that he was between her and the trees, protectively guarding her. A twig snapped somewhere close, and he pulled a pistol from an ankle holster.

"Walk faster," he told her. "Run if you have to." He was staring into the trees, his face intense and frightening.

"I'm not leaving you."

"I'm right behind you."

A dark shape moved in the shadows, and then a gigantic wolf burst from the forest, teeth flashing, its amber eyes glowing. It leaped onto Lars, who fired into its body. The wolf yelped, but the wound was only glancing, and it landed on the young Draugr with all four feet. Lars struggled against it, and the wolf's gleaming fangs snapped, trying to grab his throat.

Nika called on the rune magic inside of her and summoned a handful of golden energy. She threw it at the wolf, and the magic splashed against its side, setting its black fur on fire. The creature released Lars and dropped to the ground, rolling in the dirt to extinguish the flames. Lars staggered to his feet and emptied his gun into the wolf's head.

The silver bullets did their work, and the creature fell dead at his feet. Its body shifted from wolf to man as they watched.

"Are you all right?" Nika asked.

Lars nodded. "Yeah." He bent down and examined the body. "So, this is an Ulfen."

"Yes, and there are probably more. Let's go!"

"We have to hide this body."

"Leave it. The others will take it." She pulled on his arm. "We have to get to the house. We're not safe out here."

He hesitated, then let her pull him toward the cabin.

Chapter Six

It was finally sunset, and Erik was growing impatient. He sat in his corner booth, watching the door, and all that came through were young Draugr and their hangers-on. They gave him a wide berth, clustering against the opposite wall, staying as far away from him as they could. He had to admit that he enjoyed their fear.

Magda brought him a glass of *dreyri*, and he could feel the tingling of the powerful enchantment through his fingertips when he accepted it. He raised an eyebrow quizzically.

"On the house," she said. "Just testing a new vintage."

"Why would you give me anything?" he asked. "That's not like you. What are the strings attached?"

She smiled at him in manifestly counterfeit innocence. "No strings, Huntsman. Why would you ask me such a thing?"

He watched as she walked away, heading back toward her office. She was up to something, but he had no idea what. He decided not to drink the *dreyri*, and he pushed the glass toward the center of the table.

The door opened, and the effects of the magical ward shimmered through the room. The chatter of the younglings fell silent as the First arrived.

Bjorn was the first one through the door. He was a mountain of a man, thick and muscular, with a wiry black beard and wild black hair. He was dressed unassumingly in denim and flannel, but there was no mistaking his power. His eyes already glowed green with the preternatural Draugr fire as he strode into the room. He scanned the faces until he saw Erik, and when he did, he smiled.

Halvar and Kjeld came in next. It had been literally centuries since Erik had seen them. They looked as if they had kept up with the times, especially Kjeld, who was glued to a smartphone while he walked. Olaf followed them, his white blond hair a startling contrast to the black leather that he was wearing, complete with dog collar.

The four approached him, grabbing chairs and joining him at his table. Several of the young ones, intimidated by the arrival of such powerful and aged vampires, scurried for the exit, beating a hasty retreat.

Erik nodded to them. "Brothers," he said.

Bjorn snorted. "We have not been brothers for a very long time... *brother.*"

"The others are coming," Halvar said. "We should wait until they get here."

Kjeld put his phone away. "They're about ten minutes away." He sat in his chair and leaned back, his blue eyes narrowed as he studied Erik's face. "I didn't want to meet with you, Huntsman, not after the way you killed Ingmar."

"Ingmar was murdering humans and being lazy and messy about it. He was attracting attention that we don't need."

Bjorn snorted again. It was an unattractive habit. "You were protecting the humans, not us."

Erik said firmly, "I protect both."

"By killing the other First?" Halvar asked. "Are you trying to make yourself the last man standing?"

"That is not my intention."

The door opened and the ward sang again, and the three First who had been in Loki's company at the summit arrived. Agnar, Brevik and Dag entered together. Agnar snarled at a young Draugr couple and appropriated their table and chairs. The three dragged them over to the conference and sat down.

Dag spoke first. "I should be upset with you, Thorvald. You interrupted a very lucrative contract for us. Because of you, we didn't get paid."

Agnar agreed. "A dead Nøkken is a Nøkken who doesn't pay his bills."

He was unmoved. "Perhaps you should have better taste in clients. And I believe I have the right to be upset with you, too. Silver daggers don't feel very nice."

Dag shrugged. "Neither do bullets to the head."

"Touché."

"I suppose I should be grateful that your little pet forgot to take my head."

Erik smiled. "Yes. You should."

Brevik crossed his arms over his chest and leaned back in his chair. "Why did you call us here?"

Dag was staring at the glass of *dreyri* on Erik's table, his eyes beginning to glow with desire. Erik cupped his hands around the drink pulled it closer, letting the magic tingle in his palms, stating his ownership of the powerful liquid.

"The faery are on the march."

Halvar threw his head back and laughed, a round, loud belly laugh that drew stares from the other denizens of Snake Eyes. Erik did not share his mirth and simply waited for him to be done. Finally, when he could speak again, Halvar said, "So the faery are marching. What does that matter to us?"

"They have declared war on the Draugr, and they've gotten Ardrik's pack to fight it."

Dag looked irritated. "Faery and Ulfen are nothing compared to us. We were chosen by the gods to live forever. We are more than they are. We are more powerful than they are."

"Perhaps," Erik allowed. "The Ulfen are not to be taken lightly, not when they attack as a group. And a faery war can bring the attention of mankind down around our heads, and if that happens, I promise you, our world will burn and no gods will be able to save us then."

"I understand you, Thorvald," Olaf said. "You betray us for the humans because you fear them. You are appeasing them."

"I have protected humanity because that is what the gods charged me to do when I became Veithimathr." He did not miss the subtle insult, and he answered it. "I fear no one."

Brevik spoke next, his voice flat. "If the faery are marching, they will draw attention to themselves, not to us. We need only lay low and wait for the fighting to be over, just as we did back when the humans destroyed the last dragons."

"It won't be that easy this time," Erik warned.

"Why not?" Bjorn demanded.

"There are more humans now than in the dragon days, and everyone has a cellphone." He gestured toward Kjeld. "Everybody carries a camera and a direct link with YouTube. Nothing happens in this world anymore without a witness."

"Then we kill the witnesses."

"Dead witnesses leave bodies," Erik pointed out. "Dead bodies raise questions."

Bjorn gestured dismissively. "One of my turned younglings owns a crematorium in Oslo. We just take the bodies there. Humans go missing all the time, Thorvald. Always have, always will."

Erik was tiring of the argument. "I'm told that you've been raiding faery settlements. Why?"

"Why not?" Halvar demanded. "Faery blood is powerful, and it fetches a nice price."

"If we can conquer them, then they are at our mercy," Bjorn contributed. "This is how it has always been. Have you forgotten? You were a conqueror once, too."

Erik set his jaw. "I have learned that conquest is not always the best path forward."

"Spoken like a coward."

He leaped across the table at his former friend, and Bjorn met him halfway. Their clawed hands grasped at each other's throats, and the table between them smashed into kindling. Erik and Bjorn, evenly matched, grappled in the wreckage.

Halvar seized a large splinter of wood and raised it high, intending to bring it down into Erik's unprotected back. A flash of spell fire knocked the improvised stake out of his hand, and he turned in disbelief to Magda, whose outstretched hand still sparkled with Valtaeigr power. She gestured with that glowing hand, and the shattered glass of *dreyri* that she had given to Erik reformed, the shattered pieces knitting back together, the enchanted blood flowing back into the glass. She opened her hand, and the glass floated into her grasp.

Halvar hissed at her. "Valtaeigr bitch!"

Erik finally gained the upper hand, straddling Bjorn and throttling him with his own collar. Bjorn bucked beneath him, but Erik stuck fast, squeezing until the other Draugr's face went purple. He released him abruptly and stepped back, saying, "I am no coward."

The rest of his former brethren were staring at him, judging him. He needed to make a show of strength, and the shimmering in his peripheral vision from the *dreyri* that Magda had recovered gave him an idea of what to do. He knew that the others could sense the power in the drink as strongly as he could. He held out his hand, and Magda put the glass into it. He drained the glass in one gulp, the *dreyri* burning like fire as it coursed down his throat. His eyes swam, and stars flickered at the edges of his vision as the enchantment reached deep into his soul. He shuddered.

Dag glared at Magda. "That was linnorm blood," he accused. "You said it was gone."

"I saved a bottle for a special occasion."

Erik was reeling from the effect of the magic he had consumed, realizing too late that his forgotten caution had been well-advised. He staggered backward a step, and Magda approached him, her eyes boring into his. She was chanting.

The words were nonsense, but they made every nerve explode like fireworks, and he shook from head to toe. She came right up to him and put her hands on his chest, stacking her palms directly over his heart. She looked into his eyes and finished her chant, sneering the last word and pushing her power into him. He dropped to the ground like a sack of coal.

Bjorn, still gasping for air, looked down at his fallen foe. "What did you do to him?"

The Valtaeigr smiled. "You'll find out. Take him with you when you leave." She turned to walk back toward her office, then stopped and said, "And you're going to be paying for that table."

***

Nika had just settled back down on the bed with the book when she felt a horrible jolt surge through her. It was a lancing pain, and it made brilliant light flash behind her eyes. She gasped with the anguish of it and dropped the book, clutching her chest. Her heart felt as if it would explode, and every breath was agony. She tried to rise but her legs were like water, and she fell to the floor.

The sound of her collapse rang through the house, and Lars and Sif came running. Sif knelt beside Nika and helped her sit up while Lars hovered uncertainly, completely out of his depth. "What's wrong with her?" he asked.

"I don't know," Sif admitted. Nika leaned against the bed, and Sif cupped her face in her hands, her middle fingers pressing against her temples. She stared intently into Nika's eyes. "The Chosen bond has been broken."

"What?" Nika gasped. "How?"

Sif looked grim. "Either Erik has chosen to break it, or he has been killed."

Nika dissolved into wracking sobs. "No! No, no, no...he can't be..."

Lars grit his teeth. "Are you sure?"

"That's the only way a bond like that breaks."

Sif embraced Nika. She was howling in her grief, keening for her lost love. Tears streamed from her eyes, and they were tinged pink with blood. She gripped Sif's arms like a lifeline and wept.

Lars dialed a number on his cellphone, and all three of them could hear the other line ringing over and over. Erik's voice mail picked up, and the sound of his recorded voice was like a knife through Nika's heart.

He turned off the phone and stalked away, leaving Nika to mourn in Sif's arms.

***

Lars went downstairs and picked up his phone again. This time, he dialed Magda. The ringing lasted nearly as long as it had with Erik's number, but before voicemail picked up, she answered the call.

"*Hallå*," she said.

"Magda, what's going on?"

He could hear her walking through a noisy room, then there was the sound of a door closing. She must have gone into her office. "The meeting with the First did not go well."

"What happened?" he demanded.

"There was a fight, which I expected. Erik was outnumbered. He..." She sighed. "Lars, I'm sorry. Erik is gone."

He squeezed his eyes shut. "Who did it?"

"I -"

"*Who did it?*"

There was a startled silence on the line, and then she said, "All of them. All of the First fell on him. I didn't see who landed the final blow, if that's what you're asking."

He put his hand on his hip and lowered his head. "Are you coming back?"

"Yes. I just have to get this place cleaned up first."

"Let Benny do it. That's what you have a bartender for."

"I have a bartender to pour drinks, dear," she said. "And I've got a full house tonight."

"Magda -"

"I will be back soon. Don't worry."

She hung up on him, and he looked at the phone in disbelief.

His friend was dead.

Chapter Seven

She passed the rest of that night in stunned silence. The initial pain was gone, replaced by a bone-aching numbness that filled her with emptiness. Her lover was dead, and she could not accept it.

Dawn came, then sunset, and dawn again. She stayed in her room, sitting at the window and staring out at the driveway, hoping against hope that she would see him coming back to her. He never came.

Magda returned after three days, and Sif and Lars greeted her warmly. Nika could hear their voices in the living room downstairs. She leaned her forehead against the window pane, and a tear slid down her cheek, but she was too deeply in shock to notice.

There was a soft knock on her door. Nika neither turned nor responded, so the knock was repeated. Finally, Magda opened the door and let herself inside without an invitation. She came to Nika and stood beside her, looking out the window at the woods below. They were both silent for a long while.

"He died well," she finally told her. "He was fighting like a tiger to the last."

Nika's throat tightened. "Why did they attack him?"

Magda sighed and sat on the bed. "The Veithimathr had made no friends in the Draugr community," she explained. "For centuries, Erik and his brethren had hunted down and killed the First, along with any other vampire who stepped outside of their rule set. The other vampires had never agreed to live by those rules, though, so it was unjust. The Draugr all consider the Huntsmen to be traitors."

"He was no traitor," she said softly.

Magda continued as if she hadn't heard her. "Now all of the Huntsmen are gone. It is the end of an era." She put a hand on Nika's shoulder. "I know someone who can help you, child. You've been left alone with almost no idea how to survive as a vampire. I can take you to one of our sisters, a Valtaeigr who was made into a vampire by her lover. She can guide you. Would you like that?"

Nika wiped at her eyes. "I don't know." She took a deep breath, trying to settle herself, but it made her chest hurt and she could feel another crying jag beginning. "I just don't know."

She kissed Nika's cheek and said, "Well, think about it, dearling. I know what a bad position you're in, abandoned as you are without your sire."

Magda was almost out of the room when Nika stopped her with a question. "Did he suffer?"

She paused. "No, Nika. He didn't suffer at all."

***

When the night had nearly faded into dawn and the others were tangled in slumber in their shared room, Nika left the cabin and walked alone toward the wood. There were Ulfen in those woods, and probably faery creatures who wished her ill. She desperately wished that she could encounter one of them on the foot path through the trees. Maybe, if they were violent enough, the pain she was feeling would somehow end.

She had given up everything to come to Sweden and be with Erik. They were supposed to have had forever. Now that he was gone, she simply couldn't wrap her mind around the thought of life without him. His absence had created a hole in her heart that she was certain would never be filled again, ever. The ache of it was constant, a dull and weighty pain that dragged her down into listless staring. Life would never be the same without Erik. Life would never be life without Erik.

She was weeping again, but the wind dried the tears on her cheeks as they fell. The air was crisp tonight, feeling more like autumn than summer, and the chill seemed suitable. A sunny day or a warm, sensual night would have been insulting in the wake of Erik's death.

She heard something on the path behind her, a soft sound that barely registered above her own aching heart. She stopped and turned, but there was nothing there when she looked. There were only shadows. Nika took a deep breath and turned back into the wood, continuing her walk.

Another sound reached her, but this time it was beside her, to her left, just off of the path. Something brushed through the trees, because she could see the branches of a low-reaching fir tree swaying. She stopped.

"Who's there?" she asked.

"If my father finds you, you'll be killed," a rich masculine voice said from the shadow.

She strained her eyes, trying to see, but for some reason she could not explain, her usually infallible Draugr sight was failing her. She wrapped her arms around herself.

"Who is your father?"

Something dodged across the path right in front of her, but she couldn't see anything at all. There was a whiff of magic and musk, and then the moonlight seemed to shimmer into solidity, revealing Dominic, the Ulfen from the resort. He seemed to take form out of the silvery illumination, suddenly real where he'd been only a whisper before. He was still wearing his leather jacket and blue jeans, and the bright light from the moon gleamed off of his jet-black hair.

"My father is Ardrik," he answered. "Our alpha."

She squared her shoulders. "Well, introduce us so we can get this over with."

She lowered her head as if she meant to walk through him, and he caught her with his hands on her shoulders. "What are you doing?"

He sounded honestly confounded. She pulled away from his hands. "I want to see your father. Where is he?"

Dominic looked into the woods, then shook his head. "No. This is wrong."

Nika began to cry. "Just take me to him! Please!"

"He will kill you," he repeated.

"I know!" she sobbed. "I want him to!"

The shifter looked into her tear-streaked face and desperate eyes, and he put his arm around her. "No. I'm not sure what's happening here, but...no. Just, no."

He steered her around to face back out of the forest.

"Go back to your cabin, Rune Master. Life is not to be thrown away so easily."

She shook off his arm and turned toward him, her eyes glowing green and her long fangs ready to bite. "What do you know about it? What do you know about anything? My Huntsman is dead. I want to join him."

She fell into broken sobs, and Dominic stood awkwardly, staring at her in confusion. Finally, he spoke, and it was as if he was thinking aloud. "I have no love for the Draugr. I have no reason to want you to live." He frowned. "What do you mean, your Huntsman is dead? Who killed him?"

"The First," she answered, wiping her eyes with the heel of her hand. "They murdered him in Stockholm."

"Why?"

She crossed her arms again, holding her stomach against the bottomless pit of dark despair inside of her. "He wanted to make them stop raiding the faery."

Dominic raised an eyebrow. "He sacrificed himself to save them? Why?"

She let her fangs sink back into their hiding places above her normal teeth. "Because he was a good man."

"He didn't want the destruction of the faery?"

"He didn't want the destruction of anyone." She began to shake again. "He only wanted to live in peace and quiet in our house by the bay. He didn't want to hurt anyone."

The Ulfen looked skeptical. "He was a Huntsman and a soldier," he said. "I doubt he didn't want to hurt people."

"Just because he was good at it doesn't mean that he loved it. He was actually very kind."

"To his own kind."

"To everyone."

He took a step backward, and the moonlight shimmered over him again, obscuring him like a cloak. "Get out of the forest, Rune Master. Go home." The magical camouflage completely hid him, leaving only his voice. "I am sorry for your grief...but go home."

She heard him leaving through the woods, and she dropped to her knees, her head hanging as she cried.

***

He woke to raging thirst and a pounding head. His eyes were hot, as if coals and not irises lurked behind his eyelids. He put his hands over his face, and the effort of moving his arms was immense. He was so very weak.

Erik could hear water against wood, and he was rocking slightly. He had been a Viking long enough to know what waking on a ship felt like. He tried to sit up, but his head struck wood very quickly, and the hard rap to the head helped to clear his senses.

He was in a wooden box. It was just large enough for him to lie in stretched out, and beneath him was a layer of pine boughs and furs. He pushed up against the wooden plank above his head, and it would not budge. He pushed out against the sides of the box, but to no avail. He was just too weak to break through, and something in the pine boughs was keeping him rooted in place. He couldn't even turn onto his side.

His throat was parched, and his lips were cracked. He was desperate for blood. His belly twisted on itself in its emptiness, and he felt hollow.

It was the hollowness that helped him to remember. He remembered the fight in Snake Eyes, and Magda's hands above his heart, and the shattering of the Chosen bond. The pain of that breakage still echoed in his chest now, and he pressed his hand to the hurting place within his chest.

Why? He was unable to form any more of the thought, but that seemed to cover the subject of his focus well enough.

The ship pitched, and his box slid a few inches in the direction of his feet. He remembered high seas in the drekars of his youth, the pitching and rolling that sent most of his raiding companions to the edge to empty their stomachs into the water. He closed his eyes, and for a moment, he was back in those long-ago ships, heading for Scotland or to Spain. The memory of those raids and the pleasure of conquest stirred in his mind, and he smiled. Those had been good days.

He thought that he should have been taking a dimmer view of these memories, but he could not remember why. His mind was fuzzy, and he was confused. Something was missing, but in his addled state, he could not say what it was. It was something precious, though, and despite the fact that he could not name it, he ached for its absence.

The pine bough scent rose around him, and he inhaled the fragrance deeply. It was the smell of the old days, of fir trees and forest hunts. Within him, Vidar stirred, and the two of them, god and vessel, united in dreams of hunts and horseback rides through meadows of high grass and brushwood.

***

Lars found Nika on the forest path, lying on her side with her knees drawn up to her chest, staring ahead in utter despondence. He crouched beside her and put a hand on her shoulder. She did not respond.

"Nika," he said. "Come on. You have to come in. Erik wouldn't want this."

At the sound of her lover's name, her green eyes shifted to look up at Lars. They filled with tears. "I miss him," she said.

He gathered her into his arms and held her. "I do, too. But the ones who did this are going to pay, I promise you."

She sat like a stone in his embrace for a long moment, then finally returned the hug, clinging to his neck for comfort like a child. He stroked her back and held her tightly.

They stayed that way for a long while, and finally he rose, picking her up in his arms. Without a word, he carried her back to the cabin.

He brought her to her bedroom and put her on the bed, where she resumed her fetal position. He put his hands on his hips and considered her for a long moment.

"Nika." He could not get her to look at him, and he sighed. "Nika, I know you're hurting, but this isn't going to help anything. Giving up isn't going to bring Erik back. You haven't fed in days. Let me get you something to drink."

She shook her head. "I don't want any."

He sat beside her. "I know it hurts to lose him. Erik wouldn't want this. He would want you to continue to live, to be happy…you have to know that."

She turned away from him. He gave up and went downstairs.

Sif looked up when he entered the living room. "How is the princess?"

"She wants to die, I think."

"I'm not surprised. She was his Chosen."

He shook his head. "So?"

"When the Chosen bond is broken when one of the partners dies, the survivor pines away. She's not going to survive him for long." She turned a page in the magazine she was reading. "They can reunite in their next incarnations and try again."

Lars looked at her, aghast. "You're just - we have to do something. We can't just let her go."

"There's nothing to do," Magda said, strolling out of the kitchen with a glass of *dreyri*. She handed it to Sif. "The Chosen bond is very powerful, and the damage caused by its loss is just as great."

He frowned, looking at the drink in her hand. "Where did that come from? The keg went missing."

"I reserved it," she said, sitting beside Sif. "I didn't want to share any longer."

"You reserved it," he echoed, shaking his head. "Wow."

He went into the kitchen and found that the keg had been returned to its former place on the counter. His distrust of Magda skipped another notch. With a sour expression on his face, he filled two glasses, one for himself and one for Nika. He took them both upstairs.

Nika was still lying on the bed when he came in. He sat beside her and nudged her. "Get up." She did not respond, so he repeated the light shove and spoke again, this time more stridently. "Get *up*."

Reluctantly, she obeyed. He trusted that the scent of the *dreyri* would pique her interest, but she seemed immune to its delights. He pushed one of the glasses into her hand.

"Drink this, or I'll force it down your throat."

She finally reacted. Her face creased in an angry glare, and her eyes flashed green. "You wouldn't dare!"

"Wouldn't I?"

They stared at each other for a long moment, and she finally took him at his word. She swallowed the enchanted blood, then put the glass aside. "Happy now?"

"Immensely." He drained his own glass, then said, "The keg is back on the counter. You have two choices. You can feed yourself, either from the *dreyri* or by hunting, or I will force feed you. Understand?"

She turned away from him. "You're not very nice."

"I don't have to be nice. I just have to keep you alive."

"Why? Why do you have to do that?" She looked back at him, and tears were standing in her eyes again. "Why can't you just let me go?"

"Because I promised Erik that I would keep you safe, no matter what." He picked up her empty glass. "I mean to keep that promise, even if you fight me."

Her voice quavered as she said, "I hate you."

"Go right ahead."

He took the empty glasses back down into the kitchen, heavy-hearted but determined.

***

Dominic found his father in their pack's den, lounging with his mate. Ardrik was half-asleep, and he barely noticed when his third son rejoined them. His mate, though, the lovely Ardella, looked up and flipped her blonde hair out of her eyes, smiling.

"Hello, Dom," she said.

"I met the Rune Master."

That was enough to shake Ardrik out of his contentment. He sat up straight, unseating Ardella from using his chest as a pillow. "Did you kill her?"

Dominic hesitated. "No."

His father's eyes narrowed. "No?"

"She was despondent. She wanted to die." He realized now how stupid it sounded, and how displaced his notion of honor was in the view of his pack. His father was going to murder him. "It didn't seem right."

Ardrik rose, towering over Dominic. He was intimidating, and Dominic had always been afraid of him. He took a step back.

"It didn't seem right?" his alpha echoed.

"No, sir."

Ardella tried to salvage the situation. "Why was she despondent?"

Dominic looked at her, then back to his father. "She said that the last Huntsman was dead, killed by the rest of the First in Stockholm."

"Why would they kill him?" Ardrik asked, dubious.

"I don't know. She didn't say."

His alpha nodded. "This is good news. This is very good news. I will take this to our contact." He shifted into his full wolf form and raced out of the den.

Ardella rose and slinked over the Dominic, putting her hands on his chest, rubbing them beneath the open folds of his unzipped jacket. "You've done well, my dear," she said. "If the Huntsman is dead and the Rune Master is in mourning, our job is that much easier." She buried her hands in the black hair at the nape of his neck, and she smiled up into his eyes. "Maybe I can reward you."

He took a step away from her, disentangling himself from her touch. "You are my alpha's mate," he said.

"So? He's not here, and I'm not your mother."

"It's wrong." He took another step back. "And my father would kill me if he found out. I'm already out of his favor. I don't want to make things worse."

Ardella laughed airily and shrugged one slender shoulder. "Suit yourself. This was your one chance."

One corner of his mouth turned down. "I'll learn to live with that."

She laughed again and strolled toward the back of the den where the rest of the pack were resting. She found Alaric, his older brother, who was sleeping in his wolf form. Ardella shifted into the four-legged version of herself and curled up against Alaric's side. His brother did not wake.

Dominic sat at the mouth of the den, knowing he was not welcome to lie with the rest of the pack. He turned his back on the pile of Ulfen and looked out the den opening, waiting for his father to return.

Chapter Eight

He dreamed of a woman with red hair and woke with a deep pain in his chest, as if he had been stabbed. He put a hand to his heart and opened his eyes.

He was no longer in the wooden box, and the rolling of the sea had been replaced by the solidity of the earth. He was lying in a bed covered with furs, warm and comfortable even though his head was muddy. The room he was in was dark, but he could make out the wooden plank walls and the heavily-curtained windows. A fire was burning brightly in a fireplace on the other side of the room. There was one door, and it was tightly closed.

Erik sat up slowly, and his head decried the motion in the strongest possible terms. He swung his legs over the side of the bed and let his feet hit the floor and stay there for a moment, helping him focus on what was real. Reality, it turned out, was nauseatingly fluid, and he felt disoriented and ill. He gripped the edges of the bed and tried to will his head to stop spinning.

The door to the room opened, and Bjorn walked in, a canteen in his hand. He grinned when he saw Erik. "It lives!" he said jovially. He held out the canteen. "Hair of the dog?"

Erik accepted the canteen suspiciously. When he opened the stopper, the scent of powerful *dreyri* filled his nose, and his stomach lurched in response. He burned for blood, and despite the nausea, he gulped the elixir greedily. Bjorn watched in approving satisfaction.

When he had consumed the entire canteen, he handed it back to Bjorn and asked, "This is a stupid thing to say, but where am I?"

Bjorn laughed. "In my house," he said.

Erik put a hand to his aching head. "What happened to me?" His hand moved to his chest, hovering over his heart. "What hurt me?"

"Too much *dreyri*," the other Draugr answered. "Magda uncovered some potent ancient vintage and you drank it like it was water. You're going to be hungover for days."

He knew that young Draugr could be overcome by drinking *dreyri* that was too strong for them, but he was one of the First. There should have been no blood too powerful for him to drink. He rubbed his hand over his face. "I don't remember anything."

Bjorn beamed. "Well, why don't you join us out in the living room so we can fill you in?"

Erik rose unsteadily, and his companion put an arm around his shoulders to support him. "I feel terrible."

"It'll pass," Bjorn assured. "Just need to drink a little bit more *dreyri*, and you'll be right as rain."

They made their slow way into the main room of the house. The room was bright, the decor overwhelmingly white and chrome, and the rest of the First sat together as if they'd been having a conference. They looked up in surprise, and Dag's expression was guarded as Bjorn cheerily announced, "Look who's up?"

Agnar moved from the chair he'd been occupying so that Erik could sit there instead, and he took the offered seat gratefully.

Kjeld put his phone away. "How are you feeling, Erik?"

"Like someone dropped a mountain on me."

"That's what you get," Dag said, "for drinking linnorm *dreyri*."

Erik frowned, confused. He had no memory of such a thing. "Linnorm blood?"

A young woman with vivid red hair came into the room, joining them from another room down a short hallway. She looked familiar, but he could not say when they had met before. He should have known who she was. The woman had a shallow dish in her hand, and a pile of herbs smoldered there, the smoke dark and gray. She brought it toward him, her green eyes sparkling. A tattoo of the rune Hagalaz graced the inside of her left wrist, woad-blue against the white of her skin.

"You're Valtaeigr," he said, stating the obvious.

"Yes. You may call me Mia. I am the vessel of Lofn." She raised the smoke toward him. "Breathe deeply. It will help to clear your head."

He could sense the divine energy within her, proof of her claim of vessel-dom. That, combined with her Valtaeigr bloodline, convinced him to trust her. He took the dish from her hand and inhaled the smoke, pulling it in as deeply as he could. The smell of pine and the hint of less wholesome ingredients filled him, and instead of clearing his head, it made it fuzzier. He handed the dish back to her.

"No," he said. "Not working."

Mia made him meet her eyes. When she spoke, her voice held a timber that trapped him and drilled directly into his mind. He could not have looked away if he had tried. "You are Erik Thorvald, leader of the First, and you are here with your brothers planning a raid on the faery of Finland. You have been their leader for centuries, and you lead them with an absolute hand. There is no violence that is beyond you, and nothing that you will not do for the greater glory of your band."

She smiled and sat back, and he blinked. The spell was broken, but the suggestion had been planted. He looked at the assembled First.

"When do we raid?"

**

Nika woke to a sky full of moonlight. The clouds shimmered like pearls across the face of the moon, and the forest beneath her window was bathed in silver. It was impossibly pretty, and she hated it.

She sat on the edge of the bed and stared out the window, watching the trees sway in the light wind coming in off of the water. She thought of the house she shared with Erik, the way she'd been so excited to move in and make it theirs. Now it was standing empty, and she wasn't sure she could ever go back.

She closed her eyes and took a deep breath. Lars was right. This was now how Erik would want her to be. He would want her to live, even if that meant living without him. He had been strong and had waited for her to be reborn across a hundred lifetimes. She owed it to him to do the same now.

She wondered if it had hurt him as much as it hurt her now.

A huge wolf emerged from the forest and sat just beneath the trees, its face turned up toward their cabin. She could almost sense its amber eyes boring into hers even through the window glass. She wondered if this was Dominic, the Ulfen she had met in the wood, but something told her that it was not.

She rose and went closer to the window. The wolf looked directly at her, and then it shifted into a young man with reddish blond hair and a tight dancer's build. He was fully dressed when he assumed his human guise, and she wondered where his clothing went when he became a wolf. The palm of her right hand tingled, and she glanced down to see a tiny, glowing rune there - Algiz, standing for protection. She shook the rune away and let its energy dissipate into the air.

That was a warning, a voice whispered in her head. It was the quiet voice of Ithunn, the goddess in her pocket. *Be careful whom you trust.*

She hesitated, momentarily forgetting the wolf outside the window. *Do you know what happened to Erik?*

You will see him again, the goddess told her. It was no answer, but Nika could feel Ithunn fading back into her mind, going back to the quiet place where she sat and waited. Nika had no idea what she was waiting for, or why it still mattered all these years later, but she was sometimes grateful for the gentle presence in her head. This was one of those times.

She looked back out the window, and the wolf was gone. She opened the window and leaned out, listening to the night sounds. There were the sounds of people at the hotel and in the town surrounding it, the rustling of the wind in the trees, and the quiet shuffling sounds of the nocturnal creatures moving through the brush. She suddenly wanted to be down there. She wanted to touch something alive and hold it in her hands.

Nika went downstairs, pausing at the keg before continuing on without drinking. She could hear the mattress springs in the other bedroom, and she knew that Lars, Magda and Sif would never notice her absence. The thought was saddening and freeing at the same time.

She left the cabin and walked toward the wood, stopping briefly where the wolf had stood. She bent to examine the bent blades of grass, plucking one to pick up the lupine scent the creature had left behind. Nika's insides felt hot with contained rune magic, as if something inside of her was leaking the power to seep all through her body. She released some of it through her fingertip, letting the golden ray of sparkling runes envelop the blade of brass in her hand. It stiffened, limned with gold, then slowly softened again, humming quietly in her head. It would vibrate when a wolf was near, so now she would have ample warning if one of the Ulfen approached under its remarkable camouflage.

The path through the forest was covered with wood chips, and they crunched beneath her feet as she walked. The blade of grass in her hand was still and soft, so she continued walking without fear. Above her head, a tiny bat fluttered past, and she had to chuckle at the Hollywood vampire movies she had seen. Here she was, a vampire, and she had no affinity for bats whatsoever.

She walked for a long way, listening to the sounds of the wood, lost in thought. She finally came to a quiet spot where the brush was a little longer, and she stopped to take it in. There was an owl on the branch above her, staring at her with its great yellow eyes. Not far away, in a nest made of leaves, a family of squirrels slept, their body heat visible like a green shadow to her Draugr eyes.

A mouse was running through the underbrush, shoving leaves and sticks aside as it foraged. She stopped and crouched, watching the little creature. In the museum in Central City, there had been a pair of antique gloves lined with mouse fur. It had been very soft and very warm, and she wondered how many mice it took to make a glove.

She needed to get back to her life. She needed to go back to the house, and then to the museum in Stockholm, and try to put the pieces back together. She still could not believe that Erik was gone. The pain was less intense, buried beneath a layer of the numbness that came when a heart had hurt enough and couldn't bear to hurt any more. The numbness was not entirely healthy, but it helped give her a break from grieving so she could think.

The mouse bolted away, and too late, she realized that the blade of grass she held was stiff as a board, quivering in her grip. She rose into a loveless, clawed grip that seized the back of her neck and held her tightly and painfully.

"Rune Master?" a growling male voice husked in her ear. "You are unwise to come here unprotected."

She dropped the grass and tried to turn, but he was holding her too tightly. His strength rivalled Erik's, and it frightened her. "I'm not unprotected," she gasped.

"No," he agreed. "No vampire ever is. And no Ulfen is ever without his weapons, too."

An explosion of pain ripped through her as he slashed her back with his claws, shredding her clothes and her skin. She could smell her own blood. She cried out, and he shook her.

"Did that hurt?" He shook her again. "Do you think I care?"

She whispered softly to herself, and her hand began to glow. She held it against her body, hiding it from his line of vision, allowing the magic time to build.

The Ulfen was not finished. He slashed her again, this time across the belly, and she screamed. He laughed.

"Scream, little vampire. You and your Huntsman killed my boy."

She thought to the wolf that had attacked Lars when they'd been returning from their feeding trip, and she said, "He attacked us first!"

"The Draugr have always been the aggressors," he hissed. A growl sprang up from deep in his chest, and he turned her so she could see him.

Only inches from her face, his elongated muzzle was set with rows of white and jagged teeth, his lips pulled back in a menacing snarl. His eyes were glowing amber-gold, and he was not quite wolf and certainly not a man any longer. His in-between state was hulking, with a hunched back and long, clawed digits on all four feet. A long, bushy tail swayed behind him stiffly, and hackles stood up along his neck and down his back, just like with an angry dog. His breath was hot against her skin as he licked his lips, excited by the bloody smell of her injury.

"It's too bad you've been turned," he said. "It's been centuries since I've tasted Valtaeigr meat."

"It'll be centuries more."

She brought her glowing hand up into his face, connecting a rune-laden fist with his long jaw. His teeth clacked together with the force of the blow and his head snapped back, and in his surprise, his grip on her neck loosened. She extended claws of her own and ripped at his throat, but his hide was too tough, and she could do no more than scratch him.

It was enough to distract him, though, while she ran back toward the house.

She had come farther into the woods than she had thought, but she was faster now that she was a Draugr. She could hear large animals, more Ulfen, loping in the trees on either side of the path, but they were out of sight, completely under the effects of their camouflage. Their panting and barking and the sound of them crashing through the vegetation was terrifying, and perversely she took strength from it. The fear gave her speed, and she burst from the woods and made it to the door before the wolves could reach her.

Three Ulfen in their full wolf forms followed her from the woods, followed by the half-shifted Ulfen who had attacked her. She raised her chin. "Are you Ardrik?" she demanded. "I've heard your name."

"Then you know who is coming to kill you," he snarled.

"No. I know who I'm going to turn into a rug."

She opened the door, and suddenly Lars was there, his pistol at the ready. The Ulfen fell back, and he held the line while she got behind him. He pointed the pistol at Ardrik's face, and the alpha wolf motioned his pack mates back into the woods.

"This is not over, Rune Master," he told her. "Not by a long shot."

Nika faced him, her hand glowing once again. "Good. I look forward to round two."

The Ulfen brought up their preternatural camouflage and disappeared from view, and soon even their scent was gone. Nika put her hand on Lars' arm.

"Thank you," she said. "I thought you were upstairs."

"I was in the den," he said, "watching television. I heard their noise and came out. I didn't realize you had gone outside."

She went into the house, and he closed the door and locked it. "I needed to get some air," she said.

"You shouldn't go out alone."

Nika went to the keg and drew a pint of *dreyri*, which she drank quickly. Her hands were shaking. "So I gathered." She put the glass aside.

Lars's eyes saucered. "What the hell happened to you?"

She shook her head. "Ulfen."

He grabbed for his gun and headed toward the door. She stopped him. "Don't. I don't want you to fight with them. Like you said, I shouldn't have been out there alone."

"But..."

"No. Don't engage them on your own. You'd be killed." She sighed. "With these werewolves so close by, we should go back to Sweden."

He checked her wounds, but they were already healing shut. He nodded. "Yes...there's no reason to stay here now, not when the whole reason we came was..."

He trailed of, and she finished for him. "To celebrate Erik's birthday."

"Yes."

There was so much sorrow in that one word, so much defeat in the rounding of his shoulders, that Nika realized with a start that Lars was grieving, too. It had never occurred to her to consider anyone else's pain. She went to him and embraced him, and he hugged her tight.

"I'm sorry, Lars," she told him, stroking his back. "I've been so selfish. He was your friend for a long time, wasn't he?"

"Fifteen years," he acknowledged. "He was one of the first officers I met when I joined SOG. He was..." He took a deep, ragged breath. "He was one of the best men I've ever known. I didn't even think twice about accepting Sif's offer to turn, since it meant I would be helping him. Now..."

They pulled apart, and she looked up into his eyes, her hands on his biceps. "Now you wish you could take it back, since he's gone." Lars nodded, and she did, too. "So do I."

He embraced her again. They stood in one another's arms for a long moment, drawing strength from each other and solace in their common grief.

The quiet moment was shattered when Magda came strolling down the stairs in a silk robe, an empty wineglass in her hand. "Well, you two are a soggy mess." She went into the kitchen to top off her drink from the keg. "Honestly, you should know how these things go. Vessels are always reincarnated. He'll be back. You just have to wait for him." She returned to the room and sipped the *dreyri* delicately. "You have forever. Don't be impatient."

Lars turned to her with and said sarcastically, "Your compassion is overwhelming."

She huffed softly and headed back upstairs. "I've lived too long to be compassionate, Lars. You'll learn that lesson, too, in time."

Nika said, "I hope I never do."

Magda looked over her shoulder at her. "Keep walking with the wolves, my baby Valtaeigr, and you won't need to worry about it."

She turned and went up the stairs. Nika shook her head.

"I don't like her," she told Lars. "I don't know how you sleep with her."

"With one eye open and Sif in between us," he answered, smirking. "Honestly... I don't trust her, either. And neither did Erik."

She frowned. "She's never been very nice to him. What happened between them?"

"Sif told me that they had some sort of old history, something that made her hate him. Something from the old days."

She considered the many sins that Erik had confessed to, and she hated to think which of them might have been visited upon Magda in her youth. "Did she elaborate?"

Lars sat on the couch, and Nika sat beside him. "She said that Magda used to live in a village outside Moscow. She's Russian, not Swedish, by birth. Hakon's band apparently raided Russia, and her village was burned."

"But she survived," Nika said. "Probably not many of her family did."

"I think she was brought back to Sweden with them."

"By choice?"

"I doubt it." He rubbed his neck. "Sif said that Magda used to be his slave."

A million unsavory scenarios played in her mind, and she found herself feeling sympathetic toward Magda in her unemotional hardness. She had suffered greatly in her mortal days. Somehow, she suspected that the choice of immortality and becoming a vessel had not been entirely hers to make. Nika wondered if Erik had forced Magda to accept the ritual that brought her to be bound to the spirit of the goddess Sigyn.

"Do you know anything about her goddess?"

"Sigyn?" Lars asked. "A little. I know that she was the goddess of fidelity and victory. She was Loki's wife."

"I didn't know Loki had a wife..."

"Yeah. Two, I think. And some sons."

She leaned her head on her hand. "I don't know enough about Norse mythology."

Lars chuckled. "Well, I've been reading up. Your goddess, Ithunn, was the goddess of springtime, and she supposedly had apples that kept the gods immortal when they ate them. Vidar, who was with Erik, he was second only to Thor in strength, and he survived Ragnarok by killing Fenrir the wolf." He sighed. "We could use his wolf-killing ability now."

"Do you think that the faery will attack? Erik seemed to take their declaration of war very seriously."

He shrugged. "I have no idea. I'm actually completely lost right now. I'm trusting Sif to point the way, and what she says and does is very carefully controlled by Magda."

"They have a strange relationship."

"I guess." He looked down at his hands. "They actually love each other quite a lot."

"It's hard for me to imagine Magda loving anyone."

He shrugged. "Everybody loves somebody, for good or ill."

She looked at him. "What about you, Lars? Who do you love?"

He met her gaze. "Not a who. A what. I love my country. I've been serving Sweden all of my life. I joined the army as soon as I was able, and I've never looked back. When Sif said that there were vampires and shapeshifters and that they could only be stopped by the Huntsmen, and that all of the Huntsmen but Erik had died in America, well... I couldn't leave my country to them. I had to do something." He looked away again. "I did it for Sweden, as well as for Erik."

She put her hand on his shoulder. "You're a hero, Lars. Sweden is lucky to have you."

He smiled. "Thank you. That's a kind thing to say."

"I mean it. I have a lot of respect for men who are honorable and patriotic." She sighed. "Erik loved Sweden, too. He wouldn't have stayed in the army for literally centuries otherwise. And he had all that time to go anywhere in the world, and he stayed in Stockholm. I think that says a lot."

Lars nodded. "What about you, Nika? Are you going to stay in Sweden?"

She took a moment to think about it. "If he's going to be reborn, knowing how much he loves his country, that's where he's going to do it. I need to be here when he comes back." She tried to smile for him. "Yes. I'm staying."

"Good. I don't have many friends. I'd hate to lose you, too."

She squeezed his hand. "I'm not going anywhere."

***

Ardrik returned to the pack den in a sour mood. The other wolves were equally out of sorts, and Dominic steeled himself. As the pack omega, he knew what was coming next.

The alpha was the first to take out his bad humor on Dominic, chasing him into the back of the den and pinning him against the wall, biting at him. The others joined in, snapping and clawing. He shifted into wolf form, and they grabbed his neck and haunches in their teeth, biting painfully. He yelped and snapped back at them, baring his teeth, but he kept his tail submissively tucked.

His brother Alaric grabbed him by the ear and dragged him onto his back, flipping him so his belly was in the air, and he whined in fear and dismay. Ardrik pounced on him, snarling, and Dominic closed his eyes, ready to be eviscerated. He had never seen his father so angry.

Alaric gripped him by the throat and shook him. Stars flashed into his eyes, and he cried out in pain. The scar tissue on his neck from that long-ago Draugr bite, the one that had consigned him to this lamentable position in the pack hierarchy, helped him for once when it made his hide just a little too tough to bite through. Alaric growled.

Ardrik snipped at Alaric, and the younger wolf released Dominic. That was the signal that the beating was over for now. They left him to lick his wounds and turned away, shifting into their human forms and muttering to each other.

He stayed four-legged and as close to the ground as he could for the rest of the night.

Chapter Nine

In the old days, they would have traveled to their raiding sites in a drekar, following waterways into the center of unsuspecting villages. Now they traveled in a cargo van with tinted windows. Whatever the conveyance, when they reached their target, the effect would be the same.

Erik sat in the front passenger seat, his double-headed axe on the floor between his feet, the handle resting against his chest. He still felt empty, and his head still hurt, but he was more or less functional. He just wished he could remember anything before waking up in Bjorn's house.

They said he had swallowed *dreyri* made from the blood of a linnorm, but that didn't seem possible. He knew that the last linnorm had been slain eight hundred years ago - after all, he'd been the one to slay it, along with his brother, Gunnar. The blood that had been collected from the mighty beast had been turned over to Magda with directions to enchant it, but he had been told that the enchantment hadn't worked, and that the blood had spoiled. If he had indeed taken linnorm *dreyri*, then Magda had lied to him, which wasn't that difficult to believe. It also explained his persistent mental haze.

He looked in the rearview mirror at the Valtaeigr girl, Mia, who had come along to offer magical support to their raid. She wasn't the red-haired woman in his dream, but she was similar enough that he found it distracting. He could not shake the feeling that he should have known her, and that he should have known the woman in his dreams. Every time he tried to think of her, his chest would hurt and his head would swim, and just like clockwork, Mia would come to his side with her incense. He was beginning to wonder if her remedy was doing more harm than good.

Brevik drove the van, whistling a song from the old days. All of the First were quite merry, happy to be raiding. Agnar had even told him that he was happy Erik had chosen to raid with them again. His comment had earned him a harsh word from Bjorn, and now Erik wondered where he had been and how he had been spending his time.

As far as he could remember, raiding was the only thing he knew. He led his men into harm's way, and they returned with riches and glory. It was as it always had been. Only... it wasn't. Something was very wrong.

He rubbed his forehead with his hand, and Mia leaned forward. "Headache?"

"No," he lied. "Just an itch."

She looked unconvinced, but she sat back onto the wide bench seat she was sharing with Dag and Olaf. She was a beauty, there was no doubting that, but Erik thought there was a wrong-ness to her face, some quality that should have been there but was missing, or a quality that was there that should not have been. It made his head hurt to think about, and so he turned to look out the window.

He had done enough thinking for now.

***

Ardrik ran to the edge of a forest lake, and he lowered his muzzle to the water. By the scent, he could tell that his contact was at home. He shifted to his human form and tapped the surface three times, sending ripples through the lake to announce his presence.

After a moment, a pair of glowing yellow eyes appeared in the depths of the dark water, and then the new Nøkken ruler rose to the surface. In his natural guise, he was moss-covered and greenish, with dark veins running beneath his skin. It was hard to believe that anyone would be seduced by such a creature.

He strode to the shore and left the water, standing in front of the Ulfen alpha. He smelled of sea weed and rotting vegetation, and Ardrik suppressed a sneeze.

"What is it?" the Nøkken asked.

"The Jutland pack has arrived, and with them the Doggerland pack. We are ready to begin our operation. Will the trolls be coming?"

The Nøkken nodded. "The trolls and the frost giants will join. The others will decide after they see your success...or failure."

He nodded. "The Draugr in the cottage have silver bullets. They are ready for us."

"Then plan your attack accordingly," the Nøkken ordered archly. "We have contracted with you because of your strength, not because you are invulnerable. Every war brings casualties."

"The Valtaeigr..." he began.

"I do not care to hear about your spies and machinations," the Nøkken advised. "I care only for results. I want the Draugr destroyed, starting with the last Huntsman and the Rune Master."

"The Huntsman is dead, as I've already reported to the witches. As for the Rune Master, she is careless. We will eliminate her soon enough."

The Nøkken began to return to the lake, but hesitated and said, "And your son, Dominic. Will he fight?"

Ardrik raised his chin proudly. "None of my cubs are cowards. Even the omega will fight when he is ordered to do so."

"I hope so. I have heard that he may be...compromised."

Ardrik flushed, and he balled his fists at his sides. "His injury was years ago, and the Draugr who bit him is long dead. I made sure of that. He is no risk to you."

"If he becomes a risk, he will have to be eliminated. The witches will see to that."

He returned to the water without another word, melting back into the lake as if he had never existed at all. Ardrik returned to his four-legged form and raced back to his den.

***

Nika was sitting on the couch with the Book of Odin in the early afternoon sunlight, and Magda came and sat beside her.

"Lars tells me that you've decided not to pine away and die for want of your Huntsman after all," she said, a smile on her face. "That pleases me."

Nika closed the book. "If he could wait for me to be reborn, then I can wait for him, certainly."

"That shows a great deal of character, my dear." She touched the book with a fingertip, and Nika only barely resisted the urge to pull it away. "So, have you given any thought to what I said about your training? There is much you still need to learn."

She nodded. "I'm willing. I have to do something to fill the time until he returns."

"*If* he returns," Magda said.

"Why would you say that?"

"Nobody knows what the gods will decide to do," she shrugged. "I certainly can't predict it."

"I came back many times, and always near him. He will come back near me." Her tone was firm, and it was clear that she would brook no argument on the point. "Will I be going back to Ingrid?"

"That would be a good place to start, certainly, but I had someone else in mind."

"Who?"

Magda smiled. "My own mentor, an ancient soul named Natasha. She is of the Rus, like me, and she lives in northern Finland. She can teach you everything you want to learn, and things you haven't even guessed at."

"Natasha," she mused. "That's a modern name."

"So is Magda. So is Nika. We all change with the times."

"I suppose so." She tucked the book onto the seat on her other side, putting her body between its knowledge and the Valtaeigr who was so subtly intruding into her space. Magda noticed the way she guarded the book, and she smiled.

"Too many secrets," she said. "It will take you forever to learn everything in that book... unless you voluntarily put out your own eye and hang by the foot from the Tree of Life, that is."

Nika smiled. "Odin already did that. I just need to read his book."

Lars came into the room, a mug in his hand. Sif walked beside him, their hands entwined. Magda narrowed her eyes but said nothing. Sif saw Magda's reaction and released his hand.

"We'll be heading out tomorrow," he told Nika. "Back to Mellerstön on your own, or back to Stockholm with us."

"I want to go to Mellerstön," she replied. "I have to face it sooner or later."

It was an empty house, devoid of Erik when it had been built for them to share. She was not eager to experience the hollowness she knew was waiting for her inside, but the longer she put it off, the worse it would be. She was not someone who avoided problems, not even painful ones. She would face this challenge head-on.

Lars nodded. "Okay. I'll take you home. These two can find their own way back to Stockholm."

He smiled at Sif, who nodded. "No problem. Will you be staying on the island, or will you be coming home?"

He shrugged. "I'll probably go to Kronberg, see if there's any truth to the rumor that the SOG will accept us Draugr back into its ranks."

Nika frowned. "I don't trust them. They tried to kill Erik."

"Yeah, but they missed. And that was one rogue officer under Loki's influence, not the high command. I'll be all right."

Magda asked her, "Would you like some *dreyri*, Nika?"

She shook her head. "No. I'm going to feed in the hotel." It was something else she would have to get used to.

"Suit yourself," Sif said.

"Do you want me to go with you?" Lars asked.

"No. I need to go alone." Nika rose with the book. "I'll put this away, and then I'll go. I'll be back before you know it."

"I can watch the book for you," Magda offered. The impish look on her face said that she knew Nika would refuse.

"No, thanks. I'll just put it back upstairs."

She went up the stairs, leaving Magda's knowing smirk behind, and went into her room. She tucked the book into her suitcase and locked it, then put the key in her pocket. No suitcase would hold up to a suitably determined thief, but she doubted that Magda would do anything so crass and obvious as breaking and entering.

She glanced out the window, and she thought she saw a flash of eyeshine in the trees. She went to Erik's bags and collected one of his pistols, checking to make sure it had a full clip of silver bullets inside. He had started to teach her to shoot, but she was certainly not the marksman that he had been; still, if the wolf came up close enough, she'd be hard-pressed to miss.

She tucked the pistol into her purse and headed out to the hotel.

***

The road ran through a quiet stretch of forest, and there were no other vehicles as far as anyone could see. Even Draugr hearing failed to detect engine sounds or the noises of civilization. They were that far out into the woods. Erik stepped out of the van and looked around, drawing a deep breath of the cool air, smelling the summer scents on the wind. It was another beautiful night in raiding season, with stillness and moonlight their only witnesses. The surprise would be absolute for whoever they would be attacking.

The Valtaeigr alit right behind him, following him out through his passenger-side door, clambering over the van's gear box as she came. She dropped down beside him and put a hand on his arm. "Take off your shirt."

All of them raided bare-chested, displaying their tattoos. He did as she commanded.

The flame-haired woman began to chant, and as she did, she opened a screw-top plastic jar filled with something pungent. She began to smear it over his chest and shoulders, her hands working too quickly to be sensual. His mind tried to feed him images of another scarlet headed beauty, but her face was indistinct. He shook his head and tried harder to remember.

"No, no," Mia said, forcing him to turn his face to her. "Look here, not there."

He didn't know how she had known that his attention had wandered, but then, how did the Valtaeigr know anything? Shamans and wise women had confounded him for centuries. Clearly this one was not about to change the trend.

He focused on her, and she resumed her chant, rubbing the smelly oil into his skin. The others removed their shirts and pulled out their weapons, preparing themselves to meet glory or Valhalla tonight. Mia's eyes pinned Erik's, and though he tried, he could not look away. His skin tingled wherever her ointment touched, and he felt like he was on fire, burning to death from the inside out. His chest pained him, and he took a breath against it, trying to hide his reaction. He would show no weakness before his brothers.

"Is it done?" Bjorn asked her.

"Yes," she nodded, capping her jar again. "It's done."

"Is he with us?"

She glared at him. "The effect will last long after the raid is over, I promise you."

"It had better. We need him with us. We need him to be seen."

Kjeld help up his camera, already shooting a video. "He'll be seen, all right." He grinned at Erik. "I'll make you a star, baby."

"Fuck off," Erik growled. Kjeld only laughed.

Olaf walked out in front of the group. "The village of the trollkona Iselstad is inside this wood. She is protecting four troll children and a Huldra named Aingred. We will take the children for *dreyri* and burn the rest...." He hesitated. "Those are your orders, right, Erik?"

Kjeld filmed his face in close-up. Erik felt confused and on the spot, but he knew that with his brothers, certainty was more important than anything. He could not show a crack if he meant to maintain control. He was their leader, after all. He had always been their captain.

"Those are my orders," he affirmed.

Halvar laughed as if someone had just told him the best joke. Erik glared at him, and he fell silent.

Olaf came to Erik. "And the Huldra... what about her?"

"What about her?" Erik asked, feeling his skin tingling. He could smell the blood on everyone's breath. He could the heartbeats of the trolls in their sleeping village. His fangs extended, long and feral. "Take her however you like, for as long as you like. She is my gift to you and the men."

They exploded into grins and back-slapping, congratulating themselves on their boldness and screwing each other's courage up as high as it would go. They armed themselves with rifles loaded with incendiaries bullets, and Dag strapped a flame thrower to his back. The weapons were new, but the mentality was old. It was a small mob, but mob mentality would still rule the day.

Bjorn pressed the double-bladed axe into Erik's hand, and Erik twirled it around himself, the sharp edges whizzing through the air, first on his right, then on his left. He had always done this. It was a martial dance of sorts, a dedication of the blood he was about to spill to the Valkyries and the gods of war.

Erik raised the axe, and they looked on in breathless anticipation, crouching like runners at the start of a race. "May the gods accept the sacrifices we are about to give them." He grinned, his face filling Kjeld's tiny screen.

"GO!"

They crashed through the underbrush and found the trolls' village just a few hundred feet beyond, tucked into a little rocky valley in the woods. There were four huts, each one wide as a longhouse and just as tall, the roofs thatched and smelling of new grass.

Too wet to burn, Erik thought. *No matter. We will slaughter them where they sleep.*

They kicked down the doors and set fire to the buildings, axes and bullets putting the unsuspecting faery to their deaths. Draugr fangs sank into faery veins and screams filled the clearing. The Huldra was pulled out of the protection that the trolls had given her, and they all took a turn at her, biting and brutalizing. Her nearly lifeless body was dumped into the back of the van beside five terrified and manacled troll children, and then the bloodstained Viking vampires left, rolling down the highway with a blaze of destruction behind them.

It had taken less than half an hour to destroy twenty-five trolls and take five captives. There was no gold this time, no objects worth taking, but when they sold the virgin troll blood and finished their games with the Huldra, they would feel well rewarded.

The burning and tingling from the ointment was fading, and Erik's senses were full of smoke and blood. He felt sick.

Mia watched Erik closely. She met Bjorn's eyes, then reached up to touch Erik's neck. She spoke with a tone and timber none but a Valtaeigr could match. "Sleep."

He sagged in the seat, his chin on his bloody chest.

"Kjeld," Bjorn asked, "did you get that all on video?"

"Every single minute," he nodded. "It was just like old times. I forgot what a beast he could be. I sent it to Magda to see what she wanted to do with it."

The Huldra whimpered, and Dag said, "I think she's waking up."

Their attention turned from Erik to their captives, and still the van kept rolling on.

Chapter Ten

Nika went to the hotel bar again, since it had proven to be such a good hunting ground. There were few people there this time, and she was about to leave when Dominic walked in, looking furtively around the room. His eyes met hers, and he started to turn away.

"Dominic," she called. "Don't leave."

He hesitated, then turned back, a stormy look in his eyes. "What do you want?"

"I want to talk to you." She walked closer to him, and he stood his ground warily. She offered him a smile. "I wanted to thank you for the other night."

He nodded. "You're welcome."

"Sit with me?"

He hesitated and looked around again, then finally nodded his head. "Okay."

They took a booth in the back of the room, secluded enough that they could speak openly without fear of being overheard. The barmaid came to their table, and Dominic ordered coffee and a shot of whiskey. Nika declined. The silence stretched uncomfortably for a long moment before she found the words she wanted to say.

"You could have delivered me to your pack, but you didn't."

He folded his hands on the table. They were strong hands, square and powerful. He interlaced his fingers. "Well... you weren't in your right mind, I think, and it's not right to take advantage of someone when they're in a vulnerable position."

"That was very kind of you."

"It wasn't kindness," he objected. "It was just...what was right."

The waitress returned with his order, and then Nika said, "I don't know anything about the Ulfen. I know that your people and mine don't get along, but I don't know why. Can you help me understand?"

He poured the whiskey into the coffee and took a sip. "It's an old enmity."

"How old?"

"Centuries. Ever since the first Draugr were made." He cupped his hands around the mug. "I don't know the exact details of what happened, but I know that the First attacked a pack in Sweden and eradicated them. They drank them dry and left their bodies for wild animals to eat. That pack had never done anything to them. The Draugr just attacked for the sake of attacking."

She frowned. "That's terrible. I'm so sorry to hear that."

He looked down at his mug. "Ever since then, there's been a kind of war between our kind. The Draugr expand their numbers and their territories, and they encroach on Ulfen lands and take our prey away. It's become a fight over resources, I suppose."

"Do the Ulfen eat humans?"

Dominic looked ashamed. "Sometimes, when we can. It's harder to hide these days." He sipped his doctored coffee again. "Draugr eat humans. We're not that different that way. You must have killed your share of people."

"No," she said. "I've only killed one person, on the night I turned."

He raised an eyebrow. "That's not what I heard. I heard that you killed Loki in his Nøkken vessel."

"I just pinned him. Erik is the one who killed him." She felt a twinge when she spoke his name, and she looked away to hide the tears that sprang into her eyes.

Dominic said softly, "I had no love for the Huntsman, but I'm sorry for your loss."

She wiped her eyes. "Thank you." Nika swallowed the lump in her throat and forced a smile. "The Veithimathr were sworn to protect humanity. I'm guessing that brought your pack into conflict with them."

"Good guess."

"How old are you, Dominic?"

He shrugged. "I don't know. We don't keep track of such things. After a while, the years all run together, anyway."

"So, I guess that means you're very old, if you lost count."

"Very old," he nodded, "but one of the youngest in my pack."

"Who was ruling Finland when you were born?" she asked. "Human ruler, I mean."

He thought back. "The Russian czar, as I recall. Alexander the First."

"So, you were born sometime in the early nineteenth century."

"If you say so."

They fell silent, and he sipped his drink. She found herself staring at the scar on his throat, the obvious marks of a Draugr bite that had been meant to kill. From the look of it, he was fortunate that he still had a throat at all. Dominic noticed her attention and self-consciously turned up the collar of his jacket to conceal the mark.

"Who bit you?" she asked.

He frowned. "That's personal."

"Sorry... I didn't mean any harm. I'm just..."

"Excessively curious?"

"Something like that."

Dominic sighed. "I never knew her name. She was a female Draugr, very strong. She decided at the last minute not to kill me, and I still don't know why. I almost wish she hadn't stopped."

"Why?"

"My pack thinks I'm tainted," he said. "I'm the omega now. I'm not very welcome there anymore."

She frowned. "I'm sorry. How long has this been going on?"

"Has anyone ever told you that you're obsessed with time?"

Nika chuckled. "No, but I suppose you're right. I work in a museum, and history is important to me. I have a sort of timeline in my head all the time, and I like to put things in order."

He nodded. "You need a hobby." The ghost of a smile flirted with his lips, but it vanished as quickly as it had come. "It's been at least twenty years."

"I'm sorry. That sounds very unpleasant."

He took another swallow of his whiskey-laden coffee. "You have no idea."

She impulsively leaned forward and put a hand on his forearm. The leather of his jacket kept their skin from touching, but she could still sense his Ulfen power. "If you need a friend, I'd like to be there for you."

Dominic's eyes widened. "You're crazy." He shook his head. "If any of my pack even saw me sitting here with you, we'd both be as good as dead. Friendship is out of the question."

"Maybe we can end this war, one friendship at a time."

He pulled away. "You're a nice person. Too nice to be a vampire. But you're crazy as hell, and you don't know what you're talking about." He tossed some money onto the table and rose. "I have to get out of here. Have a good night, Rune Master."

She sighed. "Have a good night, Dominic."

He left the bar with an almost guilty slink to his walk, and she sighed. There was so much that she still had to learn.

***

The basement of Bjorn's house was equipped with holding cells and blood-collection vats. The body of a myling hung suspended above the vat, its throat slit and all of its blood long drained. Erik stood back and watched as the other First loaded their kidnapped troll children into the cells.

This is wrong.

The tingling from the ointment was gone and the mental fuzziness had returned. The celebratory mood of the other First seemed wrong and immoral, and he was deeply uncomfortable with what they planned to do.

"When they're drained, then what?" he asked.

"Then the blood is delivered to the *vala* to be turned into *dreyri*," Halvar said.

"Which *vala*?"

Bjorn pushed past him. "It doesn't matter. We handle that part of it. Mia, take him upstairs."

The Valtaeigr put her hand on his arm, and he pulled free. "No. I'm staying."

Bjorn shrugged. "If you want to see us drain them, that's fine with me."

"Faery *dreyri* is addictive," Erik mused. "Are you sure you should be doing this?"

"It keeps the customer satisfied," Dag said, grinning.

"It's lucrative." Kjeld leaned against the wall beside Erik. "The more faery blood is put into the *dreyri,* the more people drink. The more people drink, the more money we make. The more they drink, the more they need, the higher the price goes, and the more money we make. We're fucking millionaires, Thorvald. Be happy."

"We're pushers," he corrected. "We're causing harm to our own people."

"So what?" Halvar said, wrestling one of the weeping troll children into a harness. "We're the First. We can do to them whatever we want. You know that."

He frowned. "Just because we can, that doesn't mean we should."

Bjorn glowered at Mia. "Shut him up or get him back on track. It's fading."

She took Erik's hand. "Come on," she said. "You're having after effects from that linnorm *dreyri* still. Let me help you."

He shook off her grip. "I'm beginning to think that my problems are from you, not from the blood."

"Just go with her," Dag said, sounding irritated. "We have work to do."

Mia stroked the back of his neck and whispered in the secret magical language of the Valtaeigr. All of his resistance fled in a rush, and he felt weak in the knees. She took his hand again and led him, unresisting, out of the room.

She took him back into the bedroom where he had first awoken, and she guided him to sit on the bed. He obeyed, watching placidly as she bent to remove his boots and socks. He felt as if he was watching her from a distance, disconnected from his body and his senses.

Mia urged him to lie back on the bed, and he complied. She left the room for a moment and returned with a bowl of warm water and a cloth. He looked up at her as she sat on the edge of the bed, her eyes locked onto his.

With slow, sensuous strokes, she began to wash the troll blood from his chest and face, removing the evidence of that evening's slaughter. She hummed as she worked, and the sound made his brain buzz. He wanted to reach up and stop her, but he could not move.

It took all of his willpower and strength to murmur, "What are you doing to me?"

She bent and kissed him, her lips soft and warm against his. It felt wrong, and he did not return the kiss. She straightened with a frown.

"I thought you liked the Valtaeigr," she said.

He answered automatically, not understanding what he was saying. "You're the wrong Valtaeigr."

"One Valtaeigr is as good as another," she whispered.

She straddled him on the bed and continued to wash his skin. He lay immobile, completely bound in her spell. She rocked her hips against him, but his body did not respond. She leaned over him and kissed him again. This time, he was able to turn his head away.

Mia frowned. He felt her reach for the nape of his neck, and then she whispered, "Sleep."

Everything went blank.

***

Bjorn was standing near the vat when Mia rejoined them. The first of the troll children was hanging upside down over it, her throat cut, blood pouring into the container below. The Valtaeigr looked at the dying faery child impassively, then told the First, "His will is very strong. He's resisting me."

"Do what you have to do to keep him malleable," he told her. "We have to have him with us when we go to the next raid."

"I'll do my best," she said, "but I'm telling you - he knows that something's wrong. I can't keep him drugged forever."

"You can and you will." He shook his head. "Not much blood in trolls."

"I'm sure the Huldra will be more to your liking," she said, looking at the cell where the faery woman was lying in a sobbing ball.

"She has been so far," Bjorn leered.

Mia turned her back on the display. "I'm going to call our contact and see what she suggests. I didn't expect him to be so difficult to control."

Kjeld smirked. "He's Erik Thorvald. He's never been easy to control."

She walked out of the room, thinking, *We'll see about that.*

***

Nika left the hotel and walked back to the cabin, her head full of questions. She had always been inquisitive, with a dedication to learning new things that had driven her adoptive parents insane in their attempts to keep up. She knew she had been pestering Dominic, and she regretted any discomfort she had caused him, but the chance to sit and talk to a real-life werewolf was not likely to come again.

She felt a horrible twinge in her chest, and she stopped short, gasping. The pain was sudden and intense, and she was completely unprepared for it. The pain came with a sense of foreboding, and she was momentarily paralyzed by fear.

That was when she heard the wolf howl. First one wolf cried, then another, and soon dozens of full-throated howls split the night. The sound was coming from the vicinity of the cottage. She broke into a run.

Something black and furry leaped into her, tackling her to the ground and rolling with her into the edge of the forest. She snarled, her fangs and claws coming out in self-defense, but the Ulfen that had jumped on her was not attacking. He was holding her down, covering her with his own body, keeping his head low. He was huge, easily as long as she was tall, and he heavily outweighed her. She struggled to push him away, but even her advanced strength was not enough to dislodge him. She tried to bite him and came up with a mouthful of fur. He whined at her quietly, his green eyes sad in his black-furred face.

She recognized the feeling of the Ulfen, the singular shimmer of his power. "Dominic?"

He licked he face, then pressed down on top of her even more closely. He put his head down over her face, nearly smothering her in his thick ruff, and he called up his camouflage ability, hiding them both completely.

"What are you doing?" She pushed against him. "Get up! My friends—"

He whined, and she wished she could speak wolf. In the distance, she could hear a deafening chorus of barks and snarls, and then a pistol fired repeatedly. There was an animal yelp, and then a wordless shout from Lars. The cacophony was like a physical force, punctuated by the sound of smashing wood and more pistol shots.

It sounded like a war. Lights were turning on in all of the other cabins, the humans inside marking themselves as voluntary collateral damage. Nika could smell blood and smoke, and her Valtaeigr senses reeled in the rushing feeling of death on all sides. She gripped Dominic's fur tightly, tugging at it, but he refused to move.

It seemed to last forever. Finally, with noise of a hundred paws, the Ulfen raced back into the forest and the quiet was restored. Only the scent of blood and death remained. Dominic slowly picked himself up off of her, releasing her from where he had been holding her in the dirt. He shifted back into his human form as he moved.

Nika slid out from beneath him, her eyes wide with fear of what she was about to see.

"What are you doing?" she asked him again.

"Saving your life," he told her, "and ending mine."

"Why?"

He looked at her, confused and stormy, and admitted, "I don't know."

He pressed a kiss to her lips, his musky scent blocking out the unpleasantness around them. She accepted the kiss, but she did not return it. He pulled back and looked her in the eye again, solemn.

"Good bye, Rune Master," he said. "Live in safety."

She wanted to say something, but she couldn't find the words. He rose and hurried away, running back toward the hotel, still in human form. She let him go. She didn't think she would see him again.

***

The cabin where they were staying was a shambles of splintered wood and broken glass. The cabins on either side of theirs were much the same. A dead wolf lay on their porch, and three more lupine corpses littered the front room just past the ruined door. Lars' pistol lay on the floor beside a pile of ashes, all that remained of him. In the kitchen, she found more dead wolves and another pile of ash. Sif.

She was blinded by tears and wanted nothing more than to sit and sob, but there was a third member of their party unaccounted for. A quick check of the first floor did not turn up any sign of Magda, so she headed upstairs.

She smelled nothing but blood. A mortally wounded Ulfen lay in the hallway, shifted back into her human form, her hands over her belly trying to hold herself together. She had been viciously slashed by a sharp blade and nearly eviscerated. Nika knelt beside her.

"Hold on," she said. "I'll try to help you."

The Ulfen woman shuddered and gripped her arm with one hand, leaving a bloody print on her sleeve. She began, "I -"

Death took her before she could say anything more.

In the first bedroom, Nika found Magda. She was sitting on the floor, soaked in her own blood, holding a towel to her wounded neck. The Ulfen had tried to tear her throat out, but the sword she still clutched had saved her life. Nika knelt beside her and took up that sword, slashing her own wrist and pouring her Draugr blood into the open wound.

Magda clung to her, tears in her eyes, her face streaked with blood. Slowly, the vampire blood Nika shed began to take effect, and the gaping hole began to close. It took more time and a lot more blood, but eventually Magda's neck was whole again.

She clung to Nika and wailed. "Sif! Sif!"

Nika held her, understanding the pain that Magda was feeling. She kissed her hair and stroked her back while she sobbed, and tears of her own slid down Nika's face. Magda pushed her away suddenly.

"You smell like them!" she accused.

"I wrestled one outside," she said. It wasn't exactly a lie. "We have to get out of here."

Sirens of the local emergency services wailed outside, and dozens of police and other first responders clambered into their cabin and the cabins around them. Nika pushed the sword under the bed and sat on the floor beside Magda, cooking up the lie she was going to tell when the mortals arrived.

Vacation was disastrously over.

***

He spent the day asleep, haunted by nightmares of the horrible things he had done. When he woke, the sun was setting and his mouth was filled with the taste of ashes and old blood. Erik sat up unsteadily, his head spinning as it had done nearly constantly for days. There was thick smoke in the room, emanating from a dozen incense trays scattered across the floor beside his bed. The Valtaeigr concoction was still burning.

He pushed the curtain aside and opened the window as wide as it would go, then stomped out the burning incense. He used his pillow to chase the smoke out the window, then put his own head out to get a lung full of clean air.

The room he was in was on the second floor, with hard and rocky ground beneath his window. In the distance, he could see the coast line, with a trio of fishing boats out on the water, coming in for the night with their catch. If he looked to his left, he could see more of the house and the yard, including the front end of the van they'd taken on their raid last night.

They had raided a troll settlement, he remembered now. It had been bloody, vicious, and cruel. *He* had been bloody and cruel. His memory of the attack was clear in his mind, his own terrible actions lurid in his recollection. No wonder the faery had declared war upon his kind.

The thought confused him. The faery had declared war? He felt certain it was true, but he could not remember why in the world he would think such a thing, or where that information might have come from. He put a hand to his head and squeezed his eyes shut in consternation.

Erik, a female voice called in his head. *Erik Thorvald.*

He opened his eyes and looked out at the water. He could see a woman approaching, small and white and dressed in humble clothing. Her white hair floated on the breeze as she walked across the sand at the water's edge. She was speaking to him, but she was not using her voice. He realized with a start that he could see through her.

Erik, come to me, she said. *You know who I am.*

He was desperately confused. She looked familiar, *sounded* familiar, but he could not place her. He was flooded with feelings of peace and trust, but he knew that she was projecting those emotions into him. She was *vala*, and more, she was a vessel. He could see the goddess-light within her.

Yes, the woman said. She was as one with his mind, seeing his thoughts and feeling his emotions. She projected serenity. *Come to me, Vidar. I am Frigg.*

He looked over his shoulder at the door to the bedroom. It was still closed, and he could hear none of his housemates stirring. His gaze fell upon the scattered incense trays, and the woman spoke again.

They have been poisoning you.

He hauled himself up onto the window sill and jumped out. The two-story drop was of no consequence to a vampire of his age, and he landed lightly on his feet. The apparition of Frigg's vessel receded just a touch, and he understood that he was to follow her.

I will lead you, she told him. *Come to me, Erik and Vidar. Come to me.*

He went to the parked van and opened the driver's side door. The van was empty, but it still reeked of blood and carnage. He looked back at the house.

They are all dead.

He doubted the helpful specter. *Even the Huldra?* he asked.

They drained her this morning.

He pressed his lips into a grim line and got behind the wheel. It was a simple matter to hot wire the ignition. He backed out of the driveway, as slowly and as quietly as he could.

The apparition appeared in the passenger seat beside him. *I will guide you,* she said. *Drive where I tell you.*

He obeyed.

***

The police and EMTs finally left after three hours of questions, and their cabin and the ones flanking them were marked as crime scenes. Nika and Magda were checked over by the EMTs and then released with their luggage and their passports. Magda wept all through the process of packing Sif's clothes, and Nika packed Lars' and Erik's things together. The keg of *dreyri* had been shattered and its contents had leaked all over the kitchen cupboard, most of it running down the drain. They dumped the remainder and left the cabin behind, a shrine to bad memories.

They took a taxi to the dock, where the driver helped them with their baggage. They boarded Lars' boat. It seemed so much larger than it had on the trip over from Sweden, and Nika stood on the deck with her hands on her hips. Magda paid the driver for his trouble and joined her on deck.

"Do you know how to operate one of these?" Nika asked her.

"Yes. I've learned a great many things in my time." She sat at the wheel and hesitated, her hands on her lap. "I don't want to go to Stockholm yet."

Nika went to stand beside her, putting a comforting hand on her shoulder. "Where would you like to go?"

Magda wiped at her eyes. "I need to see Natasha. She's the one I told you about - the one who could help you learn more. You should see her, too."

She had nothing better to do, and nowhere to go that wouldn't echo with Erik's absence. She nodded. "All right. Can we get there by boat?"

"Yes. It'll take a while, but we can do it." She started the boat, and the engine chugged to life with agreeable speed. "Thank you."

"For what?"

"For being understanding." Magda looked at her, then away. "I was less than sympathetic when Erik died. I'm not a very sympathetic person, in general. You've been very kind to me, even though I haven't been very kind to you."

Nika leaned against the half-wall beside the controls. "I understand. You've had a hard life, and that can make a person hard."

She looked surprised. "What do you know of my life?"

"Only what Lars told me."

Magda's eyes flooded again. "Lars."

Nika impulsively hugged her, and Magda clung to her for a long moment. She whispered in a tear-choked voice, "Grief is so hard to handle."

"It is," she agreed, nodding. "It's the worst."

Magda kissed her cheek, then pulled away, wiping again at the trails of moisture on her face. "All right, then. Here we go."

She eased the boat out of the dock and into the bay, headed south.

***

Dominic made it as far as the train station before his pack found him. He was waiting for his train to arrive, ticket in hand, when he got the first whiff of Ulfen scent. He looked around but was unable to see any of the others, although he could tell from the scent that they were approaching. The train station was too loud and too filled with people for him to get any auditory hints of their progress, but when a hand grabbed him by the back of the neck, he knew it was too late to run.

The hand on his neck force-marched him into a secluded area away from human witnesses. He could feel the press of Ulfen around him, all of them moving under their camouflage, but all of them eager for his blood. They bumped against him as he was pushed into the bathroom.

"Where do you think you're going?"

Ardrik's voice was a low growl in his ear, pitiless and angry. The grip on his neck became painful, and he was forced to his knees. He cried out, but his alpha was unmoved.

"Where were you during the attack? We missed you." His father shook him, and he flopped, the nerves running out of his cervical spine compressed and deadened. "You were protecting vampires, weren't you?"

Somehow, he gathered some strength and snarled, "Go to hell."

They fell on him en masse, dozens of toothy jaws and slashing claws ripping into his flesh. He screamed and tried to protect himself by shifting into wolf form, but it was to no avail. They shredded him. He tried to fight back, but he was too outnumbered. They threw him into the air and beat him nearly senseless, attacking him until his blood stood in pools on the tiled floor.

"Enough!"

Ardrik stopped the mayhem before he was completely unconscious, possibly showing a glimmer of paternal feeling. He dragged Dominic up onto his feet and held him there, since he was unable to stand on his own.

"You are expelled from the pack," his alpha told him, his tone steely. "You are expelled from *every* pack. You are dead to us. Go to your Draugr. Maybe they will take you in. We are done with you."

He dropped Dominic onto the cold floor, and then the pack left the room, a few of them sparing the time for a parting kick or bite. When they were all gone and the room was quiet, Dominic dragged himself up onto his hands and knees, blood dribbling from his mouth.

A human man came in and shouted in surprise and alarm, then rushed to him. "What happened? My God... Help! Somebody help me!"

He wanted to push him away, but he was too weak. He fell onto his side and lay there, too spent to do anything more.

Chapter Eleven

Days passed. Travel occupied his days and his attention, and the farther he got from Bjorn's house, the clearer his mind became. He remembered the declaration of war, and his failed intervention with the First. He remembered the linnorm *dreyri* and Magda's betrayal. Worst of all, he remembered the part he had played in the decimation of the sleeping trolls in their village. He remembered the Huldra, and when he did, he wanted to weep. It had been a return to the bad habits of his past. He could never let Nika know what he had done.

He followed the directions in his head, but by now, he knew where he was going. He was headed to Ingrid's little house by the sea. The *vala* had rescued him. How she had known of his difficulty, he wasn't certain, but she had always had a knack for knowing things. He was long past questioning the Valtaeigr, but not past wondering at their ways.

He had lost his cell phone somewhere along the way. He wanted to call Nika, to tell her he was all right. The connection between them was severed, and the loss of it made him ache. He understood now that the breaking of the Chosen bond was the source of the constant pain in his chest. He hoped that she was holding up.

The road to Ingrid's house finally ended in her gravel drive, and by the time he had parked the van, she was standing in the front door, waiting for him. She had her white hair pulled back into a long braid, which she had wound into a coil on the back of her head. She wiped her hands on the apron she wore over her blue dress, smiling at him as he exited the van.

"Erik," she greeted. "I'm so glad you're here."

"I need to use your phone," he said. He caught himself, shook his head, and added, "Thank you for helping me. I greatly appreciate it."

She smirked. "A late show of gratitude is better than none at all. My telephone is at your disposal."

He gave her a sheepish smile and went into her house. It looked the same as it always had, as if no matter how much time passed, this place was a little pocket of unreality outside the stream. Her telephone was an old rotary affair, and he dialed Nika's number.

The cell phone rang and rang, and she never picked up. The voice mail greeting began to play, and he waited impatiently for it to finish. When he could leave his message, he said, "Nika, I'm all right. I don't know what Magda told you, but don't trust her. I'm at Ingrid's. Have Lars bring you on his boat. I need to see you."

He hung up and turned to Ingrid, who had closed and latched the door. She nodded to him. "Your Chosen is alive and well, although she believes that you have died. She is too strong to waste away, although she tried at first. You should be proud of her."

"I am." He sat at her kitchen table, the heart of the house. She sat across from him. "What am I going to do now?"

"First, you let me cleanse you of the effects of the spells that little harridan was casting on you," she answered. "Second, you let me get in touch with Nika and bring her here."

"That would be wonderful."

She smiled. "Would you like something to drink? I have some *dreyri* left from when you were here before."

"As long as it isn't linnorm or faery," he said ruefully.

"No. Human. Obtained from blood banks and willing donors."

He sighed. "That would be amazing."

She went down into her cellar and came back with a wooden tankard filled with enchanted blood. She put it down in front of him and sat again.

"You're probably wondering what Magda's game is in this."

"I certainly am." He sipped the drink and his shoulders relaxed, at least marginally. "I know she hates me. That's been true for centuries."

"Can't blame her."

"I don't."

"Good. But even though she's justified in disliking you, she's not justified in what she's doing now." She looked at him as he drank. "Do you even know what she's doing?"

"Other than trying to make certain that the faery have a reason to declare war? Other than trying to set up a nice little business selling narcotic blood to young vampires?"

She smiled. "Other than that."

"If there's more, I don't know what it is." He sipped from his tankard again. "I hope you can tell me. I hope you *will* tell me."

Ingrid folded her hands on the tabletop and said, "She is the vessel for Sigyn, devoted bride of Loki. You recently immolated Loki's vessel, forcing him back into the cycle of rebirth. You are also the vessel of Vidar, who is destined to kill Fenrir at Ragnarok. And do you know who Fenrir's father is?"

"Loki."

"Indeed." She nodded. "This is all about revenge. Magda hates you, and Sigyn hates Vidar, and they both want the two of you dead."

"So why enchant me and send me on that raid?" He clenched his fist. "Ingrid, the things we did - if Odin had not punished me already, I would deserve it now."

She patted his hand. "You are not responsible for the things you did while under that compulsion," she reassured him. "And Odin will not punish you, because your vow was to protect humans, not the faery."

"They were helpless," he said bitterly. "They were sleeping and we fell on them with fire."

"That was Bjorn's doing, and Mia's. Not yours. I know that you have spent years developing a conscience, but now is not the time to exercise it. Put your guilt aside until you have the luxury of time. Right now, we need to stop Magda and Bjorn."

He finished his *dreyri*. "I need to get a message to the Ulfen alpha, see if I can stop this war before it starts. If the Ulfen and the Draugr start to fight, there will be no hiding it from the humans."

Ingrid sighed. "It's too late for that, I fear. There has already been an Ulfen attack."

"Where?"

"Finland."

He felt chilled. "Where in Finland?"

She met his eyes calmly and tried to will him to stay placid. He shrugged of the suggestion. He had had enough of Valtaeigr playing with his mind.

He answered for her. "Oulu."

She nodded.

"Shit." He rose. "I need to -"

"You need to sit down. You haven't been cleansed yet. If you go back now, you'll fall right back into their clutches. We can't have that."

He hesitated, then sat again. "What do you need to do?"

"We need a ritual."

He took a deep breath and let it out in a rush. "Terrific."

***

Magda piloted the boat all the way around the southern tip of Finland and down the Neva to a slip in St. Petersburg. Nika had read about the fabulous Russian city many times, but she had never realized it was so close to Scandinavia. The gilt-edged buildings looked like Christmas cards in the sunlight, and she realized that she was gaping.

"Those are palaces from the time of Peter the Great," Magda told her. "Those were heady days. The rest of the city is very nice, but a little less grand."

"Amazing," she said, shaking her head. *I wish Erik could see this.*

A young woman with the body of a ballerina was waiting for them on the pier, her hands in the pockets of her trench coat. She was wearing sky-high stilettos and had her scarlet hair loose and cascading over her shoulders. She brightened into a smile when the two women left the boat.

"Magda!" They embraced, exchanging kisses on the cheeks. "And who is your lovely companion?"

"This is Nika Graves. Nika, this is Natasha."

They shook hands. "A pleasure."

Natasha looked down at their connected palms, then back up at Nika with a knowing look in her moss-green eyes. "The pleasure is all mine, Rune Master. So, you are the one who helped burn Loki's vessel."

She didn't know if that was meant as a compliment or a criticism. "I just cast the spell to hold him in place."

"Ah. I see. And the Huntsman burned him to death."

"Yes."

Natasha and Magda exchanged a glance, but they said nothing. Natasha asked Nika, "Do you need help with your bags?"

She glanced back at the pile of things, which included bags that had belonged to Sif, Erik and Lars. "I wouldn't mind it."

"I thought as much." She signaled to her waiting driver, and he helped them get the luggage into the back of the car. It was just this side of a limousine, and Nika was impressed. Apparently, Natasha had been doing very well for herself.

She seemed to know what Nika was thinking, for she said, "There is a lot of money in Russia these days. There actually always was, but now it's much more obvious." She slid into the car, and Nika and Magda followed suit.

The car took them to an elegant home on the outskirts of the city, surrounded by flowering bushes and a neat white fence. The driver brought the luggage into the house, then left with a tip of his cap. Natasha and Magda embraced again.

"Welcome home, my dear," Natasha said.

Magda smiled. "It's good to be back." Her smile dimmed. "The Ulfen killed Sif."

"Oh, no." She touched Magda's cheek with the backs of her fingers. "I'm so sorry."

"That wasn't supposed to happen," she told Natasha.

Nika stood awkwardly, not knowing what to say. The two women, who obviously had a great deal of history and a long familiarity with each other, continued to embrace for a long while, ignoring her. She looked at her purse, which had been left in the house during the attack and showed it. There were long claw marks on one section of the bag, as if the Ulfen had been trying to dig into it for something. She opened the flap and took out her cell phone, but the screen was filled with a spider web of cracks. It was completely broken. She sighed and put it back. She'd had the ridiculous urge to call Erik, just to hear his voice on his voicemail greeting. Now even that was lost to her.

The two women finally noticed her, and they stepped out of their long embrace. Natasha said, "Magda tells me that you still have a great deal to learn. Did you bring the Book of Odin?"

"It's in my bag," she said, nodding.

"May I see it?"

Strangely, her knee-jerk was to tell her '*no*', but instead she retrieved the book from her suitcase. Magda watched with open avarice as Nika reluctantly handed the book to Natasha. The eldest Valtaeigr opened the book and perused the pages, turning them slowly with her left hand while she cradled the book in her right.

"Amazing," she said. "I can practically feel Odin's power in these runes."

Nika nodded. "It's a very powerful artifact."

Natasha chuckled. "'Artifact.' That's right - you work in a museum, don't you?"

"Yes."

"I suppose that explains your taste for old things." She looked at Magda, who obligingly laughed at her lame joke. Nika crossed her arms.

Magda's telephone rang, and she went into another room to take the call. Nika extended her hearing, listening with Draugr senses while Natasha ogled the book.

In the other room, she heard Magda say, "Go ahead." She could hear a female voice on the other line, but she was too quiet for Nika to make out any words, even with her acute hearing. Magda sighed. "Did you at least get it on video? Good. Send it to me, and a copy to our contact. I might have more people for you to send it to later. And find him before he causes trouble."

She ended the call and returned to the front room. Nika asked, "Problem?"

"When you run a bar, there's nothing but problems." She shook her head. "I don't know what I'm going to do without Sif."

"You will do what you must until she returns," Natasha told her. "She will find you, or you will find her. I promise you that."

She seemed to be somewhat comforted by her mentor's assurances. Her phone tweeted for her attention, and she glanced down at it. She seemed pleased by what she saw. "Will you excuse me?"

"Of course." Natasha smiled at her. "Why don't you go upstairs? The reception is better there."

When Magda had left them, Natasha turned to Nika. "I think you've had a very spotty beginning of your education. I would be happy to help fill in some of the holes, if you would let me."

"I'd like that very much." She forced a smile. "I don't have anything else to do for the next twenty or so years."

Natasha raised an eyebrow. "That's a very distinct number."

"I figure that's how long it'll take for Erik to be reborn."

"Ah. Well, there's no set time table for how long a soul stays in Helheim before returning here to Midgard. Maybe it will be twenty years, maybe it will be more, but maybe it will be less." She smiled. "As with Magda and Sif, he will find you, or you will find him. It is destiny."

"I hope that's true."

"Your souls found each other in this lifetime," Natasha shrugged. "I see no need for pessimism."

"I suppose."

"Ah! But you've had a long trip. Surely you must be thirsty. Would you care for some *dreyri*? I have a selection in the wine cellar. Feel free to go down and pick out whatever appeals to you."

Nika looked around, and Natasha pointed her to the appropriate door. She tried to listen to Magda's call, but the room she had gone into was completely silent, no doubt magically warded. Nika was deeply suspicious of her hostess's motives.

"I'm all right," she said. "I'm not really thirsty right now."

Natasha was a Draugr, too, and she knew a young vampire like Nika needed to feed regularly. She could smell the lie on Nika's skin, in the pallor of her cheeks and the slight green glow in her irises that she could no longer conceal.

"I insist," she said.

She went into the basement, but not without touching the doorknob and applying a little runic magic to disable the lock mechanism. A small part inside the lock sprang out of place, making it impossible for Natasha to shut her in and keep her prisoner. She was jumpy and suspicious, and she knew it was unfair, since Natasha had been nothing but welcoming. She had no reason to suspect anyone...and yet she did.

She went down the stairs and into the wine cellar, where row upon row of bottled blood stood waiting for their drinking pleasure. Some of the bottles had more power than others, but there was one particular rack that was filled with *dreyri* that shone in her mind's eye. There was so much preternatural power and magic in those twelve bottles that it was almost painful to look upon them. She reached out and touched the dimpled bottom of the bottle with one forefinger, and a shock of power raced down her hand and up her shoulder.

It came with a vision of five Nordic-looking men, all of them sporting tell-tale Draugr teeth and eyes. The vision was from the point of view of someone these men were attacking with indescribable violence. She gasped and pulled her hand away as if it had been burned.

Natasha was standing at the top of the stairs. "Are you finding it all right?" she called.

She hesitated, then grabbed one of the bottles from a very mundane-looking rack. It had no shimmer beyond the kind *dreyri* normally had.

"Just fine," she said. "Shall I bring a bottle for each of us?"

"Just two bottles, I think," she said. "Magda doesn't imbibe."

Until her hostess had said so, Nika had not consciously realized that she had never seen Magda drinking *dreyri*. She sold it hand over fist and raked in the money for it the same way, but she never seemed to use it at all. Nika wondered how she kept herself fed.

She brought the bottles up the stairs, and Natasha led her into the library, where crystal wine glasses had been set out around a silver wine bucket. She put the bottles into the container, which was filled with water and had a heating unit attached to the bottom.

Natasha said, "I like my blood warm."

"So do I, honestly."

Her hostess uncorked the bottles and put them back into the water to heat. The aroma of the blood rose like perfume. "There are some who drink it over ice when the weather is hot," Natasha said, making idle conversation. "I dislike that, because the blood begins to congeal. I do not enjoy the feeling of thick blood in my throat."

"I can certainly understand that." She sat in a leather-upholstered wingback chair. "This is a lovely home."

"Thank you. I inherited it."

"From whom?" She hastened to add, "If I'm not prying."

"Not at all." She settled onto a settee beside the table that held the wine bucket. "I inherited it from a lover. He was a very important man in the petroleum industry, and when he passed away, he left two of his houses to me - this one and a lovely dacha out in western Siberia."

Nika chuckled. "I've never heard 'lovely' and 'Siberia' in the same sentence before."

"That's because you're American and cursed with your country's short sightedness," she sniffed. "Siberia is a beautiful place. So many forests and rivers, good fishing and hunting. It's the sort of place a person could go to get lost."

"I prefer to be found, personally," Nika said, smiling.

Natasha leaned back and crossed her long legs. She had removed her trench coat to reveal a shell-pink silk dress beneath, very ladylike and elegant, with a pleated skirt that fell around her legs attractively. "You don't know about Magda's history, do you?"

"She hasn't told me anything."

"It's a painful story."

Nika hesitated. "Then maybe you should let her be the one to tell me."

Natasha smiled, but the effect was off putting. "She was a member of the Rus tribe here along the Neva. The Viking raiders came and burned her village, and they took all of the young women captive. Magda was made a body slave."

"That's horrible!"

"Indeed. Her master used her enthusiastically for many months until she conceived a child. The daughter was born when he was at sea, and when he returned, he beat her for having the temerity to bear a girl child when he wanted a son."

Nika huffed, "As if she could control that. That's so barbaric."

"It was. He forced two more children from her, finally getting his sons when the second and third babes were born."

"I'm almost afraid to ask, but what happened to the girls?"

"She was raised by Magda and her master's mother, of course." She tilted her head. "Her master was cursed not long after the second son was born. When he returned, he forced Magda to take the blood, turning her against her will."

"That poor thing," Nika said sadly. "What a horrible fate."

"Indeed." She smiled again, and it was broader this time. She was clearly relishing what she was about to say. "Do you know who her master was?"

She steeled herself, although Lars had prepared her to hear this news. "Erik," she said.

"Precisely. So your beloved Thorvald used to be a real son of a bitch."

Nika crossed her arms. "I know he was. I also know that he changed, and that he hasn't done anything of the sort in hundreds of years. That's not who he is any longer. If he'd still been that person, he wouldn't have been made a vessel, or Veithimathr."

"That is the accepted version, yes."

"The *accepted* version?"

"Yes. The reality is somewhat different."

Nika's voice was hushed when she spoke again. "I don't care what you say. I know that Erik was a changed man, and that he would never have done such a thing now. He was a product of his time."

"If you insist." She sighed. "My dear, the first thing you will have to learn as a Valtaeigr is that men are not to be trusted. They will always turn on you. The only people you can really trust are your sisters."

Magda came into the room, her face unreadable. She sat beside Natasha. "You're telling her the story," she said.

"I am. She deserves to know."

"I'm sorry if your privacy has been invaded by me knowing these things," Nika told her.

"No matter. It's important that you know what your Erik Thorvald was really like. I know you mourn him, but I personally celebrate his demise. He has done much to wrong me."

"I'm sorry to hear that," Nika said. "But I'm confident that he was a different man now."

"Really?" Magda smiled at her, and her expression and the angle of her head were exact mirrors of Natasha. "That's cute."

Nika narrowed her eyes. "That's condescending."

Natasha put a hand on Magda's knee, silencing her. "You'll have to forgive her. She's raw right now. I'm certain she doesn't mean what she's saying. Isn't that right, dear?"

They looked at one another, and then Magda acquiesced. "That's right. Sorry, Nika."

"No harm done." She lifted one of the bottles of *dreyri*. "Shall we drink?"

Her hostess picked up one of the crystal glasses. "Let's."

Chapter Twelve

Ingrid set up one of her kitchen chairs on a tarp in her garden and brought Erik outside. "Sit here," she coached.

He sat where she bid him to, craning his neck to see what she was doing. Ingrid picked up a shallow bowl and dumped a tiny piece of charcoal into it and set it alight, then blew out the flame until only smoke remained.

"Oh, no," he objected. "No more smoke."

"Hush. Do you want to be freed of her influence or don't you?"

He scowled, feeling surly. "How do I even know that there *is* an influence? I don't feel anything."

"The name of the girl who enspelled you was Mia."

"Yes."

"She is powerful and well-trained. She's one of Natasha's girls, a Dark Sister. Natasha is their high priestess."

He shook his head. "Should that mean anything to me?"

She chuckled and sprinkled the smoldering charcoal with a powder that smelled of old blood. "Natasha is a very powerful and ancient shamaness of the Rus people. She's one of the earliest of the Valtaeigr, and she takes her immortality from magic, not from the gods. She is Magda's mother."

His jaw dropped. "Her *mother?*"

"Yes. I'll bet you thought you killed her mother, eh?" She brought the smoking tray closer and set it on the ground underneath his chair. "Sit still."

He thought back to the raid when they had taken Magda and her village, something he rarely allowed himself to do, and said, "Yes. I thought we killed all of the adults."

"Your raid killed her aunts and uncles, and her grandparents, but her mother was elsewhere when you came. Lucky for her, not so lucky for you."

She repeated her earlier procedure with another dish and charcoal, and then picked up a fan made from a bird's wing. She circled Erik, directing the smoke toward him. He coughed lightly, more from annoyance than from any actual difficulty with the smoke.

"What the hell are you doing?"

"Sit still and be quiet," she answered. "You can be such a pain in the ass."

He couldn't dispute that. Ingrid began to chant, and the words delved into his brain, making it vibrate. He shuddered against the feeling and gripped the edges of the seat, as if the chair would pitch him off at any moment. He closed his eyes. Images of the troll raid, of Mia washing the blood from his chest, of the face of the Huldra when he'd held her for Halvar... his guilt made manifest rolled through his head like a river of filth. He was ashamed.

On the heels of the shame came anger, and an urge for violence. His grip on the chair became less steadying and angrier, and he warred with himself as the impulse to beat Ingrid's brains out rose in him like bile. He was shaking with the effort of resisting it.

She seemed to sense the danger, but she did not change her spell. The chanting continued at the same pace as before, and the smoke still rolled into his face and down his throat. He squeezed his eyes shut against the daylight and against the vision of the witch who was helping him. If he'd seen her face, he could not have prevented himself from smashing it with a fist.

He had not been violent to a woman in a millennium. Whatever Mia and Bjorn's group had done to him, they had done it well.

The volume of her chanting rose, and with it the pitch, and soon she was standing in front of him, arms raised high, screaming her words into the sky. He felt himself vibrating like a crystal about to shatter, and he cried out from the pain and pressure of it.

Then, with a snap, it was gone, and he felt his soul recoil, shrinking back into himself like a tendon shrinks when it's cut. He trembled and opened his eyes, gasping for air. Ingrid was kneeling in front of him, a sword in her hand, the point pressed against his chest.

"What are you doing, old woman?" he demanded. The words came out in Old Norse, and for a moment, he was back in his mortal village, in his mortal self. His mind was disjointed, scattered.

"Saving you," she responded in the same tongue, just before she ran him through.

He howled in agony as the sword point pierced his chest, just below his heart. The sword pressed all the way through him and pinned him to the chair, where he thrashed in agony. His blood rushed out over the blade. It was darker and thicker than it should have been.

Ingrid chanted something further, then abruptly went silent and pulled the sword free. He toppled out of the chair and landed face-down on the ground, bleeding and unconscious.

***

Nika gasped as a sharp, sudden pain struck her in the chest. She pressed her hand to her sternum and stared at Natasha, wide-eyed, thinking at first that the older Valtaeigr had done something to her. The confusion on Natasha's face, mirrored by Magda, reassured her on that point. The pain was gone as quickly as it had come. In her mind's eye, she saw Erik's face. He was lying on a patch of dirt, sunlight on his skin. She shook her head, and the vision vanished.

"What was that?" Natasha asked, concerned.

"There was so much power!" Magda exclaimed.

Nika could not speak. She shook her head and held out her hand, warning them to stay back. In her mind's eye, she saw a slender golden thread extending to her out of darkness, writhing and whipping. She grasped it.

The moment she touched that invisible cord, the sense of Erik exploded in her heart, and she could suddenly feel him again. It was the Chosen bond, and it had somehow been recreated. She tugged on it, and it was solid on the other end, anchored in the soul of her beloved, which could only mean one thing.

Erik was alive.

She glared at Magda. "You said he was dead. You said the First killed him."

Magda gaped at her. "You re-created the bond."

Natasha frowned. "That's impossible."

Nika could feel all of Erik's ancient power rushing into her, filling her soul. She was drunk on it and overwhelmed by sheer impact. He was so much more powerful than she had ever known. He hid so much. She didn't know how someone could carry so much magic and seem so normal. She buzzed with it. She began to levitate.

Natasha shouted something to Magda, and the two began to try to physically restrain her. Natasha began chanting in a language Nika had never heard, and the words jangled unpleasantly in her ears. She pulled the power of her own rune magic up and around her, forming a golden shell that encased her and protected her from anything the two of them tried to do.

She tilted in the air until she was upright, and then she lowered to the floor. Her feet were still an inch above the carpet. The power she had somehow inherited from Erik filled her and pulled her out of the room and toward the door.

Natasha ran past her and slammed the door shut while Magda grabbed a rifle from a closet. Nika was unconcerned. She gestured, and the door exploded into a thousand shards, opening the way for her. The force of the blast knocked Natasha from her feet. Nika smiled to herself and floated toward the door.

Magda shot her in the back. The bullet struck her golden shield and bounced off harmlessly. Nika turned and faced her, and the look of fear that Magda wore was almost comical. She laughed and shot rune fire at her, knocking the rifle out of her grip and sending her sprawling across the carpet.

She did not stay to see the rest of their reactions. Turning toward the sky, she used Erik's power and took flight.

***

Ingrid turned Erik onto his back and wiped the black blood of his enchantment away. His wound was already healing, as she had known it would, powered by his ancient Draugr blood and his renewed connection to Nika. What she had done had more or less drained his infection and released him from the evil that Mia and her concoctions had put into him.

She poured cool water over his chest and rinsed him clean. The black blood slid off onto the plastic sheet on which she had placed him, where it could be safely contained without contaminating her herbs. She would be unable to move him on her own, so she waited for him to wake up.

He was out for a long time, but finally his blue eyes flickered open, and he stared up at her in disbelief. "You stabbed me," he complained.

"Sorry. It was the only way. They created a black bag around your heart and I had to drain it."

He sat up slowly. "That doesn't seem very anatomically likely."

"Neither do disappearing fangs or flying without wings," she retorted. "Get up and strip."

Erik raised an eyebrow. "Excuse me?"

"You heard me. Those clothes are contaminated. You have to discard them."

He gave her a sour look, but he obeyed, peeling off his blood-soaked clothing and tossing it onto the tarp. He stood fully naked before her and opened his arms to the side, displaying everything he could display. "Happy?"

She laughed. "Let me hose you down to get the last of it off."

He stood and let her spray him lightly with the garden hose, turning so that she could access all sides of him. When she was done, she beckoned him off of the tarp, and he stepped off onto the flagstone path that led to the house.

She rolled up the tarp very carefully, making certain that nothing escaped the sides. Once she was certain she had the offending contamination cocooned, she tied the tarp and set fire to it. Although everything should have been too wet to burn from the blood and water, the bundle went up like flash paper.

Erik looked at her, uncertain what to do next. He was out of his depth. Ingrid smiled and retrieved a bathrobe for him, which he put on and tied shut.

"Come in and get some more *dreyri*," she told him. "You need your strength up, and you'll be having a visitor soon."

"A visitor?" He shook his head. "I don't think I want any visitors."

"This one, you'll want to see."

They went inside, and he sat at the kitchen table. "I feel like I'm flying."

Ingrid's only answer was to laugh.

***

Mia went to Bjorn and shook him out of his inebriate haze. A bottle of troll *dreyri* lay empty beside his bed. When he finally opened his eyes, she told him, "Thorvald is with Ingrid."

"How do you know?" he asked, bleary.

"Because she just broke the last tendril of my control over him," she said. "I know it was her."

He pushed her aside and stood up, wobbly. "She's Valtaeigr."

"She is, but she never became Draugr. She's a witch. She used to be one of the Dark Sisters, but she left us years ago."

He ran a hand over his beard. "A traitor to the witches like Thorvald is a traitor to us." He dropped his hand. "Fine. We'll kill her." Mia laughed, startling him. He peered at her. "What's so funny?"

"She's the vessel of Frig and the most powerful Valtaeigr in the world," Mia said. "Not even my mother would dare to stand against her."

"Your *mother* is just a whore with a supply chain," he bit. "She's too much of a coward to do anything but hide and count her money."

"You call it being a coward. I call it being shrewd. After all, who is getting rich, and who is doing the dirty work?" She leaned closer. "My mother will never be blamed in this, and Thorvald knows you are involved. He will come for all of you."

He pushed her against the wall, his hand on her throat. She struggled as he lifted her from her feet. "Do not use your prophesy against me, little witch. I can still use you like the Huldra. Witch blood makes good *dreyri*, too."

She spat in his face, and he dropped her to the floor. She staggered once, then quickly put distance between them. "You're a fool," she told him. "A brutal, short-sighted and stupid fool."

Bjorn turned on her. "You're in my bedroom, and I'm between the door and you," he told her. "I'm an ancient Draugr, one of the First, and you're just a Valtaeigr witch. I don't like your chances right now."

She held out her hand, and a sword made of black light appeared, surrounded by shadows that writhed around the blade. Her eyes began to glow brilliant red. "I like them very much."

He waved his hand at her dismissively. "Parlor games," he spat. "I'm not some child you can impress with your smoke and mirrors."

Mia stepped forward and swung the shadow sword into him. It slashed across his chest, and he looked down in surprise at the gash it created. Blood poured out of the wound, and he looked up at her, eyes wide.

"You little -"

His words cut off when he burst into a shower of dust and ash. She watched his death with a smile, then dismissed her sword. She stepped on the little pile of his remains as she walked out the door.

***

Nika let the power lead her. It pulled her along an invisible string, guiding her to its anchor. She willed it to pull her quickly and felt the cold air rushing over her body as she streaked forward. She was exhilarated, excited and thrilled nearly beyond her ability to think. He was alive! Her lover, her soul mate, her Chosen, her master - the one man she could never live without. She wanted to cry and laugh at the same time. All of the grief that had weighted her heart before was gone, and in its place was the feeling of him, the 'Erik-ness' of his living spirit on the other end of their link.

Why couldn't he feel it? Why was he not celebrating as wildly as she? She needed to see him, to show him the wonderful truth, that they were still alive and still together. She was delirious with the inrush of all of his power, his delicious strength, the magic and the age and the experience that made him so mighty.

She could sense him now on the ground beneath her, miles and miles below. She opened her arms and flew down to meet him, pulling up at the last moment when she realized that there was a house in the way. She shook the confusion out of her head and landed in the garden. It was Ingrid's garden. She had spent many days here, learning and living. And now he was here, alive and well.

Erik opened the door and stood, staring. She went to him and wrapped herself around him, bursting into happy tears when she saw him. She pushed her hands inside the robe he wore, running them over his chest and the rock-hard muscles of his shoulders. He pulled her close and held her tight.

"Erik," she whispered against his skin. "Erik! They told me you were lost."

He kissed her deeply, and she surrendered herself to the touch, utterly his just as he was utterly hers. She could feel his heart beating against hers, both physically and through the spiritual connection they shared once again. It felt so right, and so perfect, that she could not stop crying.

Erik picked her up in his arms and carried her inside, closing the door with his foot. Ingrid rose to meet them, her face beatific with a wide smile. She held a handkerchief and dabbed at Nika's eyes, wiping away her tears. Nika reached out to embrace her, too, including her in the circle of her joy.

She sat on Erik's lap, where she kept her arms around his neck. Ingrid was chattering at her, but she couldn't hear a word over the delightful sound of his heartbeat. She smiled, and she melted, utterly undone by the beauty of his face and the sparkle in his blue eyes. She kissed him over and over.

The power that had brought her to him slowly receded, returning to its rightful owner. He grew stronger as she faded, but that was all right with her. She was happy to have his arms around her, giving her protection once more. She was where she wanted to be, and he was himself again, and he had been returned to her. Nothing else could ever matter as much.

Chapter Thirteen

Ingrid left the two lovers alone and went out into her garden. She knelt and pressed her hands deep into the earth, concentrating her magic into the ley lines that ran beneath her house. She connected with the line, a river of paranormal energy connecting all of the magical places in the world, and pushed her consciousness into it. Her body became ghost-like and followed.

She swam for what might have been an hour or might only have been a second or two, but she finally found what she was seeking. She emerged from the line in the center of a sacred grove in northern Finland. The grove was silent, but she could feel the eyes of a dozen or more faery watching her warily.

"I come in peace," she said. "I seek parley with your leader."

A voice came from the silent woods. "We have no leader."

"Then I need to speak to the alpha of the pack who defends you."

The faery whispered among themselves, and then the voice spoke again. "You are the witch Ingrid Nilsson."

"I am."

"You are the vessel of Frig."

"I am."

An aged elf, young in appearance but shimmering with the power of antiquity, emerged from the shadows. "You are harboring the Rune Master and the last Huntsman."

She saw no use in denying it. "I am."

"Why? You know of their sins against us."

"I know that the rest of the First have sinned against you. Thorvald has not, not of his own volition."

The elf looked unimpressed. "You must know about the recent raid upon the troll camp. Thorvald was part of it."

"I know," she acknowledged, "but he was enspelled. Surely you of all beings understand enchantments."

"Assuming that this is the truth," the elf hedged, "that does not excuse the murder of the Nøkken chieftain."

"He was attempting to attack the humans. The Veithimathr are bound by the gods to prevent such things. He would have exposed all of us, and all of you. His death was a mercy to us all."

One corner of the elf's mouth turned down. "I do not believe his death was merciful."

"Well, not for him. But for the rest of us."

The elf considered briefly. "I will tell the alpha that you wish to speak with him. We will be in touch."

Ingrid smiled. "My thanks, ancient one."

"Don't thank me yet," the elf counseled. "The alpha has not accepted, and it may all come to naught. Now go back the way you came. You are not welcome by everyone here."

She bowed her head. "Until we speak again."

The elf sighed. "We will not see one another again in this lifetime."

Ingrid knelt and returned to her home through the ley line. She emerged in her garden and went back into her house.

***

The delirium of power had mostly passed from Nika's mind by the time Ingrid returned to the house. She still clung to Erik, unwilling to let go of him now that she had him in her arms again. He tolerated her clinginess - even seemed to like it - and did everything he could to be gentle and reassuring.

She kissed him for the hundredth time and said, "What happened to you? Magda told me you were dead."

He frowned. "Magda dosed me with a kind of *dreyri* that acts like a narcotic, and she turned me over to the First."

Nika gasped, horrible images running through her head of what those unrepentant Vikings might have done to him. "Are you okay?"

"I am now. They had a Valtaeigr with them, and she kept using this... incense or something. The smoke made me out of my head. I don't know what it was, or what their end game was, but... I wasn't myself."

She saw a glimmer of guilt in his expression, and he looked away. "Whatever you did, it was because of the drug." She hesitated. "Right?"

"I'd like to think so."

"What else would it be?" she asked. "You're a good man, Erik."

There was doubt in his eyes when he looked back at her. "Maybe."

She embraced him, trying to drive his troubles away. "No maybe about it. What you did in the olden days, that was just because you were a man of your times. What you do now is entirely different, and the man I know would never hurt anyone unless it was in self-defense."

"Now, Nika, you know that's not true." She was surprised by his mildly scolding tone. "I'm a soldier. We're trained for the express purpose of hurting people."

She put her hand over his mouth. "I'm not talking about what you're ordered to do. I know you're in Special Forces, and you've probably killed a lot of people in the name of king and country. I get that. I'm talking about you, as a person, on your own."

He gently pulled her hand aside and said, "You have so much faith in me."

His tone was thick, and she couldn't read it completely. She nodded. "Yes. I do."

This time, he was the one who initiated the kiss. "I'm so sorry that Magda lied to you."

"I'm sorry she handed you over to them." She hesitated on the question, but she had to ask it. "Did they...hurt you?"

He shook his head. "No."

She relaxed, relieved that her worst imaginings had been false. "Good."

Ingrid returned to the house, and Nika greeted her with a smile. The old woman chuckled. "You look happy."

"I'm ecstatic."

Ingrid sat across the table from them. "I just asked the elves to arrange a parley with Ardrik."

Erik looked surprised. "A parley? What for? He's not the talking kind, as I recall."

"He needs to know that these raids on the faery are by rogue Draugr and not by all of you, and that it isn't sanctioned."

"Honestly, I don't know who would sanction anything. We don't have any central authority."

She looked at him pointedly and said, "There could be. You are Hakon's heir, and you should be their leader."

"I don't think the Draugr want a leader," he hedged.

Nika looked at him. "It makes sense. You're the most powerful, and you're a born leader. You should be in charge."

He gently put her on her feet and stood. "No. I can't be."

"Why not?" Ingrid asked.

"Look at what just happened. They controlled me. No leader worth a damn can be controlled."

"Those were extraordinary circumstances," Nika objected.

"Were they? Or is there some flaw in me that allowed it?" He paced the floor. "And it was so easy to convince me to revert to the old brutality. Was that the *dreyri* and the magic, or is that something in me that's always there? What if power makes me revert again?"

Ingrid frowned and snapped, "Stop it. This isn't like you, and it's unworthy of a Veithimathr." He stopped short, a surprised look on his face. "Someone needs to take control of this unruly lot, and to finally put an end to what the First and Magda are doing. That person needs to be you."

Nika had never seen Erik looking so flummoxed. He struggled to speak. "But... I... how do I do that? How do I take control?"

She folded her hands. "You call a congress of the Draugr and you announce it. If anyone objects, you kill them. It's that simple."

Nika's mouth dropped open. "That's brutal!"

"Violence and power are the only things that Draugr truly understand," Ingrid said with a shrug.

Erik stopped pacing and crossed his arms over his broad chest. "And how do you propose that I do that? The Draugr are all over the world. They're not all going to assemble in one place. There wouldn't be room."

Curiosity poked Nika, as it so frequently did. "How many Draugr are there?"

"Thousands," he answered. "Nobody knows the exact number."

"You call the local Draugr together at Uppsala, and I use the power of the place to broadcast what you have to say to the rest of your people," Ingrid said, as if it was the most obvious thing in the world. "Nika can help me."

She shook her head. "I have no idea how to do that."

"I can teach you."

Ingrid's words reminded her of her time already spent here, learning rune magic, and she felt a sudden flash of heat and dismay. "Oh my God," she said. "Magda and Natasha have the book."

"We'll get it back," Erik said. "I'll get Lars to help me, and we'll run a mission to retrieve it."

Nika went cold. "You don't know."

"Know what?"

"Erik... Lars and Sif are dead."

His jaw twitched as he clenched his teeth. "How?"

"The Ulfen attacked the cottage in Finland. They were destroyed." She went to him and put a hand on his arm. "I'm so sorry."

He stood in silence for a long moment, fighting his emotions. Finally, he turned on Ingrid. "And you want me to talk to them?"

She was unmoved by the ferocity in his voice. "Yes. Don't let more of your people die because of what the First are doing."

Nika rubbed his arm comfortingly. He looked at her, and his eyes were full of barely-contained rage. "How did Magda survive? She's not the fighter those two were."

She thought back. "I don't know. She was in the bedroom upstairs when I got there, and it looked like she defended herself... I guess she was lucky."

He looked unconvinced. He pulled away from her and went to the door. "I need air."

Nika began to follow him outside, but Ingrid stopped her. "Let him go."

"But he's upset," she protested.

"That's why you need to give him space. Men like Erik won't grieve in front of women."

"That's stupid."

"He doesn't want to seem weak. Remember, in some ways, he is not a modern man."

Nika sighed and returned to sit across from Ingrid. "So how do we get the book back?"

Ingrid patted her hand. "Let me handle that."

***

Erik was furious.

He stalked out of Ingrid's house and took flight immediately, his anger amplifying his native power. He went to Oulo and the cabin that they had rented for their ill-fated holiday. The place was a disaster. Police tape was strung all around the building, and debris was everywhere.

He ducked under the tape and went inside. He immediately saw the two piles of ash, disturbed but still heaped on the carpeting. He wanted to weep, but his anger dried his tears before they could fall. He scanned the room with every sense at his disposal, catching the scent of dried blood and Ulfen musk. A single Ulfen fang lay in the corner, apparently knocked out during the fight. He picked it up and held it in his hand, staring at it.

A sound on the porch, soft and almost non-existent, caught his attention, and he turned to face the door. To his surprise, Ardrik stood there, his arms crossed, his dark face locked in a pugnacious glare.

"I was watching. I thought you'd come back to this place. I'm supposed to parley with you," the alpha said, his voice a rumble, somewhere between speaking and growling. "But I would much rather slit your throat."

"Then we're agreed on that," Erik replied. "But there are things you need to know."

"Such as?"

"Such as the fact that with the exception of the fight against Loki, which I readily admit to, the Draugr raids on the faery settlements have been exclusively performed by the First." He considered the fang, then held it out to him. "One of yours?"

Ardrik looked at it, unimpressed. "It's just a tooth."

"I have enough of my own." He tossed the fang to the alpha, who caught it in midair.

He pocketed the fang and said, "You're telling me that these raids have all been done by rogue vampires."

"That's exactly what I'm saying."

"And which side of the line are you on today? Seems you tiptoed all the way over to marauder not too long ago."

Erik flushed in shame. "There were extenuating circumstances."

The Ulfen snorted. "Oh, yes. Of course. You were *enchanted*." His tone was mocking. "That's a lame excuse, vampire."

"I don't care what you think, shifter. It's the truth." He stepped closer, but stopped when they were still out of arm's reach of one another. "I'm not proud of it, and I'll make amends to the trolls if I can."

"They want you dead."

"That's one thing they can't have." He squared his stance and held his hands at his sides, ready to act if he needed to. He realized with a sinking feeling that he did not have any of his arsenal with him; if there was to be a fight, it would be strictly hand-to-hand.

"What are you proposing that I take back to the faery?" Ardrik asked. "Your assurances that your boys will stop? That won't be good enough."

"My assurances that I will make them stop, and yes, that the raids will end. What more would they require?"

"An end to the theft of faery blood for your bottles."

Erik nodded. "I can guarantee that will end with the First."

"And an end to all Draugr raids on faery settlements."

"I've already promised that."

Ardrik looked at him, his eyes hard. "And the Rune Master as our hostage until you complete your task."

Erik barked a humorless laugh. "Out of the question!"

"Then the war continues," the alpha told him, "and the next time I see you, it will be with my teeth in your throat."

"I can promise you that you have that backwards."

This time, it was the Ulfen who laughed. "Are we done here?"

"Almost." He paused to confirm that he meant was he was about to say, then continued. "The mastermind behind all of this is the Valtaeigr named Magda. She is the one conducting the bottling operation, and the one who has the most to gain from its continuance. She is using the First as her tools. She is the one you want."

"A Valtaeigr?" Ardrik sniffed. "Why would she do something like that?"

"I suspect she's part of the Dark Sisterhood."

The Ulfen sighed. "Why don't you help out a poor, dumb wolf and tell me what that is."

"The Valtaeigr who serve Hel's dark aspect are the Dark Sisterhood. They are the witches and the treacherous among the *vala*."

"You Draugr are so in love with your gods and your myths," he said dismissively. "Your superstitions keep you in the Dark Ages."

"Says the creature who lives with his pack in a cave in the woods."

Ardrik's face darkened with restrained anger. "You tell me this Magda person is behind this. Why should I believe you?"

He shook his head. "I can't say. That will be between you and your conscience."

"I have no conscience."

"I'm not surprised."

"You can't tell me that you're any different," the Ulfen sniffed.

"I can, and I am." He folded his arms. "This is my message to your faery overlords. I will stop the First. I will deliver Magda to them for punishment. The raids will end. I will enforce a truce between the Draugr and the faery."

"And in return?" Ardrik asked. "There's never something for nothing."

"In return, your pack will stop attacking my people, and the faery will stop their war."

He laughed again, but there was no mirth in it. The Ulfen said, "I will take them your message, but I wouldn't expect a positive response."

"It will be as it will be," Erik said.

"Very philosophical for a blood drinker."

"Your point?"

Ardrik shifted into his full wolf form. He growled at Erik, baring his teeth, and then loped away into the woods.

Chapter Fourteen

Erik returned to Ingrid's house by the sea, going immediately to the keg of *dreyri* that his hostess kept in the cellar. Nika followed him, concerned. His expression was steely as he pulled a pint of the enchanted blood, then drank it down in one go. She put her hand on his back.

"Are you all right?"

He shook his head. "No. But I will be." He refilled the mug and emptied it again.

Ingrid joined them, coming down to sit on the stairs. Erik did not glance back, but he said to her, "I just had that parley you requested."

She nodded. "And?"

"And I told Ardrik that I would end the raids and that I would stop the First from bottling faery blood. I also promised to hand Magda over to them for punishment, since she's the mastermind behind this whole fiasco."

"And in return, what did you ask of them?"

He filled his mug a third time. "An end to the war, and cessation of hostilities by the Ulfen."

"What did he say?" Nika asked.

"He laughed at me."

"That's not promising."

He smiled at her a bit wanly. "No, not really." He sipped the *dreyri* and sighed. "This is good, but it's lacking the life spark. I need to feed from a live human before I go."

Nika frowned. "Go where?"

"To Natasha's lair to retrieve the book, and to Uppsala to call the Draugr to a conference." He glanced at Ingrid, and she nodded at him approvingly.

"Take me with you when you go."

"No," he objected. "It's too dangerous. I know you can handle yourself, but I need you to be safe."

"Won't I be safe with you?"

"If I'm concentrating on fighting the First, I won't be able to protect you. And if I'm worried about protecting you, I won't be fighting to the best of my abilities." He put his mug aside. "I'm sorry, Nika. I don't mean to wrap you in cotton, but I just can't stand the thought of you going into harm's way."

She set her jaw. "It's my book. I ought to be the one to get it back." He looked away from her, and she persisted. "I am not helpless. Why do you think I've been learning this magic? I can use it to defend us both. You need me to counter them."

Ingrid interjected, "You are susceptible to the Valtaeigr. You always have been. If you have your own *vala* with you, then perhaps you'll be better able to keep your wits."

Nika was not going to budge on the point, and she could see that he knew it. He sighed. "Fine. Come along if you must."

She nodded firmly. "I must."

He sighed. "You are a stubborn woman."

"Good. That means I can keep up with you, because you're a stubborn man."

Erik's frown melted into a reluctant smirk, the corner of his mouth turning up. His blue eyes twinkled as he leaned over and kissed her. "I thank the gods we can't have children, because they'd be too hard-headed to bear."

Ingrid chuckled. "Pity me. I have to deal with both of you."

Erik put his arm around Nika, and she leaned against him, her hand on his broad chest. "Call your meeting," he said. "I will play the part you ask of me."

The old Valtaeigr stood and bowed to him. "My king...."

She left them in the basement with the *dreyri*. Erik's mouth turned down again. Nika rubbed her palm up and down his sternum, liking the hollow between his pectoral muscles and hoping the stroking would help to calm him. "You're doing the right thing."

"I'm not fit to be anyone's king."

"I disagree. And we've already proven that I can out-stubborn you, so you might as well just agree with me and save yourself some time."

He kissed her forehead. "If I'm king, that makes you my queen. Are you ready for that?"

She looked into his eyes. "If I'm with you, I'm ready for anything."

She hoped that those wouldn't prove to be brave last words.

***

In Finland, Olaf stood in the basement beside the vats of faery blood, watching as Magda paced and stormed. "How could you let him get away? And he's resumed his bond with her. There is no other way she could have had the power of flight. You are incompetent!"

Mia stood at the center of Magda's storm. "I'm sorry, mother. I tried to hold him, but his will was too strong."

"No man has that strong a will," she retorted angrily. "No man can resist a Valtaeigr who *tries*. By Odin's eye, I taught you better than that!"

Kjeld finished taking down the corpse of a myling. It had been a slender prize, but a prize nonetheless. "To be fair, he was under her control for a very long time, and he did things he never did even in our mortal days."

Magda glared at him. "I didn't ask for your opinion."

Olaf snorted. "You never have to ask him. It's always available for free."

She put her hands on her hips and stopped pacing. "Did you at least get the video sent out?"

Kjeld nodded. "I texted or e-mailed it to everyone on your client list. And I do mean everyone...mortals included."

Olaf raised his eyebrow. "You have mortals on your client list?"

She looked defensive. "I have pets, and some people pay handsomely for the extended lifespans that the *dreyri* can give."

Dag dragged in another myling, which was sobbing in terror as he affixed its feet to the recently emptied hook above the vat. He slashed its throat with a cold iron dagger and they watched impassively as its life drained out. The twitching lasted longer than Magda would have expected, but then, it was hanging upside down, so the blood was running to its brain, keeping it alive.

"I want -"

Her words were cut off by the sound of Ingrid Nilsson's voice in their heads. The telepathy was strong and undeniable, and they could not have ignored her if they'd tried. *All Draugr,* she said. *Hear me, all Draugr, in every land. The first meeting of the Draugr will be held in Uppsala in four days' time, at the height of the moon. All Draugr are to attend. We will speak of war.*

Dag looked at Magda. "How can she do that?"

"Telepathy spell," she said dismissively. "It's not that difficult, if you have an appropriate focus."

"And yet you still use a cell phone," Kjeld mocked.

She drew herself up haughtily. "I make use of modern conveniences to save my magic for more important things."

"Things like keeping Thorvald and his woman under wraps?" Olaf asked.

Dag waggled his dark eyebrows at her. "Whoops."

"I hate you all."

"Well, then, maybe you don't want this blood that badly," Olaf said, pulling a pistol from the waistband of his jeans. He pointed the gun at Magda. "I'm sure I can find some other Dark Sister to enchant this *dreyri* for me. Maybe it's time that Snake Eyes was under new management."

Mia stepped between them. "Olaf," she said softly. "Husband. Don't."

"Husband?" Magda echoed, looking from her daughter to the First and back again. "When did this happen?"

"We've lived together for centuries," he said. "Some things are just assumed after a while."

Dag, seemingly unable to resist needling her, asked, "Didn't you ever come to think of Thorvald as your husband? You gave him three kids."

She glowered. "He was never my husband, and I never gave him anything. Everything he ever got from me, he took."

Kjeld rubbed his finger and thumb together. "Sad violins are playing for you," he said. "The saddest and smallest violins in the world."

She spat a word of magic, and he was abruptly showered in silver dust that appeared from thin air, both aerosolized and clinging. He choked and sputtered on the toxic gas, his face turning ashen as the poison took effect.

The other First watched him gag his way into unconsciousness, none of them mustering anything beyond simple curiosity. Mia began to go to him, but Olaf held her back, his massive hand on her shoulder.

Magda walked to where Kjeld was drowning on dry land. Taking a silver stiletto out of her stylish knee-high boot, she stabbed him in the heart. He burst into ashes and fell, scattered, to the floor.

She straightened and glared at the assembled vampires. "Get me as much blood as you can. I need to get my stock up."

"You don't order us," Dag reminded her. "You were once our slave. You could be again."

She raised her hand, and the fingertips sparkled with unspent energy. "Do you want to go on the path that your friend just walked?"

"Him?" He laughed. "He wasn't a friend. And now we all get a larger share of the profits. Besides, I know that you can only cast one of those spells a day. Isn't that right, Mia?"

Magda looked at her daughter, who looked away sheepishly. "That's right," she answered.

Olaf pulled Mia into his body, wrapping one arm over her, his hands grasping at her chest. "Mia has told us many things about being Valtaeigr, haven't you?" He kissed her ear, then took the delicate upper shell between his teeth. She winced as he bit just hard enough to draw blood. "We find that with the right motivation, she can be quite a teacher."

She trembled with rage. "You will regret ever touching her."

Olaf continued to fondle her. "Not any time soon, I'll wager."

She met Mia's eyes, and the younger woman shook her head solemnly, warning her into silence. Magda backed toward the stairs.

"I will see you in four days," she said. "Bring all of your weapons to Uppsala. Thorvald and the Rune Master will be there, and we need to kill them both."

"We know what to do with them," Dag told her. "Don't worry about that."

She did not respond. With one last look at Mia, she left the basement and headed back out to her waiting car.

***

Erik stood beside the kitchen table and watched Ingrid packing up the ingredients of her spell. He had come to be very wary of incense, so he stayed well out of the smoke of whatever plant matter she was burning. She extinguished it with a candle snuffer and put it outside the window.

"Did they hear you?" Nika asked. "Did it work?"

"Did you hear me?" she asked in return.

"Well, yes."

"Then it worked." She handed Erik his cell phone. "I took the liberty of taking possession of this when you left in such a hurry."

He accepted it. "Thank you." There was a notification of a missed message, and he opened the app. The video of the troll settlement raid began to play. He immediately turned it off.

"What was that?" Nika asked.

"Someone trying to cause trouble." He looked at the list of recipients and ground his teeth. Not only were most of the Draugr that he knew listed there, but his superiors in the SOG and the Swedish military were also named. Even the personal secretary of the King of Sweden was on the list. "Jesus."

Nika raised an eyebrow and took the phone away. "May I?"

"I wish you wouldn't, but..." He took a deep breath. "It's a video of what I did while I was enspelled. It's not pretty. Please don't watch it."

He could see her warring with herself for a long moment. Finally, she deliberately deleted the message and the hateful video that had come with it.

"If you don't want me to see it, I won't look."

He embraced her, relieved. "Thank you, my love."

She held him tightly. "We're in this together, whatever anyone says or does. I don't care what happened when you were drugged and enchanted. That wasn't you. Nothing in that video was your fault."

"I don't know if other people will feel the same." He took a deep breath, steadying his nerves. He normally didn't care what other people thought of him, but in a case like this, where his actions were so heinous and his guilt was so raw, it troubled him. "Nika...I slaughtered faery children. I participated in the gangrape of a Huldra. I was brutal and beastly and..."

She put her hand over his mouth. "Stop. The First were, and the orders you were given were, but you were not. I will never believe that you were."

He pulled away. "Not long ago, you were having trouble trusting me because of my past doing things just like this. Now you ignore it? I don't understand."

Nika took a deep breath and put her arms around his neck. "I know you better now. We have lived together, just the two of us, for months and months in our little house on the island. I know you're a good man and that those days are far behind you." She kissed him, and he gratefully accepted the touch. "I know you better than you think I do. I trust you."

He pulled her in his arms and held her as if he would never let her go, nearly crushing the wind out of her in the process. Luckily Draugr could not be suffocated. When he finally released her, she put her hands on his face and kissed him again.

"I am on your side, no matter what. Let me be by your side, too."

Ingrid took his phone and pressed her hand against it, a look of extreme concentration on her face. An arc of magical energy sprang from her fingers and into the screen, then raced out into the internet. She held her hand there for a long moment, swaying on her feet, until finally the light in her hand vanished and she nearly fell. Erik shot out a hand and steadied her while Nika grabbed a chair.

She sat heavily on the seat and looked up at him through watery eyes. The strain had been incredible. "No mortals will ever see that video," she told him.

He hugged her and kissed her forehead. "Thank you, mother."

Nika gaped. "Mother?"

Ingrid smiled. "Surprise."

Erik explained, "She is the vessel of Frigg, wife of Odin, father of Vidar. When vessels were chosen, my mortal family was selected. Hakon, my father, was not worthy of bearing Odin, and so he was passed over, but my mother and I were given the honor."

She nodded. "Gunnar and Rolf were my other sons, and I had a daughter, Fulla."

"Gunnar, your partner in the Veithimathr?" Nika asked. "And Rolf, who -"

"The blood-eagle, yes." He held out his hand to her. "Forgive me for not telling you?"

She laughed softly. "Well, you've got a thousand years of stories still to tell me. I'm sure that you'll get to everything eventually."

Ingrid looked up at him. "She's too good for you, you know."

Erik smiled at Nika, his eyes warm with love. "I know that very well."

"That's a bit backward," Nika chuckled. "Usually mothers don't think the girl is ever good enough for their sons."

"Most mothers don't have sons who are as bothersome as this one is," Ingrid said with a smile. She patted his leg. "My first-born child and biggest headache..."

Erik pulled the other chair out from the table and gestured to it. "Nika, you might want to sit down. There are things I need to tell you."

She sat slowly, clearly trying to keep her face calm. She rested her hands on her thighs and looked at him expectantly.

He sighed. "Magda and I have a long history."

Nika nodded. "Lars said that she was your slave. Sif told him that."

Erik sat on the table, his expression grim. "That's true, unfortunately. When I was still mortal and still raiding with my father, we went to Russia and kidnapped several beautiful women from the Rus village we attacked. Magda was the one I took. I was harsh to her, and demanding, and... cruel, in retrospect." He could not meet her eyes. "I kept her and took her against her will, and she bore me three children...two sons and a daughter."

Her lips parted as if she meant to say something, but she closed them immediately, holding her silence.

"The boys died long ago, one in infancy, one in early manhood. The daughter was born Valtaeigr, like her mother, and she still lives." He looked up. "She's the one who enchanted me."

Ingrid said softly, "Your blood connection gives her power over you."

"I turned Magda against her will, but she and Mia - our daughter - both became vessels by their own choice. That's one thing I didn't force on them." He finally looked at Nika. "I thought you should know."

She took a moment, then said, "All right. Now I know." She smiled for him. "It doesn't change anything."

He was relieved, and he knew his face showed it. He nodded. "Thank you." He looked at his mother. "We need to go to Uppsala to prepare for the meeting."

She stood. "So let's go."

Chapter Fifteen

Alaric trotted into the pack's den and shifted immediately into his human form. His father, who was lounging with his mate, looked up expectantly.

"Well?" Ardrik asked.

His oldest son sat beside him. "The witches say they'll watch the Draugr, and they'll keep watch on the Huntsman, too, to see what he does. If he stops the raids, they'll consider calling off the war." He scratched his head. "There's no word of Dominic anywhere."

Ardrik glowered. "Forget your brother. He is dead to us." His mate, who was in her wolf form, licked his face. He stroked her silvery fur. "And what are the Draugr doing?"

"All accounts are that they're flooding into Sweden in droves. Every Draugr in the world, it seems, is coming."

"A war party?" the alpha asked. "Are they assembling their army?"

Alaric shook his head. "My contact says that the Huntsman has called a meeting of all Draugr at Uppsala, where the old temple was."

Ardrik narrowed his eyes and thought about the news. "Strange. I wonder what he's doing."

"I have no idea. My contact says that the Draugr have never been assembled this way before."

One of the other females, who was sitting nearby with a book, asked, "Who is your contact?"

"One of the Dark Sisterhood."

She frowned. "Can you trust her?"

"As much as you can trust anyone who isn't Ulfen," the pack beta shrugged. "I believe she tells me the truth."

"Are you fucking her?"

He grinned. "When she lets me."

Ardrik chuckled. "That's my boy."

***

Erik and Nika stood beside Ingrid in the garden. She was bent and listening to the earth, hearing something that neither of them could detect.

"What is she doing?" Nika asked him in a whisper.

He shook his head in bewilderment. "I have no idea."

Finally, Ingrid smiled and pushed her hands into the soft soil. The feeling of energy like static electricity filled the air, and the hair on the back of Nika's neck began to stand up. She wrapped her arms around herself and looked into her mentor's face.

"Ley lines," Ingrid said. "They connect points of power all over the earth. Early humans could detect that power, and that's why they built their ceremonial spots on the nexus spots, the places where the lines intersect. There's a line that runs right through this garden."

She held up a hand to Nika and beckoned her to kneel beside her.

"Put your hand in the ground, just here," she directed. "You'll be able to feel the line."

"Should I...?" Erik began.

"No boys allowed," Ingrid said with a grin. "Valtaeigr only."

He fell silent and stepped back to watch, his arms folded. Nika gave him a smile, then returned her attention to Ingrid.

"Hand in the ground, child," she encouraged.

Nika pushed her hand into the dirt where Ingrid had pointed, and almost immediately, she could feel the rushing of energy flowing past beneath her fingertips. It was impossibly fast and stronger than she expected. Her entire arm began to vibrate and buzz with the feeling.

"Through the ley lines, a suitably talented Valtaeigr can travel to other points. There is a nexus in St. Petersburg, not far from where Natasha keeps her house. That's where they have your book."

"Are you sure?" Erik interjected. "We need to get some -"

"Shush!" his mother scolded.

"...intel."

"I'm sure. Don't doubt me." She nodded to Nika. "Push your hand into the flow. Feel that energy, that river of power. Now... will your body to dive in and swim along." She laced her fingers with Nika's free hand. "I'll go with you so you don't get overwhelmed. You won't be able to travel alone for a very long time, but with me to guide you, you'll be safe."

Erik shifted his stance, his expression skeptical. Both women ignored him and concentrated on their task.

"Is this rune magic?" Nika asked.

"No. This is something else. This is witchcraft."

"But I'm not a witch," she protested.

"Yes, you are. Now... dive."

Ingrid went first, her physical body dissolving into motes of light that swarmed like tiny flies, then diving into the ground where her hand had been. As the older *vala* disappeared, Nika began to dissolve, as well, and she gave a cry of surprise just before bursting into a shower of golden sparks that followed Ingrid down into the line.

Erik shouted and stepped forward, but the two of them were gone as if they had never existed. Trying to trust his mother to bring them home safely, he went back into the house to wait.

***

The current drew them swiftly along, and Ingrid, who was very experienced with this mode of travel, swam even faster. Nika felt herself - although how she was feeling anything was a mystery to her - flying along behind Ingrid, their hands interconnected, their motion smooth and fast as a skiff on the water.

She was full of sensations - tickling electricity, an almost religious awe, the rush of speed, pressure in the head that wasn't even real any longer. She also felt fear, but she could feel Ingrid with her, and the presence of the veteran Valtaeigr was comforting. She followed where her elder led

Suddenly they were real and whole again, standing on two feet connected to solid legs, an inch deep in the soil of a flower garden. She looked around herself in wonder, seeing a huge edifice of yellow and white with a colonnaded entry way. She and Ingrid were in the lawn, just off the side of the brick approach to the building.

"Where are we?" she asked, gasping for air now that she had lungs again.

"St. Petersburg Botanical Garden," she answered, pulling her feet out of the ground. It was difficult at first to break through the undisturbed turf; it was almost as if their feet had been planted like bulbs and they were the flowers that had bloomed. Nika had never felt so much like a flower in all of her life.

Ingrid held her hand. "Well done," she congratulated. "You handled that first travel brilliantly. When you're finally powerful enough to do that on your own, you'll have no trouble."

She stepped up onto the bricked walkway. "Are we close to Natasha's house?"

"You tell me. Can you find the book?"

Nika closed her eyes and reached out with her mind, extending invisible fingers to grasp toward the tendrils of power that surrounded the Book of Odin. She could not pinpoint its location, but she felt enough that she could discern a direction. "This way," she said.

They left the grounds of the garden and headed east along Reki Karpovki and across the Neva. The humming in Nika's ears grew louder the closer they came to St. Sampson's Cathedral. The church's three-story gate house was pale blue with white trim, a confection in color that looked almost too sweet to be real. She went through the wrought iron gate and into the building.

A square of paving stones to the left of the gate had been disturbed, and she pulled them aside. There was a hiding place beneath the stones, and in that hiding place, a familiar shape wrapped in cloth. She reached in and pulled the Book out into the light.

As soon as she lay hands on it, the sound of a gun cocking sounded behind her. Ingrid crossed her arms and stood by silently as Natasha, her raincoat belted tight around her slender waist, stepped out of the wing of the gatehouse.

"I knew you would come," she said, speaking English. "And Ingrid, too."

Nika clutched the book to her chest and faced her, lifting her chin. "In the flesh."

"I have friends who would pay dearly for your head... or your ass."

"I suppose they'll have to be disappointed."

Ingrid put her hand on the small of Nika's back and subtly pushed her to the side, close under Ingrid's arm. Natasha stepped closer, her stiletto heels clicking as she walked.

"That remains to be seen." She aimed the gun at Nika. "Put down the book, or I will blow a hole in your head."

"Where's Magda?"

Natasha smiled, her scarlet lipstick stark against the ice white of her teeth. "Not your concern. I said put down the book."

Ingrid whispered in her mind. *Overpower her.*

Nika frowned. *She's older than me and probably much faster. Stronger, too.*

I'm not talking about physically. Think like a vala.

The Book of Odin hummed against her chest, and she looked into Natasha's eyes. Their gazes connected, and she smiled wider.

"No."

Natasha raised the gun, but her hand went numb before she could pull the trigger. Her eyes widened in surprise as she felt an unseen hand slip inside her own, followed by a spectral body that slid into place, arms in her arms, feet in her feet. She let out a strangled cry, but there was nothing she could do. Nika's will had been made manifest and was in control.

"Tell me, Natasha," she said, "what was the plan? Were you and Magda going to widen your empire of narcotic *dreyri*, coasting to power and money on the backs of a thousand addicted vampires? Were you going to use my blood as the crowning vintage? Or maybe Erik's? Or were you going to try to make him your slave, to get revenge for the years of slavery he put Magda through?" She saw a flicker of response in Natasha's mind, and she nodded. "So that was it. Death for me and slavery for him, then he would be thrown literally to the wolves. You would appease the Faery and the Ulfen and you'd get your revenge. It's a nice plan, I must congratulate you. You just forgot one thing."

She stepped forward and pulled the gun out of Natasha's hand. Ingrid stepped back, showing with her body language that she would let Nika handle this as she chose. Nika put the gun against Natasha's forehead.

The other Valtaeigr, High Priestess of the Dark Sisterhood, trembled in her struggle to break free from Nika's control. She was strong, but not quite strong enough, and all three women knew it. Nika smiled.

"You forgot that I don't die that easy."

She yanked away her control just before she pulled the trigger. The high-velocity bullet took Natasha's head apart, and she dropped to the paving stones, never to rise again.

Nika had meant to pull the trigger, and had intended to end Natasha's threat. Still, she had never killed anyone, much less as point blank range. She felt all of the color drain from her face and her knees went watery.

A scream sounded from the street, and Nika snapped to. She put the gun into the pocket of her jeans. "Let's go back, Ingrid."

"Yes," the old woman said, as sirens began to wail. "Let's."

Nika turned to head back toward the garden, but Ingrid dragged her in another direction, past a trendy microbrewery and a sports bar. She pulled her through a cafe and out into a tiny green patch of grass at the base of the building.

"Hold on," she said, and she turned them both into energy and dove back into the ley line. They hit it at speed and careened through the links, hitting nexus after nexus, twisting and turning so quickly that Nika lost all sense of direction. Ingrid kept moving forward, never stopping, not even when the line they followed seemed headed directly into a blazing inferno of spiritual power.

Don't let go, Ingrid coached her, and then they plunged into those flames, the brilliant white of the light surrounding and penetrating them, coating all of the tiny echoes of their spirits with an energy that spoke with a hundred voices. They were being crowded by a thousand personalities, a thousand words rattling through their heads, and Nika had the disconcerting feeling of being grabbed at by scores of hands. Then, as quickly as the chaos of that light had begun, it was over, and she and Ingrid were once more on the solid ground, this time in a clearing surrounded by ancient trees.

"Sorry," Ingrid gasped. "Didn't mean to go through the graveyard."

"Graveyard?" Nika sputtered. They both fell onto the ground, panting.

"Dead human souls travel the ley lines, too. Sometimes they're unhappy to see us. I should have warned you."

Nika shook her head and rolled onto her back, the book still tightly grasped in her hand. "It's okay. I should have warned you that I was going to shoot her."

"It surprised me," Ingrid admitted. "I would have expected that from Erik, not you. Of course, you *are* American..."

"Gun control is great until you have to shoot somebody," Nika said, closing her eyes.

Ingrid chuckled. "Don't get too comfortable. We're a long way from home, and we're not in safety yet."

"I'm glad you didn't say we're not out of the woods," Nika grinned, gesturing at the trees. "I would have had to hit you."

They laughed together, and then Ingrid rose up onto her knees. "Come forward, sisters. Meet the new Rune Master."

There was a shimmer in the woods, and then the sound of leaves rustling, and from all sides, a group of women emerged into the clearing. They were all shapes and sizes, all colors and ages, and they all moved cautiously into view. Some were dark-haired and young, some gray-haired and bent with age. One was tall and statuesque and the stereotypical Swedish goddess. They all looked at Nika with frank and open gazes, appraising her.

"Sisters of the Light, I present Nika Graves, Chosen of Erik Thorvald and Mistress of Odin's Runes." She turned to Nika with a smile. "Nika, these are the witches of Hel's bright half."

One of the witches, a tall and stout woman with gray streaks through her long brown curls, stepped forward and put out her hand. "Welcome, sister."

Nika accepted the handshake. "Thank you."

Her acceptance of being called sister to these witches caused them all to visibly relax, and the one who was still holding Nika's hand said, "I sense no duplicity in her."

With that, they streamed forward, surrounding her with hugs and words of welcome. Ingrid looked on with a smile.

***

It was more than a day since Ingrid and Nika had vanished into the ley lines, and Erik was doing his best to stay calm.

He could not seem to reach Nika directly, but their Chosen bond was intact and untroubled, telling him that she was in good health and possibly even happy, wherever Ingrid had taken her to. He hoped they got the book back with minimal difficulty, and mostly he hoped that Magda was not there when Ingrid and Nika arrived.

He had to be in Uppsala in three more nights. There was not much time to get things arranged, especially not if he was going to have to work alone.

The most important thing for him to do would be to ensure that there were no humans around with his vampire kin began to arrive. The very young ones were unable to spend more than twelve hours without a kill, and there would be many youngsters at the congress. That was a lot of killing that would need to be covered up. Better, he thought, to just prevent it. To that end, he went to Karlsborg Fortress and called on the SOG.

He wasn't foolish enough to call on the actual SOG, just on the stores. He "borrowed" a uniform and just enough paperwork and ephemera to give his planned ruse the stamp of authenticity. His last act was to liberate a jeep from the garage and take it out of the Fortress and on the road.

He drove to Gamla Uppsala Museum and parked the jeep, its Swedish army insignia and plates plain to see, in front of the main door. He adjusted his olive-green beret with its SOG patch and walked into the museum lobby.

There was a clerk at the information desk, a bit apart from the ticket-takers. He walked up to her.

"*Hej*," he greeted. "My name is Captain Thorvald, SOG. I need to speak to the museum director, is he here?"

She looked up at him with surprise and excitement in her pale eyes. "Uh... Yes, Captain. Right this way."

She led him past the ticket-taker and into the director's office. The director, a middle-aged man with an athletic build, met him halfway across the room with a hearty handshake.

"Welcome to Gamla Uppsala Museum, Captain," the director said. "I'm Sven Nordstrom. How can I help you?"

"Mr. Nordstrom," Erik greeted, shaking his hand. "I need to talk to you about closing the facility for the next 48 hours."

Nordstrom's jaw dropped. "Closing? But..."

"I realize that this is a peak time for tours, and I'm very sorry about the inconvenience. The Supreme Commander of the SAF would not make this request unless it was very important." He gestured toward a tour bus that was being boarded just outside the window. "We need to stop these tours immediately and clear the site."

"What is this about?"

Erik met his eyes seriously, and tiny pinpoints of green Draugr fire flared in their depths. The human's mind acquiesced and believed every word he said. "I cannot share certain details - top secret. But the Supreme Commander has reason to believe that it would be unwise for tourists to enter the Gamla Uppsala site for the next 48 hours. They need to be cleared immediately."

Nordstrom stared blankly at him for a heartbeat, and Erik feared he may have mesmerized him too deeply. The man shook himself slightly and said, "There won't be any harm to the site, will there? This is a rich historical and archaeological site. It is invaluable."

"I understand that, and that's why we're trying to keep it, and everyone else, safe." He sighed and forced the man to meet his eyes. He'd had enough of subtlety and bowing to human free will. "Clear. This. Site."

Nordstrom shivered once, then moved to obey, placing phone calls to tour guides and docents. Erik went and stood in the main lobby, watching as the flow of tourists was stopped, reversed, and sent back out to wherever they had come from. It all happened in an admirably orderly manner, and it was swiftly carried out. The army could not have done the job better.

He was watching the last of the humans being loaded up into their tour buses when he caught the scent of an Ulfen nearby. He looked around and saw her standing at the entrance, her thick blonde hair plaited into a single braid and lying thick on her shoulder. She nodded to him when she was certain that he had seen her, and he squared his stance, facing her. He did not pull a weapon.

She walked to him, keeping a safe distance away, with a support pillar nearby in case she needed to duck for cover. Erik intended to use the ticket desk for cover if it came to that. She looked unarmed, but he had learned never to underestimate the wolves.

"Huntsman," she greeted. "I am Ardella."

He nodded to her in response, civil but not exactly friendly. He said nothing.

She shifted on her feet, cagey, and said, "What are your people planning for Uppsala? We heard that you are calling a great meeting, the first of its kind."

"I told your alpha and that I would be ending the raids. This is part of that."

Ardella took a cautious step forward, and he held his ground. "The Faery do not believe that you mean it."

"Then the Faery should watch and see."

"What are you really doing?"

She was closer now, and he could have reached out and touched her. He knew that he should have backed up and put more space between them, but he thought that might look like an admission of weakness, so he stayed where he was.

"I told you. Ending the raids and dealing with the First at the same time."

"I have a contact who says that two of the First were recently killed."

He kept his face expressionless. "Which two?"

"Bjorn and Kjeld."

The news surprised him. He had expected Bjorn to be the last of them to go. He had always been spectacularly wily. "Who is your contact?"

"A member of the Dark Sisterhood who has broken ranks to side with Faery."

"Why would she do that?"

"She developed a conscience. She says she inherited it from her father."

She looked aside, and he saw a tiny tattoo on the left side of her neck, just below her ear. It was Hagalaz, the symbol for destructive and uncontrollable natural forces. It seemed an appropriate rune for a werewolf to wear. She touched the symbol, knowing he was looking at it, and then she turned back to face him.

"Remember this sign, Huntsman. My contact wears the same symbol."

He had seen that tattoo once before. "Mia," he said.

Ardella looked impressed, but only for a moment. "The very same. Good memory."

Erik hesitated, then took a gamble. "If your pack wants to witness what I do, have them come to Uppsala when the Draugr meet. Stay outside the circle of the royal mounds and watch. If they see what I do, they will believe that my words have been sincere."

She looked skeptical, but said, "I will tell my mate. I can't guarantee he will come."

"You can only do what you can do," he said. "Ardrik is known for his hard head."

She smiled briefly, brilliantly, at the mention of her alpha's name. "So you know him."

"We've spoken."

Nordstrom came and distracted Erik by announcing, "The tourists have all gone. The site is clear."

"Thank you. You may go."

The museum director did as he was told and left the museum, heading for home. When Erik turned back to speak to Ardella, he found that she was gone. He sighed and went back out to the jeep.

***

Nika and Ingrid returned to the house late in the night, the Book of Odin once again safely in Nika's possession. The house was quiet and still and they found Erik sleeping in front of the fire. Ingrid kissed Nika on the cheek and went up to the loft, leaving the two of them alone.

Nika put the book on the kitchen table and curled up beside Erik, her arms around his waist. He stirred at her touch and opened his eyes.

"You're back," he mumbled.

She kissed his shoulder. "Yes. Natasha is dead."

"Pardon me if I don't weep."

He turned in her arms so that he was facing her, his hand brushing a stray hair out of her eyes. She smiled at him and touched his face.

"Tomorrow night everything changes," she whispered.

"What do you mean?"

She ran a hand down his chest. "After tomorrow, you'll be king."

He chuckled and pulled her into his arms. "Then nothing changes but a word."

"You'll have more responsibilities," she said. "You might not..."

"Might not have time for you? Is that what you were going to say?" He looked into her eyes. She looked away, and he turned her face back toward him. "I will never, ever put you last in line, my love."

"I just..."

He silenced her with a kiss, showing her in action what his words were failing to convey. She put her arms around him and tangled her fingers in his blond hair, kissing him fiercely. He teased her lips with the tip of his tongue, and she opened for him, letting him inside. He explored her mouth with leisurely passion, his hand running down her side to cup her firm buttock and pull her closer still.

He kissed her until she was dizzy from it, and she rolled him onto his back. He looked up at her, and the love in his eyes allayed all of her fears. She knelt over him, straddling his hips, her fingers running lightly down the midline of his body. He shivered, and she smiled.

They undressed each other in the firelight, the glowing flames warming their skin. He cupped her breasts almost reverently, and she pressed herself against the growing heat between his legs. She teased him for as long as she could stand it, rubbing their bodies together until they both demanded more. He groaned when she let him slip inside of her, and she tipped her head back with pleasure.

They took their time. They kissed and touched, long, languid trails of fingertips and lips, and all the while their bodies were joined as one. He took her hands in his, and she interlaced their fingers, squeezing gently. She began to rock, slowly at first, then with more speed as the feeling grew sweeter. He pushed up into her, rising to meet her downward motions, and it was like heaven.

Sensation demanded speed, and they moved faster, desperate for each other and for the release they could only find together. When the moment came, it was a tidal wave of purest ecstasy, and then they were spent, lying in one another's arms in a happy haze.

Chapter Sixteen

At the time appointed, they gathered on the burial mounds at Gamla Uppsala. A series of hills were the only remnants of the mighty temple that had once stood here, but in his mind's eye, Erik could still see it as it was in its grandest days. The tallest hill was surmounted by a makeshift wooden platform that had been erected for the purpose, and Erik stood there with Nika at his side, watching as hundreds of Draugr filled the meadow. He had his double-headed axe there with him, his hand on the grip, the blades hones and shining.

The wind blew in from a stand of trees to the side of the fenced-off field, and it carried with it the scent of the Ulfen. The other Draugr sensed it, too, and there was a low murmur through the crowd. Nika took Erik's hand and squeezed it nervously.

There was a flutter in the assembled vampires, and then a rush of power announced the arrival of the rest of the First. Olaf, Brevik, Dag, Halvar and Agnar strode up to the base of the hill, moving as a unit. It was almost as if they had come to raid the meeting. In their midst, Magda and Mia walked side by side their faces grim. Magda was wearing the black of mourning.

When all of the vampires had finally arrived, Erik was stunned by the sheer numbers of them. He had no idea that there were so many Draugr in the world. The meadow below the burial mounds was thronged with faces, most of whom he did not recognize. He would have felt more confident in his plan with fewer Draugr to contend with; when a group was as large as this one, it could become unpredictable and dangerous. Mob mentality was a frightful thing when the mob was made up of vampires.

Brevik shouted up to him, his voice raised so that all of those in attendance could hear. "Tell us why you called us, Thorvald."

He looked out over the group of vampires. "I am Erik Thorvald, the son and heir of Hakon, our first king." He heard a low murmur, and he waited for it to pass. "I have come to claim his crown."

The murmur became a roar of surprise, outrage, and even acclamation. The other First looked at one another in disbelief, and Olaf said to Mia, "What did you do to him?"

She shook her head, staring up at her father in consternation. "Not this."

Magda crossed her arms and stared up at Erik with a hateful look upon her face. "King," she spat. "I will not live under his thumb again."

Dag looked around the group, his eyes drawn toward the forest. "Why are the Ulfen here?"

Agnar shrugged. "If all of your enemies were gathering together, don't you think you'd want to see what they were doing?"

Erik held up his hand, and the Draugr fell silent. A group of young vampires, men and women who had probably been turned in just the last year or so, swarmed forward, their eyes bright with excitement. They were like fans at a rock concert, rushing the stage. He wondered if this was how rock stars felt. It was not a disagreeable sensation.

He gestured toward Nika. "This is my Chosen. She has mastered the rune magic of Odin, and she will rule at my side."

Nika looked at him in surprise, and he smiled at her. *Didn't see that coming, did you?* he asked her in her mind. She shook her head.

One of the young ones jumped up onto the platform with them and turned to face the crowd. "Hail King Erik! Hail King Erik!"

His chant was taken up by his friends, then by the other young ones, until it spread through almost the entire crowd. Erik had never dreamed that it would have been so easy to take control. A suspicion touched him, and he looked at Nika, asking her telepathically, *Do you have something to do with this?*

My sisters, she said. *They're making them...malleable.*

He asked, *Does that include the First?*

With a little more effort, she nodded, *it can. Would you like us to raise the power?*

He smiled grimly. *Please, as long as you can exclude me from the effects.*

She took his hand, and he could feel the shimmering warmth of rune magic between their palms. *Guaranteed.*

Then let it happen.

She shifted her focus briefly, and then he felt a shimmer of power course over him. There was an almost-visible frisson in the assembled Draugr, and they surged forward, crowding closer to the platform. The only place that wasn't filled in by young ones was a pocket around the First, who were standing together directly in front of him. Nobody crowded the First.

He gestured to his former brothers and their Valtaeigr escorts. "Come up here," he called them.

Olaf grinned. "He's calling us! The glory days are going to be back!"

Out of all of them, Dag and Magda looked the least convinced. He turned to her. "I'm not taking part in this," he told her. "This feels wrong."

"I agree," she said. "Mia, come with us. We're leaving."

Her daughter looked stunned. "But we can't leave."

"Can't you feel that? The witches are here, and they're trying to affect our minds. I will not accept him, ever, and especially not when I'm forced. I have had enough of that to last a hundred lifetimes." She grabbed Mia's arm. "Come along!"

The three of them broke away from the First and headed toward the road, leaving the increasingly frenzied acclamation of the new Draugr king.

Erik saw them as they began to leave. "Stop them," he told Nika. "They can't get away, Magda especially."

He saw a hard look come into his beloved's eyes, and she raised her free hand. It began to glow with runic fire, and the young ones thronging before them cheered like spectators at a fireworks show. She threw the magical ball into the air, and it exploded above Dag and Magda's heads. Mia pulled free of her mother and ran back to vanish into the throng, so she escaped when the magic turned into a glowing net of runes and magic that fell over Dag and Magda, pinning them in place.

The rest of the First joined him on the platform, the four of them standing in a little clump beside him. The crowd burst into applause and cheers. There was a wild, bacchanalian edge to it, and Erik began to fear the excessive enthusiasm of his new subjects. It was hard to control one person at a time, let alone a thousand. For the first time, he doubted if he was doing the right thing.

"You all saw the video," he said. "Magda and Kjeld sent it."

There was another cheer. They were applauding the depredation of the faery. That would never, ever do.

"The things that were done in that video were wrong and are henceforth forbidden. If anyone raids against the faery from this time forward, you will answer to me."

A murmur crawled through the crowd, and he saw them looking at one another in confusion.

"My part in that debacle was the result of enchantments cast by Dark Sisters and traitorous Valtaeigr. I was wronged, and in the process, the faery were wronged. The faery have committed to going to war with us over these attacks."

"Then let them!" someone in the crowd shouted. "War! We are Draugr! We will fight!"

"You will fight and you will die," he snapped. "The faery are far more numerous than we are. Look around you. This is our entire population. The faery are worldwide and are so numerous that they could never fit into one place. They would destroy us. And they have at their sides the Ulfen and the other shifters."

As if to emphasize the point, Ardrik's pack made themselves visible on the outer edge of the forest, close enough that they could charge and attack in less than a heartbeat. A ripple of fear and confusion spread through the crowd, and the Draugr drew inward, retreating from the wolves. Ardrik threw his head back and howled, and answering howls rose into the night air on all sides. They were surrounded.

"There will be no more raids on faery," Erik shouted again. "And drinking of faery blood and faery-tainted *dreyri* is forbidden!" He picked up his axe and looked at the First. "Kneel."

Agnar looked at him, tears in his eyes. "But...brother..."

"I am not your brother," he bit.

Compelled by the power of the witches, they knelt. Erik looked at Ardrik and nodded to him. The alpha nodded back in understanding.

He gestured to the runic net and the two would-be escapees that were held within it. "Bring them here."

"I'll do that," Nika said, her voice quiet but firm.

The net closed around them, and though they fought the suggestion, Dag and Magda were forced to walk back to the platform. They struggled against every step, straining with every fiber of their beings, but the power of the Rune Master was too strong. Magda screamed in rage when they reached the platform. Nika forced them to kneel, as well.

"Look upon these traitors," he told his people. "The *dreyri* that they have been giving you has poisoned you. They are enemies of us all."

He released Nika's hand and took up his axe. With a mighty swing, he severed Olaf's head at the neck. The ancient vampire exploded into a shower of dust and ash, and the crowd cheered. Brevik and Agnar followed their brother to the afterlife in the same manner. Halvar began to weep.

"Please, brother," he begged. "Please. No."

Erik was unmoved. Halvar died.

Only Dag and Magda remained, and they both glared at him with deep ill will. If they could have reached him, he knew, they would have happily torn him into pieces. Quietly, he said to Magda, "I do not blame you for the hatred you hold for me. I earned every bit of it. I *do* blame you for the excesses that it drove you to, and the crimes you have committed."

He signaled to Nika. The net of runic magic vanished, and Erik swung his axe. Dag was lost in a puff of ash, and Magda screamed in impotent rage as the blade fell on her neck.

It was over. Nika and Erik stood alone on the platform once more. He took her hand and raised it into the air. The Draugr in the crowd chanted his name.

"Erik! Erik! Erik!"

The shouting and celebrating continued for what seemed like hours. Finally, he gestured for silence, and the crowd obeyed.

"From this moment on, we are at peace with the Ulfen and the Faery. Any acts against them will be acts against me, and you will fare no better than these Draugr here at my feet." He rested his axe on the ground and folded his hands on the grip. "Return to your homes. Go in peace."

The Ulfen alpha came forward and shifted into his human form. He called out, "I will tell the Faery what I have seen. The war will end."

Erik inclined his head toward him. "Thank you."

Ardrik turned back into his wolf form and raced into the cover of the trees, his pack following closely behind. Erik pulled Nika closer and put an arm around her shoulders, dropping a kiss on her temple.

"Are you ready to be my queen?"

She put her hand on his chest and looked up at him with a smile. "I would follow you anywhere."

He kissed her deeply as the crowd dispersed. "Don't follow me," he whispered. "Walk at my side."

"Gladly."

They embraced again, relieved to have finally ended the threat of war, and relieved that the danger of Magda and the First had been defeated. Nika stroked his back with both hands, and he relished the sensation of her warm touch.

"What do you think," she asked as they finally separated, "about taking over Snake Eyes and making sure the barrels and whatnot of faery blood are all destroyed?"

"That was definitely on my list of things to do," he nodded. "But there's something else that we need to do, too."

She frowned. "What's that?"

He grinned. "What good is being royal if you can't have a royal wedding?"

She gasped. "Are you serious?"

"Of course. Why would I joke about something like this?"

Nika smiled, and the smile became a grin that threatened to split her face in two. "Are you seriously asking me to marry you?"

"No, I was talking to the axe. Of course I'm asking you to marry me!"

She threw her arms around his neck. "Yes. Yes, yes, yes, a thousand times, yes."

He pulled her into a kiss to seal the deal.

*****

THE END

Rune King's Daughter

Rune Series Book 4

Amelia Wilson / J.A.Cummings

Contents

Prologue
- Chapter One
- Chapter Two
- Chapter Three
- Chapter Four
- Chapter Five
- Chapter Six
- Chapter Seven
- Chapter Eight
- Chapter Nine
- Chapter Ten
- Chapter Eleven
- Chapter Twelve
- Chapter Thirteen
- Chapter Fourteen
- Chapter Fifteen

Epilogue

Copyright © 2017 by Amelia Wilson/J.A. Cummings
All rights reserved.

In no way is it legal to reproduce, duplicate, or transmit any part of this document in either electronic means or in printed format. Recording of this publication is strictly prohibited, and any storage of this document is not allowed unless with written permission from the publisher. All rights reserved.

Respective authors own all copyrights not held by the publisher.

Prologue

When the train slowed at the station, she barely waited for it to stop before she leaped on board. The passengers who were trying to exit the train gave her nasty looks as she pushed past them, but she cared little for their opinions. She only wanted to get the hell out of Sweden.

She sat in the middle of the car, more than arm's length from any of the windows, just in case someone tried to punch through and grab her. Her father was powerful and had many, many soldiers who would be more than happy to drag her back to him for punishment. She had seen the things he was capable of doing, and she wanted no part of it.

The car exchanged riders with the platform, and several men and women, and even a few children, pressed in past the doors. She crossed her legs and clutched her duffel bag on her lap, her hand covering her face. She let her fingers stroke the tattoo of Hagalaz on her neck, a nervous habit she had developed since her father's woman had become Rune Master. She nervously studied the people who climbed on board, but to her vast relief, there were no Draugr among them. She felt like she could almost breathe again.

Then he walked in.

He was no Draugr, but he was just as unwelcome to her as a Draugr would have been. He was tall and dark, with long hair and a black leather jacket that was more than a little worse for wear. It looked like someone had taken scissors to it, totally shredding the motorcycle club logo on his back and severing the attached belt. The dangling buckle bounced against his muscular thigh as he walked in and sat on a bench in the other half of the car. There was something strange about him, a shimmer around him that prevented her from seeing his true nature. He wasn't human, but she wasn't able to see what he was, which was so much more frightening.

She realized that he was staring at her, and the hand that she held to conceal her face began to tremble. He looked away, maybe to trick her, maybe to be polite. It was so difficult to tell. She gathered her bag and rose, determined to wait for the next train, but a trio of Draugr men appeared on the platform. One of them, dressed in an immaculate black suit and a matching woolen coat, both far too warm for the heat of the evening's summer weather, lit a cigarette and shook out the match. His eyes locked onto hers, and he took a long drag, then breathed out smoke in a long stream that he sucked back in through his nostrils. He pointed at her.

The doors closed. The train began to pull away. The Draugr and his companions, who were in suits of a less-expensive variety, just watched her as she was carried away from them.

What are they doing? she asked herself, panicking. *What are they waiting for?*

She looked back and watched them as they receded, vanishing around the bend as the 9:15 from Stockholm to Paris sped away.

She clutched her bag, looking at the dark-haired man in the shredded jacket. A lock of blonde hair, recently bleached to conceal her native red, fell into her eyes, and she brushed it away. She shouldn't have cut her hair. It got in the way too easily now, which she would not have expected. Maybe she should have cut it shorter. Maybe she...

She took a deep breath and realized that the man in the shredded jacket was staring at her again. Maybe she should have flown.

The DSB train line she had chosen was her cheapest option, but it would take 20 hours to get to France, including a three-hour transfer in Germany. There would be stops in Malmö, Copenhagen, Hamburg, Cologne and then Brussels before it finally reached Paris tomorrow night. She clutched her route map and tried to stop shaking. There would be five options to bail out on this train before she committed to the final destination, five opportunities to run if the man in the jacket didn't stop staring.

Why is he just staring?

She whispered words of magic, and she tried to put up a protective enchantment. The man saw her spell and chuckled, unimpressed. She wanted to scream.

She jumped to her feet and headed back through the train toward the dining car. Hopefully she could find a private berth that she could sneak into before the man in the jacket caught up with her.

She looked over her shoulder. He stood up, too.

She walked faster, heading through the sliding doors at the end of the car, passing the connector and going into the next car. She cut through that car, and then the next, moving quickly. There were no private cars that she could break into, unless they were on the other end of the train, which meant that she would have to pass him to find out.

Taking a deep, steadying breath, she turned around and faced back the way she had come. A man and woman, speaking quietly to each other with their heads together like lovers came into the car. They were the only people moving around, other than her. The seats were nearly full, all the way from this car through to where she had been sitting. That knowledge gave her some comfort in knowing that the man in the jacket wouldn't be fool enough to attack her with so many witnesses.

She hoped.

A cold breeze blew past her, and she looked for an open window. There were none that she could see. She gritted her teeth and slung her bag over her shoulder, shoving her ticket and train itinerary into her pocket as she did. She was getting so tired of being afraid.

A hand grasped her elbow, and she nearly screamed. She spun toward whoever had grabbed her, but there was nobody standing there. The man in the seat beside her looked at her with disapproval, clearly thinking she was drunk or high or something equally foolish. She looked at him and wanted to beg him for his help, but he was only human and would be worse than useless. She tried to turn away, but the hand on her elbow - the invisible hand - held her fast.

"Stop running and walk back to the car you came from," a deep masculine voice said in her ear. "Nod if you'll cooperate."

She had no choice. The hand on her arm was like a vice, and she was not strong enough to break free without resorting to magic. Doing something like that would be suicide in a place as filled with humans as this car. She nodded.

"Good. Walk."

She felt another hand take hold of the collar of her jacket, and the hand on her elbow let go. She could have pulled free, could have dropped the bag and struggled out of the jacket and tried to get away... but no, that would have accomplished nothing. She could not get away from this invisible captor without starting a riot.

She walked.

Step by step, he force-marched her back to the first car, depositing her back onto the seat. She felt his hand release her, and then he was sitting beside her, fully visible. His dark hair was hanging down over his golden-brown eyes and his shredded leather jacket was stained with old blood. She could smell it.

"What do you want?" she whispered, terrified.

"I think that we can help each other," he said. "You are Valtaeigr."

"And you are..."

"Ulfen." The corner of his mouth turned up, somewhere between a smirk and a sneer, and he added, "Mostly."

He didn't feel Ulfen. She wanted to ask him why that was, but instead she stayed silent, sullenly holding her bag between them, trying to shelter behind it as if it were a shield. The Ulfen did not take offense. Indeed, it seemed as if he understood. He sat back in his seat and consulted his own ticket and itinerary.

"I figure we'll be out of their immediate territory once we get to Cologne," he said. "There's currently no pack there. I don't know about Draugr."

When she spoke, her voice was a husky whisper, filled with dread. "The Draugr are everywhere."

"Not everywhere. Most of them are still in Sweden, I believe, waiting to celebrate the royal wedding." She could feel her expression sour, and she looked away. He chuckled. "Not a fan of the new king, I see. Or maybe it's his intended you don't care for."

She didn't respond to his implication. "Is there a pack in Paris?"

"Of course. And in Brussels, and in Copenhagen." He tucked the itinerary into his jacket's breast pocket. "I was planning to get off at Cologne. You could get off with me."

"There are vampires in Cologne."

"Maybe. But there are more of them in Paris. I thought you'd know that."

She cursed under her breath. Of course there were. She wasn't thinking.

"You smell like a runner," he told her. "Your fear is coming off of you in clouds. You might want to reel that shit in."

"Well, you just jumped me from under camouflage, so pardon me for being a little nervous," she snapped.

This time, against all odds, he actually did smile. He offered her his hand. "Dominic, formerly of the Pikkarala Pack."

"Formerly?"

He smiled more broadly, revealing a set of white, even teeth. "When a person introduces himself, it's customary to introduce yourself in return."

She sighed, irritated with herself and with him. "Mia."

They shook hands. His skin was warm and calloused. He had done a lot of manual labor in his day, she thought, or perhaps the roughness of a werewolf's paw pads translated to the palms of their human hands.

"Pleased to meet you, Mia."

"If you say so." She crossed her arms. "I don't want your help."

Dominic nodded. "All right. Far be it from me to force you to accept my company." He rose. "Have a good trip, Mia."

He walked back to his seat and sat down, looking out the window. He was ignoring her now, which seemed strange after he had spent so much time staring at her so fixedly. Paradoxically, she almost missed his attention.

It didn't matter. The last thing she needed was a werewolf hanging around when she was trying to get to America.

There was a thump on the top of the car, barely audible over the noise of the wheels on the track. Dominic looked up, immediately on his guard. The thump was followed by a series of slow, deliberate footfalls, moving across the roof until they stopped directly over Mia's head.

It was the Draugr.

The Ulfen rose and rushed to her, grabbing her hand and pulling her after him into the next car, moving in the direction opposite the one she'd been traveling in before. She clung to her bag and followed him, preferring the company of a strange werewolf to that of the vampires who were hunting her on behalf of her father. They burst through first one set of doors, then another, traversing three cars in their flight. The Draugr footsteps followed them on the roof, keeping pace all the way.

"Pray for a tunnel," Dominic told her.

He found a toilet and pulled her inside with him. There was barely room for both of them to stand, especially since he was so broad. He pressed up against her, his chest against her back, his pelvis tight against her buttocks, and he wrapped his arms around her. She could feel his camouflage envelop them both, and she held her breath, although she knew that it made no difference if she were breathing or not.

The footsteps continued past them on the roof, running farther down the car before they stopped short and turned. The Draugr circled back, then hesitated. He had clearly lost the scent. His footsteps raced away.

"Is he gone?" she asked.

"Shh."

They heard the car doors open, and the same footsteps stalked down the aisle. They hesitated outside the toilet, and Dominic covered her mouth with his hand to keep her quiet. She grabbed his hand with hers, simultaneously clinging and trying to tear it away from her face. He resisted her efforts, and then, miraculously, the Draugr outside the door walked away.

They listened until the footsteps vanished completely in the rushing of a car door as the Draugr abandoned the train. Mia sagged against the wall and closed her eyes. She nearly dissolved into tears; only her pride and her unwillingness for a werewolf to see a Dark Sister in tears allowed her to keep her composure.

Dominic released his hold on her mouth and backed up as much as he could in the confined space. "He's gone," he told her.

She slid away from him, stepping out of the toilet and into the aisle. He followed her. "Whose blood is all over your jacket? Your last kill?"

He looked insulted and tossed his head. "Mine."

When he moved his jaw, she saw a raised scar on his throat, the clear mark of a Draugr attack that had not healed well. She had never seen an Ulfen who didn't heal from a vampire bite.

"What happened to your throat?"

"Don't be stupid," he grumbled. "You know what that is."

"Why didn't it heal?"

He popped the collar of his jacket, hiding the mark. "I guess I'm just lucky that way." He walked away from her, but after he'd gone a few feet, he turned back to face her. "You're welcome."

She didn't respond right away. She just went back into the toilet and closed the door, locking it behind her.

Chapter One

Erik sat in what had been Magda's office at Snake Eyes and looked at the pile of ledgers on the desk. Nika crouched behind him, rummaging through the bookshelf, pulling out more of the leather-bound record books and piling them up beside the first. She stopped and stood beside him, one hand on her hip, the other on his shoulder. He snaked an arm out and encircled her legs with it, his hand on her thigh.

"That's the last five years," she said. "Do you have any Draugr accountants that we can pay to go through this mess for you?"

He sighed and flipped through the pages of the top book on the pile. "They're not actually a mess. Magda was very precise and deliberate. Her records are pristine." He turned another page, then closed the book. "But you're right. I am no accountant, and I can't begin to figure out whether this place is in the black."

Across the room, another vampire sat cross-legged, examining a list of invoices. She was dressed in blue jeans and a Detroit Red Wings hockey jersey with a big number 5 on the back. Her hair was spiky and dyed improbable colors. Her ears had each been pierced five times, and a gold hoop pierced her left eyebrow. She had a tracery of tattooed cobras around her wrists like permanent bracelets. She looked like any other millennial in Stockholm...except for the fangs. "Oh, Snake Eyes is in the black," she said. "But whether it stays that way once the supply of illegal *dreyri* runs out is anybody's guess."

"Elke," Nika asked, "how much faery blood is left?"

She squinted up at her. "Enchanted or unenchanted?"

"Both."

She scratched her head where the hair was pink. "Unenchanted, about seventy barrels' worth."

Erik was horrified. "Seventy barrels?" he echoed. "Good gods!"

Elke nodded. "And enchanted, about five hundred barrels and about a thousand cases of bottles. The Draugr population won't have to go cold turkey on its faery blood addiction just yet."

Nika moved her hand to the back of her man's neck. She tried to gently rub away the tension that she could feel building there. He was going to be developing another one of the headaches that dealing with his new kingship kept causing him. She bent and kissed his temple, literally blowing a healing breath against his skin, the air coming out of her laced with tiny glowing runes. The arm around her legs squeezed in silent gratitude as the nascent headache evaporated.

"We won't have them go cold turkey," she said, knowing that his initial plan had been to destroy the enchanted faery blood. "A bunch of vampires with the DTs would be a nightmare. We ought to start mixing the faery blood with the human-based *dreyri* until we can wean them off of it."

He sighed. "You're right. I hate it, but you're right. Until then, I want to maintain strict controls of the stock." Erik sat back and Nika ran her fingers through his blond hair. "I want to make certain that we are the only place where the Draugr can get this shit."

Elke stood, unfolding in one smooth motion that revealed her pre-turning past as a competitive gymnast. "Sure thing, boss. I'll go double check the locks. You two should be the only ones with a key. By the way, the staff are running a little betting pool."

Erik glanced at Nika, and she smiled at him. He looked at his assistant. "What betting pool?"

"That Mia will be brought back here before the wedding. There's a lot of money changing hands."

His expression soured. "I don't want people betting on my daughter's well-being."

"Nobody said anything about her well-being," Elke said with a shrug. "Just whether she'd be back."

Nika chuckled. "Okay, I'll bite. What are the odds?"

"It's 3 to 1 that she'll be back before the wedding, 5 to 1 that she'll be back afterward, even odds that she'll make some sort of dramatic appearance on the day itself, and 17 to 1 that she'll vanish forever."

Erik sighed. "And where have you put your money?"

Elke grinned. "Dramatic appearances. I'm a sucker for that stuff."

In spite of himself, he smiled back. Her impish good humor had an infectious effect on his moods, an unanticipated but very valuable fringe benefit to her installation as his assistant. Nika was glad she had that effect on him. "Get out of here, you little turd," he said.

She giggled and skipped out of the office.

"She's incorrigible."

He guided Nika to take a seat in his lap. She went willingly, draping her arm around his neck. She kissed him. "Totally true. Now, Mister Captain Thorvald King of the World sir, how would you like to get some lunch? We've been in here for hours, and if I don't get a break, I'm going to hit something."

He smiled at the string of names and ran his hand over her scarlet tresses, stroking the soft waves that ran from the crown of her head to the small of her back. Since she had been turned, her hair had grown much fuller and longer, and he loved to touch it almost as much as she loved receiving that touch.

"Okay," he agreed. "Let's go take a break."

"Excellent."

She started to stand up, and he pulled her back down. "I thought maybe..."

"No way. If you want to make love, you're going to have to take me to a bed, or at least a couch."

"There's a couch in here."

She tapped the end of his nose with her fingertip. "No. No office nookie. I am sick of looking at this place." She hopped up onto her feet. "Air, Your Majesty. I need some, right now."

He let her pull him out of the chair, a smirk on his face. "I can't go out there. The bar is full of Draugr who all want something."

Nika linked her arm with his. "I'll protect you."

"Promise? I'm scared."

She looked at him, and she burst out laughing, unable to maintain the charade. The thought of a warrior like Erik being afraid of toadies was too much.

"What?" he asked. "There are vampires out there."

"You giant goofball!"

Erik laughed and slid his hand down to take hers. "All right, since you say you'll protect me, I'll be brave."

"Stop!"

"There's just one thing I need to know," he said.

She raised one slender eyebrow. "What's that?"

"Did you seriously just use the word 'nookie?'"

Nika laughed and gave him a soft slap on the arm, which made him chuckle. "You are such a brat!"

"Yes," he nodded. "It's part of my charm."

"I never said you were charming."

He grinned. "Touché."

They made their way out into the bar proper, leaving the private office and going into the open front area of Snake Eyes. The room was filled with Draugr, some old, some very young, all of them jockeying for position and trying to attract the attention of their new king. One of the Draugr, a startlingly beautiful woman with raven hair, bowed to them as they entered the room.

"Your Majesty," she said, her voice throaty. She cast her dark eyes down, flirting outrageously.

Erik more or less looked past her. "Good afternoon, Maria," he greeted. He took Nika's hand and walked her out of the bar, headed for the bright light of day outside. As they passed the assembled Draugr, Nika could feel the weight of their stares on them, and she could almost taste their barely-restrained yearning for favor. Erik walked past them as if he didn't see them, but Nika couldn't replicate his calm self-assurance.

Courage, Erik told her through their Chosen bond. *They would never hurt you. They wouldn't dare.*

I'm not really afraid of them hurting me, she responded in kind. *I feel like a rock star waiting for the fans to rush the stage.*

Erik chuckled and held the door for her, his touch making the ward jangle through the club. He was the only surviving member of the First; the ward would respond to nobody but him, now. She stepped out into the sunlight, enjoying the warmth on her skin. She was grateful that the Draugr weren't the sort of vampires that Hollywood movies showed. She would have been very sad to never see daylight again.

He joined her on the sidewalk, slipping his arm around her. His hand settled comfortably on her hip and she leaned into him.

"Let's eat in a sidewalk cafe somewhere," she requested. "I love the feeling of the sun today."

"Your wish is my command." He kissed her temple. "I know just the place."

Chapter Two

They walked a few blocks south of the club until they reached a little restaurant with cheerful yellow tables and white umbrellas. The hostess seated them and handed them brightly-colored laminated menus. Erik smiled at Nika as they got comfortable.

"I'll bet you never would have believed that life as a vampire could be so sunny," he said.

She laughed. "No, indeed. Based on all of the movies I've seen, we should be bursting into flames or something."

"I try not to do things like that," he said drily.

Once they had ordered their lunches and the server had taken the menus away, she reached out and took his hand, holding it on the table top. "So, do you want to talk about the wedding?"

"I expected that we would eventually," he smiled. "I think that weddings belong to brides. Just tell me what you want, and I will make it happen."

"Don't you have any opinions?"

"As long as we're married at the end of the day, nothing else matters to me."

She brought his hand to her lips and kissed his fingers. His hands were so masculine, broad and strong, just like the rest of him. There was nothing about Erik that didn't entice her. "You're so sweet," she told him.

"Just being honest." He touched her face gently, his eyes warm. When he looked at her like that, she was convinced that nothing could ever be wrong in the world. "So... you must have a thought or two."

"A few," she admitted. "I want my friend, Tamara Jackson, to be my maid of honor."

"Tamara," he repeated. "I know you've mentioned the name, but I don't think I know her."

"You met briefly, just before the Rune Sword was stolen. She was the one I was at the exhibit with."

He snapped his fingers. "Oh, yes! The one who wanted you to call her." He smiled devilishly. "Tell me, did you ever make that call?"

"Not right away," she admitted. "Things were a little busy, if you'll remember."

"I remember very well."

"I called her once we got settled in Mellerstön. She was mad at me - boy, was she mad! - but we got everything straightened out. Once I told her about you, she was full of questions and relationship advice."

"What did you tell her?"

Nika smiled and brushed an errant lock behind her ear. "I told her that I was swept off my feet by a hot Swedish Special Ops soldier who stole my heart and whisked me away to his homeland."

"Ah! The truth, then," he grinned.

"And nothing but the truth."

He leaned across the table and kissed her. Their lips lingered, and it was only reluctantly that they parted. Their moment was interrupted by the arrival of their food, and they settled back into their chairs again.

Erik cut into his open-faced sandwich and asked, "So, Tamara as your maid of honor. Why don't you call her and invite her to come to Stockholm? We can put her up in a nice hotel."

She stirred her soup. "That sounds great. Who do you think will be your best man?"

He hesitated, and she saw a flicker of sorrow on his face. All of his friends, his brothers, were dead; the losses had been so recent, she wondered if he'd even had time to properly grieve. She suspected that the loss of men he'd known for literally centuries would take a long time for him to accept.

Finally, he said, "I don't know. I'll figure it out, though."

"Are you okay?"

He smiled for her, but it looked forced. "Fine. How's your soup?"

"Hot." She hesitated. "But I guess it can't really burn me anymore, can it?"

"Nope."

He watched as she took a tentative spoonful; although it was certainly hotter than she would normally have liked, it didn't cause her any pain, and the taste was not obscured. She shook her head. "I guess I still have a lot to get used to."

"It'll come in time," he reassured her. "You only turned a few months ago. It'll be hard to overcome a lifetime of habits learned as a human, and nobody expects you to do it over night. Nobody else has."

"Not even you?"

"Especially not me." He took a sip of his water, then asked, "So, about the wedding... do you want it to be in a church, or at the courthouse? Or maybe Ingrid should officiate in the old style?"

She considered the question. "Well, since you're not Christian, it seems kind of silly to have a church wedding."

He shrugged. "It's up to you. It's whatever you want."

Nika looked at the rune tattoo on her arm, then said, "I think, all things considered, we should have an old-style wedding, with Ingrid doing the honors."

For someone who had claimed to not care about the details, Erik looked awfully pleased with what she'd said. She chuckled to herself.

"All right, then," he said. "I'll give her a call and let her know."

Erik's cell phone interrupted their conversation, playing Roger Daltrey's voice singing "Who are you?" He scowled at the offending object and swiped the screen to take the call.

"*Hej*," he answered.

A man's voice responded. "I know where your daughter is."

Nika leaned closer, although she could hear the other speaker perfectly well thanks to her augmented hearing. Their eyes met as Erik asked, "Who is this?"

The man laughed. "Someone who wants to prove his worth to his king."

"Where is Mia?"

"Expect a text."

The call ended abruptly, and Erik frowned. Nika asked, "Did you recognize that voice at all?"

"No." He watched his phone expectantly, and finally he was rewarded by an incoming text with a photograph attached. He opened the photo and they looked at it together. The photograph showed Mia with her hair bleached blonde and cut short. She was leaving a train, her elbow being held by a young man in a tattered leather jacket. Nika gasped.

"That's Dominic. He's Ulfen. I met him in Norway."

"Is he a threat?"

"He saved me from his pack the night they killed Lars and Sif."

"That can't have made him very popular with Ardrik." Erik studied the photograph, specifically the signage and objects in the background. "I can't tell where this picture was taken, and the number that sent it is unlisted. I need to figure out where she is."

Nika sat back. "When we were on that stage in Uppsala, when you executed the First and Magda... what were you going to do with her?"

"It depended."

"On what?"

"On whether she was acting of her own free will or if she was being compelled by my brothers." He shook his head. "I can't believe she would have done those things to me unless someone ordered her to do it."

Nika pressed her lips together and measured her words. "She was part of Magda's great conspiracy to make me think you were dead, and she made you do things you hate yourself for. She's a card-carrying member of the Dark Sisterhood. She's got a lot of black marks on her in my view, and when you're hurt, and when I'm hurt, I don't forgive easily."

He pushed his food away. "I'd like to think that she had no choice."

"I know. But I know Valtaeigr abilities, and I know that we're not as easy to force as you might think. If she didn't want to enchant you, and if she didn't want to be an active player in the slaughter of the faery, then she wouldn't have."

"She was under Bjorn's control," he objected mildly. "He didn't give her much of a choice, and neither did Magda."

Nika was unconvinced. "She still needs to pay for what she did to you."

"Not if she was compelled."

"Why are you so willing to give her the benefit of the doubt?"

"She's my daughter," he protested mildly.

"Yes, and she showed her daughterly love by hazing you out of your mind and taking away your free will," Nika said archly. "She's one of the ones responsible for this addictive *dreyri* mess. You don't owe her anything but a kick in the ass."

"That's harsh."

"I won't apologize."

"I'm not asking you to."

She sighed. "Erik, unless I miss my guess, you never showed any real interest in her before, not for centuries. Why the sudden concern?"

He put his phone aside. "I was a bad father when she was born, and I remained a bad father for centuries. She was her mother's daughter, and as you say, she became one of the Dark Sisters. That's enough for me to want to know where she is, so we can keep her from harming us with her power." He sighed. "The truth is, I want to make things right now. I know it's probably too late, and I know that probably too much time has passed, but I need to correct my past mistakes."

"What about her mistakes?" she asked. "Shouldn't she have to correct those, too?"

"Yes. As you say, she has a lot to answer for, but I'd like to hear her side of the story before I pass judgment. I just need her to stop running first." He looked at her intently. "You really hate her, don't you?"

Nika couldn't meet his gaze, so she looked at her soup instead. "I hate what she did to you."

"As do I. But before I do anything to her, I need to know how much was her idea and how much she was forced into by her mother and her lover." He put his napkin beside his half-eaten lunch as his appetite for mortal food evaporated. "I hope you understand."

"I understand." She pushed her soup away, too, and signaled the server for their check. "I hope you get to hear her explanation. It had better be good."

***

They walked back to the club, but avoided going in. Instead they climbed into Erik's souped-up Koenigsegg Agera, the newest of his automotive toys. He loved fast cars, and he drove like a demon when he got outside of Stockholm. Within the city, though, he obeyed posted rules and regulations, preferring to avoid issues with the police.

He had been honorably discharged by the SOG and they had stopped hunting him like a criminal or a deserter, so they had been able to move back into his comfortable and very modern home in the neighborhood of Vasastan. The garage door slid open whisper-silent as they pulled into the drive, revealing his Humvee and Aston Martin DB11. The three-car garage, an embarrassingly luxurious affectation, was fully heated and with runway lights set into the floor.

Nika chuckled. "I always feel like we're going into the Bat Cave when we come home."

Erik smiled and pitched his voice as low as it would go. "I'm Batman."

"Honey," she laughed, "if you're any superhero, you're Thor."

He waggled his eyebrows. "Let me show you my hammer..."

She threw her head back and laughed again. "Stop! You nerd!"

He only smiled in response.

The garage door closed and locked behind them, and he parked the car in its designated spot. Erik went around to open Nika's door, then gave her a hand out. She smiled. "Such a gentleman."

"I try." He closed the car door without relinquishing her hand.

They walked into the house, where he pulled her toward him. She went willingly, interlacing her fingers behind his neck as they kissed. His hands settled onto her hips as he held her tight. When they parted, she looked into his eyes.

"I just don't get you," she said.

He frowned slightly, confused. "What do you mean?"

"You can be such a giant dork, but yet you're this powerful vampire, and you're so gentle but I've seen you fight like a monster." She shook her head. "It's like you're multiple people sometimes."

Erik smiled and kissed her again. "I'm just one person. You're not so straight-forward, yourself."

"Sure I am."

He chuckled. "To yourself, maybe. But you fascinate me." He kissed her again. "You're everything to me, Nika."

She embraced him, pressing against him. He wrapped his strong arms around her waist and held her close, his cheek leaning against her scarlet hair.

"I love you, Nika. I love you more than time and more than life and more than everything in the world."

Warmth spread through her, and she held him tighter. She reveled in the feeling of his muscular body beneath her touch, and in the power that thrummed through him and into her, their souls' connection vibrating. The closer they were, the more their bond shimmered, and the closer she felt to him. Sometimes, especially when they made love, she felt like she could get caught in an endless feedback loop with him, her soul sending energy to his soul while his soul sent energy to hers. She realized now that she relied on those moments, and she was amazed by how much she needed him.

He stroked her back with one hand, and she leaned back to look into his bright blue eyes. She had never seen any man as beautiful as Erik.

"You look happy," he whispered.

"I am."

He kissed her, his mouth claiming hers with passion and desire. She opened for him happily, accepting his gentle exploration. She shivered, and he gathered her in his arms, sweeping her off of her feet. She clung to him, feeling safe and sheltered in his strength.

Erik carried her up the stairs to the master bedroom, where he placed her gently on the bed. He knelt at her feet, looking up at her with an expression that burned all the way through her, igniting her body with a need for him that was breathtaking in its power. His hands stroked her thighs, and she spread them for him, letting him in closer. He smiled.

They helped each other undress, peeling away the layers of clothing and revealing the treasure within. She lay back as he finished turned back to her, the last garment discarded. His body was a sculptor's dream, from his broad shoulders to his well-defined abdomen to the hills and valleys of his muscular thighs. His cock was even beautiful, she thought, straining for her attention and perfectly shaped. She took it in her hand and gave it a lazy stroke, and she was rewarded with another beatific smile on his handsome face.

"I could look at you forever," she whispered.

"As long as you touch, too, I'm okay with that."

He leaned over her, one knee on the mattress between her thighs, his hands on either side of her head. He bent to kiss her while she kept working him with her hand. He moaned into her, and she squeezed him gently, her thumb running over the weeping tip.

"I want you so badly," he moaned.

She opened her legs for him. "Then take me."

He went happily, and she sighed in pleasure and delight as he filled her. She tightened around him, and he gasped breathily, his face pressed to her neck. Nika wrapped her arms around him, one hand reaching down to his buttock to urge him in deeper.

His thrusts were slow and controlled, and she wrapped her legs around his hips. He was so careful with her, so gentle. He made her feel special and protected, and when she was wrapped around him like this, she finally felt complete.

They rocked together slowly, deliberately, awash in the passion and delight. She could feel him trembling with the effort of holding back. She tangled her hands in his blond hair and told him, "Faster."

He complied. He drove into her harder, faster, with more energy and purpose. She friction and the heat thrilled her, and she tipped her head back with a moan of ecstasy. He grazed her throat with his lips, then with the sharp tips of his fangs. She groaned and tugged his hair.

"Oh, yes, Erik..."

His breath was hot against her skin, his body burning inside of hers. She arched against him, the first wave building deep inside of her, his long cock buried in her body as far as it would go. She needed him in every way, needed to have more of him. She groaned and whispered his name, then sank her fangs into his shoulder.

He jerked when she bit, his body surging even more powerfully into hers. She drank from him, his powerful blood tingling on her tongue. He was filling her in every way he could, and the sensation of feeding while making love was overwhelming. Her head swam, and her climax exploded around them, shattering her into a wailing mass of pleasure.

Erik shuddered against her and came hard, his hips snapping into hers until the sound of flesh on flesh was loud in the room. She moaned as a second orgasm ripped through her, and she pulled free of his neck with a cry. He took her through her climax, never stopping until she finally fell still. He collapsed on top of her in a sweaty, satisfied heap.

She loved the feeling of his weight on her body and his cock still deep inside her. She almost liked this moment of afterglow more than the climax that came before it, because in this moment, there were no pretenses, no separations, no distance. They were one body and one soul, and she reveled in the closeness.

He pressed his face against her neck and bestowed a gentle kiss to her pulse point, saying without words what words could never have said. She held him as tightly as she could, burning and alive and in love.

Chapter Three

Mia and Dominic walked through busy Paris streets. She had considered trying to lose him, but nobody could track like a wolf, and anyway, she didn't want to be unprotected in this city. Dominic wasn't her first choice of traveling companion, but he was strong and clever, and he had already been useful to her once. She might as well let him hang around.

The Ulfen walked quietly beside her, keeping his thoughts to himself. She wondered why he was no longer with his pack, and why he had chosen to leave his home. He'd said he was from the Pikkarala Pack, which meant he was from the largest Ulfen pack in Finland. He didn't look Finnish, that was certain. She stole a look at her companion. His skin was like cafe-au-lait, and his eyes were a striking golden-brown, almost the color of honey. His hair was black, lustrous and thick, a little long and given to messiness. He was athletic and trim, with compact and useful muscles, not the sort of useless brawn that steroid junkies and bodybuilders sometimes had. He was built for strength and speed, not just for show. As for the rest of him...she looked at him with her Other Sight, through the eyes of her Valtaeigr power, and she examined the radiance of his soul. He was Ulfen, yes, but there was something different about his spiritual signature, something dark and contentious that called out to her. As a Dark Sister, she was a specialist in shadows, and Dominic had shadows aplenty.

"Mia," he said suddenly. "Look up."

She did as he suggested, and she saw a trio of people standing on the roof of the building they were walking past, watching them. Even from this distance, she could sense the shimmer of Draugr power around them. They were vampires, but they were relatively young - the oldest was probably turned just after the Second World War. Still, they would be more physically powerful than she was, and most likely more powerful than Dominic. Her mouth ran dry. Any Draugr could overpower any Ulfen in a one-on-one fight.

"What do we do?" she asked.

"We find a house or a flat to duck into," he said. "They're Draugr - they still need to be invited before they can come in."

"If we break and enter, doesn't that negate the sanctity of the ownership ward?"

"Not for them." He took her elbow and guided her off of the sidewalk and into a block house filled with apartments. He hesitated at the post boxes and sniffed at them before selecting their target. "2B. They haven't picked up mail in almost a week. They're either on holiday or they've moved."

"If they've moved, then there's no owner, and the Draugr can follow us in."

"Well, pray that they're on a cruise."

They jogged up the stairs to the unit in question, and Dominic produced lock picks from the inner pocket of his jacket. He applied the picks to the lock for a gratifyingly brief moment before the door clicked and swung open. He reached inside and found the light switch. The ceiling lights flickered once, then came on, illuminating the room. The apartment was still furnished; he smiled and pulled her inside.

"Looks like we're lucky. It's still occupied."

She followed him into the apartment, and he closed the door behind them, locking it securely once again. Dominic hesitated by the door, listening, while Mia went further into the apartment and sat on the couch.

They held their silence for half an hour, listening for the Draugr to approach. No footsteps came up the stairs, and they were too far from the roof to hear anyone walking there. It was quiet and serene, and she dared to hope that they might have eluded their pursuers.

Mia felt the need to say something, just to break the silence. Her nerves were frayed. "You're very good with those lock picks."

Dominic looked at her, surprised. After a moment, he said, "I've learned a few tricks here and there. I've done a lot of traveling."

"Not fond of your pack?"

He grimaced. "My pack is not fond of me. Last time I saw them, they made a chew toy out of me. I'm lucky I'm still alive."

"Are you the omega?"

Dominic sat beside her on the couch. "Yes."

She thought to the books she'd read about werewolves. "So, does that mean that you're waiting to be taken as an Alpha's mate? And that you can get pregnant, even though you're male?"

The look he gave her was withering. "No. It does not. That's just a lot of foolishness."

She smiled. "I had to ask." She turned to face him, her knees drawn up, her arms braced around them. She leaned her back against the arm of the couch. "Why did you want to come to Paris?"

"I didn't. I wanted to get off at Cologne, remember?"

"But you stayed on."

"Because you stayed on." He shrugged. "I couldn't very well let you go unescorted."

Mia tilted her head, studying him. He had a handsome face. "Why not?"

He took a breath. "Because I already stepped in to protect you once. That means I'm committed. I'll keep you safe."

"Why?"

"I don't know why the Draugr are hunting you, but anytime the vampires are hunting someone who isn't also a vampire, I get worried. I don't want to see you get hurt."

"Do you think I'm innocent?"

He snorted softly. "Nobody is innocent, especially not Dark Sisters."

"Ah. So you know what I am."

"I know what you were." He ran his hands over his thighs, the gesture replete with nervousness. "I also know that you're a lady, and I won't allow a lady to get hurt if I can defend her."

She smiled. "Very chivalrous."

"I believe in honor, even though very few other people do."

The door to the apartment crashed open, and they both leaped to their feet. A trio of Draugr barreled into the room, dressed like mafia hit men in their black trench coats and black pinstripe suits. Dominic pushed Mia behind himself and growled at the vampires, shifting into his half-wolf form.

"Close your mouth, dog, before I close it for you," the Draugr in the center of the group sneered. "Paris is a wolf-free zone. Didn't you get the memo?"

"We're just passing through," Mia said. "We won't be here long."

The three Draugr stepped forward, crowding Dominic, who would not back down. Mia climbed onto the couch and stood behind him, her hands tingling with readied magic. Dominic snarled again, and he snapped his powerful jaws at the main Draugr, who flinched. The Ulfen chuckled at the vampire's reaction.

One of the other Draugr poked a finger into Dominic's throat, scratching at the bite scar that showed through the dark fur. "What's this?"

He bit at the vampire, who pulled his hand back. The third Draugr sniffed at him. "You're not even a born wolf, are you? You were turned with a bite."

"What's it to you?" Dominic demanded. "And how did you get in here?"

The lead vampire smiled. "We own this building. We fucking own this city. And we don't like the smell of dog in our streets." He laughed. "But who's this luscious morsel you're protecting? Is she your bitch?"

Mia raised her hand, and it glowed white with magical power. "I'm nobody's bitch, vampire. Back off."

The three of them thought that her display was extremely funny, and they roared with laughter. Mia's eyes narrowed in irritation, and she flicked the ball of power at the trio. It hit the lead vampire in the chest and exploded like a grenade, showering all three of them with eldritch fire. They barely had time to scream before they turned to dust.

Dominic reeled back, startled. "Jesus!"

"Not Jesus. Hel." Mia shook her hand, dispelling the excess magic she had summoned. She looked at him. "Shift back. We have to get out of here."

He resumed his human appearance, and she nodded. "We can't stay here, not if the vampires own this building, and we have to find someplace where they can't catch your scent."

He thought hard, then said, "I know just the place."

She let him take her by the hand and pull her out of the apartment. He led her back out into the street. "Have you been to Paris before?"

"Yes, a long time ago."

"Do you remember where to go?"

He was moving at speed, and she struggled to keep up. "Yes."

He took her around a corner and then between two buildings, dragging her after him. The daylight streets were full of everyday Parisians, all of whom looked more than a little annoyed by the ragged twenty-something shouldering them out of his way. His path took them through side streets, alleys and across a busy thoroughfare until finally he was trotting down a sidewalk with a will. Mia was about to dig in her heels when he dragged her into a cafe and sat at a table in the back.

She sat obediently enough, but then asked, "Where are we? What are we doing?"

He pulled out a burner phone and dialed a number, taking the digits from incised graffiti in the top of the wooden table. "I'm finding us a safe place."

"Where?" she demanded. He didn't answer, listening instead to the ringing of the phone he had called. She let magic spark on her fingertips and she grabbed his arm.

"Where?"

Dominic yelped and pulled his arm away, the sound so lupine in nature that other diners turned and looked. He glared at her and turned his back toward her, sheltering the phone. She could hear a woman answer.

He spoke in rapid French, a language that she had never troubled herself with learning, and the person he had called spoke back. A brief exchange followed. Mia offered a helpless smile to a waitress, who brought them menus and gave Dominic a scathing look before she left, pointing at a sign that clearly said "No Cell Phones" in seven different languages.

Dominic ended his call and put the phone away. He looked at the menu, and Mia prompted him. "Now what?"

"Now we wait."

He kept nervous eyes on the doorway, but she was hungry and decided to order a pastry and some coffee for both of them. When the food was brought to their table, he handed over a credit card, which the waitress swiped using an iPad mini. She handed the card back to him with a smile.

"Enjoy your coffee, Mr. Mills," the waitress bid him, her English perfect.

Dominic smiled and answered in kind. "Thank you."

When he smiled, it made him look handsome and approachable, almost trustworthy. Mia looked away. When the server was finally out of earshot, she asked, "What are we waiting for?"

"Our guide." He turned that smile on her, and she wished he wouldn't. "I told you I would find a place where they couldn't sniff me out. We're going to the Catacombs."

"The Catacombs? You're taking me into a medieval tomb?"

"Something like that." He drank his coffee black. She shuddered after one sip and added more sugar to her own cup. "They won't be able to smell me over all of that rot and decay."

"Well, good for you." She finished her cup and stood. "I don't want to go where it smells like dead things. I don't think I need your help anymore."

"You say that now. What if the next set of vampires recognizes you?" He shook his head. "Not all of them are going to be as far out of the loop as the bunch you killed. Nice magic, by the way. Remind me to stay on your good side."

"I recommend it." She sat back down reluctantly. "So what happens if some of the Huntsman's men come for me? Do you plan on protecting me from them?"

"Yes." He sipped his coffee.

"Why?"

He shrugged. "Something to do."

"I don't believe that."

"Draugr are the sworn enemy of my kind," he told her. "At this point, opposing them is instinctive. If they want to hunt you down, then I want to keep you away from them. Besides, I know why you're running, and I've already said so."

She crossed her arms on the table. "And why are you running?"

"I already said that, too." He finished his coffee. "It's better to be a lone wolf than an omega."

"Doesn't that put you at odds with your father?" she asked.

"First off, you're not in a position to talk about daddy issues," he teased, a smirk lighting his face. "Second, he's not my father, even though that's pack terminology for him. He's just the wolf who bit me."

Mia raised an eyebrow. "So the Draugr wasn't lying?"

"No."

"Interesting."

The door to the cafe opened, and a serious-looking woman entered, dressed in cargo shorts and a plain white T-shirt. She was tiny and elfin, with dark hair pulled back into a severe bun. There was a camera around her neck, and she was fiddling with her cell phone. She walked directly to their table.

"Naomi?" he greeted.

"Dominic." They shook hands, and she sat at their table. She eyed Mia.

"This is Mia," he introduced. "She doesn't speak French."

The woman sighed and responded in English. "What you're asking isn't simple. If the gendarmes see us going into the catacombs, we'll be arrested."

"That's why I called you. You can get us in discreetly, and you can guide us."

Naomi sat back and scratched at a scab on her knee. "I can get you in, for a price," she said.

Mia leaned forward. "What price?"

"Euros," she said simply. "You might say that I'm a material girl."

"I have Euros," Dominic said. To Mia, it smelled like a lie, but she kept silent. "How much do you need?"

"To get you in? Five thousand."

"That's ridiculous."

"Do you want to get in or don't you?"

Dominic sat back. "I don't want to get in that badly."

Naomi snorted. "Don't you?"

Mia interceded. "One thousand to get us in. Five thousand if you guide us."

Dominic glared as his companion. "For God's sake..."

The cataphile examined Mia in silence, then asked, "Where do you want to be guided to? Just on a jaunt to get a little scare into your cute little bones?"

"I want you to guide us to a safe place in the catacombs, where we won't be discovered and where we can lie low for a while," Mia answered evenly, not rising to the bait.

"Lie low? You in some kind of legal trouble?"

Dominic said, "Let's just say there are some people we'd like to avoid."

She thought about the offer for a moment, then said, "One thousand to get you in, five thousand to hide you, five thousand to bring you back out."

Dominic scoffed. "Eleven thousand euros? Are you out of your mind?"

"I must be, if I'm letting you get me involved in whatever trouble you're having. I don't need any drug cartels or human traffickers breathing down my neck."

Mia considered telling her that traffickers and drug dealers were the least of her worries, but she decided against it. She sighed. "Fine."

"Up front."

"No," Dominic said. "Six thousand up front, the last five when you bring us back out. I'm not stupid."

Naomi smirked. "That remains to be seen. Fine. Meet me outside this cafe at midnight. I'll take you then. Make sure you have the cash, or the deal is off."

She and the Ulfen shook on it, and then Naomi walked back out of the cafe. When she was gone, Mia turned to him. "And where do you think you're going to get eleven thousand euros?"

"You're the one who upped the ante." He held up the credit card he had used to pay for their snack. "But as for the money, Mr. Mills will help us with that."

"You're a thief!"

"I'm inventive and I have a strong survival instinct," he defended. "Come on... let's go get ready. We need supplies."

Chapter Four

Erik and Nika returned to Snake Eyes after their long lunch, although neither of them was really that enthused about going back. The sun was angling lower on the horizon, casting long shadows across the paved square in front of the club. The Draugr population in the bar was swelling, and it would just keep getting bigger as the night drew closer.

The ward on the door throbbed as soon as Erik put his hand on the handle, and he looked at Nika with a sheepish smile. "I wonder if we should get that taken off," he said.

"No way," she objected. "I like feeling when you walk in, and it gives the young ones a thrill. It also makes any trouble makers shape up before they cause too many problems."

"You're a young one," he teased. "Does it thrill you when I touch the door?"

She kissed him. "Ask me again when we get home and I'll show you."

He held the door for her and watched the sway of her hips as she walked in ahead of him. "That thought won't be distracting at all."

She laughed and threw him a bright smile over her shoulder. He followed her closely, his hand on the small of her back.

There were no mortals in the club yet, no goth thrill seekers, no Draugr pets. The usual barflies were sitting on their stools, glasses of *dreyri* in their hands, sipping the enchanted blood and jockeying for position. All eyes had turned toward the door when the ward jangled, and they all stared as their king, the first king many of them had ever known in their vampire lives, made his way into the room.

Nika took his hand, and the runes on her forearms tingled. She frowned and glanced down at them, seeing a slight sparkle in the lines on her skin. Erik saw the look on her face. "What is it?"

"Strange," she said. "I've never felt that before."

"Felt what?"

"My runes." She showed him her forearm. "Do you see it?"

He looked, but it was clear that he saw nothing out of the ordinary, even though she still saw magic coursing over the lines of Perthro and Sowilo. "I guess whatever you're seeing is for Valtaeigr eyes only," he said.

"I guess so." She rubbed her hand over her bare arm, and the prickly sensation subsided. "Weird."

"Maybe we could ask Ingrid about that."

"Maybe..."

He sat in a corner booth, choosing to stay among his people instead of going back to the drudgery of accounting in the office. Nika sat beside him, her legs curled up onto the seat, and when he put his arm around her, she leaned into his broad chest. A waitress came to the table, a young Draugr who had been turned only a few months ago.

"Sami," Erik greeted. "Top shelf *dreyri* for me and my queen."

The girl smiled. "Coming right up, sir."

Nika rested her hand on his shoulder and looked into his eyes. "Top shelf? Are we celebrating?"

He smiled. "Every day we are together is a celebration."

She kissed him. "You're corny as hell, but it's adorable."

"Thank you, I think."

The door opened, and instead of the low, throbbing hum that accompanied Erik's touch, there was a sharp feeling like being jabbed in the ribs. All of the Draugr reacted to it, and Erik immediately slid out of the booth to face the newcomer.

A large man with shaggy dark hair and a muddy overcoat stood in the doorway, looking around with an unreadable expression on his bearded face. He was no Draugr, but he was cloaked in power. Nika's arms tingled again, and she rose to stand at Erik's side.

The man's eyes locked onto Erik's, and he strode across the room. The assembled Draugr gave him space, letting him cross unimpeded and watching to see what he would do. When he got up to the vampire king, he extended a hand.

"Huntsman," he said, his voice heavily accented.

Erik accepted the handshake. "You have me at a disadvantage."

"Call me Vladimir. I am here from Leningrad."

"They call it St. Petersburg now," the vampire told him. "I think you've just dated yourself."

"Perhaps I have. The Soviet days...they weren't so bad."

He had been with the SOG during the Cold War, and Nika knew that his views of the Soviet Union were very different. He crossed his arms and kept his opinion to himself. "What can I do for you, Vladimir?"

"I am a tracker," he said. "I come to offer my services to you to find the Dark Sisterhood."

"That's not all you are," Nika said. She could feel magic clinging to him like road dust.

"No," Vladimir admitted. "I am a witch."

Erik nodded. "Come into my office."

He turned and walked away, showing his back in full view of his people, his open body language stating plainly that he had no fear of this newcomer. It was a display, but it was effective. The watching vampires relaxed. Vladimir followed him, and Nika brought up the rear, not more than arm's length away from the Russian witch.

Once they were in the office, Erik sat behind the desk and gestured to one of the guest chairs, which Vladimir occupied by dropping heavily into the seat. Nika closed the door, then went to stand at her man's side.

"Now, why would you come all the way to Sweden from Russia?" Erik asked. "And what makes you think I can't find the Dark Sisters on my own?"

The Russian smiled. "I think you would have her already if you could."

"You're talking about Mia," Nika said.

"Yes."

Erik sat back. "I know where she is. I can have her retrieved in a heartbeat if I wish it." It was a lie, and both he and Nika knew it, but there was no way that Vladimir could have known.

"So why is she not here?" the man asked.

"Have you ever been a father?"

Vladimir shook his head. "No."

"Sometimes you have to let your children run a little bit, make some mistakes, before you come to their rescue."

"She's not running to be free," he objected. "She's running to hide."

"What's your interest in this?" Nika asked.

The man looked up at her, his dark eyes flat and almost expressionless, like a doll's eyes that had been painted on. "All of the other Dark Sisters are dead," he said. He turned his face back to Erik and grinned like a piranha. "I killed them, all but your former slave and your daughter."

Erik looked unimpressed. Nika admired his ability to keep his cool. "You killed them," she said. The man nodded proudly. "Why?"

"They were responsible for many pains to my people," he said.

"And who are your people?"

He smiled. "I told you already. I am a witch."

Erik raised an eyebrow. "And?"

Nika said, "The Dark Sisters and the witches have a rivalry. If you are a male witch, then you're defending your coven. Am I right?"

"Smart and beautiful," Vladimir nodded, his eyes shining as he looked at her.

"And taken," Erik pointed out.

Vladimir raised his hands in a gesture of harmlessness. "I wouldn't presume to try anything with your Valtaeigr, Huntsman."

"Good. Then you're smarter than you look."

Nika sighed. The posturing was flattering, but this was not the time or the place for Erik to revert to his Viking ways. "How would you track her, and what would you do with her when you find her?"

Erik's icy gaze was locked on Vladimir's face. "He's not going to be tracking her, so the question is irrelevant."

The Russian witch grinned. "If you insist." He reached into his pocket and pulled out a business car. "If you change your mind, this is how to reach me."

Erik made no move to accept the card, so Nika came forward and took it from his outstretched hand. Magic sparked from him into her fingertips, electric blue and snapping like a live wire. She jerked back, and Erik lunged out of his chair.

Vladimir grinned. "Sorry. Static."

"That was no static." The Huntsman surged forward, fury in his eyes. "What did you do to her?"

"Nothing! Nothing, I swear! It was... she is powerful, no? We touched fingers and my power combined with her power and it was just a spark. One spark. No harm, okay?"

Nika put her hand on Erik's powerful chest and held him back. "It's okay. I'm not hurt."

He clearly wanted to rip off Vladimir's arm and beat him with it, but he stilled and reined in his anger. She turned to the Russian witch. "Thank you for your offer of help. How long will you be in Stockholm?"

"Another week, at least. I have business here."

Erik asked, "What sort of business?"

Vladimir smiled and stood. "Things that do not concern the King of the Draugr." He backed up a step. "I'll show myself out."

Nika kept her hand on Erik's chest until the witch was out of the office and the door was safely closed behind him. He took a deep breath and blew it out. "I don't like him."

She chuckled. "I noticed."

He took her fingertips and kissed them. "Are you hurt?"

"No, I'm fine. I was just surprised." She smiled for him, then glanced at the door, which still shone with magic that formed the faint outline of the Russian's body. She would not have been surprised to learn that he was wearing some sort of active enchantment.

Erik saw where she was looking, and he shook his head. "I don't trust him. He will bear watching."

"By whom?" she asked. "Who can you trust that much?"

He looked away, his troubles showing on his handsome face. "I don't know."

***

In Paris, Dominic used three different stolen credit cards and a raft of travelers' checks that had come from who knew where to purchase two sleeping bags, two backpacks, a Coleman stove, food and a change of clothes for both of them. They both loaded their backpacks and shrugged the straps over their shoulders.

"So how are we supposed to come up with the fee she's going to charge?" Mia asked.

"I kind of wish you'd thought of that before you got excited with negotiating," he said sourly, "but I have a plan."

She followed him as he went to Deutsche Bank, walking in as if he owned the place. His confidence belied his scruffy exterior, and she found that the guards let him pass without a second glance. She hurried to stay with him.

He went to a teller and began speaking in fluent French. As she listened to the bank employee replying, she recognized that Dominic's accent was slightly different, and she thought she knew why. She kept her conjecturing to herself while he produced a Canadian passport with his actual picture inside, showing him younger, cleaner and better groomed. The teller handed him a signature card, then left to confer with her manager.

"French Canadian," Mia said when they were alone. "Am I right? You're from Montreal."

"Quebec City, actually," he said. "My pack leader is a wealthy man with an account here. I don't know if he still has money in it, but we're about to find out."

There was a strange bitterness in his voice, and Mia cocked her head slightly, considering him. She whispered a few words of magic and reached out toward his mind, but he gave her a warning glare and blocked her out. She gave him her brightest smile.

"Sorry. Just curious."

"Well, stop. That's rude."

The teller returned with a large stack of cash, and after some more discussion, she allowed him to sign another document and handed him the money in two thick envelopes. He nodded to her and took Mia's elbow.

"Let's go," he said, glancing up at the surveillance cameras over the doors.

They returned to the street, and she asked excitedly, "Did you get all of it?"

"And then some." He folded the envelopes and tucked them into his waistband, over his stomach and under his shirt. "We'll be able to get anywhere you want to go once we get out of Paris. For now, let's go find Naomi and get down to the Catacombs before the vampires start wandering."

They went back to the cafe and waited on the sidewalk for the cataphile to appear. She finally showed up an hour later, walking quickly and glancing over her shoulder.

"Do you have it?" she asked without preamble as soon as she reached them. Dominic nodded, and she said distrustfully, "All six thousand?"

"As promised," he said. He handed her one of the envelopes, warm from its hiding place inside his clothing.

Naomi accepted with her lip curled in distaste. She counted the money, then said, "All right. Follow me."

She led them through the back alleys and side streets, constantly on guard. Dominic and Mia followed, and her anxiety was contagious. Mia found herself looking up at the roofs of the buildings they passed, watching for Draugr among the chimneys. Once she thought she saw something move, but when she looked more closely, it was gone.

"Hurry up," Naomi coached, leading them through a wooden door in the back of a bakery. She closed and locked it once they were inside.

There was a single electric bulb hanging by a wire, and she turned it on with a pull chain. The yellow light it cast was weak, barely illuminating the square of floor beneath it and doing nothing to chase away the shadows in the corners. Their cataphile guide crouched and dug her fingers into the wooden planks on the floor, pulling several away and exposing a stone slab set with an iron handle.

She crouched over the heavy stone and pulled it aside with difficulty. Dominic leaned down and grasped the edge of the stone with one hand, moving it easily out of the way. She gaped at him in surprise for a moment, but then her expression changed to one of wary distrust.

"After you," he said.

Naomi dropped down through the opening, and Mia and Dominic followed. They found themselves in a dank tunnel that smelled of mildew and rot. The cataphile pulled a flashlight out of her pocket, and Mia retrieved her flashlight from her backpack.

Their guide led them farther into the subterranean recesses beneath Paris, going down a long spiral staircase of rusted metal. Finally, they turned a corner and came face to face with stacks of human bones. Mia could sense the rustling of unrested spirits, and she summoned a protection rune that she hid in her palm. Dominic sniffed the air.

"The scent is thick," he said. "They won't find us down here."

"The catacombs are part of a mining system that was abandoned a long time ago," Naomi told them as she led them forward past rows of staring, eyeless skulls. "There are hiding places in the mines that the catacomb tours won't get near."

They followed her for what felt like hours. The macabre surroundings gave Mia the creeps, and she drifted closer to Dominic. He put a hand on her shoulder and gave a companionable, reassuring squeeze. She resisted the urge to look at him.

At last, Naomi brought them out of the ossuary and into the ancient mines. A side chamber had been carved out of the bedrock, and it was equipped with wooden crates upended like stools around a central fire pit.

"If you're going to build a fire, keep it very small. There's no ventilation down here, and the smoke will blind you. You'll also use up your oxygen and you'll die."

Mia looked around the little space and crossed her arms, rubbing her hands over the opposite biceps. The ghosts were thick and unwelcoming. "How long do we have to stay here?"

Dominic said, "Only for tonight. In the morning, when they're sleeping, we can leave Paris."

"I'm not coming back for you tomorrow," Naomi said. "I have things to do. I hope you memorized the way back."

"You're being paid to bring us back out," the Ulfen reminded her.

"Then stay until I can come back." She started to walk away. "I hope you brought extra batteries."

She disappeared into the darkness, leaving them alone.

Mia glared at him. "This was your bright idea? Hiding from the undead in an open grave?"

"They'll never find us here."

"How are you so certain? This is a public place, so there's nothing stopping them from coming down here. They'll know that we're hiding somewhere, so they might think this is the best place to look. I think we're in the worst possible place."

He sat down on one of the crates and stretched out his long legs. "You're just saying that because you're freaked out by the ghosts."

She opened her mouth to reply, but the words died on her tongue. "So, you can feel it, too?"

Dominic nodded. "My family has a tradition of mediumship on my mother's side. There are a lot of ghosts here. Maybe we can recruit them to keep watch for us."

Mia rolled her eyes. "Right. Because that's so likely." He looked up at her, studying her with narrowed amber eyes. After he had stared for a long moment, he snorted softly and looked away. She frowned. "What?"

"Nothing. I just almost forgot that you're one of the Dark Sisters." He rubbed his hands on his jeans. "How many faery children have you killed? How much of their blood have you enchanted?"

She leaned down, her face inches from his, angry with him for his tone of voice. "Dozens and dozens."

He met her gaze, and his eyes flared with Ulfen power. He was not intimidated - not that she'd expected him to be. "Nice," he said. "How do you live with yourself?"

She straightened and crossed her arms. "Very easily."

"It must be nice to have no conscience."

She turned her back on him and busied herself getting out the Coleman stove and her sleeping bag. "You should try it sometime."

He grumbled, "I'll pass."

"Passing judgment, dog?" she mocked. "You weren't too high and mighty to attach yourself to me on the train. You knew what I was then."

Dominic frowned. "I thought you might have been running because you were forced to be in the Dark Sisterhood. Now I think you went willingly."

"When you've been held down for all of your life, would you pass up the chance for power, real power, when it's offered to you?"

He gave her a scathing look that carried the weight of secrets. "Yes."

"Well, I guess I'm not as good of a person as you are." She rolled out her sleeping bag with a snap and settled down in it, her back to him. "Tomorrow, you need to go your way and let me go mine. I don't want your protection."

Dominic snorted. "Fine."

"Fine."

***

Nika picked up the phone and dialed Tamara's number. After a few rings, her friend picked up. "Hello?"

"Hi, Tam. It's Nika."

"Hey, long lost. How's Sweden?"

"Beautiful. Hey... I have a favor to ask."

Tamara sounded like she was smiling. "Shoot."

Nika hesitated, suddenly nervous about her friend's reaction. "Will you be my Maid of Honor?"

There was a long hesitation, and then Tamara squeaked, "You're getting married? What?"

"Yeah," she laughed, happy. "We haven't got the date set yet but Erik would like you to come to Stockholm and visit. We'll put you up in the hotel, and he'll even pay for your plane ticket. What do you say?"

Another long hesitation made Nika worry. "I'd say that he's a little controlling..."

"Oh, stop. He is not."

"He makes you leave your country, move into his house, and he's holding the purse strings...You're not even working anymore. What's up with that? I thought you'd never leave the museum business."

Nika sighed. "I'm finishing up a sabbatical, that's all. Then I'll be back at work. And he's really rich, so why shouldn't he pay for a few things?"

"How did he get rich on a soldier's salary?"

"God, but you're suspicious. He's from old money, okay?" She almost laughed at how accurate that term was. "And he's not that kind of person."

"He's a special ops guy," Tamara objected. "I've heard stories that they beat their wives and stuff. How do you know…?"

"He has a violent past, yes, but he's never going to do anything to me."

"Are you sure?"

Nika smiled. "Completely sure."

"Then test him."

"What do you mean, test him?" she asked, confounded. "Tamara, you're crazy."

"No, I'm not." She could hear her friend warming up to her own topic. "Listen, the one thing that a man who's going to hurt his woman will always get mad at, and that's being told no when he's in the mood. Right?"

"Right." Nika didn't like where she was going with this.

"Especially a guy who's been used to having it whenever he wants it. I doubt you've been telling him to shove off, have you?" Her tone was teasing, but it masked something very serious.

"If you saw him, you wouldn't say no, either," Nika said. "But I'm listening."

"He's a macho dude who's used to getting it anytime he wants. Make him wait. If he just lets it go because you say so, without getting mad, then he's worth keeping. But if he gets mad or starts to get violent, then you're coming back to the States with me. Deal?"

She shook her head. "You're crazy. You know, if he were that kind of guy, I wouldn't be with him."

"Maybe. Maybe not."

She sighed. "Fine. I'll test him. But he's going to pass."

"I hope so, for your sake." Tamara yawned. "Listen, email me when you're ready for me to come over and I'll see if I can take some time off. I don't know how happy Stuie will be with me skipping out on the bar, but I'll do it for you. Just let me know."

"Thanks, Tam. I appreciate it."

"No problem."

The call ended, and Nika sat with the phone to her lips for a moment. Images rose in her mind from the video that had been taken during Erik's foray into brutality against the faery. She remembered his stories of what he had done in the bad old days, and the hatred that Magda still bore for him until the moment she died had been based in her experiences as his victim. Erik had a history, and it was dark, and had resurfaced not that long ago.

She wanted to blame Mia and her magic for the change in him, and for the horrible things he had done to the poor Huldra that had died in the hands of the First. Was she sure of him? Was she certain that under duress, he wouldn't revert back to those horrible behaviors again?

She sighed. She wasn't certain, but she would like to be. She would go forward with the test.

Chapter Five

Mia was sleeping with her back still facing Dominic, her bleached blonde head pillowed on her arm. He was listening to the shuffling sounds in the caverns and thinking about his childhood in Canada when everything went silent. The ghosts stopped moving, and even the distant dripping of water seemed to stop. He stood and shifted into his full wolf form, his clothing vanishing into his four-legged form. He backed up and bared his teeth, waiting.

He smelled them before he saw them, even though his eyes were well accustomed to seeing in the dark. He growled as three men in black came into the chamber. Mia woke and scrambled to her feet, disorganized and uncoordinated as she struggled to rise.

"What is it?"

The Draugr on the right smiled. "Hello, Mia."

She froze, but Dominic lunged. He leaped onto the Draugr and buried his long teeth into the vampire's neck, tearing out his throat with one powerful jerk. He swallowed the flesh in his mouth and kept biting, tearing out his spine and ending him. The vampire vanished into a cloud of dust.

The Draugr in the middle pulled a long dagger with a silver blade and slashed Dominic in the side. He yelped and leaped away, landing close to Mia so he could protect her as the third vampire approached her from the other direction. She held up her hands, and the protective rune she had placed on her palm earlier in the day flared, lighting up the entire chamber. Flames danced over her skin, creating a glove made entirely of fire, and she began to whisper in a language Dominic did not understand.

The Draugr with the blade stepped forward, grinning. "Come here, you stupid fucking dog," he said, his tone light despite the harsh words. "Some play with papa."

Dominic snarled and snapped at him, his hackles risen as high as they would go. He kept himself between Mia and the vampires, and the man with the blade feinted forward. He nearly lost his hand, and he shrank back. The Ulfen's fangs were bared, his nose wrinkled while his tongue darted in and out of his mouth in agitation. In the dark room, his eyes burned yellow, a counterpoint to the red eyes of the Draugr.

"Your father wants to see you, little girl," the third vampire said. "Call off your dog and come peacefully and nobody will get hurt."

She interrupted her chant long enough to laugh at him, then continued. He bent and picked up a rock from the stony ground.

"Last chance, Mia."

Dominic snapped at him again, his growling louder.

The vampire pulled a pistol from his pocket. "I'll shoot the wolf. I have silver bullets."

"Go ahead," she said, finally breaking off her incantation. Her hand still burned. "He doesn't mean anything to me."

The man with the blade asked, "Then why are you running with him?"

"Because he was useful at first and now he won't go away," she snapped. The flames around her hand brightened, flaring up as if someone had thrown gasoline on her fire. "Now this is your last chance. Leave me alone!"

"Where do you think you're going to go, Mia?" the knife-wielder taunted. "Don't you think the Huntsman will find you? That's what he does – he tracks down people and kills them."

Dominic took one stiff-legged step toward the Draugr with the pistol, his back arched menacingly, warning him to back off. The man stepped back, but his pistol remained trained on the wolf.

"Come and see my boss," the blade user said. "Leave this animal behind and come discuss the possibilities we can offer you here."

The fire leaped from her left hand to her right, the arc of its passage glowing orange in the dark. "I'm not Draugr. I'm Valtaeigr, the last surviving Dark Sister. You can offer me nothing that I want."

"Sanctuary," the man with the pistol said. "Protection when the Huntsman comes for you."

She hadn't been born yesterday. "In return for what?"

"That's why you need to talk to our boss."

She considered the offer, then looked at Dominic, who was still protecting her fiercely. "What about him?"

In answer, the Draugr aimed the gun and fired. A slug buried itself in the werewolf's side, and Dominic fell to the ground with an ear-splitting yelp. Mia stepped back to prevent him from falling on her, and she stood over him uncertainly. Finally, she extinguished the flame on her hand.

"All right," she said. "I'll talk to him. You have me cornered anyway."

The man with the gun grinned as Dominic whined in pain. "You could have dusted us at any moment," he said. "I know what you Dark Sisters can do."

"Maybe," she said. "Maybe I didn't want to."

The Ulfen metamorphosed back into his human form, lying in a fetal position with his hands clutching his lower abdomen. She stepped over him without another glance.

"Take me to your boss, then. And you had better not be lying about sanctuary."

They walked away, leaving Dominic lying on the floor in a pool of blood. He tried once to rise from the floor, but the pain overwhelmed him and he collapsed.

***

Mia looked back once at the Ulfen who had tried to protect and help her, and she felt a stab of regret that he was injured. She supposed that was what he got for getting involved in other people's business. She'd never asked him to stand up for her against the Draugr. That had been his own bad choice. She was a little amazed that the silver bullet hadn't killed him outright, and she would have liked to have known why. She supposed that was just one question that would never be answered. Soon he would dead, and his pain would be over. She hoped he died soon.

The Draugr knew their way around the Catacombs, and really, she should have expected that. They were the sorts of creatures who enjoyed death and all of its trappings. She was grateful that they knew a faster route. She didn't want to stay down there with the bones and the ghosts.

They brought her up out of the underground, using the tourist entrance. She shoved her hands into the pockets of her jacket and followed them to a big black car. The man who had shot the gun opened the back door for her, and she slid inside. They closed the door and went away, leaving her alone.

Or... perhaps not alone. She could smell the scent of the Draugr everywhere; since this was their car, that wasn't a big surprise. She and the driver were the only ones in the car, but she felt a presence there, someone close and watchful, and a shimmer of magic tickled the edges of her mind. Mia brought her hand up and began to cast, but someone invisible grabbed her wrist.

"No magic," a man's voice said.

"Nice, coming from someone under a magical cloak."

"My car, my rules."

"Show yourself," she bit, pulling free.

There was a chuckle. "All in good time."

She crossed her arms and legs and sat back in the seat. She was aware that she was pouting, but she really didn't care. She'd been having a rash of very bad days, and it was enough to make anyone cranky.

Her unseen companion chuckled again. "You're a real piece of work, missy." His voice was a pure baritone, his accent American.

"Who are you?"

She could hear the smile in his voice as he answered. "You can call me Derek." There was a hesitation. "You cut your hair. I liked it better when it was red."

Mia clenched her teeth. "Fuck you."

Derek laughed and said again, "All in good time."

***

In Sweden, in the house they had recently purchased, Erik was lounging on the bed in a pair of silk shorts watching Nika prepare for bed with a smile on his face. She walked slowly toward him, brushing her lustrous red tresses, smiling back, dressed in a white satin chemise.

"What are you looking at?"

He smiled. "I'm looking at you."

She put the brush aside and knelt on the bed. "Like what you see?"

"Always."

He held out his hand for her, and she took it, letting him pull her into his arms. She pillowed her head on his broad, muscular chest, letting her fingers play along the peaks and valleys of his defined abdomen. Nika kissed his warm skin and breathed in his masculine scent and the undefinable magic that was indisputably his. She felt it all the way down to her toes, and it made her tingle.

Erik kissed her tenderly, his lips light as a whisper against her own even while his arm was strong around her shoulders. It was a heady combination of gentleness and power, and it made her happy. She looked up into his bright blue eyes and ran her fingers through his tousled blond locks.

"You, my love, are absolutely gorgeous," she told him.

He smiled. "Thank you. I think – " He was interrupted by his cell phone, which suddenly blasted out the techno ringtone he had assigned to identify calls from Elke. "Seriously?"

Nika snickered and leaned over him to retrieve the phone. "Hello?"

"Hi, Nika," Elke said brightly. "Listen, remember that guy that I've been seeing?"

"Why are you calling me on Erik's phone to talk about your boyfriend?"

"Because yours is turned off. Anyway, he works for 3 Sverige. That's a cell phone network here in Sweden."

Nika rolled her eyes. "I know. That's who I have my phone through."

Erik shook his head and dropped it back onto the pillow, looking up at the ceiling and holding his arms out in a 'why me?' gesture. She struggled not to laugh.

"Oh, okay," Elke continued. "I wasn't sure. So, I sent him the data from Erik's phone with the call about Mia, and he traced the call."

Now Erik was much more interested in the conversation. He sat up, his eyebrows rising. Nika nodded to him. "Where did the call come from?"

"It was on a phone that was purchased through 3 Sverige in Copenhagen, and it's on a universal card. Based on pings and triangulation and all that jazz, he says that the picture was taken is Paris."

Erik frowned. "Paris?" he echoed.

"Hi, boss!" she chirped, well aware that with his Draugr hearing he was already party to the conversation. "Yeah, Paris. And in Paris, guess what?"

He sighed. "Elke, spit it out before I shake you."

She giggled. "That might actually be fun."

"Elke..."

"All right, all right. Paris, you might remember, is split between two Draugr groups. The Draugr chief of east Paris didn't come to Uppsala. In fact, he stayed there and cemented his holdings by taking the territory of the other Draugr chieftain in west Paris, who did go, and who's still here in Sweden. He's also being really chummy lately with a coven of witches based in Bordeaux."

"Chummy in what way?" he asked.

"Well...he's been acting as their muscle under a kind of Mafia-style agreement."

Erik shook his head. "The hell he is. Get me all the information you can about those Draugr in Paris and get it to me on my desk in the morning, and about the witches in Bordeaux. And I want to know where in Paris Mia was seen."

"You got it, boss."

He gently pulled the phone out of Nika's hand and spoke into it. "And stop calling tonight unless it's a complete emergency."

His assistant giggled again. "Sure thing. You two have fun, now!"

He ended the call and put the phone aside. Nika leaned forward and kissed him, then got under the covers and lay down with her back against his side.

"Good night, sweetheart," she said, unable to keep the grin out of her tone.

She could sense his confusion in the silence, but finally he said, "Good night." He turned out his bedside table light and rolled over until they were lying back to back. She smiled and leaned into his warmth, then settled down to sleep.

Chapter Six

Dominic hauled himself onto his hands and knees, feeling the silver burning in his gut. It should have killed him. He didn't know why he was still alive. He whimpered in pain, the sound still wolf-like even though his form was human. He squeezed his eyes shut, hard.

The sound of footsteps approached, and he tried to move away from the door, but his hand slipped in the pool of blood beneath him and he fell onto his side. He lay there, gasping, staring at the entry to the little rock chamber.

A human man in a muddy overcoat with shaggy, unkempt hair appeared in the doorway. He looked down on the felled Ulfen with a kind smile, even though he shouldn't have been able to see him in the utter darkness.

"Well," he said, his voice thickly accented. "I came expecting to find a runaway Valtaeigr and I find a wounded wolf instead."

Dominic tried to speak, but he couldn't make the sound come out. The man came closer and crouched beside him.

"That's a bad wound," he said conversationally. "I'll bet it feels as awful as it looks."

The Ulfen whined and tried to scoot away from him, but the man out a hand on his shoulder and held him tight. The heat of magical power shot into him from the stranger, and he was completely paralyzed.

"I don't know how much a hurt Ulfen is like a hurt animal, but I can't have you biting me while I try to help you, can I?" The man had a Russian accent, and his scent was ruddy and rich, like blood in black soil. He rolled Dominic onto his back and pulled a black-handled knife out of his pocket. The ritual blade glowed with powerful magic. "This will only hurt for a minute. I'm sorry I can't make it not hurt at all."

He pulled Dominic's shirt up and his jeans down to expose the bullet entry wound. With a quick, almost apologetic smile, he cut into him and reached his blunt fingers inside through the incision. The Ulfen tried to howl in pain, but the paralysis extended to his voice, and he was forced to stay silent. After an eternity of probing, the man finally pulled out the bullet and tucked it into a pocket.

"There," he said. "Good as new. Almost."

He bent and lifted Dominic onto his shoulders as if the Ulfen was weightless, and he carried him out of the Catacombs.

***

The car pulled through a guarded gate and into a private estate on the outskirts of Paris. As soon as the gates were locked up again behind the vehicle, the one calling himself Derek materialized on the seat beside her.

He was shorter than she would have expected, with chocolate brown hair and equally dark eyes set in a face with skin so pale he seemed to be made of milk. He was in an elegant suit with a black wool overcoat covering it, but he seemed to have no difficulty with the heat. Now that his magical concealment was dismissed, she could tell that he was an old Draugr, secure in his power.

"Welcome to my home," he said with a pleasant smile.

She glowered at him. "Am I a prisoner?"

"Not yet."

"What do you mean?"

He smiled more broadly. "Your ultimate fate depends greatly upon the choices that you make, and the reactions of your father."

"Did he send you?"

"Quite the contrary. This is going to be a huge surprise for him." The car stopped, and he exited, offering her his hand to help her out. She took it reluctantly.

Derek led her up the front steps and into a palatial mansion that was clearly centuries old. A human woman met him at the door and collected his coat, and another asked Mia for hers. She shook her head and kept it, and the woman simply walked away.

He took her to a sitting room filled with antique furniture and exquisite art. She sat in a wingback chair while he made himself comfortable on a loveseat facing her.

"I am Derek Dupin, the chieftain of the Paris band. Have you heard of me?"

"Should I have?"

He smiled. "Perhaps not. But soon everyone will know who I am." He crossed his legs and sat back, his arms across the back of the loveseat. "Now that your father has so helpfully destroyed all of the First, I am now the second oldest vampire in existence. I will not bow to him."

Mia snorted. "He'll make you."

"No," he said with a shake of his dark head. "Not if I have you at my side."

She narrowed her eyes. This was beginning to sound a great deal like the arrangement she had endured with Bjorn. "At your side in what way?"

"As his daughter, you are his heir and princess of the Draugr kingdom. You are also the last surviving Dark Sister, and therefore the strongest link to the powers of Hel. I am proposing an alliance, one that will benefit us both."

"What sort of an alliance?"

"A marriage of convenience," he said with a shrug, as if he were discussing a coffee date. "If we wed, we will be the heirs to his kingdom, and if anything unfortunate should happen to him, we will be in a position to take it all. All of the power. All of the territory. All of the money. And we will be able to resume making faery *dreyri* and reaping the financial benefits of a population addicted to what only we can provide."

"What makes you think he won't just kill you when you make your demands?" she asked. "I assume you're going to make demands."

Derek smiled. "He wants to be king, doesn't he? Part of kingship is diplomacy. I have more experience in that field than the Huntsman does. I can work him into a position where we will have everything we want."

She was not convinced. "And what do I get out of this?"

He was prepared with an answer. "An end to running. All of the power you can take. Respect due to you for your particular skill set. Protection from the Huntsman and his Rune Master."

He finished speaking and waited for her to respond. She stared at him, their eyes locked, for a long time while she ran his suggestions over in her head. Finally, she said, "If I agree to this, there's one more thing I want."

Derek beamed. "Anything for my future bride."

"I want the Huntsman's head on a pig pole."

His dark eyes gleamed. "That is a gift I would be happy to deliver."

Mia considered for a moment longer, then smiled tightly. "You have a deal."

***

Nika slept fitfully. In her unquiet dreams, she saw Mia and a Draugr she did not know standing on a battlefield, facing Erik. The two Draugr were in ancient armor, swords in their hands. Nika herself stood at Erik's side, her rune magic tingling in her hands. Mia had magic of her own prepared.

The faceoff took place in an empty field beneath dark skies heavy with thunderclouds. The lightning added power to their magic, and a soaking rain slicked the ground. Erik and the Draugr fought, and Mia concentrated her magic on her father, weakening him. Nika could not get her magic to work. She was forced to sit by helplessly while her lover was hacked to bits, dying before her eyes.

She jolted awake and reached for him, but his place in the bed was empty. She sat up, alarmed. "Erik?"

There was no answer, so she tried again through their Chosen bond. *Erik?*

In the study, he responded.

She slipped from the bed and padded through the house to where he sat in the dark, his face ghostly in the glow from his laptop's screen. "What are you doing?" she asked.

"Trying to get things in order with the club and everything else." He ran a hand over his face. "This is not my strong suit."

She went to him and embraced him, her arms tight around his neck. He held her wrists gently in his hands and looked up at her.

"Are you all right?"

Nika sighed. "I had a horrible nightmare."

He pulled her onto his lap, and she put her arm around his shoulders, happy to be there. He circled her waist with his arms and said, "It was only a dream. Whatever it was, it didn't happen, and we're as safe and sound as we've ever been."

"That's what I'm afraid of." She sighed and leaned her head against his, looking at the spreadsheet on his computer. "These books are going to be the death of you. Why don't we just hire an accountant?"

"Do you think we'll be able to find one who'll keep quiet about all of our business and who won't get freaked out by what we are?"

"Probably. Money helps some people accept anything and keep any secret. We have how many Draugr, though? Surely one of them is a CPA."

He smiled. "I'll tell you what. If you can find a Draugr accountant, I will hire him or her on the spot. Deal?"

"Deal." She patted his shoulder. "Anything is better than seeing you wrestle with numbers like this."

Erik shrugged. "It's not as if I ever went to school. It's a miracle I can understand these things as well as I can." He was quiet for a moment, then he asked, "Who did you see in your dream?"

"Mia," she said. "You and me. A Draugr man I've never seen before. It was very dark and rainy and you were fighting and... I couldn't get my magic to work. I couldn't help you. You...you died."

"Ugh." He kissed her. "It was only a dream. Here I am, as alive as I was the day you met me, and I doubt your magic will ever fail you in real life."

"Don't the Norse believe in dreams?" she asked.

"We did. And sometimes I still do. If it concerns you, call Ingrid and have her interpret it for you. She's a *vala* of many talents."

Vala was the ancient Norse word for "wise woman," and his mother was certainly that. She had taught Nika about rune magic and about what it meant to be Valtaeigr. She had also proven to be a powerful ally against their foes.

"I'll call her in the morning."

"Good idea." He reached out and closed the laptop. "Enough of this. Let's go back to bed, shall we?"

She kissed him, and she longed for more, but if she gave in to her own urges tonight, it would mean she'd have to start her test all over again, and she didn't want to do that. The sooner this test was over, the happier she'd be - for a number of reasons.

Erik could tell that she was thinking, and the way he was looking at her, she worried that her thoughts had been showing on her face. She couldn't let him know that he was being tested.

"Chosen?" he asked, his voice gentle but guarded. "Is something troubling you?"

"Just the dream," she lied. She got up off of his lap and took his hands in hers. "I'm just tired and I'd like to go to sleep."

He rose and put his arm around her. "Then sleep you shall."

Together, they walked to the bedroom and went back to bed. They slid under the covers and she curled up under his arm, her head on his chest, her hand on his stomach. He kissed her hairline and ran his hand along her arm, stroking her soft skin from shoulder to elbow. His heartbeat was strong in her ear, the drum beat of his life and his love. She kissed his chest.

He put his arms around her and pulled her closer, moving her easily with his steady strength. She ended up lying on top of him, her belly against his hips. He looked at her with adoration, and she kissed him deeply.

His body responded to the touch, and she could feel him hardening against her. She longed to touch him, to feel him inside of her, but she reminded herself of the things he had done in his mortal days and while under Mia's control. She pushed away and put some space between them.

He looked at her in confusion, little lines appearing between his eyebrows. "Nika, what is it?"

"I'm just tired, that's all." She pulled further away and lay down without touching him. "I just want to sleep."

He took a deep breath and pressed his hands against his face. "All right," he said at last. "I'm sorry."

"It's okay," she said, smiling, pleased that he was taking her rejection so well. She cuddled into her pillow, facing him. "Good night, Erik."

He arranged his pillow and sighed. "Good night."

It took hours for both of them to fall asleep.

Chapter Seven

The man took Dominic through ley lines, traveling in an unreal dream state between the physical and the imaginary. The Ulfen still paralyzed and in pain, wished that he could close his eyes against the swirling phantasms that played around them as they moved. There was no such relief for him, however, and he did his best to hold on to his mind.

Luckily, the trip was short, only ten minutes or so of being more spirit than flesh and yet more flesh than spirit. He emerged gasping on the man's shoulder. The air smelled of Sweden.

The man carried him through a doorway and up a flight of stairs. They went through a fire door and into the corridor of a hotel. His helpful abductor produced a key card at the fourth door on the right and carried him inside.

He was dumped inelegantly onto one of the two beds in the room, and the man removed his overcoat, which was now heavily stained by Dominic's blood. He tossed it aside and stood over the injured Ulfen, his hands on his hips.

"Now, let's have a look at you, little wolf," he said.

He stripped off Dominic's torn leather jacket, which he examined minutely, then tossed on the floor. He pulled off the paralyzed man's motorcycle boots, his socks, his bloodstained jeans, his torn and bloody T-shirt and his briefs. When Dominic was naked on the bed, the man knelt over him, pressing his hands against the bullet hole and the larger incision he had made.

He chanted in Russian, and Dominic could feel healing energy pouring into him. Part of his spirit rose to meet that energy, binding with it, pulling it into himself with abandon. It was blinding pleasure combined with welcome relief from suffering, and his breath caught in his throat.

"There, there, little wolf," the man cooed. "Let Vladimir take all the hurt away."

He could do nothing else. The Russian witch worked his magic, then pulled away, wiping his hands on Dominic's T-shirt. He looked down at him, studying the vampire bite scar on his throat and the dimples on his shoulder from Ardrik's teeth.

"So you were bitten by a vampire and you were bitten by a werewolf. Which bite came first, I wonder? And did you know when you were bitten that you were born a witch?" He leaned forward. "I think that's the truth of you, isn't it? And why the silver didn't kill you. Silver is a friend to witches."

Dominic tried to will him to release his paralyzing hold, and somehow, Vladimir got the picture. He straightened and clapped his hands twice over the Ulfen's face, and the spell holding him motionless shattered. The first thing he did was to slide out from under the Russian witch and try to cover his nakedness.

Vladimir chuckled. "A modest wolf. Now I've seen everything. You can use the shower to wash off the blood. I'll get you new clothes. Yours are ruined."

Dominic took a step toward the bathroom, then turned and said, "Thank you for helping me."

The Russian witch nodded. "You can pay me back in time."

He preferred not to speculate on what form that payment would take. He went into the bathroom and locked the door.

***

When he left the bathroom after a self-indulgently long shower, he found Vladimir sitting on the bed nearest the windows, watching television. A set of department store bags waited on the closer bed, alongside his boots and his jacket. Dominic hesitantly looked inside and found replacements for the garments he had lost, nearly identical to what he'd had before. He dressed.

"So which was it?" Vladimir asked, muting the television set. The movie he'd been watching continued to play with the sound turned off, silent images flashing across the screen.

"The werewolf bite came first," he said. "The vampire bit me about twenty years ago."

"Why didn't she kill you?"

"How did you know it was a female vampire?"

Vladimir smiled at him and tapped his index finger against his own temple. "I know many things, little wolf."

He sat on the bed to put on his socks and boots. "I don't know why. She bit to kill, obviously, but then she pulled away. Maybe I don't taste very good."

"Or maybe she realized you were a protected witch and chose not to cause any more devilry."

Dominic frowned. "Protected? By what?"

"By the Great Lady and by the Horned One." There was reverence in Vladimir's voice as he named his deities.

"Sorry," he said softly. "I just don't believe in gods and goddesses."

The Russian laughed. "Well, they believe in you!" He gestured toward the bed. "There's money in there for you, if you want to take it. You can go back to Finland and your pack, or you can leave Scandinavia all together. But first I want to know what you know about the Dark Sister."

He took a breath. "She's hard. She was taken by Draugr in Paris. I don't know where they went."

"What do you mean, 'she's hard'? Do you mean she's hard-hearted? Is she mean?"

"Something like that." He picked up a bank envelope that had been beside the clothing bags. A stack of Euros two inches thick stared up at him, and he pocketed it without counting the amount. "She doesn't regret anything she's done, and she has no love for her father or his intended bride. I think she's a little scary."

Vladimir nodded. "All of the Dark Sisters were. They gave their souls to Hel and to Niflheim a long time ago. Your friend is the last of their sisterhood."

"I never said she was my friend. She was a lady in trouble, and I tried to help her out."

"Did you try to do anything else?"

Dominic looked insulted. "Of course not! I'm not a monster."

"No, you're an omega werewolf, and your only chance to get laid is outside of your pack. I wouldn't have blamed you for trying – of course, it would have been like trying to mate with a cobra, but to each their own." He turned back to the television. "Did you catch the scent of the vampires who took her?"

"I'm a werewolf, not a bloodhound."

"Of course. You keep telling me all the things you're not. I wonder, do you know what you are?" Vladimir laughed. "Well, have a good life, little wolf." He turned the sound back on. "You can go."

He wasn't sure how to react, so he just picked up his jacket and left.

***

Erik rose from bed just before dawn and stood at the bay window in the living room, overlooking the water and the glowing sunrise. He held a mug of *dreyri* mixed with coffee in his hand, and the heat of the mixture gave the enchanted blood a more palatable taste. He had grown accustomed to drinking cold blood, but he had never grown to like it.

He could hear Nika's slow and steady breathing in the bedroom, and he knew that she was too young as a Draugr to awaken yet. He had hours to pass before she would rise from their bed. That gave him time.

He thought about Mia, and about the misery that had been her childhood. He thought about his brothers, especially Gunnar, to whom he had been closest in both age and affection. He had never expected to face life without Gunnar at his side. They had been through everything together, from boyhood training at their father's knee to the ritual that had made them Veithimathr, huntsmen of the gods. They had worked together as partners and brothers and friends for centuries. Now Gunnar was gone, and Erik had need of his advice and company.

In a perfect world, Gunnar would still be alive and would be preparing to stand with Erik when he married Nika. The concept of a "best man" was a curiously modern one, and they would have laughed about it together. In Norse weddings, the man and woman approached the gods alone to seek their blessing and to solemnize their decision to be together. It was strange that modern people needed to involve another man and another woman as glorified servants to take the same oath that Norse couples were strong enough to take on their own. Still, if he'd had to choose some other man to play a part in his one and only wedding, it would have been Gunnar, and they would have smirked at the ridiculousness together.

Nika expected him to have someone standing with him when they took the weak and watered-down vows that marriages began with these days. He couldn't disappoint her, so he had to choose someone to take the role. The problem was that he had literally no one left to ask.

He had destroyed the First for their role in instigating the war with the Faery and for the way they'd forced his daughter to steal his will away. He didn't want to believe that Mia had cast the magic to deprive him of his free will because she'd wanted to do it. Still...

He drained his blood and coffee cocktail. It was time to be honest.

He had been an absentee father. Worse than that, when he'd been around, he'd been horrible. He had been abusive to Magda, and Mia had been on hand to witness the things that Erik had done to his body slave. If she didn't hate him with every fiber of her being, she was not truly Norse. He should have expected her to go with her mother, to learn dark magic and plot for centuries for revenge.

He had to admit the truth. She had meant to enslave and dishonor him. Somewhere, he was certain, she was still plotting his demise. So why was he searching for her now? Nika was right. It was too late to make things right, and Mia would never forgive and forget. She couldn't. In her place, he certainly would not.

So, he thought sadly. *This will end with me putting my own daughter to death. The only surviving child of my body.* He rinsed his mug and put it in the dishwasher, obedient and domesticated as a lapdog. He was filled with distaste. *What has happened to me?*

He left a note for Nika advising that he was going for a walk and put on his jacket. After a moment of hesitation, he picked up his axe along with his car keys and left the house.

Chapter Eight

Erik drove to Gunnar's house and opened the door. The house belonged to him now, technically, under the terms of the deed, but in his mind it would always belong to Gunnar.

From the outside, the house looked like any other suburban Stockholm dwelling, albeit one with heavily curtained windows. That illusion was shattered by the first glimpse through the door. The inside of the house had been completely remodeled, the interior walls removed and wooden pillars installed to replace the load-bearing joists. The house had been remade in the image of an ancient Norse longhouse, with furs and wooden planks on the walls. A bed in the corner was covered with more furs, and wooden benches and elaborately carved oaken chairs surrounded a central fire pit. A hole had been opened in the roof to release the smoke. Weapon racks and shields lined the walls, and it was as close to home as Erik would ever come again.

He sat in Gunnar's chair, the biggest and most intricately carved seat in the house. It was shaped like two crouching dragons, their wings forming the back, their back-sweeping horns making the arms. Across from him was another beautiful seat, carved in the image of two antelopes. He had spent many hours sitting in that antelope chair, talking to Gunnar while they drank mead and *dreyri*.

He sighed heavily and leaned forward, his elbows on his knees, hands dangling. Between his hands, his axe rested with its double head on the floor boards. He gave the weapon a lazy spin, watching the blades rotate.

"What ails you, brother?"

He jerked, startled by the sound. Across the room, shimmering and wispy gray like smoke, he could see Gunnar standing, his arms crossed across his mighty chest, his feet firmly planted on the ground. Erik gaped, and Gunnar laughed.

"What's the matter, Huntsman? Never seen a ghost before?"

Erik stammered, "I... Gunnar!" He rose slowly, his axe dropping to the floor. "Is it really you?"

"In the not-flesh." He smiled briefly, then turned serious. "I was sent to you with a message from the All-Father. You cannot go forward and backward at the same time."

He was stunned speechless. *A message from the All-Father?* he thought, incredulous.

His brother's ghost smiled again. "Say something."

"I..." he tried. "I understand."

"Do you?"

"I think so." He blinked his cobwebs away and smiled. "I've missed you."

Gunnar waved his hand dismissively. "Eh, I'm always around. Especially in this place."

Erik sat again, watching as his brother's form flickered like a candle flame in the breeze. "I can't turn Mia back toward the good, can I?"

Gunnar smiled sadly. "You cannot go forward and backward at the same time."

"I'll take that as a no."

"What's done is done, brother," the ghost said. "And you should know that you have friends and allies in places you might not expect."

He chuckled. "You could be a little less cryptic, you know."

"No I can't. It's in the ghost rules."

"Bastard."

Gunnar grinned, then said, "My time is short. Remember that you can always find me here if you need me." He began to fade. "Be well, Erik."

A gust of cold air brushed his face, and then the ghost was gone.

***

Nika woke just before noon and found herself alone. Erik's note was perfunctory and she wondered if he'd been angry when he wrote it. After a breakfast of cold *dreyri* and a quick shower, she picked up the phone and called Tamara.

The phone rang several times, then her friend's sleepy voice came on the line. "Hello?"

"Hi, Tam."

"Nika, it's five in the morning. Time zones are a thing." There was the sound of rustling, and then she asked, "Is everything okay? How's the test going?"

"I think he's getting irritated. He wasn't here when I woke up this morning."

Tamara yawned. "Well, he works for a living, right? Maybe he went to work. Speaking of, shouldn't you be doing that?"

Nika sighed. "I told you, I'm still on sabbatical."

"Must be nice. Bartenders don't get that kind of perk."

She sat on the couch. "Do you think you can come to Stockholm soon? I mean... to stay?"

There was a long pause. "You want me to immigrate?"

"Just get a tourist visa. You can stay for six months, and then we can figure it out after that."

Tamara sounded sorely tempted. "I'll need a job."

"Erik is rich, and we own a bar in town now. We can get you set up there if you want. You were a bartender in college, right? We'll pay better than what's-his-name, that idiot you work for." She picked at the edge of the sofa. "I miss you, and I really need a friend."

"Honey, what's the matter?"

She hesitated, then said, "There's a lot that I have to tell you, but it would be easier to tell you in person. Please, like I said, we'll buy your ticket and everything. We can put you up in our house, or we'll get you a hotel room, whatever you want."

She realized that she sounded desperate, and Tamara had been her friend for too long not to pick up the clue. "Okay. I'll get things worked out on my end and I'll be there as soon as I can."

"Thanks, Tam. I really appreciate it."

"No problem." They both knew that it was a huge problem, but they chose to let it slide. "I want to travel, anyway."

Nika smiled, relieved. "Thank you so much."

Her friend yawned again, then said, "You can make it up to me by introducing me to some Swedish hotties."

She laughed. "You've got it."

Tamara groaned as she hauled herself out of bed. At least, that's what it sounded like she was doing, from the sounds of moving fabric and the creaking of a bed spring. "So, are you going to buy my ticket?"

"Of course."

"Good. I'll email you the deets once I get them figured out." She yawned again. "I'll see you soon, sweetie."

***

Dominic wandered down a street in Stockholm, not at all certain where he was or where he was going. He was surrounded by Draugr, their coppery scent filling his nose everywhere he went. He supposed that the vampire population was elevated in preparation for the vampire king's wedding to the Rune Master.

A few vampires passed him on the sidewalk, and they looked at him in shock. He turned away and kept walking, trying to avoid an incident. He wasn't certain how bold these Draugr might be, and whether they would try to attack him in the middle of mortal company. He couldn't be too careful, though, as a lone Ulfen without a pack to protect him.

A slim arm hooked around his, and he looked down into the elfin face of a tiny Draugr woman with brightly colored hair and multiple piercings. She grinned up at him. "Hey, handsome," she greeted. "Looks like you might need a friend."

He blinked in surprise. "Uh...maybe?"

"I'm Elke," she said. "And you are?"

"Dominic."

"Nice to meet you, Dominic."

"Likewise."

She pulled him off of the sidewalk and into a bookstore with a colorful display in the window hawking the latest best seller. He followed her, letting her drag him by the arm into the far corner of the store, were there was a couch and a coffee table set up for casual readers to enjoy. She folded herself up on the cushion and made him sit down beside her.

"Those guys were going to take you into an alley and roll you," she told him. "They think they're really tough, and taking down a werewolf would add to their street cred."

He blushed, although he didn't know why. "Thanks for watching out for me."

"No problem. That's what I do – I'm an assistant." She giggled at some private joke. "Do you mind if I ask you a question?"

Dominic shifted on the couch. "Could I stop you?"

"Probably not." She called up a photograph on her cellphone and handed it to him. It was him and Mia, leaving the train in Paris. "Where did you leave her?"

He sighed. This question again. "She left me. Actually, some other Draugr came and took her. I don't know who, and I don't know where."

"Too bad." She tucked the phone back into her pocket. "My boss really wants to find her."

"Your boss?"

"The Huntsman. Her daddy."

He stood. "I don't want anything to do with him, or his wife, or Mia. I'm done."

"Maybe, maybe not." Elke rose, too. She only came up to the middle of his chest. "My boss will want to talk to you."

He brushed past her. "I don't want to talk to him."

"Do you really want to go back out there?" she called after him. "They know I work for him, and they won't jump you while you're with me. If you go out there, you're a dead dog...if you'll pardon the expression."

His steps faltered, and he turned back to face her. She smiled broadly, brazenly displaying her fangs in the early afternoon light.

"Good boy," she said.

He returned to the couch, rankling. "Could you please lay off with the dog references? What is with you people, anyway?"

She shrugged. "It's in our blood," she said, wickedly pleased with her own joke.

"Apparently." He rolled his eyes and sat down again. "Aren't you worried that you might cause a scene with those teeth out in the open like that?"

Elke grinned again, making no effort to hide her fangs. "No. This place is Draugr-owned and operated, and no humans make it this far back in the store."

"Why not?"

"The staff has to eat."

"That's...disturbing."

She laughed. "Oh, right. Like you've never eaten a human being."

"Actually, I haven't. Well..." He hesitated, then amended his comment. "Not on my own, anyway."

"Uh-huh. That's what I thought."

She came closer to him and straddled him on the couch, her legs closing around his with a vise-like grip. She was all muscle. He considered trying to evade her, but realized that he had nowhere to go. He was behind enemy lines.

Elke grinned at him like a predator and tugged his T-shirt out of his jeans. "I'm thirsty," she said. "And I've always wondered how werewolves taste."

He caught at her wrists, but she shook him off easily. Draugr were physically stronger than Ulfen. "I don't know about most vampires, but I'm told I taste horrible."

He lifted his chin to show her the scar on his throat. She stopped and stared at it, then laughed.

"I'll be the judge of that."

Before he could stop her, she had sunk her fangs into the soft flesh of his neck. Pain raced through him like lightning, and he bucked beneath her. She held on tight, not budging an iota as she gripped him with her jaws and thighs. Elke grabbed his wrists and pinned them to his sides as she fed. He struggled to free himself, but she overpowered him easily.

Dominic groaned as the pain began to give way to an entirely different sensation, one that was unexpected and unwelcome. His cock hardened and strained against the denim of his jeans, tenting the fabric and pressing painfully against the zipper. She chuckled in the back of her throat and reached down to free him from his confinement, not releasing his vein, which she stroked with rhythmic passes of her hot, wet tongue. Images rose in his mind of that tongue on other parts of his body, and he had no doubt that the thoughts were placed there by her. He had no wish to think such things.

She got him worked loose and took him in her hand, stroking the shaft with fast, quick jerks. He shuddered beneath her and his vision swam, stars sparkling in the outer fields of his vision. He tried desperately not to enjoy her touch. She worked him faster, rotating her grip and running her thumb over the weeping head, rubbing him just hard enough to give pleasure with just a hint of pain. She squeezed his balls in her other hand, tugging at them until he groaned. She stroked his taint with her finger and intensified the hand job she was forcing onto him. He began to shake.

She stopped pulling blood from his wound, although she left her teeth buried in his flesh. He was too far gone to even notice. Dominic cried out raggedly and came in hot spurts, coating her hand and his own stomach with his seed. He moaned in pleasure and defeat.

Elke finally released him and sat back, licking her fingers clean. "Good boy," she said breathlessly, her face flushed. She bent down and licked the white trails from his hard-muscled abdomen. "Almost as good as blood."

He tried to speak, but the blood loss worked against him. His amber eyes rolled up in his head and he passed out.

Chapter Nine

Erik went to Snake Eyes without going home. The throbbing of the ward on the door startled the younger Draugr who had assembled there for their morning cup of blood, and as he walked past them, he had to wonder why they weren't out fending for themselves.

He stopped and looked around. "Don't you idiots hunt anymore?"

They looked astonished. One of them, a red-haired man with a smattering of freckles across his nose, stammered, "N-no..."

"Why not?"

The redhead looked away, embarrassed. "Human blood doesn't taste as good as this."

He looked at the bartender, Helaine. "Really? All faery *dreyri* all the time?"

She nodded. "That's all they ask for. If they have the coin, they get the drink."

Erik scowled. "God damn it. They're cut off from the strong stuff. Give them regular *dreyri* or nothing at all."

There were mumbled protests, but he ignored them.

He stalked into his office and sat at the desk, hating it. He wasn't a desk job sort of person and never had been. Since his abrupt discharge from Special Ops, he had been more sedentary than at any time in his life, and that had him feeling agitated today.

The reports that he had asked Elke to compile weren't on his desk. He pulled out his cellphone and glared at it while he punched in her number. His assistant's phone rang twice, then a mechanical voice answered and told him to leave a message. He hung up in disgust.

Not two minutes later, Elke came into the office with a man's body slung over her shoulder. She dumped him on the couch, and Erik recognized Dominic immediately.

"Look what I found," she chirped.

"What did you do to him?"

Elke shrugged. "Eh. I fed a little. I might have overdone it."

He went to the unconscious Ulfen. He could hear Dominic's pulse, slow but rhythmic, and from his scent and the cold sweat on his brow, Erik could tell that the Ulfen was very depleted.

"Nice. You almost bled him out."

"He tasted really good," she defended. She reached into her messenger bag and pulled out a manila folder. "Here's that info about Paris that you wanted."

He took the folder and sat at his desk. "If he dies, it's on you."

She sat down in one of the chairs facing him and propped her ankles up on the desk. "Take it out of my salary."

Erik looked archly at her boots and raised an eyebrow. "Really?"

She put her feet back on the floor.

He reviewed the information she had provided. The two most powerful Draugr in Paris were Derek Dupin and Laurentia Moselle. Dupin ran the Paris on the east side of the Seine, and Moselle ruled the west. There had been no love lost between the two of them for as long as anyone could remember. Both Dupin and Moselle had been turned during the years of the Black Death, and their age and power helped them to hold their territories in iron grips. Dupin was ambitious, though, and had taken advantage of Laurentia's presence at Uppsala to stage a coup. He now possessed all of Paris, on both sides of the Seine, as Elke had told him on the phone. The information available indicated that it had been a largely bloodless take-over.

According to the information Elke had provided, Laurentia had busied herself over the years with collecting magickal texts and vat after vat of supernatural blood. She and her men had drained countless faeries, shifters, witches and other inhuman creatures into enchanted barrels that prevented both coagulation and decay. She was like the Draugr version of Elizabeth Báthory, drinking her fill but bathing every night in blood to suck up the life force it contained, soaking in more than her stomach could hold. She was a vain and greedy woman, and she collected power and hid in the bowels of her mansion while the world went by.

In his opinion, both Dupin and Moselle were too corrupt to rule.

"Moselle is here in Stockholm?" he asked her.

Elke nodded. "Yes. She's staying with Maria."

"Bring her here."

"Yes, sir." She hopped up and gave him a quick and sloppy salute. "Hey, if my wolf there wakes up, can I have him?"

"No."

"Killjoy."

"Live with it."

Elke opened the office door and nearly collided with Nika, who was on her way in. Both women laughed in surprise, and Elke stepped aside to let Nika enter unimpeded. Elke winked at Erik and closed the door as she was leaving.

Nika hesitated when she saw the sleeping Ulfen. "Is that Dominic?"

"Apparently. Elke found him and brought him here. She fed from him first, so I think he might be under-sanguinated right now." He put the folder aside and smiled. "Good morning."

"Good morning." She came around the desk and kissed him, then pulled away before he could touch her. He frowned.

"Nika, is there something wrong?"

She smiled brightly, and it felt patently false. "No," she said. "Not at all."

He sighed. "You're lying."

Nika looked shocked. "I... I just thought maybe you were upset with me."

"I should be asking you the same question."

She sat down in the chair that Elke had just vacated. "Why would I be upset with you?" Erik sat back. "You tell me. What did I do? You seem like you don't want me anymore. Like right now, I tried to put my arm around you, and you pulled away, like you pulled away from me last night. Is there something you need to say?"

"No."

He sighed. "Why don't I believe you? Nika, answer me. Do you still want me as your lover?"

Nika looked down at her hands, evidently finding it difficult to speak. "I do still want you, but I want to know that there's more to our relationship than sex."

He felt affronted. "If you're doubting that, after everything we've been through together, then we have bigger problems than I thought. Of course there's more to us than sex. By Odin's eye, Nika, I've waited for you through lifetimes. I went without properly feeding for years and years because I wanted to prove to the gods that I deserved to have you back. Centuries. Don't you think I would have given up by now if sex was all that I was after?"

She couldn't meet his gaze, and her voice was small when she said, "I needed to be sure of you... after what you did with the other First..."

His stomach tightened. "You mean what happened to the Huldra."

She tried to speak, but could only nod wordlessly.

"You yourself said once that I was not responsible for that, because I was under the influence of Mia's enchantments. That's why you hate her, if I'm not mistaken."

"I needed to know if you would take no for an answer. You never did with Magda."

"We've talked about my past, and about my sins. What happened with Magda was many, many years ago, and I know now that it was wrong, but at the time..." He sighed. "I have promised that I would never hurt you. If my word isn't good enough for you, then I don't know what else I can do to prove myself to you."

He rose and collected his coat. Nika stared at him, shocked. "Erik, I'm sorry. I was..."

"If you think that I could ever raise a hand to you, you mistake me."

"Erik..."

He walked out of the office without looking back.

***

Mia and Derek stood in the *mairie*, the government office that oversaw civil marriages. She was wearing a long white lace dress and white satin heels, dressed like a bride. He was in an impeccable suit. His two goons, the ones who had dragged her from the catacombs, were waiting to act as witnesses, dressed in suits of their own. One of them was filming the proceedings with his cell.

The actual wedding was short and dry, as emotionless as the couple themselves. The functionary performing the ceremony barely looked at them until after they had signed the register and all of the paperwork.

"There," Derek said when it was over. "Our alliance is complete."

The Draugr with the cell snickered. "Not quite complete, boss."

Mia glared at him. "I understand what's required of me." She turned back to Dupin. "Let's go back to the house and get this over with."

He smirked. "Most women don't greet the thought of lying with me in such a negative light."

She snorted. "Most women have a choice."

"You had a choice, my dear."

"Not a good one."

"It was a choice, all the same." He held the door for her, smiling. "After you."

They left the office and walked directly into a smiling man in a muddy overcoat. "Mia," he said. "You've been a bad, bad girl."

She recognized him immediately. "Assassin!" she hissed. Magic flared at her fingertips, and she flung it at Vladimir's face. The Russian batted it away, magic of his own surrounding his hands.

Dupin and his men pulled guns from beneath their suit coats and opened fire. The bullets bounced harmlessly away, and Vladimir ignored them, focusing his attention on the Dark Sister before him.

"I went through a lot of trouble to find you," he said. The magic around his hands was intensifying, glowing a sickly green and crawling up toward his elbows. "You almost got away."

She bent and slipped a knife from inside her boot. "I still will." She added her magic to the blade and threw both at him, snarling words of power. The knife penetrated his defenses, striking him in the shoulder. His magic flickered, and in that instant, Dupin fell upon him with fangs and claws.

Vladimir pushed his hands, still crawling with green magic, into Dupin's face, and the vampire howled in pain as his skin blistered and split. Dupin reeled away, and Vladimir vanished into the ground, her knife still stuck in his body.

Mia went to her new husband and cast healing magic for him, augmenting his innate Draugr ability to recover from injury at lightning speed.

"Where did he go?" one of their companions demanded.

"In the ley lines," she said, irritable. "He's running, but he'll be back."

"Who was that?" Derek asked her.

"Vladimir. He's a witch hunter." She searched the spot where Vladimir had disappeared, hoping that he hadn't taken her knife with him, but it was nowhere to be seen. "Damn."

"Did Thorvald send him?" her husband asked.

"I have no idea. Most likely." She glanced around. Their tussle was attracting a crowd of bewildered humans. "Get the car. We need to get out of here before the police arrive."

Chapter Ten

Nika dialed Erik's number, but the call went straight to voice mail. She bit her lip. *Why did I listen to Tamara?* She knew that her doubts had hurt him deeply and all she wanted was to make amends. She tried again, but again he failed to pick up. She swore and tossed the phone back into her purse.

Tamara was on a plane already, flying from America to Sweden. She couldn't have reached her if she'd tried. The thought that she might have ruined things with Erik haunted her, and she wished he'd pick up the phone. She put her head into her hands and began to weep.

A moment later, a groggy male voice asked, "Rune Master, why are you crying?"

She gasped and turned to look at the couch. She had almost forgotten that Dominic was there, and now he was looking at her, his amber eyes cloudy, his face pale. He struggled to sit up as she wiped her cheeks.

"I... it's personal."

He nodded slowly. "Sorry. Didn't mean to pry."

She waved her hand at him. "It's okay. It's not ... what happened to you?"

The Ulfen rubbed his hand over his neck, and he said, "One of your vampires happened to me." He looked at his hand as if he expected it to be bloody, then dropped it into his lap. His expression took on an edge of shame and embarrassment. "She said her name was Elke."

"Ah. That's right. Erik told me." She went to the bar and poured a glass of whiskey, which she brought to him. "Drink this. It might help."

He sniffed the liquid suspiciously, then shook his head. "No, thanks. I don't think I need alcohol right now."

"Water, then?"

"Sure."

Nika went to bar and got a glass of Perrier for him. He accepted it when she brought it back. He sipped it, then grimaced at the mineral burn. She sat beside him.

"You were with Mia."

"Yes." He leaned back, slouching on the sofa, the glass cradled in his hands. "I was trying to help her hide from the vampires in Paris, and we got separated. They found her, shot me, and then I was picked up by some Russian named Vladimir."

She raised an eyebrow. "Interesting..."

"He healed me, then sent me on my way with new clothes."

"Why Paris?"

"That's where she wanted to go. I don't know why. I wanted to get off the train in Cologne, but I couldn't leave her." He looked down into his glass. "Maybe I should have."

"Do you know where they took her?"

Dominic shook his head. "No, and everybody can stop asking me. I volunteered to protect her because I'm an idiot. She didn't lift a finger to help me. Now I'm back here in Sweden, and I just wanted to get the hell away..." He looked at her. "Ulfen aren't very welcome in Stockholm, you know."

Nika tried to look sympathetic and encouraging. "I know... why don't you go back to your pack?"

He grimaced. "No, thank you."

"Can werewolves even survive without a pack?"

"This one will." He put the glass aside and rose unsteadily. "Listen, thanks for the water, but I have to get out of here."

The door opened, and Elke came back in with a handful of papers. She grinned like a predator when she saw Dominic standing there. "Hey, handsome." He blushed furiously and looked away, and Elke handed the papers to Nika. "This is the invoice for the delivery that just came. Thought you'd like to look it over."

She glanced at it, her heart completely not in the task. "Whatever. You take care of it."

"Where's Erik?"

"He... left."

"Huh. He wanted me to bring Laurentia Moselle here, but she needed time to get washed up and ready to see him."

Nika sighed. "Maybe you should find him and give him that message."

Elke nodded, no doubt aware she was being dismissed but not caring. "Sure thing!" She strolled over toward Dominic and reached up to brush some of his dark hair from his forehead. He jerked back.

"Don't touch me."

She pouted. "That's a hell of a way to treat someone who just gave you such a good time."

He took a step away, a low growl in his throat. Nika frowned and rose. "What's going on?"

"Who knows?" Elke shrugged. "Dogs these days. See ya, lover."

She strolled back out of the office, and Nika turned to the Ulfen. He was standing with his fists clenched, ready to fight, his eyes looking more wolf-like than human.

"Dominic," she said gently. "Are you all right?"

He turned to her and forced his wolf traits to recede. "Fine," he said, although he was clearly lying.

"I don't believe you."

"I don't care what you believe. Can I go?"

She stepped out of his way. "Of course." Nika watched as he headed toward the door at speed, the taint of fear altering his rich animal scent. Just as he passed her, she put out a hand to stop him. "If you need help, I can help you."

He stopped and looked at her hand, which she removed from his arm. "I don't need anybody's help. I just need to get out of Europe."

He yanked the door open and all but ran out of Snake Eyes. Nika followed him down the hall. Several of the young Draugr rose, attracted by his flight, ready to give chase.

"Stop it," she snapped. "Sit down and leave him alone."

They turned surly eyes to her, but they obeyed. Being the King's woman and the Rune Master gave her more sway than she should have, given how recently she had turned. She knew that it was fear of Erik's reprisals that kept them obedient. Her heart sank like a stone. She was nothing in this new world without him.

And she might have chased him away.

***

Erik went to Maria's townhouse not far from the Royal Palace in Stockholm. Back in the day, when the palace had been occupied by Gustav III, Maria had been his Spanish mistress, installed in the very apartments she still occupied. She had even performed in plays written by the monarch. Erik remembered those days with a certain fondness.

She opened the door herself when he knocked instead of sending her butler to do the task. Her beautiful face was composed and smiling when she curtsied to him, her gesture briefly transforming her bathrobe into a ballgown. "Your Majesty," she said, lowering her dark head in respect that was only a little mocking.

He smiled. "Good morning, Maria. I've come to speak to your houseguest."

Maria stepped aside and said, "You may enter."

They both knew that the traditional Draugr greeting probably wasn't necessary, but he hadn't actually crossed her threshold for over fifty years. Her earlier welcome may have worn off, and it was better to offer an extra invitation than to let him suffer the embarrassment of bouncing off of an invisible force field across the doorway.

"Thank you." He stepped inside and looked around. "It's always 1792 in here."

"I preferred those days," she said. "I was happiest then. Laurentia is still bathing. As you know, sometimes the oldest of us are not so quick to move about."

Erik snorted softly. "She's hardly one of the oldest of us, and if I can haul my ass around at dawn, she can certainly get up at noon."

"Not all of us are as blessed with Viking tenacity and boldness as others," a smooth female voice said from the salon door.

Laurentia stood there, a pale blonde figure wrapped in a plush white robe. Her fox-brown hair cascaded down her back and over her shoulders like a silken waterfall, and her large blue eyes were artfully lined and accented. Her pink lips curved up slightly and she said, "To what do I owe the honor of both a summons and a visit, my lord?"

"I have news that you need to hear. Dupin has taken Paris."

Laurentia's mouth went slack, and her face, already pale, became ghostly. Maria went to her side and took her hand. "What?"

Erik nodded. "I'm sorry to be the bearer of bad news. Intel says she took your territory while you were attending the assembly in Uppsala."

Her brows knit together and she bared her feral teeth. "My city will never be his."

"Well, at the moment, it is," he said, "along with my daughter."

Maria sighed. "So that is where Mia has gone to. He keeps dark company, Erik."

"I know." He walked further into the room and sat down in one of Maria's wing backed chairs.

The deposed leader of western Paris stepped forward. "What do you intend to do about it? You are the only Huntsman left and the Draugr here in Stockholm are an inebriated mess. If Dupin chooses to oppose you, he will have the force to take the night, and with Mia at his side he will have the witches' approval."

"I have the Rune Master."

"So what?" Laurentia demanded. "A barely-turned vampire with no real sense of her own power, still playing at being a mortal, unaware of what she could really be? Your Rune Master has the skills but none of the experience. If she were as old as you, she would be a force to be reckoned with. As it stands, she has too much to learn."

"I am aware of how young she is, and how inexperienced."

Maria ventured, "She needs real war to harden her to what she's meant to be."

"I will decide what Nika needs," Erik said, his voice calm but his eyes sharp. "I intend to take Paris back from Dupin, and you, Laurentia, will need to fight for it, as well. Do you have any forces who are loyal to you?"

She hesitated. "I... I don't know."

He nodded. "And that is why you've lost Paris."

Laurentia rushed to him, kneeling at his feet, her hands gripping his knees imploringly. "Give me back my city! I have always lived in Paris, my whole existence, through everything the mortal and immortal worlds have done. Do not make me an exile!"

Erik looked at her coolly. "Your people did not defend your right to your territory. Why would I support you, if you are so weak?"

"Because... I beg of you."

"I have been begged before."

He felt annoyed with her supplication. He remembered another time, centuries ago, when he had been in a similar position: a victor with a vanquished and deposed leader groveling at his feet. He had worn leather and furs then instead of denim, but the accidents of power were much the same. In his mind's eye, he could see the stony castle in Kiev and the groveling king whose body would later float down the Dnieper, Erik's axe marks in his head.

Those had been bloody days.

"I will give you anything you ask," Laurentia continued, pressing her hands against him. She gripped the waistband of his jeans, her face desperate. "I will...ah...anything."

He had not been sex-deprived long enough for that offer to be enticing. He pushed her away with disgust.

"Get up." She slinked away, and he said, "I will retake Paris from Dupin because it pleases me to do it, and because he has allied with my enemy."

Maria said softly, "Do you mean the coven in Bordeaux, or Mia?"

Erik's eyes were flinty as he looked up at her. "Does it matter?"

She wisely demurred, "No, sir."

He turned his attention back to Laurentia. "Can I look to you for support in this?"

"Of course. I want my city back!"

"What do you offer me, apart from sex?"

She blushed and clenched her fists. "I would give you gold. Ancient gold. My coffers are full of it. And I will give you full freedom of the city..."

"Your gold belongs to Dupin now, and I have full freedom of every city already." His tone dared her to disagree. "What else?"

She looked bereft. "What else do I have?"

"You have an archive and a wine cellar, if I recall." He saw the recognition dawn in her eyes, followed closely by a strangling horror that she tried unsuccessfully to conceal. "Do I have your attention now? If I give you Paris, which you dearly want, then I need you to give me what I want."

"The blood."

"And the books. And the totems and the relics and the magical items." Laurentia's jaw set, and he grinned unkindly. "Did you think we didn't know what you were doing all these years? There was nobody to object before, but now I'm here, and I am objecting. Give me the rank riches you've collected with your crimes and support me in removing Dupin, and I might forget your excesses. I might let you rule Paris as a whole on my behalf – under my laws. Unless you think the price is too high."

Maria came to Laurentia's side and clutched her hand. The deposed chieftain agonized long and hard while Erik stared her down. Finally, she spoke.

"I agree to your terms. You are a cruel man, Erik Thorvald."

"At least we understand one another." He rose. "You will fight at my side so that I can see the amount of effort you put forth. If I am not convinced of your loyalty and your desire to retake your city, I will make other arrangements."

He walked toward the door, and she hissed at his back. "I hate you."

Erik smirked and looked back at her. "I don't care." He nodded to Maria. "Good day."

Chapter Eleven

Nika sat in the airport coffee shop, watching the news on the terminal television. Nothing ever really changed in the human world. New wars replaced old ones, new politicians repeated old lies and the rich kept getting richer. The same was probably true in the vampire world, as well, but with less news coverage and fewer witnesses.

Tamara's plane would be landing soon. Nika was eager to see her old friend again. They had known each other since high school, and they had seen each other through all of the ups and downs ten years could bring. Tamara had been her closest companion and confidante, Nika had trusted her with everything.

Now she was wondering if maybe she had trusted her a little bit too far. She feared that she had erred by putting Erik through Tamara's loyalty and morality test. He had stormed out of the office at Snake Eyes yesterday afternoon, and he stayed away all night without even a call. Now it was the next morning, and there was still no word from him. She was worried something had happened to him.

She was worried that he might have left her.

She checked her phone for the nineteenth time, and there were no texts or missed calls. The clock told her that Tamara's plane was likely in its final approach, so she finished her coffee and left to stand by the customs station where her friend would emerge.

Nika contented herself with people-watching to pass the time while she waited. She had always thought humans were interesting creatures, but now that she saw with Draugr eyes, they were so captivating. Their life force glowed around them like halos, all blues and greens and golds, with a thin line of red near their skin that varied with the health of the person. A very healthy man, for instance, had a thick scarlet line, and an ailing child's line was very, very thin. She supposed it was like a visual representation of how much blood that human had to offer, so the vampire in her could select its meal accordingly.

She hadn't hunted since Finland, and she disliked the exercise. She could well understand why so many of the Draugr in Scandinavia had come to depend upon *dreyri* for their sustenance. It was so much easier to obtain, and quicker, and with the enchantments that had been placed upon it to preserve the donors' life force and to prevent decay, it was far more satisfying. Real blood fresh from the vein carried a more sexual edge, a more animal quality, and it had its appeal, she supposed. She'd much rather drink champagne from a crystal glass than try to swallow the pressings from the bottom of a wine barrel. The comparison of *dreyri* to living blood was that stark to her.

Dreyri gave its power more quickly than fresh blood, probably again due to the magic that it bore. She thought she should probably learn how to perform that enchantment so that they could continue to have bottles and casks on hand to sell through Snake Eyes. It was a pity that there wasn't a recipe or a set of directions lying around in Magda's ledgers.

A group of Draugr walked past her, their power far less than Erik's but much greater than hers. The sole woman in the group, wisp-thin and painfully pale, glanced at her with disdain as she passed with her immortal entourage. Nika wondered if they didn't recognize her, or if they just chose to disrespect her in Erik's absence. She decided to let it go.

"I would have forced them to acknowledge me if I was their queen," a man said behind her. She turned and found Vladimir standing there, still muddy and disheveled. "But then, maybe I wouldn't have."

She turned away from him. "I didn't want to start a scene."

He moved up to stand beside her. "So polite of you. Very proper." He glanced around at the throngs of humans scurrying about them. "Probably a very sober choice."

Something about him irritated her. "What do you want, Vladimir?"

"I wanted to let you know that I am going to kill that last Dark Sister. I know your master doesn't want me to do it, but I thought you might like to get her blood on your hands, for old time's sake."

He was grinning like a fool when she turned to look at him, and the expression was chilling. He was so eager to deal death. Nika said, "I appreciate the invitation, but I don't like killing. I've rarely done it and I don't care to do it again."

Vladimir shrugged. "Suit yourself. I quite enjoy it."

"I can tell."

He leaned against the wall beside her. "So, if I kill the Dark Sister, will you keep your master from retaliating against me?"

"First of all, he's not my master. He's my fiancé. And second of all, if he decides he really wants to kill you, there's nothing I can do to stop him." She sighed and looked at him again. "He warned you off. Isn't that enough to make you stop hunting her?"

"No." It was a straightforward answer, but she didn't expect his bluntness. "The Dark Sisters and some of your Draugr have decided that *dreyri* from witch blood is also very tasty, and they decimated the coven in Kiev and Rostov, along with others. They drained them dry and took their blood for their infernal drink, and I mean to make them pay. Your master's – your fiancé's – little girl is one of the most powerful and evil of the Dark Sisters, and she personally presided over the draining of my children. All of my children. Do you know how many of my children they killed?"

Nika's mouth was dry. There was mania behind his eyes. "No idea."

"Thirteen. Lucky thirteen. She destroyed my family." He turned and looked toward the customs gate, where the new arrivals from America were being screened. "And now I mean to destroy her."

She knew she should have supported Erik's decision to leave Mia alone. She knew she should have done her part to warn this Russian madman off of the trail. She also knew that she couldn't do that. "Then destroy her," she said, her voice flat. "I don't want to participate, but I think it needs to be done."

Vladimir turned and kissed her on both cheeks. "A brilliant decision, my queen, and when I kill her, I will bring a token of her power to you as my patron."

He took a step backward from her, and she shook her head. "I'm not your patron."

He vanished from sight without responding.

She turned back toward the customs gate just in time to see Tamara, who rushed toward her with her arms out wide. "Nika!" she exclaimed.

They met in the middle of the concourse with a tight embrace. "So good to see you!" Nika enthused.

Tamara stepped back and pushed her blonde hair out of her eyes. "You look fabulous! Sweden suits you."

"Thank you." They hugged again, and then Nika asked, "How was your flight?"

"Boring, I guess. I slept through most of it." She adjusted her purse, which was falling off of her shoulder, and said, "Let's go get my bags and you can show me your new world."

They walked together to baggage claim, dodging bodies as they went. Tamara was wide-eyed and excited, looking all around them with the childlike sense of wonder that Nika had always envied in her. They reached baggage carousel and waited with the rest of the incoming travelers.

"So," her friend asked, "how's what's his name?"

Nika chucked. "Erik is fine. He's a little bit stressed out by his new job, but he's all right."

"And how's the test going?" She groaned, and Tamara nodded sagely. "That good, huh? He hasn't hurt you, has he?"

"No, just the opposite. He asked me what was wrong, and I ended up telling him about the test. He got really upset with me for not trusting him."

Tamara shrugged. "Well, you know how it is – the people who are loudest about telling you to trust them are usually the ones who are least trustworthy."

Nika shook her head. "You really don't like him, do you?"

"He took my best friend to another continent. You might say I'm holding a grudge." She grabbed a suitcase and stepped back. "I only took two weeks off. I'm not ready to move to Sweden completely yet."

She was disappointed, but she understood. "Not a problem. Let's just try to make this vacation the best one you've ever had, right?"

They snagged her second piece of luggage, and Nika led her out toward the parking lot. Tamara struggled with her heavy suitcases, but once she got them righted on their wheels and extended the telescoping handle, she was able to manage. Nika took control of one of the weighty bags.

"Wow, what did you pack? Gold bricks? Did they have to charge you extra for these?"

"A little," Tamara allowed. "So, for someone who's getting married soon, you sure seem down in the dumps."

She shrugged one shoulder, which was entirely unconvincing. "I'm okay."

"Liar."

Nika took a deep breath and led the way to her – well, Erik's – parked car. "Like I said, I told Erik about the test, and he didn't take it well."

Tamara whistled. "Nice wheels!"

She smiled at the Aston Martin, and at the gleam in her friend's eyes. "Thanks. Erik's a car guy. He likes things that go fast."

"I'll bet he does."

She opened the back door and busied herself with lowering the handles and tossing the suitcases onto the seat. They flew in with enough velocity that they bounced against the opposite door. She turned back to Tamara and saw her friend gaping at her, her mouth literally hanging open.

"The hell, Graves?" she finally said, using her last name the way they'd done as a joke back in school.

Nika hesitated. "Uh...what, Jackson? Just because you can't handle it doesn't mean I'm weak." She mentally castigated herself for not being more careful. Sometimes it took an effort to conceal her new Draugr strength, and she had forgotten to hide it. It was just her luck that Tamara was bright enough to catch on.

Tamara shook her head and got into the passenger seat. Once Nika was settled behind the wheel and driving away from the parking structure, she said, "So by 'didn't take it well,' what do you mean?"

"I mean he stomped off and didn't come home last night," she admitted.

Her friend went still and silent for a moment, then said, "Honey..."

"Don't say it. He doesn't have anybody else, and he's going to come back, and we'll work this out." She clenched her jaw briefly, but the pressure and the agitation made her fangs come out, and she quickly pulled them back in. She wanted to tell her friend about her new life, but there were more subtle ways to do it. "I'm betting he'll be at the house when we get there."

Tamara crossed her arms. "I'm glad I'm going to be staying with you. If he gets out of line, I can knock him on his can." Nika laughed, and her friend insisted, "Seriously! I've learned some tricks from the bouncers at Paradise. I can handle a guy who's out of line."

"If you say so." She merged into traffic, leaving the airport behind. "You might be able to handle a regular guy, but Erik is something else all together."

"Oh, yeah?"

"Ex-special forces. Yeah."

Tamara nodded. "Well... even a special forces dude has balls that hurt when you kick them."

"You wouldn't!"

"If he does anything to hurt you, hell yes, I would."

Nika glanced at her friend, amused by the truculent tone and the fire in her eyes. "It's so good to see you," she said.

***

Mia and Derek celebrated their marriage with a long, *dreyri*-soaked feast at his estate for his Parisian Draugr. When the sixteenth hour of the party passed, Derek finally took her hand and leaned toward her.

"Let's go make this official."

Her stomach twisted. She knew that there would have to be some sort of consummation of this marriage, but until now she'd kept even the thought of it at bay. Now with her new husband eyeing her with lust and his vampires watching them keenly, she knew that the time had come.

Well, she thought. *I'm not without some tricks of my own.*

He led her upstairs to the master bedroom and locked the door behind them. Nervousness tickled her spine, and her fingertip tingled with preparatory magic. She held it in reserve so she could call it up at speed if she needed to defend herself.

Derek was not unattractive, she supposed, although he was shorter than she liked her men to be. She much preferred the big, beefy types like Bjorn, men who made her feel engulfed when they held her. There was a certain amount of danger to a man like that, and she enjoyed the risk. With Derek, while he was certainly powerful thanks to the antiquity of his vampire blood, he was closer to her own size. She stood a chance of escaping him if he tried to overpower her. She found that disappointing.

Mia sat on the edge of the bed and kicked off her high-heeled shoes. He smiled at her and took off his suit coat, draping it over the back of the chair that sat at one of the room's two vanities. He loosened his tie and began to open his shirt as he walked closer to her.

"You're very beautiful," he told her.

"Don't pretend this is a love match," she responded coldly. "You don't need to compliment me or sweet talk me. I know what this is."

He raised an eyebrow. "It was merely an observation, wife," he said. "I'll keep such things to myself next time."

"Good." He pulled his tie loose and considered it for a moment. She could practically read his mind. "Don't even think it."

He chuckled. "Don't even think what?" he teased. "Tell me, what do you think I was thinking? It might be revelatory of your own state of mind."

She stood and turned her back on him. "Zipper, please."

Derek came close behind her and grasped the zipper tab, pulling it down slowly. "You're pale enough to be a Draugr," he said.

"I thought you were keeping your observations and compliments to yourself."

"Who said it was a compliment? I prefer my women with a little blood in them."

"Well, if you object, we can just call this off," she snapped.

"Not so fast. Nobody's calling a halt to anything." He grabbed the dress and yanked it down off of her shoulders, using it to pin her arms to her sides. "Do the Dark Sisters bleed, I wonder?"

She should have fought against him, or said something sharp. Instead, she shuddered, and not from revulsion or fear. Her breath hitched in her throat, and she could feel Derek alter his stance behind her, pressing closer.

He whispered against the back of her neck, taking advantage of the access offered by her shorn locks. "What is this about, hmm?"

She started to pull free of her dress, but he held her fast, preventing her from moving. She had learned long ago that a Valtaeigr, even an immortal and ancient one, was no match for a vampire's strength.

"Let me finish undressing and we can get this over with."

Her words sounded stronger than she felt, and she was grateful that the fluttering in her stomach wasn't telegraphed to her voice. He seemed to hear it all the same.

Derek gripped her arms tightly and pulled her back against him, his erection prodding her. He put his face against her head and inhaled deeply, and she shivered. He chuckled in the back of his throat.

"I see you, little Sister," he said, his voice deep and thick. "I think you want power but only until someone can take it away from you. I think you want a man who can push you and pull you and take away your free will. Don't you? I think you want a man who can control you." He grabbed her earlobe in his teeth, piercing it with the sharp points until a tiny drop of blood welled up. He licked it away, and despite her best efforts to stay stoic, she moaned. "Oh, yes. I see you. I see you all too clear."

"Fuck you," she tried, but it came out sounding almost hopeful.

He wrapped one arm around her chest and the other around her hips, and he picked her up and put her face down on the bed. His weight pressed down on her, pushing her into the mattress and pinning her tight. She shivered again, unable to stop trembling. He dragged her skirt up and pushed her legs apart with his knees, and while she made a token grumble of objection, she obeyed.

He kissed her neck, his lips just above the pulse point. Bjorn had taken her blood many times, and she knew exactly where the fangs would go and how they would feel sliding in. She stayed still, yearning for that sharp invasion, wishing he would just bite her and get on with it.

Instead, he held here there, his chest against her back, the weight of his body keeping her in place, as if she would have tried to move. His hands busied themselves with her filmy thongs, breaking the elastic that held them together and tossing the garment aside. He stroked her with demanding fingers, and she whimpered.

"That's the sound of a passionate woman," he whispered to her. "That's the sound of someone who likes to be held down and handled roughly."

His finger breached her lower lips, and she moaned, "Hurry up and do it."

Derek worked his fingers inside of her. "Hurry up and do what, wife? Tell me what you want me to do."

"You know what I want." Her words came out as little more than a breath.

"I want to hear you say it."

Mia sighed brokenly, giving up the pretense. "I want you to fuck me. I want you fuck me so hard I can hear it."

He laughed and complied. He pulled his hand free, and then he was sheathed inside her all the way to the root, thicker than she expected. He began to snap his hips, and the sound of flesh slapping flesh filled the room, accompanied by Mia's ecstatic moaning. She came almost immediately, shrieking in her pleasure as he held her down.

"Oh, yes," he panted into her ear. "Oh, yes."

His fangs stabbed into her neck, and she cried out in aguish and delight, her eyes rolling backward. Penetrated by him in two places, she gave herself over to him completely, her magic enveloping them both. He grunted in surprise but kept his rhythm, slamming into her while he filled his mouth with her blood.

She could feel her magic sink into him, blazing a trail through his mind and spirit, leaving her essence everywhere it touched. She marked him as her own, binding his spirit to hers. He would never again be satisfied by any other lover. He would never again be happy unless she allowed it. She branded his soul with the glowing sigils of her power, her Hel-born gift raking into him and burning into everything that was truly Derek.

He came, filling her with his dead seed, and she felt his body quake. He moaned against her neck, his mouth still locked to her vein, and she blazed the final connection.

She whispered as he came down from his orgasmic high. "This is how a Dark Sister and Valtaeigr claims her man. This is how we are connected from now on." His fangs slid out of her flesh, but their bodies stayed connected. "You are mine."

Chapter Twelve

Erik pulled into the driveway at his mother's home, his tires crunching on the gravel as he parked. Ingrid was kneeling in her flower bed, digging in the dirt, and she looked up with a smile when he got out of the car.

"To what do I owe this honor, Your Majesty?" she asked, grinning, wiping her fingers on her skirt.

He smiled back. "I need your advice."

"Of course. Come inside."

They went into her little house, and Erik sat at the kitchen table while Ingrid busied herself with putting a kettle on the fire. A bouquet of fresh flowers in a blue glass vase sat on the window sill, and their fragrance filled the room. The place felt peaceful and comforting, and he was grateful for it.

Ingrid sat across from him. "What's troubling you?"

"Nika."

She looked surprised. "In what way?"

"She doesn't trust me." He leaned back in his chair, his hands falling onto his thighs. "She says she's been testing me to see if I'll listen when she tells me she doesn't want to make love. It's like she thinks I'm going to turn into some sort of ravening beast..."

Ingrid nodded sagely. "And this hurts you."

"Of course it does. After everything I've gone through, all the years I've spent waiting for her to reappear... how could she think I'd ever hurt her?" He shook his head. "You would think she would know me by now. I don't know how to react. Mother, help me. What do I do?"

"You pass the test."

"That's it?" he asked, dismayed. "I just accept this insult and roll over?"

She met his eyes with a steady gaze. "If you want to keep her, yes. Surely she's worth humbling yourself a little."

He frowned. "I'm so tired of her not trusting me. This keeps coming up again and again."

"Trust is hard to earn," she said. The kettle began to whistle, and she rose to pour some tea. "Once you've earned it, she will be yours completely. This is just one last hurdle. Surely you can cope with a little denial."

"That's not the point. I'm not upset about the lack of sex. I can live with that. It's the lack of trust." He sighed. "But you're right... she's worth it to me to put up with this."

She put a cup in front of her son and sat down with one of her own. "Love and marriage aren't easy. People think that once you fall in love, that's the end of it, and it's all hearts and flowers from then out. But it's not. You have to work at relationships, and you have to keep winning your love every day."

He smiled ruefully. "I'd be satisfied with not feeling like I'm losing her every day."

Ingrid took his hand and squeezed it. "Erik, this is only temporary. I promise you. Once she sees that you are the man she wants you to be, she will be satisfied and the tests will end."

"I hope you're right."

She grinned. "Between the two of us, which one of us knows women better?"

"Point taken." He chuckled. "There's another thing."

"I thought as much. You'd never come to me for just one question." She sipped her tea. "Let me guess. Mia."

"Yes. There's a witch from Russia named Vladimir who wants to hunt her. He says he's killed all of the other Dark Sisters. Is this true?"

Ingrid's eyes unfocused for a moment as she called upon her Valtaeigr abilities. Finally, she nodded. "It's true. She is the last. Vladimir, you say?"

"Yes."

"Be careful of him. He's a powerful witch hunter and not to be trifled with."

He frowned. "Witch hunter? Not a witch?"

"No. He's a warlock, not a witch. He has witch-like powers, but he uses them against the witches. He is a traitor."

Erik nodded. "Then I should eliminate him. He's a threat."

"Not to you."

"No, but he might be a threat to the Valtaeigr, and I can't have that." He cupped his hands around the tea cup, not interested in drinking it but enjoying the warmth. "If he kills Mia, he may turn to you and your sisters next."

"It's entirely possible," Ingrid agreed. "But you will not be able to destroy him. Only another magic user can do that. I think you know who I mean."

"Nika. The Rune Master."

"Yes."

"She won't kill him. She's on his side."

Ingrid raised an eyebrow. "For now."

They were quiet for a long moment, Ingrid drinking her tea, Erik holding his. Finally, he said, "One more thing."

"Ah! The trifecta."

He smiled. "The young ones in Stockholm are completely addicted to the faery *dreyri*. They don't even hunt anymore. Nika thinks we should slowly wean them off of it, water it down with other blood and serve them that way, but I think we should just destroy it all."

"Bad idea."

"Why?"

"Because you'll have a revolt on your hands. I know you want the young ones to live like proper Draugr, but they need to be hand-held to get there." She finished her tea. "If they're truly addicted, and if you deny them their fix, then there will be chaos. You already know this."

"But will weaning them do the trick?"

She took her cup to the sink. "It should, as far as getting them off the juice." She rinsed the cup and then came back to her seat. "What else?"

"Paris. Derek Dupin has taken all of the city because Laurentia Moselle has been here. I told her that she had to fight beside me to take her territory back, and in return, I get her vats and her relics and everything." He swirled the brown liquid in his cup. "She's not the fighting kind. She's not going to be able to take her city back. Should I take it back for her?"

"No. Take it back for yourself. But remember - Vikings have historically had a terrible time in Paris."

He smiled at a distant memory. "I don't know. I remember enjoying the place, and we got what we wanted."

"Of course you did." She folded her hands on the table. "What else?"

Erik smiled. "I'm sure I'll think of something."

"Well, when you do, you know where I am."

He went to the sink and poured his tea down the drain, then rinsed the cup as she had done with hers. "I saw Gunnar," he said, not turning around.

He heard Ingrid gasp at the sound of her dead son's name. "His spirit?"

"Yes. In his house." He turned and leaned against the counter. "He said he came with a message from Odin."

Her eyebrows shot up toward her hairline. "Indeed! And what was this message?"

"'You cannot go forward and backward at the same time.'"

"There's logic to it, certainly." She put her chin in her hand. "What do you think he meant?"

Erik shrugged. "I was hoping you could help me."

She considered the question for a moment. "Well, the most obvious thing is that you can't go back and try to be a father to Mia now. The second most obvious thing is that you must remember that Nika is not Berit, even though the soul is the same. You can't expect her to behave the way Berit would have. She's been reborn and has a new life now, and a new personality." She looked into his eyes, and he could feel her peering straight into his soul. "You need to ask yourself if you love her because she's Nika or if you love her because she used to be Berit."

Her words made him go cold, either with anger or with regret. He couldn't say. "Of course I know that. I love Nika for who she is, not who she was."

"Just be sure of it," his mother said softly. "Be very sure."

He ran a hand over his face, a hundred contradictory thoughts and emotions roiling inside of him. He muttered, "Why did I ever think being king would be a good idea?"

Ingrid went to him and put her hands on his shoulders, and for a moment he felt like a child again. He pulled his mother into an embrace, and she rubbed his back as she reassured him.

"You wanted to be king because you knew that your people needed a leader, and because you knew that you were the right man for the job." She pulled back and cupped his face in her hands. "You are smart, and strong, and you have a good heart. You will be the best king they could ever hope to have."

"Thank you, *kära mor*," he said.

She kissed him on the cheek. "You haven't called me 'dear mother' since you were a little boy."

She looked so touched that he wondered why he'd been stingy with his affection for all these years. "I think it's overdue," he whispered. He kissed her forehead. "You've always been good to me, even when my father wasn't."

"Your father was a hard man," she nodded. "He was very rough on you and your brothers."

"Just rough enough for the time. He made us strong."

"Perhaps." Ingrid stepped back and looked into his eyes again. "When the time comes to face Vladimir, or to face Mia, I will be at your side. I will help you and Nika overcome this challenge." She smiled. "And maybe I'll call my future daughter-in-law and tell her a thing or two about trust."

"Thank you."

"Don't mention it." She patted his chest. "Have I ever told you that you've always been my favorite?"

He smiled, warmed. "No."

She winked at him. "Good."

Like so many other things between them over the years, the words were left unsaid, but the intention came through loud and clear.

***

Mia sat in Derek's office as he received the good wishes and wedding gifts of two of the more powerful Draugr left west of the Seine. She ignored the vampire politics, uninterested as long as they knew who was in charge. Derek accepted their obeisance with noblesse oblige, then sent them on their way.

She looked up when they were alone. "When do we declare ourselves to my father?"

Her husband looked startled. "Declare ourselves in what way?"

"As opposing him for rulership of the Draugr, of course." She stood and strolled to where he was sitting, hitching her hip up onto his desk and letting her miniskirt ride up to show her trim thigh. "He's unfit to be king, and I can cast magical rings around his so-called Rune Master. We need to depose him."

He smiled at her, his dark eyes glinting. "You're ambitious, that's certain."

"Without ambition, you stay what you always were."

"The daughter of a slave, born in slavery?" he needled.

"Yes," she said. "Or a failed priest with a habit of using the confessional for sexual liaisons with parishioners."

"Touché." He leaned back and smiled at her. "I'm impressed that you know about my past. Have you been asking after me?"

"The Valtaeigr in general and the Dark Sisters in particular make it our business to know all of the power brokers in the supernatural community." She shifted to sit in front of him, her feet on the arms of his chair. She was giving him a good look at the part of her he liked the best. "I know a great deal about all of you."

Derek smiled. "I'm sure you do."

***

Nika brought Tamara to the house in Stockholm, parking the Aston Martin in is designated slot in the Bat Cave. She opened the door and carried in her friend's bags, which she put on the floor at the foot of the stairs.

"Welcome to our house," she said. "Boy, have I got a hundred things to tell you."

"You can start with telling me how you got to be so strong," Tamara said. "In St. Louis, you needed help taking out your garbage."

"Ha! I was never that bad!"

She smirked. "Maybe not, but you were never like this. Am I going to have to check you for blood doping or something?"

"Sort of..."

Nika hesitated, not at all certain how to proceed with this. She wanted to tell her the truth, needed to tell her, but she didn't know how to go about it.

"Show me around," Tamara said, saving her from the moment.

She gave her the fifty-cent tour, taking her through the airy rooms upstairs and down, ending by taking her out into the back yard where she had put in an herb garden. Her friend nodded, impressed. "Nice. Small, but nice." She grinned at Nika. "No nursery?"

"No. Kids won't be happening." She heard her own voice sounding more serious that she had intended.

Tamara hesitated, and she said, "Is there something wrong? You always wanted kids before."

"Well... I can't have any. And neither can Erik."

Her friend looked at her in silence for a moment, then said, "Well, you must save a lot of money on birth control."

Nika laughed. "That is so you. Always finding the bright side!"

"I do my best." She flopped down in one of the wooden lawn chairs. "So... tell me about him. I remember what he looked like in his suit and stuff, but give me the dirt."

Nika sat in the other chair and smiled. "He's funny, and smart. He's also really brave and strong. He's got a really good heart and a sense of honor, and he's loyal to his traditions and his people. He's... everything."

Tamara rolled her eyes. "Oh my God, but you have it bad."

"I'm supposed to be in love with him," Nika defended herself. "I'm going to marry him, after all."

"Well, that's great and all, but tell me the dirt. Does he have a bad temper? Is he bad at paying the bills? Is he good in bed?"

"No, no, and very."

"'Very?' That's all I get?"

She smirked. "I don't kiss and tell."

"Since when?" Tamara chortled. "You practically gave me a blow-by-blow with… what was his name?"

Spencer, she thought, but aloud she said, "I don't remember."

"Bullshit."

Nika only smiled and shrugged. "Once you go Viking, you don't go back."

"I'll bet. Got any spare Vikings laying around?"

"Well… there are a lot of men in Sweden, but I'll let you pick out the ones you want," she teased. "I was never good at setting up blind dates for you."

Her friend shuddered. "Jeez Louise, do you remember that loser you set me up with in senior year? Harvey?"

"He was sweet."

"He was a mama's boy who gave Norman Bates a run for his money."

"Oh, come on. He wasn't that bad."

Tamara snorted. "Says you. You didn't have to kiss him."

Nika's cell rang, and she nearly jumped out of her skin. She grabbed it quickly. "Hello?"

Erik's voice came to her. "Did Tamara's flight come in on schedule?"

"Yes, she's sitting here in the garden with me." She hesitated. "Are you all right?"

"Fine." He sounded like nothing untoward had happened. She wondered what he was thinking. "I'm driving back down from Ingrid's and won't be home for another hour or so. Have fun if you take her out on the town, but be careful."

"I will." She hesitated. "I love you. You know that."

"I know. And I love you, too."

The call ended, and she turned back to her friend. Tamara asked, "Was that the man of the hour?"

"Yes. He was up at his mother's house and won't be back for a while."

"Cool. More time for us to visit without boys interrupting."

Nika chuckled. "Oh, believe me. He is no boy."

"So I gather." She turned to face her. "So, what's with the super strength? Did you get bitten by a radioactive spider or something?"

Her palms suddenly felt clammy. "Well... I was bitten by something. Or someone, I should say. Do you remember all of those movie marathons we'd have around Halloween?"

Tamara frowned, confused. "You mean all of those Christopher Lee vampire movies? The Hammer flicks?"

"Yes."

"Yeah, I remember. What about them?"

"Remember when we said we thought it would be cool but scary if vampires were real?"

Her friend's face was a mask of confusion with fear creeping in at the edges. "I'm starting to pick up what you're laying down here, and I don't know if I like it."

Nika looked away and called forth her Draugr self. Her eyes glowed red, and her teeth lowered in her mouth, sharp and gleaming. She looked back at Tamara and smiled.

"It's actually pretty cool."

"Jesus Christ!" Tamara leaped up and backed away. "What the - how the - Jesus!"

To add to the shock, and to get it all out of the way at once, Nika summoned her runic magic and let glowing Futhark figures dance in the air between her hands. She looked up at Tamara and said, "I've been through a lot of changes since I left St. Louis."

Tamara began to speak, but her voice came out as a helpless squeak before she fainted dead away.

Chapter Thirteen

When Erik got home, Nika was sitting alone on the living room couch, her knees drawn up to her chest. She was chewing on her thumbnail and fretting so hard that he could practically hear it.

He put his keys on the console table near the door and walked into the room. As soon as she saw him, she leaped up and rushed to him, wrapping her arms around him in a tight embrace. He hugged her just as tightly.

"What's wrong?" he asked.

"I'm sorry," she said, her eyes filling with tears. "I was stupid to test you. I didn't mean to upset you."

Erik sighed and kissed her forehead tenderly. "I want you to be comfortable with us," he said. "If that means that you need to test me until you believe in me, then you can test me."

"But I do believe in you," she said softly. "I don't know what I was thinking."

"You were thinking that I've done horrible things in the past, and that I did horrible things under Mia's enchantment. You were wondering if I'd go back to my old ways. I understand." He stepped back. "Where is Tamara?"

Nika put a hand to her forehead. "I screwed up."

He frowned, confused. "How so...?"

"I showed her my Draugr side, and my magic." She smiled awkwardly. "I didn't know how else to tell her, but I wanted her to know."

Erik shook his head and chuckled. "Dramatic, but effective, I guess. How did she take it?"

"She fainted."

"Oh. Whoops."

She sat down again. "I put her in the guest room, and after she woke up, she locked the door. She hasn't come out since."

He sat beside her on the couch and put his arm around her. She snuggled into his chest, a look of relief on her face. He kissed her hair. "Well, she can't stay in there forever. Eventually she'll have to use the restroom, or she'll need to eat."

"She hates me," she moaned.

"She doesn't hate you. She's probably just processing the information. It was probably a lot to take all at once." He chuckled. "That's my Chosen - dramatic to the end."

They sat together for several long, quiet minutes. Finally, she said, "Were you at Ingrid's the whole night?"

"No. I was working a little, too. There's going to be a fight soon, and I need to get our people prepared for it."

She straightened and looked into his eyes, concerned. "A fight? What kind of fight?"

Their conversation was interrupted by his cell phone. A new text message had arrived, and he opened it up immediately. The sender was Derek Dupin, and it contained only a URL. He glanced at Nika, then tapped the link.

His smart phone took him to the internet. The website in question was a blank black screen with an embedded video. Nika leaned closer so she could see, too, as he activated the video. The recording was a little shaky, obviously having been taken on someone's handheld device, but he knew was he was seeing. It was his daughter marrying Dupin.

Erik let out a huff of breath, somewhere between a snort and a laugh. "Well, that's interesting."

"Who is that man?"

"His name is Derek Dupin. At least that's what he goes by these days. He was in charge of the Draugr in the eastern half of Paris." He turned the video off and scrolled through the web page. There was nothing else to see. "He took control of the western half while his rival was here attending the moot in Uppsala."

"Why is she marrying him?"

He turned off the phone and tossed it onto the coffee table. "He's marrying her, not the other way around, and he's probably doing it to consolidate his position. He's got a magic user at his side now, which makes it that much harder for the western Paris leader to take her territory back."

Nika sat back. "That's the fight you were talking about."

"Yes."

"Well, if you're going into a fight with a magic user, you need one of your own. I'm going with you." She suddenly went pale. "Erik, my dream..."

He nodded. "Perhaps it was a premonition."

"But... you died in my dream."

He touched her face, wishing he could caress away her horror. "It was a warning. We will take precautions, now that we know what might happen."

A fat tear slipped down her cheek. "I'm not losing you," she whispered. "I refuse."

Erik pulled her into his arms, and she buried her face in his shoulder, crying. He stroked her back to comfort her because he had no words that could ease her fears. The truth was that if it was his time, there was nothing he could do to stop it. The Norns decided when a man's time ran out. The only power he had was to make the most of the time he was allotted, and he had been given more time than almost anyone else. He was content.

There was a creak at the top of the stairs, and Tamara descended a few steps, her face ashen. She stopped and said, "Did you do this to her?"

"Do what?" he asked. "You'll have to be more specific. Welcome to Stockholm, by the way."

She took another step down. "Why is she crying?"

"Because I will be going to war and she is afraid." He kissed Nika's hair, and she sat up, trying to compose herself. She wiped at her face, and he told their guest, "But I don't think that's what you meant at first."

She set her jaw and saw, "Did you make her into a vampire?"

"Ah. There it is. Yes, I did, but with her full agreement and consent."

"So you're a vampire, too."

"I am."

Tamara gripped the banister, her knuckles white. "Are you going to kill me?"

"Absolutely not. I haven't killed a human in hundreds of years."

Nika said, "Tam, he's not a monster. Neither am I. I'm still the same person you've always known...just different."

She came down the stairs the rest of the way and came to stand in front of the couch, just outside of arm's reach. She peered at Erik, then at Nika. "You look human."

He nodded. "We can conceal our Draugr nature."

Tamara frowned. "Draugr? What is that?"

"That's the Old Norse word for vampire."

"Old Norse," she said. "So you're, like, a real Viking."

Erik smiled. She was warming up to them, and the more she expressed her curiosity, the less she feared him. "I was. I don't go a-viking so much anymore."

The human looked from Erik to Nika and back again. "Dude, you are totally robbing the cradle here."

Nika laughed and stood up, opening her arms to her friend. "Do you forgive me for scaring you?"

Tamara hesitated, then hugged Nika, and the last of the ice shattered. "Yeah, I suppose. Now I have a whole new set of questions I need you to answer."

He rose from the couch, and their guest eyed him warily. "I'm going to go to bed," he told them. "I need to get some rest. You two have fun catching up."

Nika held out her hand to him, and he took it, pressing a light kiss to the knuckles. "Do you want me to come up?" she asked.

He looked from his fiancée to the woman who had convinced her to test him, then smiled. "No, that's fine. I've been up since yesterday morning, so I'd really like to get some sleep. Take your time."

She smiled at him gratefully, and he went up the stairs to their bedroom.

***

The room was silent.

Mia slid from her husband's bed after making certain that he was completely under the control of her enchantment. He would not be waking any time soon.

She pulled a piece of chalk out of her bag and knelt on the floor, drawing a circle and a series of intricately interconnected runes. She chanted while she drew, words of Old Norse falling from her lips in a breathy hiss. Power began to shimmer over the white lines, making them dance and sway like figures behind a wall of heat distortion. When she had surrounded herself with the magic of summoning, she bit into her hand until it bled and let the blood drop into the middle of her circle.

The scarlet drops sizzled as if they'd hit a frying pan, and smoke rose in the shaking air. A cold breeze blew across her cheek, and it carried the smell of death and the grave. She squeezed more blood out onto the floor, then spoke in a louder voice.

"Oh Hel, great goddess of the dead and of revenge, I call on you now. My enemy sleeps. Show me his weakness that I might exploit it."

In front of her, hovering in midair like the screen from a dismantled television, an image of Nika appeared. She was sitting on a couch, speaking with a blonde woman Mia didn't recognize. She frowned. This was not her intended target, but sometimes Hel spoke in secret ways. Perhaps her goddess was telling her that Nika was her true enemy.

"Goddess, Hel, Dark One... guide me."

Nika's image was surrounded by a thin gold light, and from that light came another, like a tenuous and gossamer thread, that extended up through the ceiling above her head. Mia pushed the power of the spying image forward, following the thread through the ceiling and the floor above it, finding her way into the bedroom where her father was lying in his bed.

Erik was covered to the waist with bedclothes, but where he was exposed, he was naked. The owl tattoo on his chest shimmered with magic, and she wondered what was suppressed inside those black lines. He had his eyes closed, but he was not yet asleep.

She whispered words of hate and magic, and a glowing dart made of red energy appeared in her hand. She focused it, aiming it at her father's heart, and with a final command word she let it fly.

***

Nika hesitated in her conversation with Tamara. "Did you feel that?"

"Feel what?"

"Like someone is watching us." She shuddered and rubbed her hands over her arms, chafing her skin against the cold she felt in her soul. The runes on her forearms buzzed and glowed, and she was filled with the need to go to Erik.

She rose like shot, moving with as much speed as her Draugr nature could provide. Tamara shrieked in surprise and jumped back.

"Wait here," Nika commanded, and she took the stairs two at a time.

She felt shaky inside, full of adrenaline, convinced something was very, very wrong. She burst into the bedroom, startling Erik out of his drowsiness, and saw a circular blur over the end of the bed. Something red was pushing through, and she was filled with anger when she saw it.

"*Svik*!" she hissed in Old Norse, the word rolling up out of the goddess who rode along inside her soul. Ithunn spat the word for treason through Nika's lips, and she pointed her finger at the blur. A blast of golden energy shot out and struck the red object, and the whole assemblage – blur, red dart and feeling of being watched – vanished into thin air.

Erik sat up in bed, confused. "What the hell was that?"

"Someone is trying to kill you," she said, "using magic. And there's only one person with the ability and the motive to do that."

He set his jaw. "Mia."

"Apparently, that was her wedding gift to you." She turned to him, her face flushed with the residual rush of the magic she had wielded. "Are you unhurt?"

"I'm fine. How did you – "

"I felt it from downstairs." She sat on the edge of the bed and stroked his face. "She has to be dealt with, Erik. I know you want to show her leniency because she's your daughter, but..."

He took her hand and held it to his chest, just above his heart. "I know." His face was grim. "It's time."

***

In Paris, the dart was turned back by Nika's blast. It reversed course and flew like a bullet toward Mia. She dodged out of the way just in time to avoid being skewered in the chest, but her own weapon still lodged in her shoulder. She gasped in agony as the prepared assassin's dart burned its poison into her own flesh.

"Impossible," she whispered, trying and failing to dispel the dart. It refused to obey her.

She closed her eyes and tried to still the rapid beating of her heart. If her pulse stayed fast, it would speed the poison through her system that much more quickly. She racked her brain for someone who could help her.

"Ingrid," she said aloud, calling on the grandmother who had helped to raise her when she was just a tiny girl. "Ingrid, help."

There was no response, but she could feel her the ancient *vala* turning away from her. She burned in fury at the betrayal.

Her head was swimming, and it took all of her strength to crawl toward the bed. Mia clutched the bedspread and used it to drag herself up until she was face to face with Derek, who still slumbered under the effects of her spell. She banished the enchantment and watched as his eyes flew open.

"Mia," he said, his voice husky. "What happened?"

"Rune Master," she said, her lips and tongue thick. "Attacked me."

He grabbed the red dart, ignoring the way it burned his hands. He pulled it free and threw it against the wall, where it became embedded. He put his hands on Mia's wound, trying to stop the blood.

"I'll kill her," he said angrily. "That bitch!"

Mia was rapidly succumbing to a fever that burned painfully from her shoulder through to her head. Her stomach flopped in nausea, and she started to sweat. "Derek," she breathed.

He looked down at her, and she could feel the weight of his gaze. He shifted to lie down beside her, curling close to her almost protectively. She was drifting off into oblivion when his fangs thrust into her neck.

She cried out at the new pain and tried to push him away, but he was too strong. He was pulling at her vein with a will, drinking her blood as if it was the sweetest water and he'd been lost in the desert. Her strength vanished, consumed along with her blood, and she fell still, barely aware of the thready beating of her own heart.

Something hot and salty was pressed to her lips, and she tried to turn away. Derek held her head still and forced her to open her mouth. She felt the thick splash of blood on her tongue, and she suddenly knew in horror what he was doing.

He was turning her.

Chapter Fourteen

Dominic sat in the airport terminal, a ticket for New York in his hand. All around him, humans bustled about, loud and smelling of blood and sweat. A thousand scents filled his nose, and he had to think about something else to avoid being overwhelmed by it.

A familiar figure in a muddy trench coat sat beside him. Vladimir smiled at him. "Going away?"

He should have been surprised that the Russian had found him, but somehow, he wasn't. "Yes."

He peered at Dominic's ticket. "New York. Thriving town, New York."

"It's just a stop over."

"Ah. I see." He sat back and stretched out his legs, crossing his ankles. "Tell me, Ulfen, what will you do when you get to New York?"

He glanced at Vladimir, wondering what game he was playing. "I don't know. Vanishing, I hope."

"There are a few werewolf packs in the city. You knew that, right?"

Dominic sighed. "I do now."

"You might want to cultivate a little favor with them... or you might want to leave town quickly. Of course, you might find that they'll be very welcoming if you come with a powerful ally."

"What are you talking about?"

The Russian smiled. "I am a hunter. You are a hunter. I propose that we join forces and work together."

"Why would I want to do that?"

"Because I can keep you from ever suffering as an omega again," he answered coolly. "I know how unpleasant life as an omega can be. Surely you don't want to go back to that position in a new pack."

Dominic looked away. "I don't intend to join any pack. I'm on my own for a reason. And I don't intend to join up with you." He hesitated, and his curiosity got the best of him. "What do you hunt?"

"Witches, mostly. Demons. Things that go bump in the night a little harder than they should." His smile vanished, and he said seriously, "Someone needs to protect humanity against the threats of the supernatural."

He looked down at his ticket and considered the offer. It was tempting. If he agreed, it would give him a purpose, something that his life was sorely lacking. Vladimir was powerful, and he could do the things he said he could, preventing Dominic from ever again falling to omega status in a wolf pack. He took a deep breath.

"Are you done hunting Mia?"

Vladimir nodded. "For now. She's no longer my concern."

"Why?"

"Because." He smiled again. "What do you say? Partners?"

Dominic looked at him. "Does it pay?"

"In satisfaction and adrenaline." He winked. "But don't worry - you'll never go hungry."

He had nothing to lose. With a nod of his head, he extended his hand to Vladimir. "Partners."

Vladimir shook his hand firmly. "Welcome to my world."

***

Erik finished dressing and strapped on the harness that held his axe. The bedroom still felt electrified with the magical exchange that had taken place, and his skin prickled with it. Nika stood nearby, watching intently.

He picked up his phone and called Elke. His assistant picked up on the third ring, and a cacophony of noise in the background nearly drowned her out. "Hello?"

"Call a meeting of the six oldest Draugr, including Moselle, one hour from now at Snake Eyes."

"What's up, boss?"

He felt grim and determined, and his voice reflected his mood. "We're taking Paris."

"Tonight?"

"No, next month. Yes, tonight. Call it and be there, yourself." He hung up and turned to Nika. "You're sure about this?"

"Absolutely. I'm not letting you face her alone."

Tamara appeared in the bedroom doorway. "What's going on? I heard a - is that an axe?"

"It is." Erik turned to her. "I'm sorry to do this, but we have business to attend to and have to leave. Help yourself to anything in the house. Hopefully we'll be back in the morning, or in a few days, depending."

She frowned. "Nika? What is he talking about?"

"We have to go, and we're sorry to desert you," his fiancée reiterated. "If you get some sleep, we'll probably be back by the time you get up."

Erik unlocked his gun cabinet and began arming himself with firearms loaded with silver ammunition. He handed a pistol to Nika, and she slipped it into one of his shoulder holsters.

Tamara's eyes saucered. "You're handling a gun?"

"It's only for emergencies," Nika explained to her friend. "In case something happens and I need to defend myself with deadly force."

"What the hell kind of business are you getting into?"

Erik answered. "The vampire kind."

***

The clientele had been cleared from Snake Eyes so that the elder Draugr could meet without young interruptions. When Erik and Nika arrived, the six oldest vampires in Sweden had been assembled. Maria was there with Laurentia, who stood at the side of the room with an air of dismay.

Elke stood at the bar, chatting with a 15th-century creation named Niklas, and she waved to her king when his touch on the door handle made the wards ring.

They went to the bar, and Elke said, "They're all here. The best and brightest of the Stockholm bloodsucking community. We have Annika, who's only a little younger than you, and Christian and Niklas." The vampire in question nodded his blond head when his name was spoken. "Markus and Lena are here, and Maria. And I brought Moselle, like you asked."

"Thank you."

Nika could feel them looking at her, judging her. For most of them, this was their first close encounter with the new Rune Master. She tried to keep her face impassive and to display calm self-assurance, but she stayed close to Erik anyway.

He vaulted up onto the bar and looked out over the group. Nika hovered near him, and Elke did the same, both of them standing in front of him.

"Tonight, we take Paris," he said without preamble. "Derek Dupin has taken the territory belonging to Laurentia Moselle, and he has allied himself with Mia, the last Dark Sister. We're going to kill them."

Markus, who was seated at one of the tables, leaned forward. "If Moselle isn't strong enough to keep her territory, why should we be bothered to win it back for her? Let Dupin keep it. And I don't care about the Dark Sisters."

"You should care about Mia," Nika said. "She tried to kill Erik tonight."

"Such is ever the fate of usurpers." A dark-haired woman with flashing green eyes smirked. "I do not concern myself with assassination attempts on petty dictators."

Nika could feel cold anger rolling through her from Erik. "Petty dictator," he echoed.

The woman nodded, unafraid. "We Draugr have existed for centuries without a king. We have no need of a king now. The young ones might be impressed by your posturing, but that's only because they're in a drug-addled stupor. Once you relieve them of their *dreyri*, they'll turn on you."

"Like you're turning on me now, Annika?" he asked. Nika had heard that rumble in his voice before. This mouthy vampire had better watch her step.

Annika rose from her seat at Markus' table. "I can't turn on you when I was never with you. Have fun with your little riot."

She turned and walked away, audacious and insulting. Erik limbered his axe and flung it at her, and it embedded in the wall in front of her, the handle quivering. Annika flinched in spite of herself and turned to face him.

"Do you want this back, or can I keep it?"

Unexpectedly, Erik smiled. "Why do you always have to bust my balls?"

She wrenched the axe out of the wall, taking bits of plaster and drywall with it. She threw it back, and Nika ducked. Erik caught it in midair. "Because it's in the shield maiden handbook," Annika said.

"I never got any handbook," Elke said, grinning.

"Maybe when you're older," a buxom blonde said, moving forward to sit at the bar. She must have been Lena, Nika deduced. "So, what's the plan?"

Erik said, "Derek Dupin has an estate outside of Paris. We don't have to take on the whole city, just him and his groupies. The first thing we're going to do is get a headcount on the number of vampires and goons he has working in his house. The second thing is we're going to go in and kill them all."

Maria shook her dark head. "A typical Viking plan, all onslaught and no subtlety. I thought you had experience with stealth."

Erik responded calmly, "I do. But I also have experience with the element of surprise." He pulled out his cell phone and hit a button on it, saying, "Bring it."

The front door opened, and another Draugr, this one a male with shocking bleached white hair, dragged in a heavy crate. He stopped in the middle of the Snake Eyes dance floor and ripped the lid away with his claws, exposing a set of military-issue automatic rifles.

"Courtesy of the SOG Special Unit," Erik said. "Each of these is equipped with a double-drum magazine filled with silver bullets. That's 100 rounds per clip. The beauty of an automatic rifle is that you don't have to really aim all that well - just press the trigger and spray. You'll eventually hit something."

Markus went to the crate, his eyes gleaming red in excitement. "Do I get to keep it when this is over?"

"I have no trouble with that," Erik shrugged. "But if you use it in a way that brings undue attention to us or does excessive damage to humans, I'll take issue with you very directly."

Annika snickered. "He means he'll beat your ass."

"I mean I'll kill him."

Markus did not look up. "I know what he means." He picked up one of the rifles and ran his hand down the barrel lovingly. To Nika, it looked like he was considering making love to the thing. "She's beautiful. Did you know I was a sniper during the Second World War?"

Elke rolled her eyes. "Yes, Markus. We all know. You've banged on about it to all of us a hundred times."

He ignored her. "Just think of how many Nazis I could have killed back in the day with a gun like this."

"I hope you can still shoot," Erik said mildly.

The veiled insult shook Markus out of his reverie. "Fuck you, Thorvald. I'm a professional."

The Draugr king smirked. "So I've heard. You make a nice, tidy living at it, too."

The other vampire grinned. "It pays the bills."

"And then some."

Lena, blonde with the heavy bosom, spoke up. "So how are we going to get a headcount on his house without him knowing?"

"That's where Nika comes in."

The black-haired vampire who hadn't spoken yet said, "I was wondering when she would be useful."

Nika glared at him. "Christian, is it?" He nodded.

He crossed his arms over his barrel chest. "You call yourself the Rune Master. But shouldn't that be Rune Mistress?"

"Master is a title of ability, not gender," Erik said coldly. "And disrespect her again and I will slit your throat. This is your future queen."

Christian snorted. "If the only way you can get obedience from your people is by threatening them, you're in a poor bargaining position."

"That would be true, if I were bargaining, but I'm not. I'm ordering, and you are obeying." Erik jumped down off of the bar and walked toward the other vampire, his eyes turning blazing red. Christian did a good job of concealing his nervous reaction to the ancient Draugr's anger, but they all could smell it seeping out of his pores. Erik stopped with his nose practically touching the other man's. "Any questions?"

They stared at one another for a moment, then Christian looked away. "No."

"Good. Nika, if you please..."

She took a deep breath and tried to remember the lessons that Ingrid had taught her. She spread her hands out flat in front of her, thumb to thumb, then spread them straight out to the sides. A flat sheet of golden energy formed, showing an image of a city. She concentrated on feeling Mia's power signature, on tracking her down in the massive energetic noise of humans in Paris. Soon, she had pinpointed the building where she was lying.

Nika manipulated the image with sharp gestures of her hands, flicking her fingers and expanding the view of the estate to be a semi-transparent model of the real thing. She could see people walking or sitting in every level of the house, from attic to basement. She could see the doors and windows, where the furniture was located, and who was armed and who was not.

In the master bedroom, she could see Mia lying in motionless, gripping a pillow to her stomach. On the floor beside her bed was the dead body of a woman in torn and grimy clothes, her head scarf in disarray. She looked like a refugee who had come to grief. The reason for the body's lifelessness was obvious – her throat had been completely torn away. Not one drop of blood had been spilled, though, and despite the corpse, the bedroom was immaculate.

Lena whispered. "That's a turning kill."

Erik put his hand on the small of Nika's back. *Excellent work,* he told her telepathically.

She smiled but did not speak, afraid that if she did, she would break her concentration and lose the image. She expanded the scrying view until she could see not just the house but also the grounds of the estate. More men were milling around in the vineyards and gardens around the mansion, carrying automatic rifles of their own. Markus pointed his finger at one, gun-like, and pulled an imaginary trigger.

The door to Snake Eyes opened, and Ingrid strolled in, adjusting her white crocheted shawl over her shoulders. She smiled at her son.

"I am here on behalf of the Valtaeigr," she said. "I will help you get to Paris if you need it."

"We call can fly," Maria said. "We're old enough."

"Speak for yourself," pouted Elke.

"We will all go to the estate and draw their attention out of the house and to the front lawn. While they're distracted, Nika and Ingrid will go into the building and confront Mia." Erik looked at his assistant. "I need you to stay here and make sure that nobody comes into the club. We're closed tonight. Keep it that way."

"The young ones will be howling for their *dreyri*," Niklas warned.

"Let them." Nika looked up at Erik, and his icy blue eyes were fixed on the targets on her scrying mirror. He looked firm and in control. "Arm yourselves, and take extra clips. Let's go."

The vampires helped themselves to the weapons from the SOG, and as they filed out, Nika collapsed the floating image into a tiny cube that she held in her hand. The rune tattoos on her forearms were ablaze, and her eyes, instead of Draugr red, were glowing with the golden light of runic magic.

Erik kissed her deeply. "You are magnificent," he whispered.

She smiled for him. "Go get 'em, tiger."

He grinned and picked up a rifle for himself. He slotted the double roll magazine into place and nodded to her. "That's the plan."

Markus held out a hand to Ingrid. "Come fly with me."

"No. We will be going through the ley lines." She met her protégé's eyes. "We have unfinished business, I think."

"May the gods hold us in their favor." Erik turned to Laurentia Moselle, the only one of the Draugr who had failed to select a rifle. "Are you fighting for this city, or am I taking it for myself?"

She looked at him coldly, her face a mask of defeat and disdain. "You are taking everything from me anyway. My relics, my vats, my treasures... what will stop you from taking my city, too?"

He nodded. "If you fight at my side and act like you want to keep your position, you will be allowed to rule Paris in my name."

"As your puppet?"

"As my vassal and ally."

She sneered in silence for a moment, then said, "I prefer a pistol. Do you have one?"

Erik pulled his own pistol from its holster at his waist and handed it to her. For a moment, Nika's mind was filled with the image of Laurentia pointing the gun and pulling the trigger there in the club, but she only took the weapon into her small white hand. Without another word, she walked out through the front door, following the others out and up into the air.

"One more kiss," Erik said, coming to Nika to claim her lips once more. "I will see you when this is over. Be safe." He turned his gaze to his mother's face. "Both of you."

"We know what to do, Huntsman," Ingrid said softly. "Worry about yourself."

Chapter Fifteen

Erik led his Draugr to the estate, landing in the front lawn with their rifles at the ready. Markus, always eager to let some lead fly, immediately sprayed the front of the building with a volley of bullets.

"I think they know we're here," Lena said drily.

"Fan out," Erik ordered. "Markus, establish over watch and do what you do best."

The vampire grinned. "With pleasure." He flew to the roof of the mansion and lay on his stomach, sighting down his rifle and waiting for a target.

He didn't have to wait long. Vampires and humans armed with automatic rifles of their own poured out through the front door while others raced around from the east side of the building. A silver bullet hit the ground just in front of Erik's toe, splattering his boot with mud. He laughed.

They're out, he told his Chosen. The coast should be clear.

***

The building had been built directly over a node in the magical confluence. No doubt the intention had been for the inhabitants to gain power from the nearness of the ley line, but it actually just made them easier to find.

Nika and Ingrid emerged from the ley line in the center of the first-floor office. She spoke to Erik through their bond. We're inside.

She could hear his voice throbbing with adrenaline. Stay safe. Good luck.

The sound of gunfire was loud outside the house, and Ingrid grimaced. "It sounds like a war zone."

"That's because it is. Come on."

They left the office and crept toward the stairs leading to the upper levels. There were voices in the corridor approaching them, and Nika pushed Ingrid into a broom closet. The clatter of soldiers passing grew louder, then faded as the group of armed defenders hurried by. When the noises had ceased, Nika opened the door cautiously.

A man in a three-piece suit stood in front of them, facing the closet door with a pistol in his hand. Derek Dupin pointed his gun at Nika's face.

"Rune Master," he growled. "You are not welcome here. How did you get in? You weren't invited."

Ingrid pushed Nika back. "I brought her through the ley lines. There are no thresholds there and your invitation wards don't protect you against Valtaeigr."

He chuckled mirthlessly. "More magic. I'm growing sick of magic."

"Then why did you marry a Dark Sister?" Nika asked. "You're her pawn, you know. She's enchanted you."

"Lies."

"Are you sure?" Nika asked. "I think that if you were really certain, you would have shot by now."

Mia appeared on the stairs, descending slowly in her bare feet, her pale face dotted with the sweat of her turning. She glared at the two women in the hallway.

"Bring them to me," she ordered Dupin. "The old one first."

Nika looked at Ingrid and shook her head. Ingrid nodded. She retreated back into the closet.

"What are you doing, you old hag?" Mia demanded. Nika could feel her calling on her magic, but the power sputtered and sparked around her hand like a car engine that wouldn't start. She shook the useless energy off in annoyance.

Nika raised an eyebrow. "Problem?"

"Derek," the Dark Sister snapped. "Bring them!"

The Paris chieftain stepped forward menacingly, and Ingrid disappeared into the ley lines. Nika raised her hands and shot rune fire at him, but he dodged out of the way. A section of the wall behind him cracked and began to smoke.

Mia pointed at Nika and shouted words of magic. Her fingertips blurred for the briefest of moments, and then all of her power evaporated, sparking around her once again. She cursed and fled up the stairs. Derek covered her escape, drawing a long cavalry saber from a sheath at his waist. He held it up.

"Come on, Rune Master," he said. "Show me what you have."

She squared her shoulders. "Don't make me kill you, Dupin," she warned. "I'll do it. Mia is dead already. She's got no magic left, and Erik is here to kill her. Don't sacrifice yourself for her. She isn't worth it."

One corner of his mouth drew up in a sardonic smirk. "If she is dead, then I have nothing left to live for." He swung the saber, and Nika ducked. The blade caught her ponytail and a handful of chopped red hairs fell to the floor around her.

"Bastard," she swore, backpedaling. She came up with both hands glowing, and a stream of runes flew out of her palms, hot and whistling through the air. He dodged to the side, and another wall took damage.

A burst of machine gun fire ripped through the air. The fight was just outside the door. '

"Hear that?" she mocked. "That's Erik, coming to finish her."

"That's my men defending me. We outnumber your Huntsman and his friends."

He charged her, his saber swinging wildly. She ducked underneath his arm and grabbed his chest as she went by, pumping runes and lightning into him. Derek stiffened and screamed, then burst into flame from the inside out. In less than a heartbeat, he was gone, leaving only a pile of gray ashes on the floor.

Nika didn't take time to relish her victory. She took up his saber and went up the stairs, two at a time.

***

The estate's defenders were putting up a stronger defense than Erik would have anticipated. They fought like true believers, not like hired thugs. He wondered what promises they'd been made that had secured such devotion.

Ultimately, it didn't really matter. Devoted or not, they would be dying all the same.

He was sheltering behind a stone pillar on the front portico. Lena trotted to him, her mouth and chin red with someone else's blood. "There are more in the back."

"How many more?" A burst of gunfire made the pillar erupt in a shower of splintered rock and dust, and he turned away to protect his face. Lena threw her arm up over her own eyes and came away speckled with tiny cuts that healed almost as soon as they appeared.

"Twenty, maybe thirty," she reported.

Down the porch, hiding behind another pillar, Moselle was crouching, her borrowed pistol in her hands. He had not seen her fire a single shot.

"Take her with you," he said, gesturing with his chin toward the former chieftain of Paris.

Lena scoffed. "Really? Are you trying to get me killed?"

"I didn't say defend her. Either she fights for her land or she dies." Loudly, he said, "Moselle! Moment of truth! Go with Lena to the garden and prove you want Paris!"

She turned an angry look toward him but held her silence. He stepped out from behind his pillar and returned fire, covering for Lena and Moselle as they moved out. He heard a loud laugh from the other side of the lawn as one of the defenders took the opportunity to mock him.

"Missed me!" the man shouted in French.

Erik got a glimpse of the man's head. He was a human, but with augmented abilities. A Draugr pet, no doubt, someone that Derek had been feeding vampire blood to keep him living and enhanced. Erik fired once and caught him in the forehead, splitting his skull. The man's body dropped.

"Not that time," he said.

He could feel energy pass by under his feet, something that he'd never felt before. He sidestepped, startled by the feeling, almost expecting to see the ground bubbling with the passage of some great monster. Nothing happened physically, and he shook his head.

Nika, he called. *Are you all right?*

Fine. He could feel her running. *I killed Dupin.*

He smiled in grim satisfaction. *Excellent. Mia?*

Nika's voice was firm and pitiless in his mind. *She's next.*

***

Ingrid surged through the ley lines. She normally the eldritch conduits only for travel, but today she needed more. She swept through the lines, gathering in as much power as she could hold. Her passage was fast, and she was unprepared for an obstacle.

Someone else was traveling the lines, and they collided with a stunning crash that sent them both spinning backward down the paths they had been taking. Ingrid recovered her senses and reached out to identify who or what she had encountered.

The witch hunter Vladimir was in the lines, and she could feel his anger at her inadvertent interruption. A surge of fire blasted down the conduit, and she leaped out of the ley line to avoid it. She found herself in the catacombs of Paris, an unpleasant enough place that was nevertheless better than being dead. Vladimir had struck to kill.

She ducked back down into the ley line. Vladimir had rushed past her position and was heading at full speed toward the fight. Ingrid followed him, sucking in power as she went. The Russian witch hunter was doing the same, and the lines were dim from their dual assault. The node beneath Dupin's estate was just ahead, and she saw it flare as Vladimir shot through it.

She followed him just a moment behind.

***

Nika reached the top of the stairs just in time to see Mia disappear into one of the rooms, the door slamming shut behind her. She increased her speed and burst through the door, her Draugr strength giving her all the impetus she needed to disregard the flimsy barrier.

Mia spun to face her, her brand-new fangs extended as she hissed. She stepped into the center of a magical circle drawn onto the floor. There was no response from the circle, not even a shimmer acknowledging that she had stepped inside. Nika shook her head.

"Give it up, Mia. Your powers have deserted you."

The Dark Sister picked up a ceremonial dagger. "I will never surrender to you."

"Maybe not, but you're done all the same."

As Nika spoke, she felt the ley line node shift twice. She could sense two new magical presences, and she could identify Ingrid immediately. The other felt familiar, and she could guess who it might have been.

Mia took advantage of Nika's distraction and launched herself at her, tackling her to the floor. She tried to seize her throat in her teeth, but Nika wrenched herself out of the way, leaving Mia with a mouth full of her shoulder instead. Blood flowed, and Mia drank greedily. Nika gloved her hand in magic and pressed it against the Dark Sister's forehead, where it steamed and sizzled. Mia released her with a shriek and backed away, a hand-shaped burn on her face.

Vladimir burst through the remnants of the door, his face grim. Ingrid was right behind him. Nika pointed at him, her hand glowing.

"Stop right there!" she commanded. "Ingrid, hold him!"

The elder Valtaeigr wrapped him in silvery threads of energy and slowed his progress into the room. The Russian snarled at her. "Release me, bitch!"

"No. This one isn't yours."

Mia was backing away, fear in her eyes. She looked around the room frantically, searching for anything that could be used as a weapon. Nika stalked her, keeping her away from the fireplace. She brandished the saber she had taken from Derek's ashes.

"You have caused a lot of trouble," she told Mia. "More trouble than you're worth. If we were mortals, I'd want to see you behind bars, but since we're not, there's only one thing to do."

Mia stood tall, her eyes flashing defiantly. "If you're going to kill me, then kill me. Don't talk me to death."

Nika took a deep breath and drew back the saber. Mia stared at her, unflinching. *I can't do it,* she told Erik.

Through their Chosen bond, she got a rush of activity and anxiety, and she could hear more gunfire in the back garden. He finally responded, *What?*

I can't kill her. I can't just... murder her.

He sounded mildly annoyed. *Then hold her there until I can reach you. I'm a little busy right now.*

Nika swallowed hard and put the point of the saber against Mia's throat. "Sit down."

"No."

There was a sudden tearing sound, and then Vladimir was free. He lunged at Mia and brought her down to the ground, his hands alight with green fire. Nika stepped back, her mind going fuzzy and making her dizzy.

Mia struggled out of Vladimir's grasp and flipped them so that she was on top, straddling the Russian's torso. She bared her new Draugr fangs and struck like a cobra, sinking deep into the witch's vein. She pulled a mouthful, then spat it out, her lips burning. Vladimir laughed at her.

"Witches are poison to vampires," he said.

She grabbed his head and tried to twist it, but a silver net of energy cast by Ingrid descended over them both, stilling their combat and holding them in place.

The older Valtaeigr came to Nika's side and pressed a finger to her forehead. The fuzziness in her head vanished with a snap, and her field of vision filled with the image of shattering green glass.

"Enchantment," Ingrid explained. "You've had it on you for a while."

Nika thought back to the shock when Vladimir had touched her in Erik's office. "Clever."

Running feet approached, coming up the stairs and down the corridor. Erik burst into the room, his rifle in his hands, his eyes wild. He saw the net and stopped, looking at Nika and Ingrid.

"You're all right?" he asked.

His mother nodded. "Fine."

Erik walked closer to the two figures trapped beneath the magical net. "Mia," he said softly.

She turned and hissed at him, her eyes burning red. "Huntsman. Come to play?"

"You hate me," he said.

His daughter ground her teeth, her long fangs flashing. "I would kill you if I could."

He sighed and shot her, putting a silver bullet into her brainpan. She dissolved into dust, coating the infuriated Russian witch hunter.

"She was my kill!" Vladimir protested. "Mine! You had no right!"

Erik lowered his gun and ignored him. He turned to his female companions.

"The fight is over. The others have left. The mortal authorities are on their way, and we have to get out of here, now." He looked back at Vladimir. "Leave him here."

Ingrid whispered words of magic, and the net constricted, then vanished. By the time it had fully disappeared, the witch hunter was insensible, rendered unconscious by her power.

Nika shook her head. "I have so much to learn."

"Indeed you do." Ingrid linked arms with the two of them. "But first, let's get back to Stockholm."

She took them into the ley lines and left the carnage behind.

Epilogue

The wedding was on a glorious summer day in Uppsala. They both underwent a ritual bath meant to wash away their unmarried selves and prepare them for their new existence. In the absence of family, Nika was attended by Tamara and Elke. Erik stood alone, but he carried Gunnar's sword.

Ingrid spoke to her as they approached the hill where the ancient shrine had stood. "Normally, you would have your father's sword with you. When Erik gives you his sword, you are to hold it in trust for your sons, and give your father's sword to him to take the place of the one he's giving up for you. Since you won't have any sons, the sword will be yours."

Nika adjusted the bridal crown that Elke had given her, an elaborate thing made of braided gold. It was heavy, but at least it wasn't made of wheat like it would have been in the old days. She wouldn't have enjoyed wearing cereal grains to her wedding.

"I don't have a sword," she said.

Tamara stepped up to her with a wrapped bundle. "Yes, you do."

Nika took the bundle from her and pulled away the cloth. Inside was the Rune Sword, the one that had brought the two of them together at the very beginning.

"Oh my God," she breathed. "How did you get this out of the museum?"

Elke smiled. "I know a werewolf with excellent thieving abilities."

They went to the ritual space, where Erik stood in a scarlet tunic and black leather pants. His black boots reached to his knees, and a golden torc adorned his neck. She had never seen a more beautiful man, and he took her breath away.

When he turned to look at her, in her embroidered white gown and with the bridal crown upon her head, he smiled, his eyes aglow. He looked at her as if she was the most wonderful thing he had ever seen. She smiled back at him.

Nika walked to him, passing through a crowd of Draugr and Ulfen and faery who had come to see the Rune King's wedding. Her eyes never left his face, and his gaze at her never wavered. Despite the hundreds of attendants, she felt as if they were alone in this moment.

Ingrid said prayers to the old gods, and they exchanged the swords. She could see the moment that Erik recognized the Rune Sword, and he blinked in surprise. She nodded to him with a silent smile, and he happily exchanged his sword for hers.

There were more prayers, then gold rings for them both, and then Ingrid bound their hands with a golden cord. She intoned words of ancient Norse that Nika did not know, but their import was clear. It was a blessing, and it was most welcome.

Ingrid smiled at them. "I now pronounce you man and wife."

Erik gently squeezed her hands and pulled her closer, and she leaned into him. In the brilliant sunlight of midday, they kissed, and then Erik looked at her with eyes shining with unshed tears.

He whispered to her. "Welcome to forever."

CPSIA information can be obtained
at www.ICGtesting.com
Printed in the USA
LVHW111631150820
663283LV00001B/134